The War

Randy Boyd

The War

Library of congress Cataloging-in-Publication Data
The War/Randall Boyd

Registration Number
Txu 1-747-918

Effective Date of Registration
March 17, 2011

10   9   8   7   6   5   4   3   2   1

First and foremost, to God be all the glory.
Secondly, I would like to dedicate this book to
my Book Launch Team: Sheila Boyd,
Wanda Boyd, Jaylee Graves, Amy Cooke,
Michael Mulford, Brandi Matthews,
Lucy De Rojas, Shane Thomas, and
Norma Parks.
THANK YOU TEAM!

Ephesians 6:12

For we wrestle not against flesh and
blood, but against principalities, against
powers, against the rulers of the darkness
of this world, against spiritual wickedness
in high places.

Revelation 12:7-9

7 And there was a war in heaven: Michael
and his angels fought against the dragon;
and the dragon fought and his angels, 8
And prevailed not; neither was their place
found any more in heaven.
9 And the great dragon was cast out, that
old serpent, called the Devil, and Satan,
which deceiveth the whole world: he was
cast out into the earth, and his angels
were cast out with him.

Prelude

Heaven: Thousands and thousands of years ago...

Long before the foundation of the earth was spoken into existence, The Kingdom of Heaven stood in all its glorious splendor. The clear blue skies that silhouetted the mountainous regions were far more deep and vivid than humankind could ever truly conceive. The flourishing vegetation possessed a richer, fuller green than a simple human mind could possibly fathom. That is due to the fact that the frail eyes of man are not capable to withstand the beauty that God's kingdom possesses. Behind the enormous, stark white walls, so bright that they appeared to be made from Holy light, only a spirit had the ability to withstand the kingdom's true magnificence.

Cazzbein, a mere angel in the service of the Lord Jesus Christ, was such a spirit. Before there was the concept of time within the realm of man, God Almighty reigned over the Kingdom of Heaven with complete and utter harmony. Seated at His right hand was His Son, Jesus Christ, who ruled with every bit as much authority as His Father. Both Father and Son governed the Kingdom of Heaven with peace, honor, and most of all, love.

In charge of the Angelic Host was by far the most prominent angel Heaven had to offer. His name was Lucifer, the anointed cherub, and Field Commander over all of the Angelic Host. Lucifer was the highest exalted angel in all of Heaven, with eminence and honor surpassed only by Christ Jesus.

Lucifer was by far the most beautiful angel in all of heaven. The gorgeous cherub possessed long, black hair that flowed down past his sculpted shoulders, and neatly trimmed, dark beard that etched his masculine features. There was no doubt the handsome angel was a charming sight to behold.

As always Lucifer was adorned in his stunning red chest plate that he wore over a gown made of the deepest, darkest ebony. His mere presence produced a Holy illumination so bright that it paled all the other angels' light in comparison.

Sadly, his Holy prominence did not last forever. Lucifer found himself troubled by certain events that had taken place during the creation of the Earth. With his vanity fueling his thoughts, the mighty angel felt as though he should have played a much more significant role during the undertaking, since it was he, after all, that was one of God's highly exalted. When the cherub at last heard that man was being created in the image of God and His Son, his pride had been deeply struck. A seed of jealousy then pricked Lucifer's heart. Over time, that same seed festered into a seething hatred for the Lord Jesus.

No longer able to control his intense revulsion, Lucifer began covertly assembling an army for a rebellion. Utilizing his authority within the Angelic Hierarchy, the anointed cherub was able to sway one third of the Heavenly Host to his cause. When God Almighty at last called for a day of celebration to be composed in order to commemorate the creation of the Earth, and pay honor to Jesus, Lucifer saw his opportunity to unveil his displeasure.

Cazzbein, on the other hand, was filled with a sense of happiness as he entered the audience hall. The construction of the Earth was a massive undertaking after all, and a grand celebration seemed appropriate. He watched with a childlike fascination as his brothers and sisters gathered into the magnificent chamber and waited patiently for the festivities to begin. Across the way Cazzbein spotted his longtime friend Gunthar, taking in the splendor in the same manner as he. As he made his way through the crowd to stand next to the burly angel, Lucifer took that moment to speak the first words of anger ever uttered within Heaven's glorious walls.

"I will ascend into Heaven, I will exalt my throne above the stars of God: I will sit also upon the mount of the congregation, on the sides of the north: I will ascend above the heights of the clouds; I will be like the most High!" The beautiful angel declared, with hostility dripping from every word.

"Blasphemy!" the Archangel Michael spat, just before Lucifer's followers began brandishing their weapons.

Cazzbein could not believe what he was hearing. If the words echoing throughout the courtyard were true, then Lucifer, the anointed cherub, had just waged war against God Almighty. At first the thought of war in Heaven seemed impossible, but with a third of all the angels quickly beginning to join forces with the renegade, the idea became all too real.

It may have been his dashing good looks, or the impressive rank in which he held that lured the other rebellious angels to follow his cause. However, Cazzbein believes they were simply misled by the lies being spewed forth from Lucifer's deceitful tongue. Either notion did not change the fact that Heaven was about to erupt into turmoil.

The once peaceful kingdom, which had always been illuminated brightly with God's loving presence, suddenly turned as dark as the blackest storm clouds. While thunder rolled unpleasantly throughout the lush green fields, Cazzbein could only assume the transformation was caused by the anger God was feeling toward his arrogant servant and his army of mutinous followers. The guardian angel was shocked to see that some others of his angelic kin also brandished magnificent weapons of warfare. Their once fair and beautiful faces turned to sour scowls as they dared to draw near the throne with malicious intentions in mind. It was only when they had breached the open courtyard, pouring through the glorious gates leading to the audience hall, that Cazzbein realized he needed to make a decision. He could either join the insurgents, which consisted of a great number of his most beloved companions, or stand and fight for God, his creator.

The decision was an easy one to make. With a heavy, but determined heart, Cazzbein pulled his two brilliant scimitars from their scabbards, lighting the courtyard brightly with their breathtaking radiance. The mere essence of the blades was so spectacular that the traitorous angels thought as though they were peering into the sun at daybreak. "Come if you dare, disloyal swine!" Cazzbein growled. "But hear me when I say…I will protect my Master at all costs!"

The approaching force was taken aback by the vivid proclamation, and eyed their golden-haired brother for a brief moment as they harbored a twinge of fear within themselves. No one in attendance wanted to cross blades with Cazzbein, whom many of them considered the finest sword bearer among them. Nevertheless, the goal was clear in their darkened hearts, and they would do whatever they must to get through the defiant angel.

Four of the mightiest Archangels, Michael, Gabriel, Raphael, and Uriel, stood behind the mass of warriors quickly trying to formulate a defensive strategy once they knew which angels were friend and foe. But before any battle arrangements could be finalized, the renegades were upon them.

A thunderous crash echoed throughout the square as the two forces collided into battle. The sound of cold steel on steel reverberated off the tall white walls as each side's extraordinary weapons met in macabre play. Some of the angels took the fight to the air, circling overhead, locked in combat with one another, while others chose to remain grounded, refusing to relinquish a mere inch of terrain to their adversaries.

Cazzbein worked his blades with sheer and utter poetry, whirling one scimitar inward to parry an attack, and then thrusting forward with the other for an assault of his own. The dazzling attack routine achieved him several lethal strikes against the mass of oncoming enemies, only to leave him facing a swarm of new opponents in the place of the many he had already defeated.

Although all the combatants on the battlefield fought as though they had no fear of death, the thought of being defeated in battle and having to face God's judgment was an all too real consequence. Cazzbein proved that fact several times over with many wicked thrusts of his scimitars. Every lethal strike he landed caused his injured enemies to fall lamely to the ground, where they were helpless to do anything more than wait for God Almighty to hand down their punishment.

With that dreadful display clearly in mind, Cazzbein pressed onward with unrelenting fury. It was difficult stepping over the wounded bodies of his numerous fallen opponents while also trying to keep his thoughts in check. Nevertheless, since there was no other alternative presenting itself, Cazzbein managed to fight on the best he could, even though he knew one mistake caused by the subtlest of hesitations could be his last.

It did not take the valiant angel long to cut himself out a section of open ground in the melee to better maintain his swordplay, but he could not help but feel troubled when he witnessed his former comrades littering the ground at the hands of his weaving scimitars.

They made their choice, he reasoned, *as did I.* With that grim uncertainty finally settled, Cazzbein leapt back into the fray with renewed vitality.

The spectacular battle went on for what seemed like only a few days, but to the human time frame it could have been a thousand years. The advancing forces put up a tremendous fight, but were held at the courtyard, never coming within any real threat to the throne. After the greater majority of rebel angels had been defeated, it did not take long for the rest of their mutinous kin to surrender their weapons and give up the fight.

A mighty blast then came from Gabriel's trumpet, clearing the battlefield of all combatants except for Lucifer and Michael. Michael was by far the superior of the two, but somewhere within Lucifer's arrogant mind he thought he could beat him. As the two squared off, Michael raised his greatsword in the air to signal he was ready to begin the duel. The gesture was honorable, but Lucifer only viewed it as a chance to gain the advantage.

Before the noble Archangel could bring his sword down to defend himself, Lucifer sprung into action, cutting a deep gash under Michael's ribs with a razor-sharp dagger. Although in pain, Michale still had the awareness to bring the hilt of his greatsword crashing down into Lucifer's nose. The sickening crunch could be heard everywhere as Lucifer's once flawless visage was marred.

Shocked and hurt, Lucifer dropped his weapon and pinched his throbbing snout together with both hands in a feeble attempt to thwart the unpleasant sensation. Seeing his enemy staggered, Michael pressed onward, hoping to rid the wicked fiend from all existence. However, the evildoer was not ready to end the battle just yet.

Seeing his nemesis rushing in, Lucifer pulled a trident off the ground that had belonged to an angel that had fallen in battle. He wildly swung the weapon in a long arc, merely trying to keep Michael at bay. The move had served its purpose, and now both opponents found themselves on even ground once more.

For several long moments the two enemies crashed their weapons together, showering the ground all around them with brilliant sparks. From a spectator's vantage point the fight looked as though it could go either way. Lucifer, however, knew that his strength was fading as quickly as his ambitions. With one last swing of Michael's greatsword, Lucifer's three-pronged spear went flying from his hand, disarming him once and for all. Seeing that he was wholly defeated, Lucifer conceded. The uprising had at last been crushed.

After the ferocious fighting was over, a strict judgment was passed down upon all the angels that had fallen from grace. They were immediately led to the gates of Heaven alongside their defeated leader, Lucifer. Cazzbein could not help but notice the fear in which they held within their once sparkling eyes, and wondered what must have been going through their minds at that moment. Their once radiant glow that had been empowered to them by their maker was stripped away, and they stood before everyone in attendance like an artificial representation of their once glorious selves.

The magnificent gates of pearl creaked open eerily as the horde of renegades approached. The breathtaking

splendor of the Kingdom of Heaven was all these creatures
had known since their creation, but now the unfamiliar
world of Earth beckoned to them with a haunting silence.
One by one the disloyal angels were cast out of the gates,
where they plummeted to the unknown world far below
like bolts of lightning. Cazzbein and his brethren let loose
blissful cheers of joy as they watched the betrayers descend
downward, pleased that the battle was finally at an end.
However, little did the rejoicing angels realize, the long
War for the Souls of Man had just begun…

Chapter 1

Earth: Present day...

Cazzbein was powerless to do anything more than watch as Scott took yet another long drink from his glass of alcohol. The guardian angel stood atop the dirty bar surface looking down upon Scott while he sipped his bitter brew, and a glimmer of pity seemed to glisten in his clear blue orbs as he considered the aged human. Cazzbein knew the old man's life would be required of him this night, and that thought troubled the angel greatly.

The spiritual guardian had been placed in charge of Scott's wellbeing sixty-seven years ago, and knew the human had never accepted his Master's gift of eternal life. Instead, after Scott's wife had left him for another man several years ago, he embraced an addiction to alcohol in order to drown out his sorrows and other miseries. Cazzbein couldn't help but shake his head at the reasoning. The alcohol never helped Scott deal with the grief of losing his wife, and it certainly did not aid him with any of his other problems. In fact, the booze added even more troubles to the already long list of difficulties in the man's life.

Cazzbein stooped down for a moment and looked into Scott's bloodshot eyes. Even though the angel was mere inches from the human's face, the man still could not see him, because Cazzbein was watching him from the spiritual realm. Nevertheless, that did not change the fact that the guardian was indeed present, and very concerned.

He noticed Scott shudder for a moment as if an unexplained chill had just come over him. The cool sensation was brought on when Cazzbein's glowing aura graced the man's skin. Although it had been inadvertent on this occasion, Cazzbein had used the feeling to get people's attention before. Nevertheless, other than a vigorous rubbing of his arms in an attempt to ward off the icy sensation, there was no other response.

Seeing that he was getting no positive reaction, Cazzbein bore his steely gaze straight through the man's frail chest cavity. The angel's powerful eyesight passed through flesh, blood, and bone until he found what he was searching for. The guardian could see that Scott's heart had already begun to flutter irregularly. The stress of the alcoholism and harsh lifestyle had finally taken its toll on the vital organ and it was about to fail.

The guardian couldn't help but think back over all the years of Scott's life and wonder why the man had never abandoned his self-destructive habits. The conclusion of this evening's events would be far more pleasant if he had. As Cazzbein reminisced about Scott's better days, a dark shadowy mist began to rise from the dirty floor of the tavern. Just like Cazzbein, the eerie smog was hidden from the eyes of the human patrons in attendance, due to the fact that it was every bit a part of the spiritual realm as he was.

The angel had seen the murky fog take shape countless times and had been expecting its arrival with immense dread. The gloomy vapors swirled for a moment as they formed a large circle, and then, without so much as a sound, the middle of the smog fell through as if the floor beneath the haze was no longer able to hold any physical characteristics.

Cazzbein recognized the murk as the gateway that leads into outer darkness. The portal itself was so black that even the darkest of shadows being cast throughout the barroom were pale in comparison. After the dramatic presentation had ended, another being of the spiritual world emerged, soaring out of the gateway under the power of its filthy wings. This being, however, was a creature of incredible evil.

The demon flew around the perimeter of the barroom for a moment, taking in the new scenery, before executing an impressive head-over-heels maneuver, and then, with skills more graceful than a swan, landed quietly on the dirty ground beneath him as if the tactic had been mere child's play. Cazzbein recognized the wicked friend immediately as his once old friend Vermillion, one of the fallen angels that had rebelled against God.

The wicked creature had many shapes it could have taken, but on this occasion, it chose to use its true form. He stood nearly six and a half feet tall, and had a lean chiseled physique. His features were fair and smooth with a flawless appearance, yet his black eyes lacked any pupils, and were as cold and unfeeling as a serpent's. His head, which once held a beautiful blonde mane, was now bald and barren of any hair at all, and his pearly white smile was now tarnished and gray.

His once lovely wings were also shabby and unclean; no doubt a consequence of the curse God had bestowed upon him and his other rebellious kin. Cazzbein could not help but notice how Vermillion and all the other fallen angels seemed to lack the once radiant luster that they had possessed before they were cast out of Heaven, which led him to wonder what other penalties they may have had to endure for their disloyalty.

Vermillion cast his snake-like gaze in Cazzbein's direction, and a wicked grin spread across his fair visage when he saw the guardian angel standing protectively over the drunken human.

"Greetings to you, my dear friend Cazzbein." The demon said mockingly, while stooping into a low bow.

Cazzbein did not dignify the sarcastic greeting with a response, but instead, the angel thrust his glistening silver breastplate outward while extending his wings to their full span, demonstrating his dominating presence. Cazzbein stood two inches above seven feet, and his physique was toned, with muscles honed for swordplay. His hands rested easily on the hilts of two scimitars sheathed comfortably at his hips, waiting for the moment that he might have to bring them into sight against the derisive creature standing before him. The swords were brilliantly crafted weapons possessing artistically fashioned hilts, with razor sharp blades that appeared as if they had been created from the purist light imaginable. The only thing more dazzling than gazing upon the sword's magnificent exterior, was watching the blades in action whenever they were wielded in the angel's capable hands. Both angels and demons shared the opinion that Cazzbein was the fiercest sword bearer in all the spiritual realm.

Vermillion caught notice of Cazzbein's hands, laying almost threateningly on top of the deadly blades and he was quick to discontinue his disdainful line of communication. Instead, he turned his attention toward the intoxicated man seated within their presence. The demon leaned in and glanced at the human's forehead, and a sinister chuckle escaped his evil lips.

"This one does not bear the seal of God on his forehead." He was quick to declare, drawing an irritated expression from the angel. "Your failure is most appreciated." The insulting words were like a smack in the face to Cazzbein, and he proceeded to give his retort by unsheathing his blades with lightning quick reflexes. The tip of each scimitar rested upon the demon's esophagus after the incredibly quick maneuver was finished. The tactic had been executed with such blinding speed, that the only evidence it had been performed at all was a resonant ring made by the blades as they exited their sheaths.

Vermillion's eyes opened wide with disbelief, and he dared not make a move toward his own weapon lest he welcome Cazzbein's brilliant blades to penetrate his throat. Although the demon was a creature of the spiritual realm and could not be physically killed, he could, however, be slain in battle and then cast into the pit of outer darkness before the Day of Judgment. There he would be imprisoned for quite a long time before being cast into the Lake of Fire that was created for Satan and his fallen kin. The thought of that was far more horrific than any notions of death.

"Speak, but one more insult to me, swine," Cazzbein warned. "And I will cut your tongue from your foul mouth." The look of malice that flickered to life in Cazzbein's clear blue orbs convinced the demon to refrain from any more slander.

Wisely, Vermillion bit his lip, and then slowly backed out of range of the deadly blades. After he was sure he was far enough away that the swords would do him no further harm, Vermillion rubbed a dirty hand on his neck where the weapons had been. To his disgust, a wisp of smoke, which resembled a dark shadow, was slightly trickling from a small wound. The shadowy matter happened to be the demon's life essence, and the sight of the precious substance exiting his body angered Vermillion dearly.

He subtly entertained the thought of brandishing his wicked sword, in an attempt to repay the gesture. However, the intelligent creature of darkness knew that not even ten demons could possibly stand a chance against Cazzbein in swordplay, so the thought, although hard to digest, slowly faded away into nothingness. Nevertheless, the utter hatred the two spiritual beings held for one another was still quite evident.

It was then that Scott's convulsing body caught both their attention. His heart had finally taken its last beat, and the man had at long last realized how fragile his life really was. He stumbled from his barstool all the while clutching his chest in anguish. He then collapsed to the floor where he drew the attention of the other drunken patrons. They rushed to his aid, but little did they know their help would do him no good. Scott was dead.

In the spiritual realm, Vermillion and Cazzbein watched as Scott's soul escaped the fleshly shell that had been his covering all the years of his life. The human now stood in the spiritual realm with them, as the look of disbelief etched his concerned features.

"Where am I…?" He managed to ask.

"Your new home, human." Vermillion answered, with the look of cruelty washing over his fair visage.

With that reply, a wave of shadowy-like figures poured out of the dark portal. They had no particular shape, and no decisive characteristics to mark them, they were simply dark spirits that came to claim their prize.

With utter brutality they grabbed hold of Scott. Their touch was sticky, like nothing Scott had ever known on Earth. It reminded him of the most unrelenting adhesive imaginable, yet it was bitterly cold. Their savage grip was like iron, and with every limb they grasped, Scott was sure it would be viciously torn from him. The evil spirits tugged at their new acquisition with unimaginable strength, and although Scott knew he was fighting for his pure survival, he could not slow their pace no matter how hard he fought. They were drawing him into the pit of eternal darkness, and Scott was powerless to fight them off. The helpless soul looked at Cazzbein for one fleeting second as the dark forces pulled him by. Scott knew that a creature so beautiful could only be an angel. "Help me!" He screamed over and over again, in a blood-curdling shriek.

Cazzbein could only watch though. Everyone on Earth is given the same opportunities that Scott was given, so there were no excuses. You either accept Jesus Christ's gift for eternal salvation, or you reject it. There is no middle ground.

"I tried." Cazzbein muttered under his breath, more for his own ears to hear than anyone else's in attendance. The guardian recalled countless times that he tried to get Scott's attention to make him aware of the fact that God's message was all around him. There were many occasions that Scott had driven by churches, or changed the channel on the television when an evangelist was preaching, and even ignored the Holy Bible that was placed in motel rooms, and doctor's offices. Whether Cazzbein liked it or not, by making no decision at all, Scott had in reality already made his decision, and therefore sealed his fate forever.

The angel, who normally possessed a strong, confident demeanor, now bore the expression of heartbreaking sorrow. Cazzbein never delighted in seeing sinners receive judgment for their sins, and he knew God did not either. However, that did not change the fact that punishment would be swiftly enacted if an unrighteous soul entered into the spiritual realm. Within himself, the angel knew what was far worse for a sinners unsaved soul than the painful torture it would endure for all eternity, was the fact that there would no more hope for them to cling to. Anything could be tolerated for a time, so long as you knew there was hope for you to hold on to. But, without God's loving grace, Cazzbein knew there was no further hope for those lost souls who entered into the gates of outer darkness.

Scott's agonizing pleas for help continued even after the dark spirits pulled him into the portal, and then, like all the tortured souls before him, the screams grew even stronger as they ultimately realize their fate is forever sealed.

"My work here is done." Vermillion said with finality. Then the demon slowly backed towards the portal while continuing to hold Cazzbein in his snake-like gaze. With his hand still clutching the wound on his neck, he gave the guardian angel some final words, "I will not soon forget our meeting this day, Cazzbein!"

Looking for some response from the angel, Cazzbein merely shot his enemy a grin, pleased with the work he had performed on the demon's neck, and then returned his magnificent blades to their scabbards with no outward signs of concern. The patronizing gesture only served to make the demon all the more livid, as he plunged himself back into the dark portal in which he emerged. As if on cue, the murky gates closed eerily behind him, and then, with a tremendous sound of booming thunder, the portal was sealed.

After the evil beings had made their exits, Cazzbein took one last look at the human's gathered around Scott's deceased body. *Such careless creatures they are,* he thought. *How could such fragile little beings, who were not omnipotent by any stretch of the imagination, take their short lives for granted so much?*

The answer would elude him this night, just as it had the last several thousand times he had asked himself that same question. With nothing more to do here, he took to flight on his gorgeous white wings, and headed back to his master's kingdom for another assignment.

Cazzbein soared high above the tavern, slipping through the ceiling as though the structure was nothing more than air to him. Into the night sky the angel flew with purpose. He looked down for a moment as he ascended into the clouds and saw hundreds of his Holy brothers and sisters all doing the duties that were assigned to them.

Each and every one of the angels watched silently from the mysterious boundaries of the spiritual realm, waiting patiently for their services to be needed. All of his siblings were assigned a certain task to perform, and each and every one of them would perform that task when the time came without question or complaint.

After he drifted through the fluffy mass of nighttime clouds, he caught sight of the magnificent kingdom of Heaven. Its awe-inspiring radiance washed over him more intensely than the beams of a thousand suns. Its tall white walls stretched on even further than his exceptional eyesight could bear witness to. Till this day the guardian angel found it amazing that he had been created within the walls of the magnificent kingdom, and had protected the mighty structure from harm, but still had not seen its splendor in its entirety. Nevertheless, he was pleased beyond all reason to be a part of the wonder that took place within its pearly gates.

Cazzbein could see a countless number of other angels flowing in and out of the splendid entrance, as some went on their way to their next assignment, and others, like himself, came back to receive another mission of their own. The spiritual being had been sent on so many assignments in his long existence that he had stopped counting eons ago. The amount of projects meant nothing to him anyhow. It was the success rate of his handiwork that signified any true importance. Yet, it was that same success rate that troubled him. With the world falling further and further into sin, it was becoming more difficult to secure victories for his Master, and that thought bothered him more than words could express. Even though Cazzbein knew that it only took one saved soul with as little faith as a tiny mustard seed for God to work many wonders through, the angel still desired more of the humans to repent.

What good is it to be sent forth on a mission to protect one of the humans if they never allowed themselves the pleasure of being added to the flock? He wondered.

Even though the answer to that question escaped him, Cazzbein knew God's love for the fragile little beings went further than anything the angel could ever comprehend. Therefore, he would perform his duties to the best of his abilities, and leave the rest up to his Master.

Once inside the mighty gates, Cazzbein was filled with an even greater sense of peace than he had had just moments ago. Whenever he was inside the sheltered walls, an enormous sensation of refuge would come over him. Nothing could penetrate the massive fortifications, he knew, which is why the feeling of tranquility was so much more evident to him than when he was outside the enormous walls. Cazzbein could not help but pause for a moment and consider the splendor that surrounded him. Earth had its beauty because the hand of God created it. However, not even Earth's most serene locations could compare to this magnificent kingdom that even words could not begin to describe.

"Amazing isn't it Cazzbein?" A familiar voice called, tearing his attention away from the grandeur. Cazzbein turned to see his longtime friend Gunthar watching him with his powerful arms crossed in front of his massive barrel shaped chest. Gunthar stood a few inches taller than Cazzbein. They both shared long, flowing manes, however, Gunthar's locks possessed a sandy-blonde color. Cazzbein chose to let his long tresses flow gracefully down his backside unopposed, Gunthar on the other hand, wore his locks tied into a tight tail so that he could better see his enemies when he wielded his massive war hammer in battle.

Gunthar was by far the strongest angel Cazzbein was familiar with. The powerful guardian adorned himself with a superb golden breastplate that he wore over a flowing white gown, and as always, an impressive war hammer was strapped to his backside. Across the bridge of his nose Gunthar had his name marked in fine angelic script. The translation was known only to him and his Master, and when spoken, would give the angel power to vanquish a small number of demons. However, the power could only be used once every hundred years.

"Well met, Gunthar!" Cazzbein greeted, clasping his friend on one of his broad shoulders.

"What brings you back to paradise?" Gunthar inquired, rubbing a hand down his powerful jaw line.

"The same reason you are here, I would imagine, my friend." Cazzbein answered slyly.

"If you are here for another mission," The sturdy angel began. "Then, yes, we are here with the same motives in mind."

As the two guardians reacquainted themselves with each other's company, they happened to walk by a large elegantly decorated fountain with the waters inside so pure and clear that they could see straight down upon the Earth below. The glowing blue orb seemed to linger soothingly in the dark silhouette, peacefully revolving on its unseen axis as it brought each and every continent into the sunlight of daybreak and then slowly back to night again. The sight of the slowly transpiring panorama was enough to make them both pause and take notice.

"Look at it, Gunthar." Cazzbein said, in a tone that sounded as though he were losing himself in the vastness of it all. "From here it looks so peaceful…"

"I know what you mean, my friend," Gunthar answered, as he heaved his huge war hammer from around his shoulders to reveal thousands of tiny gashes whittled into the handle. The muscular angel was careful to point out two cuts that were more recently made than any of the rest. "However, the world of man is not to be taken lightly. I had an unpleasant encounter with two of those traitorous fallen angels, but after our meeting, the only sign of their wretched existence is the two gashes in my handle."

Cazzbein smiled at his friend's entertaining comment. He knew that Gunthar kept an accurate score of all the demons that had fallen to the mighty war hammer, and the several thousand marks made upon the weapon's handle would provide evidence to that fact.

"Gunthar," Cazzbein said, pausing to make sure he had his friends undivided attention, "How have your assignments been turning out as of late?"

The strong angel shrugged his shoulders at the question.

"If you are inquiring about success, then I would have to admit I've seen better days." He answered solemnly.

"Yes…I know exactly what you mean." Cazzbein said grimly. "Just once I would like to be sent on an assignment to watch over someone that isn't so careless, or who isn't so difficult to communicate with."

"I agree." Gunthar admitted. "However, the humans have become far too distracted these days, with their fast-paced lifestyles."

Cazzbein nodded his agreement. Gunthar's words made him think about Scott, and the distracted way of life he had lived. If he wasn't preoccupied with work, or women, or his disgruntled daily grind, it was the alcohol that blurred his vision.

"Sin is running rampant down there." Gunthar said, tearing Cazzbein from his thoughts. "And it's all because of those rebellious traitors!"

"Exactly!" Cazzbein agreed. "Why, just on my last mission, I had a…"

"Cazzbein!" Came a familiar call from behind, which made the angel discontinue his previous statement.

Cazzbein turned to see another of his comrades, Anthony, running toward him with a rolled-up scroll in his slender hand. Anthony was every bit as old as Cazzbein and Gunthar, yet he seemed to possess a much more youthful demeanor than either of the two. There was a spring to his step, a little more rosy color around his cheeks, and a tad bit more innocence twinkling inside his radiant green eyes. His light blonde hair was cropped short, and he wore no armor, yet for some reason, Anthony chose to wear a small, silver mace fastened to the belt he wore around his waist.

The weapon almost seemed out of place as it dangled by the youthful looking angel's side, since no one can remember Anthony ever having to bring the weapon to bear. Anthony was mostly used as a courier, and had rarely been to Earth. His duties, more or less, consisted of delivering messages between the angels. Yet, on some rare occasions, he might be asked to deliver a message to someone in the world of man. Still, that was an infrequent event. Since speed was Anthony's main attribute, his Master adorned the young-looking angel's feet with modern day sneakers. This gave Anthony an even greater advantage in swiftness over his other angelic kin, and also added to his already youthful appearance.

Cazzbein and Gunthar, on the other hand, were battle-hardened warriors, ideally created for combat. Their skills were much more suited for the likes of the human world, where fallen angels sought to destroy them. It's quite possible that the lack of experience is what kept Anthony's young-looking eyes flickering with their youthful aura.

"Oh joy! If it isn't little Anthony! Gunthar remarked sarcastically to Cazzbein.

"Easy Gunthar." Cazzbein cautioned. "He is still our brother, is he not?"

Gunthar could only roll his eyes, and shrug his massive shoulders for his reply to Cazzbein's question, nevertheless, his artificial sentiments were heard loud and clear. Cazzbein was well aware of the fact that Gunthar was not only the strongest angel he knew, but also the most loving. Cazzbein often commented on how he felt that there was a greater dose of love placed into larger angels, and Gunthar was surely no exception. That is why he knew

Gunthar's comments toward Anthony were purely counterfeit, and were only expressed so that the gentle giant could hide his tenderness.

"You're finally here!" Anthony shouted, once he was within earshot of the two guardians.

"Finally?" Cazzbein asked, referring to the fact that he arrived only moments after his last assignment had expired.

"There's no time to explain!" Anthony said abruptly, as he handed the scroll to Cazzbein. "Everything you need to know is in there."

Cazzbein unrolled the scroll, eager to find out what Anthony's great haste was all about. After the first few lines, the angel's crystal-clear orbs opened wide showing his concern to his friends standing nearby.

"What is it?" Gunthar asked curiously.

"My next mission is about to start under some very dangerous circumstances."

"Go with him!" Anthony urged Gunthar. "He may need your assistance."

The muscular angel turned his attention back to Cazzbein, who was looking around at the marvelous kingdom he would have to leave behind once more. Although his visits were brief, Cazzbein cherished every moment he could spend within the fabulous walls with great bliss. Even though he didn't desire to leave, he knew that his services were needed. So with a steadfast resolve, Cazzbein enfolded the scroll and brought his attention back to his companions.

"Anthony is right," He said somberly. "I may need your help."

With that said, Gunthar nodded his head in support. However, he could not help but wonder what could be so troubling to his friend that he would feel compelled to bring along a companion for aid. Cazzbein was more than able to handle most any situation that could arise. That thought meant little to the powerful angel though. If Cazzbein needed assistance, then he would get it.

"Follow me." Cazzbein said.

Being the multi-tasked creatures that they were, the angels were sometimes required to be at many places as quickly as possible. They were able to do this the same way a sunbeam lights the Earth. Although there may be only one ray of sunlight, it is still able to cover a large portion of the world, quite the same way an angel can travel to so many destinations in so little time.

With no more than a subtle thought the two guardian angels faded from sight, leaving nothing but a faint bluish outline of their figures to mark that they were ever there. When the silhouettes faded into nothingness, Anthony was relieved, because he knew two of the finest guardian angels he could have sent were well on their way.

Chapter 2

Jody Brooks didn't consider the evening to be any different from any other given night. The small town of Loves Park, where she was born and raised, was normally calm and peaceful, and on this night, there was no exception. The stars speckled the nighttime horizon like thousands of sparkling diamonds laid out on a dark piece of velvet, giving the evening a much more peaceful appearance than usual. The summertime breeze, although warm and a bit dry, blew gently through her long auburn hair, bringing a moment of brief satisfaction. The calm wind was pale in comparison to the air-conditioned atmosphere of the 24-hour grocery store in which she exited, but seeing as though she needed to get home, Jody had no choice but to step out into the heat anyway.

Although she greatly disliked having to walk through the vacant parking lot at night, especially when the lighting was of such poor quality, the young woman knew she would have no time to pick up her necessities in the morning without being late for work. So, since it was nothing more than a minor inconvenience, and a two-block detour out of her way, Jody sacrificed the time and went to the deserted supermarket before heading home.

The young woman was barely in her mid-twenties, but already she had a great sense of maturity about herself. While most of her friends were still indulging in the late-night drinking, dancing, and promiscuous lifestyles in which they lived, Jody chose to focus her attention toward her home life. Not so long ago, the young woman's parents had died in a fatal car accident, leaving her unaided in the cruel world. However, her lonely status was soon about to change.

Jody's belly was swollen with child. She was already late into her eighth month, and would be giving birth very soon. The thought of raising a child alone terrified Jody, but seeing no other alternatives, the young woman faced the brutal facts and decided to meet the task with committed determination. Jody had been raised in a Christian home with good upstanding principles. So to her, there were no other options but to give birth to the child and raise it in the same manner in which she was brought up. Although her parents tried their best to get Jody to abandon the out-of-control lifestyle in which she was living and surrender herself to God, the young woman unfortunately had to learn the hard way.

In addition to losing her parents, getting pregnant was far too much of a burden for the young woman to tolerate without the helping hand of God in her life. Jody only wished that her parents could have lived long enough to see that all their painstaking efforts to bring her to Christ worked out in the long run.

Jody could not help but think to herself that her rundown Chevy Cavalier looked incredibly lonesome while sitting all alone in the abandoned parking lot. Even though she stood several yards away from the automobile, its dark burgundy paint could be seen flaking away under the effects of rust it had acquired throughout its long existence.

The young woman tried feverishly to fish the vehicle's keys out of her purse with her free hand, while managing not to drop the overloaded bag she clung to in her other hand. As she struggled, little did she know, her meticulous efforts were being carefully examined under the watchful eyes of several evil beings from the world of outer darkness.

"Are you sure this is the one in which we seek, Hunter?" Dartamus, the smallest and most devious demon among them, asked their leader.

Hunter, by far the most cunning one in the group, did not immediately reply to his shifty eyed companion. Instead, he held one of his elbows in one hand, while tapping a slender finger on his smooth chin, deep in thought as he examined the scene before him.

Something seemed amiss to the crafty demon. Jody was a devout woman, and Hunter could clearly see the Seal of God glowing vividly on her forehead. The Seal was placed upon all of God's children after accepting the gift of everlasting life. The flowing insignia served as a warning to all the creatures of darkness that the bearer would be wholly protected if any of them attempted any wrong doings. Seeing the emblem shimmering in the night was more than enough to confuse Hunter.

Could there have been a mistake? He thought. Attacks upon humans bearing the Seal of God were not only uncommon, they were rarely successful. Nevertheless, his orders were indeed clear. This woman fit the description perfectly. There was no doubt in the demon's diabolical mind that this female was the one of whom his master spoke of. Hunter now understood why his master thought it necessary to send such a large assemblage of henchmen to accompany him on the mission. However, the dark creature also knew that if he or any one of his servants were to attack the young Christian woman, it would take much more than the fifteen demons in his group to fend off any guardians that would arrive to aid her.

The noisy sound of a garbage truck's hydraulics being put to work stole Hunter's attention. Maybe he and his assorted crew of underlings would not have to assault the human directly after all.

"Dartamus, see to it that the garbage truck takes care of this fair lady for us." Hunter said calmly, as a malicious grin formed upon his smooth visage.

The underhanded little demon knew exactly what Hunter was suggesting, and returned an evil grin of his own as his reply. Without another word, Dartamus wafted like a fog in a gentle breeze toward the vehicle with wicked intentions in mind.

Oblivious to the many villainous eyes watching her every movement, Jody managed to pull her keys from her purse and unlock the passenger side door to her beat up Chevy. She placed the overloaded bag of groceries in the seat, satisfied to be relieved of the heavy bundle, and then proceeded to close the door while clutching her aching back.

Jody leaned up against the old Chevy to catch her breath. As the woman rested her weight upon the vehicle, she took a moment to recollect about how easy it had been to perform the simple tasks she once took for granted before her pregnancy. Simply walking across the long parking lot used to take no effort at all, yet now Jody felt as though she had just ran a marathon. How thankful she would be when she was once again able to do simple chores without being sapped of all her energy.

While Jody took the time to regain her vigor, Dartamus sought to take advantage of her weakened state. The conniving little demon located the lines that supplied air to the brakes of the garbage truck, and with one swift tug he managed to wrench them free from their home. After doing so, the rig's emergency system kicked in, locking the brakes in place once again. This quandary proved to be little hindrance to the demon though, as he pried the brakes open with his unimaginable strength, leaving the vehicle powerless to stop. He then ordered several of his evil kin to push the semi into a steady roll, which they did with little effort.

The driver of the truck was horrified when he heard the hissing sound of the diesel's brake lines spewing out air. His worst fears were realized when he slammed a heavy foot down on the brake pedal only to discover that there was no pressure to slow the truck's pace, and to make matters worse, the diesel was on a collision course towards a helpless pregnant woman. Seeing that the brakes were doing no good, the driver immediately hit the horn on the steering wheel in an attempt to warn the helpless woman to get out of the way of the oncoming semi, which had picked up considerable speed under the strength of the powerful creatures of darkness.

The deafening sound of the truck's horn startled Jody. She turned in the direction in which the sound came only to stare confusedly into the bright beams of the semi's oncoming headlights. The large vehicle had picked up so much speed that Jody was unable to move out of the way in time. With no options presenting themself in the short time she had left, Jody did the only thing she could think of that would calm her fears. The young woman closed her eyes and prepared to meet her end in peace.

It was then that Cazzbein burst onto the scene. With brilliant speed that could have left a lightning bolt in his trail, the guardian angel plunged into danger's way, giving no care for his own well-being. He quickly thrust himself between Jody and the runaway semi, positioning himself squarely in the center of the truck's huge bumper. The impact was massive, but with his teeth gritted and his determination unyielding, Cazzbein was not moved an inch. The cold hard steel of the semi's sturdy frame buckled and contorted around the angel's body, surrounding him in an envelope of twisted metal. The sound of glass shards and debris crashing to the ground could be heard all around him, and Cazzbein could only hope he was in time to save the young woman.

After Cazzbein was sure the truck's momentum had ceased, he turned to find Jody. He was greatly pleased to see that the young woman was alive and well. However, the reason behind her well being surprised him. It was true that he stopped the runaway semi before it could do any damage to Jody, but he was shocked to see that a third angel had intervened. The third angel, whom Cazzbein was unfamiliar with, was a beautiful female, with strawberry blonde locks, and sparkling green eyes. She had pulled Jody to the side and sheltered the woman from the falling fragments by wrapping her wings around the human's body like a feathered cocoon. Not so much as a shockwave from the crash had penetrated the anonymous angel's embrace.

Bewildered, Cazzbein had no time to ask questions. He knew the demons that had been the cause of this turmoil still needed to be dealt with, and he intended to do so with great pleasure. Pulling his scimitars from their scabbards, the angel turned his attention toward them with a gleam of anticipation in his eyes.

Cazzbein was further relieved to see that Gunthar had already vanquished several of the deceitful creatures. The angel then almost chuckled aloud when he realized his friend would be adding even more notches to the already impressive collection of swipes on the massive war hammer's handle.

From all human perspectives, the parking lot was barren, except for the driver of the demolished garbage truck and Jody. However, to the spiritual beings that were present, the blacktopped surface was a very real, and very active battlefield. Cazzbein looked past Gunthar, who was battling a large group of the evil demons single-handedly, and caught sight of the leader, Hunter. Through all the chaos of the surrounding skirmish, the evil spirit held his composure in an almost eerie calm. In the demon's slender hands he held a menacing looking saber and serrated dagger with many jewels decorating its silver hilt. Judging from his posture, Cazzbein could tell Hunter eagerly awaited the moment they would lock blades.

Hunter was a remarkable creature. Throughout the centuries he remained as true as he could to his former angelic form without openly offending his demonic kin. Hunter had a trim physique with each and every firm muscle taut for warfare. His stark white hair was long and straight, flowing gracefully down either side of his gray feathered wings and ending just shy of the small of his back. He adorned himself in black, studded leather armor that he wore over a loose-fitting dark gown, much like that of his angelic kin. His vivid, lavender eyes resembled gemstones and sparkled with excitement as he anticipated the impending duel.

Cazzbein knew Hunter well. Before the evil being fell from grace, his reputation as an able sword bearer was legendary among all the angels in Heaven. The tales of his exploits were renowned, and he was held in high esteem. But since that darkened day so many centuries ago, Hunter has put his malicious blades to use sowing seeds of cruelty. Some would argue that hunter was second only to Cazzbein in the art of swordplay. Hunter, on the other hand, felt in his own blackened heart that he was the better of the two, and was eager to settle the issue once and for all.

"Well met, Cazzbein," Hunter greeted, as he stooped into a low bow. "I have been longing for the day when I could meet with you in battle."

"Then you have been craving for the day of your demise, foul creature," Cazzbein replied flatly. "For you will not take pleasure in the outcome of this meeting, I assure you."

With that said, Hunter lunged forward with the tip of his saber leading the way. The attack had a twofold purpose. First it was executed to test the angel's reflexes, and secondly, to end the contest with an easy kill, if at all possible. Cazzbein deflected the strike with little effort though and once again the combatants found themselves on even ground.

Hunter was indeed impressed with what ease Cazzbein used to repel the attack. The guardian angel's reflexes were undeniably swift, just as the rumors had acknowledged. Nevertheless, even with the lightning quick speed that had just been displayed, Hunter pressed on, showing no visible signs of apprehension.

With a rapid succession of thrusts Hunter came in fiercely, charging in with his dagger, and then swiping out wide with his saber. Cazzbein recognized the attack routine and realized immediately what the demon was trying to accomplish. The dagger assault was merely thrown into the mix so that he would have to keep his eyes away from the real danger, which was Hunter's saber. The second Cazzbein became too distracted with averting the dagger's serrated blade, the saber would swoop in for a killing strike.

Cazzbein knew exactly what Hunter was trying to achieve with this method of attack, so therefore he knew how to defend against it. Twirling his body away from the dagger, Cazzbein was then able to block the jagged edge with the scimitar in his right hand, leaving his left blade free to cut a clean gash just above Hunter's exposed left knee. The demon let loose a cry of pain before backing off a few paces, amazed once again by the angel's impressive speed, and the skill in which he wielded his scimitars.

"The first strike is indeed yours, Cazzbein." Hunter spat, glancing at the shadowy life's essence seeping from the fresh wound.

"As will the killing blow, I assure you." Cazzbein answered confidently, drawing a disgusted look from his adversary.

Cazzbein was hoping to anger Hunter with his disdainful words, so that he could draw the demon out of his rhythmic fighting style. If Hunter could be made to lose his temper, then maybe he would exchange blows in a more erratic fashion, giving Cazzbein the edge in their duel.

Unfortunately, Hunter saw through the ruse, and was able to keep his feelings in check. He came in again with a series of thrusts that left Cazzbein with a taste of respect for his well-trained opponent. Hunter's speed was unlike anything Cazzbein had ever encountered in battle before. The lethal tips of his weapons came dangerously close to their intended target, only to be parried by each of Cazzbein's scimitars. This time it was Hunter who twirled his body around with a double blade slash to Cazzbein's left side. The guardian angel was barely able to get one of his scimitars up in time to ward off Hunter's saber, but the serrated dagger was left unopposed and cut a deep line into Cazzbein's left bicep.

"Now I have returned the favor, guardian." Hutner sneered, as he licked a portion of the angel's essence from the blade of his dagger in order to mock his enemy. Cazzbein was speechless. Never had he felt the sting of an opponent's weapon.

Truly Hunter is a force to be reckoned with, he thought, as he inspected the wound.

The angel had never seen his own life's essence running freely from an injury before. It appeared to him as tiny bits of light trying to escape from behind a solid surface. The pain stung him terribly, but not nearly bad enough to get him to discontinue the fight. Trying to keep his own anger in place, and ignoring the throbbing sensation he now felt in his arm, Cazzbein raised his scimitars for another sequence of attacks.

He didn't have to wait long. Hunter ran in with an intense fire in his eyes. With his weapon's first taste of striking Cazzbein, Hunter was enthralled in the battle, and could almost sense a victory well within his grasp. Cazzbein remained vigilant, and had warded off several of the oncoming swipes, before a very large fist slammed into hunter's face, knocking the demon to his backside, where he then slid several feet away.

Gunthar had chased away nearly all of Hunter's party, and proceeded to take the fight to the most powerful dark spirit yet remaining on the field of battle. However, with his back turned, two demon underlings decided to take advantage of the situation, raising their weapons against the large angel for their vicious attack. They may have very well succeeded with their efforts, if it had not been for two very precise arrow shots sinking into their torsos, causing them to crumble into nothingness.

When Gunthar traced the arrows' flight pattern back to the source, he saw the unknown angel standing defiantly with bow still in hand. With a show of camaraderie, the strawberry blonde angel nodded her head at Gunthar. Recognizing the sentiment, the powerful angel returned the gesture with gratitude.

As the two angels showed their amity, Hunter pulled himself from the ground, rubbing his cheek with the back of his dagger wielding hand. Seeing that his small band had been driven away, leaving him to face the guardian angels all alone, Hunter decided that discretion was the better part of valor, and turned to take his leave.

"We will meet again another day, I assure you Cazzbein!" The foul demon hissed. "Then we will indeed see who is the better between us!"

"I shall look forward to it, fiend!" Cazzbein shot back.

With the look of intensity still burning wildly in their locked gazes, Hunter vanished into the wind like a wisp of smoke being carried away in a gentle breeze. When the dark creature was finally gone Gunthar noticed that Cazzbein was injured.

"You've been wounded." The giant angel commented.

Cazzbein turned his attention to the cut only to see that his life's essence was still trickling from the open gash.

"It will heal." He stated solemnly.

Gunthar could tell from his friend's tone that he should not bring mention to the injury again. Instead, he turned his interest to Jody, to see if she had survived the incident. While the battle had been going on, the paramedics and police had arrived on the scene and rushed Jody into an ambulance. The third, and unknown angel, was standing outside the rear doors, still watching over the young lady with her arms crossed over her bosom.

"Greetings, by brothers." She said, when Gunthar and Cazzbein approached. "My name is Glistinia."

"You must be Miss Brooks' guardian." Cazzbein acknowledged. "How did she fare this night?"

"The runaway semi posed no problem, thanks to you." She answered. "However, the sudden shock has sent her into labor, where I am afraid she is not doing so well."

Cazzbein used his extraordinary vision to peer through the ambulance walls so that he may view the contents first hand. The paramedics were doing their jobs flawlessly, taking great care of Jody. Unfortunately, the young lady had slipped into unconsciousness, and they were delivering the baby by cesarean.

"I do not understand." Gunthar admitted. "If you are the young woman's guardian, then why were Cazzbein and I sent here?"

Before Gunthar's question could be answered, the sound of an infant's crying filled the night, as a newborn baby boy took his first breath of air.

"It was not Miss Brooks whom we were sent to protect my old friend." Cazzbein replied, as he put an affirming hand to one of the powerful angel's broad shoulders. "We were sent here to make sure little Ethan was brought safely into the world."

*   *   *   *   *

On the other end of the parking lot, a quite ordinary looking man had watched the display in its entirety. His eyes were of such a blue clarity that they almost seemed to glow in the darkness as he took the sight in with great interest. He murmured something aloud, as if having a conversation with himself, and then ran an anxious hand through his jet-black hair. It wasn't until he heard the infant's cries that a pleased smile spread across his face. With what could only be described as the look of relief upon him, the man pulled the hood of his jacket over his head and walked away from the commotion, all the while exchanging dialogue with some unseen individuals.

Chapter 3

Twenty-four years later…

Ethan Brooks stared out at the horizon, in deep thought, while sipping his morning coffee. Nothing at all seemed to phase the young man as he watched the dawn's sunbeams glistening off the large beads of freshly fallen dew that covered his back lawn. Even the melody of the many singing birds that filled the overhead sky could not break his concentration, as the feathered creatures awoke, and began the business of their day. In fact, it wasn't until he downed the last bit of his java that he showed any concern at all.

Long gone were the events from that dreadful night in the grocery store parking lot. Although the angel, Glistinia, had secretly protected his mother from an instant death, the trauma of the incident mixed with the physical pain of childbirth was too much for her to endure. The paramedics were able to sustain Jody just long enough for her to hold her new son in her arms and give him the name that he would bear for the rest of his lifetime. Then she was carried off into Heaven by the angel, Glistinia, where she would spend all eternity in paradise. Even though Ethan was not with his mother for very long, the circumstances of that fateful evening would forever change the outcome of his life, whether he was aware of it or not.

Turning his attention away from the pleasant outdoor scenery, Ethan took his empty mug to the kitchen and ran a bit of warm water through it, so the dark colored beverage would not stain his favorite cup. He then placed the mug on the counter next to his .40 caliber Glock. Plucking the pistol off the dark, granite countertop, Ethan slid the 15-shot clip into the handle and then chambered a bullet. Afterward, he removed the clip, added another bullet, and then injected the clip back into the pistol, upgrading the weapon to its maximum shot allowance of sixteen. When he had finished, Ethan made sure the safety was engaged and then strapped the weapon into the holster that he wore under his left arm.

"Don't forget these, *detective*." His wife's voice came from the other side of the room. It did not escape Ethan's attention that she used great emphasis when announcing his new title.

"I like the sound of that." Ethan said, as he turned to see Becky standing in the doorway holding his "old blues".

"Detective Ethan Brooks does have a nice ring to it." She commented, as she hung the old police uniforms on the refrigerator handle by the wire hanger on which they were neatly draped.

"Let's just see if I make it through the first day." Ethan commented, while rubbing a hand through his thick, dark brown hair. He looked at his reflection in the glass that was mounted within the kitchen cabinet door and fussed with his locks, trying to get the spiky style just the way he liked it.

Becky smiled at her husband behind his back, because she recognized the fidgeting for what it truly was. Ethan was nervous, due to the fact that it was his first day on the job as a detective, and the sudden care in his appearance was merely a way for him to ease his anxieties.

"Your hair looks fine, Mr. Brooks." Becky said playfully, as she wrapped her arms around her husband's neck, being sure to make eye contact with his reflection within the glass that served as his mirror." "Feeling nervous?"

"Is it that obvious?" He asked, staring into the mirrored image of his wife's big blue eyes.

Becky spun her husband around and looked straight into his five o'clock shadow he kept on his face. "If you could handle all those years as a patrolman, I'm sure you'll do just fine as a detective."

"I know you're right." Ethan agreed with a sigh of relief. "It's just that, I've been dreaming of this day for a long time, and I don't want to blow it."

"You're not going to blow it." Becky assured, with a wink. "You breezed through the academy, caught the attention of the top brass with your skills as a patrol officer, and nearly aced the detectives exam. If anything, you're liable to earn another promotion."

"I wish I shared your confidence." Ethan replied.

"You'll be fine." Becky said, before giving her husband a soothing kiss on the lips.

Ethan considered himself to be a very fortunate man, as he held Becky in his arms, admiring her. Not many men could boast that they married their high school sweetheart. However, here he was with her slim waist wrapped up within his affectionate embrace, her long blonde hair laying as straight and perfect as it had been before they went to bed last evening. His feelings had only grown for the woman since he first met her some seventeen years ago when they had worked together at a motel on their very first summer job. Ethan still remembers how her tanned, shapely legs had drawn his attention while she was wearing her maid uniform, and now those same beautiful stems teased him every morning from underneath the hem of her housecoat.

"You know this new position is going to be hard on you too, right?" He asked with a smirk.

"How so?" Becky inquired.

"Well, there's going to be a lot more laundry for you to do now that I'm wearing civilian clothing all day." Ethan joked.

"I think I can manage." The young woman replied with a grin of her own.

"Way to take one for the team, babe." Ethan replied, before giving her a kiss on the forehead. "Now, as much as I'd like to stay here all day, I'd better get going. What kind of first impression would I make if I showed up late on my first day?"

"I agree." Becky added, before relinquishing Ethan from her hug. "Just imagine how many bad guys would get away if you played hooky."

"I shudder to think." Ethan snickered, while slipping into his gray, hooded jacket. After doing so, he then clipped his detective's badge onto his belt, making his outfit complete.

"What time do you think you'll be home?" Becky asked.

"I have no idea." Ethan answered, while heading toward the door.

"Aren't you forgetting something?" Becky questioned.

"What?" Ethan asked, before turning to see his wife pinching his wedding band between her slender fingers.

"Actually, babe, I wasn't going to wear it to work anymore." He admitted, with the sound of regret in his tone.

"Why not?" Becky asked.

"Don't take it personally, "Ethan began. "It's just that I have no idea what kind of scumbags I'm going to be dealing with, and I don't want to advertise that I have a family they can hurt."

"Oh." Becky replied, with a nod. "That makes sense."

"This is the kind of job where I *literally* don't want to bring any of my work home with me." He added, before giving the woman a kiss on the lips. "Now, have a good day, and I'll see you sometime tonight."

"I love you." Becky said, as Ethan exited the front door.

"Love you too…" The young man replied, as he made his way to the sedan waiting in the driveway.

Becky watched as her husband climbed behind the wheel, started the vehicle, and then slowly drove off down the street. She had put on a brave front for Ethan's sake, but in truth, she was a nervous wreck. It was always hard for Becky to watch her husband head out each morning when he was merely a patrolman, but now that he was a detective, it seemed to cause those fearful feelings to multiply. Being the devout Christian that she was, Becky did the only thing she knew to do that would help her husband in his dangerous profession… She prayed.

*　　　*　　　*　　　*　　　*

As Ethan drove down the street, little did he know he was being watched under the scrutinizing gaze of a spirit of darkness. The grotesque underling clung to a limb of a nearby tree like some sort of oversized, deformed bird until Ethan's vehicle had driven out of sight. Then the bulbous little creature known only as Dartamus, jumped off his perch and wafted through the air toward his destination. His gnarled face was twisted into a wicked scowl, as he scoffed at the human from the invisible confines of the spiritual realm. The little demon cursed his misfortune for having to perform such meaningless tasks with many vile blasphemies as he made his way back to his master under the power of his undersized, leathery, bat-like wings.

With his goal clearly in mind, Dartamus flew with great haste through the neighborhood even though he dreaded seeing his master again with every fiber of his being. Dartamus' bloated body flew with much more grace than one would expect. He twisted his way through row after row of houses and parked cars, before leaping behind a large oak tree, making sure to remain in the shadows as he did so, even though his blackened skin was far more dense than the shade he utilized for cover. His bulging, yellowish eyes darted back and forth in his misshapen head as he made sure there were no unwanted sentries to witness his presence. After all, these were times of war, and one had to take all precautions while traveling, lest they meet with an untimely demise at the hands of one of God's Holy Angels. When he was satisfied with his assessment, a crooked smile, made up of many rotted teeth took shape on his distorted face before he leapt into action once more.

With speed that seemed impossible for the plump demon to achieve, Dartamus raced his way down the street until he came to an abandoned house at the end of the block. Never slowing pace, the evil spirit flew straight through the wall as if it were made of nothing more than air.

On his arrival he was surprised to find the lower level of the structure empty. He quickly searched all the rooms on the ground floor and still turned up nothing. After doing so, the demon decided to make his way to the upper portion of the house where he then found his master, Hunter staring calmly out the window with his arms folded neatly behind his back.

"Do you see them, Dartamus?" Hunter asked, already feeling the weight of his servant's stare on his back.

"Do I see…what…master?" The little underling asked, in a timid tone.

"As I examine the skyline, I see more and more of our brothers and sisters heading eastward." Hunter replied, casually.

"What does it mean?" Dartamus asked, curious to know the answer.

"It means that our master is preparing himself for something big." Hunter responded in a placid tone.

"Do you think it's *the time?*" Dartamus inquired, referring to Armageddon, the last battle of the war.

"I do not know." Hunter answered flatly. "Regardless, if it is or if it is not, that does not alter our current mission. What news do you bring?"

"Ethan Brooks has left to begin his workday, master." The plump demon replied.

"And did you see…*him*?" Hunter asked.

"Cazzbein?" Dartamus clarified. "No master. I did not see the angel."

"What is his game?" Hunter asked aloud to himself, through gritted teeth. "The human does not even bear the Seal of God, yet he is protected by one of the fiercest warring angels in existence."

"His wife bears God's mark as did his mother." Dartamus reminded him. "It must be their prayers that have granted him such fine protection."

"No!" Hunter replied, in a heated tone, as he turned to face his subordinate for the first time during the conversation.

"God has some sort of special purpose for this human. It just has not revealed itself as of yet."

Dartamus did not immediately respond. The underling merely watched his master, unsure of what he was going to do next.

"Forgive me master." Dartamus groveled. "I meant no harm."

Hunter had always regretted his decision to rebel against God Almighty, and knew that his time on earth was limited. Most of Hunter's brothers and sisters knew the depth of his disappointment and held him in contempt for his thoughts, yet dared not openly speak out against him for fear of his lethal blades. He felt that the only reason the more powerful demons among the demonic hierarchy tolerated him at all was the fact that they were outnumbered by the angels by a full third and could not spare him. Nevertheless, no matter how much he lamented his decision, he had tossed his lot in with Lucifer, and he would follow whatever course of action his kin asked of him to the dismal end.

"It matters little." Hunter said, the rage slowly fading from his dazzling orbs as he turned his attention back to the scenery outside the window. "This assignment is proving to be as humdrum as the thousand that have preceded it."

"Master...?" Dartamus queried, confused by the sudden change in temperament.

"We need to face the truth, Dartamus," Hunter began.

"Our time in the world is nearly over, and when it is, we will be cast into the Lake of Fire for our transgressions."

"B-But Lucifer is confident that he can rally the humans into aiding in the final battle…" Dartamus countered. "Don't you see? We have a chance at winning the war!"

"Lucifer's overconfidence is why we will spend eternity in Hell." Hunter spat.

"Your words are dangerously close to treason…*master*." The underling warned, as his twisted hand moved toward the hilt of his sword.

"I would hate to have to terminate your many centuries of servitude to me, Dartamus, but I assure you, if you dare to unsheathe your weapon against me, you will be spiraling into the lowest depths of the Abyss before you ever know what happened." Hunter threatened, without ever having looked at his subordinate.

The dangerous edge in Hunter's voice caused Dartamus to reconsider his initial thought. Just as slowly as he had moved his twisted, clawed hand toward his sword, he backed it away.

"As always, I am just frustrated, my old friend." Hunter continued, as he turned to consider the deformed servant. "The prince of this region is shifting the position of our armies, and yet again, here we lie dormant."

"Forgive me for pointing out the obvious, master…" Dartmus began, choosing his words carefully as he spoke.

"Speak your mind wretch!" Hunter barked in a volatile tone.

"It just seems to me…that if you showed a little more loyalty to the cause…we would be called upon more frequently." The sniveling demon replied, hesitantly.

Hunter's fair visage instantly contorted into a look of disgust.

"Is my contempt for this war so open that even a slack jawed buffoon like you manages to see it?" He asked aloud, not really expecting his cohort to answer. "You are right, though. I regret with every fiber of my being that I chose to rebel against God Almighty. But that matters little now. No matter how deep my remorse runs, it will never change the outcome of my fate. The best course of action now is to get back within the good graces of Mistress Vixanna."

The mere mention of Vixanna's name caused Dartamus to recoil in fear. Every visit he remembers having with the hostile demon has not bode well for him, ending in one form of punishment or another. If that was the best course of action Hunter could fathom, then he would much rather continue to remain hidden from the eyes of the demonic hierarchy.

"But master, Mistress Vixanna has no good graces." The imp commented.

"Maybe not to a loathsome underling like you." Hunter replied with a snarl. "But to one possessing skills with the dual blades such as I, she will purr like a kitten to see me."

Dartamus did not share his master's optimism and could only hang his head at the comment.

"Do not look so disheartened, Dartamus." Hunter said, soothingly. "I am certain she has forgotten all about our last visit."

*   *   *   *   *

Tyler Lynch was seated behind the wheel of his custom, charcoal gray "69 Chevy Caprice, halfheartedly watching a drug deal go down across the street as he skimmed through the contents of an important file. Every now and again his well-trained eyes would focus in on the illegal activities transpiring a mere thirty yards away from where he was parked, just to make sure the deal was still going down, and then he would read a few more lines from the paperwork in his hands.

Tyler had never been accused of being the compassionate type. He was raised on the streets from birth and considered himself to be a true product of society. It took no time at all for someone with his caliber of thinking to use his quick wits to find a loophole in the system that would allow him to conduct his lawless, money-making schemes, while still remaining hidden from the eyes of the police. He was able to pull the wool over the eyes of the law enforcement officers so skillfully only due to the fact that the crafty young man was in fact one of them. Even though the young detective had a wall full of commendations, Tyler was as crooked as a knotted-up tree limb. He had what he considered the best of both worlds; a quick and easy way to make a lot of money, and an airtight alibi to cover his tracks.

As Detective Tyler Lynch continued his observation, the passenger side door to his vehicle opened up and a rough looking black man with long hair slicked back in a tight ponytail climbed inside, raising no concern to him.

"Yo, ain't we gonna do something, or are we just gonna sit here all day?" Detective Booker Briggs, asked, gruffly.

"I'm watching what's going down." Tyler replied, glancing over to the scene and then back down again.

"What's in that file that's so important, anyway?" Booker inquired. "You haven't gotten your nose out of it since we rolled up."

"The captain's throwing some new meat our way." Tyler answered, as he passed the file to his partner.

"Ethan Brooks…" Booker said aloud, after reading the name that was typed out on the file's heading. "What do we need another member for?"

"It could mean only one of two things…" Tyler began. "Either the anti-gang task force is proving itself to be effective and the top brass want to expand us, or the new guy's working for Internal Affairs."

"I.A.D.?" Booker asked, his tone growing noticeably concerned. "Are you serious?"

"Serious as a heart attack." Tyler responded coolly, as he rubbed a hand over his smooth face.

"Are they on to us?" Booker had to inquire.

"I don't think so." Tyler answered. "The kid's way too young to be working for I.A.D.."

"How we gonna be sure?" Detective Briggs queried.

"The same way we always know…" Tyler responded, in a placid tone. "We get him to become one of us, or we break him. Nobody likes working with a squeaky-clean boy scout with no secrets to hide."

"Yeah, it tends to make everyone nervous." Booker agreed.

"So, we get him to do some things in our presence that he wants to keep secret, or we send him packing." Tyler continued.

"Or…maybe the new guy makes a rookie mistake and gets himself killed." Booker said, in a tone lacking any feeling.

"Well, Booker Briggs, is that any way to be?" Tyler asked, in a mock southern accent.

"Yeah." Booker replied, in a very serious intonation, while watching their suspect climb behind the wheel of his rust spotted Bonneville.

"I know." Tyler concurred as he removed his Beretta 9mm from its holster and unlocked the safety. "Now let's bust this fool."

Just as the words had escaped Tyler's lips, the suspect's car drove by. The detective then returned his gun to its holster and fired up his Chevy's engine. The souped-up motor purred as each of its eight cylinders worked in unison. He pulled the vehicle away from the curb and followed closely behind the suspect, as the shiny spokes from his rims sparkled in the sunlight. The Caprice was a superb undercover vehicle, because it blended in so well with the gangbangers cars that roamed the streets in the more crime ridden areas of town. In fact, no one suspected the customized Chevy was an unmarked squad car until it was put into action, and by then it was too late.

Booker fired up the dash mounted red and blues before giving the wailer a few quick squeals. Even with the light and siren exhibition they had to follow the perp for a couple of blocks before he finally decided to pull his car to a stop. After he did, the two detectives sprung into action, jumping out of their vehicle and rushing up to the Bonneville with guns drawn.

"Get out of the car, cornrows!" Tyler screamed, as he yanked the car door open with his free hand.

"Yo, man! What'd I do?" The surprised black man in the driver's seat asked, with his eyes opened wide in disbelief.

"Absolutely nothing!" Tyler growled, before grabbing the man by the back of his neck and throwing him roughly to the hard pavement. "And it tends to get men angry when I tell somebody to get out of their car and they do *nothing*!"

"Spread 'em out!" Booker ordered, referring to the suspect's arms and legs.

"Man! This ain't right!" The suspect yelled angrily, as he complied with the demand. "I'm gonna file a complaint on you two!"

Tyler knelt down on the suspect, placing a knee hard into the small of his back, and then began to frisk him for any possible weapons and the drugs he knew he would find. When he reached his fingers into his front right pants pocket and felt the familiar touch of a Ziplock baggie and evil grin formed on his face.

"Who you going to complain to, dope fiend?" Tyler asked in a gruff tone, before pulling the baggy full of crack rocks out of the man's pocket, dangling it in front of his face to tease him.

"Well, well, well, partner, we got enough dope here to put him away for twenty years on a distribution charge." Booker chimed in.

"No man! That stuffs purely for recreational purposes! I ain't selling it!" The man shouted frantically.

"Well, you might be able to prove that if we find a crack pipe in your car." Tyler added, with the sound of mock sympathy in his voice. "That would bring your sentence down considerably.

With that said, the dirty cop began searching the man's vehicle for the smoking utensil he was sure he was going to find. He combed the car carefully and not only found one crack pipe, but three. He then climbed out of the vehicle and held them in his hand so that the suspect could see them.

"I guess he was telling the truth, partner. These pipes will take a lot of years off his sentence when his lawyer sees them." Tyler said in an overly calm tone, before dropping the little glass tubes to the ground and crushing them to powder under his foot. "That's why we have to make sure there never make it back to the station house."

"Hey man! You can't do that!" The suspect yelled irately.

"Looks to me like he just did." Booker said, in a matter-of-fact tone.

"Come here!" Tyler barked, as he pulled the suspect from the ground by his braids and then flung him face down on the hood of his own car hard enough to make a dent. "You still want to file that complaint? Who's going to listen to some crack fiend like you anyway?"

"Especially when we tell 'em down at the precinct we caught ya slingin' dope to kids." Booker was quick to add.

"Why are you guys doing this?" The man asked, in a much more relaxed tone than before.

A cocky smirk formed on Tyler's lips, because he knew he had broken yet another suspect. "Today's your lucky day."

"Do you wanna go to jail, or do you wanna go home?" Booker asked. The pair of crooked cops had played this cat and mouse game more times than either of them could remember. That is why Booker knew exactly when to chime in.

"I wanna go home." The man said pitifully.

"Then I want a name." Tyler demanded, through gritted teeth. "Who's your supplier?"

"If I tell ya that, I'm a dead man…" the suspect groaned.

"If you go to prison, you're a dead man." Booker commented, before returning his gun to its holster.

"Either way, your future's not looking too promising." Tyler said wickedly, as he pushed the barrel of his Beretta into the suspect's neck. "Give me the name."

The man quickly weighed his options out in his mind, and then a defeated look washed over his sweaty face. "The Spanish Kings all call him Evil. I don't know his real name."

"Well, that's a start." Tyler said.

"Glad to see you can play ball with us." Booker put in.

"I'm cutting you loose now." Tyler added before removing the suspect's wallet from his back pocket and sneaking a peek at his driver's license for a name and address.

"But remember, Tyrone Jenkins"... you breathe a word of this to anyone, and I'll make sure some of Evil's Spanish King buddies come to pay you a visit at 421 Independence Avenue."

"They tend to not like rats." Booker warned.

"Yeah. They have a funny way of making them disappear so that they can't testify against one of their brothers in court." Tyler continued.

"Go figure." Booker put in for good measure.

"Now get out of here before I change my mind." Tyler growled, before turning loose of the man's neck. "And don't let me see you around here anymore."

When Tyrone realized that the officers were finished with him, he wasted no time in jumping back in his car and speeding away. The two cops watched as the rusty Bonneville sped off down the street and turned the corner.

"I think that went rather well, don't you?" Tyler asked, as he returned his Berretta to its holster and walked back to his car. "Better than could be expected." Booker agreed, as he followed suit.

"Now let's go pay Evil a visit." Tyler said, before turning his Caprice around, heading back in the direction they had just come from.

Tyler pulled the car to a stop directly across the street from where he had been parked only moments ago when the drug deal was being conducted. As if they had traveled the route a thousand times before, the two detectives then got out of their vehicle and walked up the sidewalk to the front door of a tan, two story house and gave it a few hard knocks. After a few moments the curtain moved and someone on the other side of the door eyed them. Then, as expected, the deadbolt clicked and the door opened.

"Man, what do you guys want?" A five-foot seven-inch Latino asked, in an irritated voice.

"You know what we want." Tyler replied, pushing his way past the short Latino to step inside.

"Another crackhead dropped your name to us, Evil." Booker said calmly, as he followed his partner through the door.

"So, what do ya want me to do about it?" Evil asked, after closing the door and nonchalantly taking his seat on a black leather couch.

"I want you to protect our product." Tyler said, as he whipped the bag of crack rocks into Evil's lap.

"There's plenty left." The Latino replied, tossing the bag on his coffee table. "You didn't have to shake the guy down."

"Never hurts to sell it twice." Tyler added, as he took a seat in a recliner directly across from Evil.

"How much did we make?" Booker asked, as he lit up a cigarette.

The look on Evil's face told the two detectives he was about to withhold information. Even before the gangbanger opened his mouth Tyler began to grow angry.

"About $250."

The room was filled with a thunderous sound as Tyler slammed the flat of his hand on the coffee table. "Who do you think you're fooling you little weasel?"

"Alright! Alright! Chill out!" Evil flinched. "We made $500!"

"You mean me and Booker made $500." Tyler corrected.

"Come on Tyler, don't be like that dog." Evil whined.

"Be like what?" Tyler questioned, heatedly. "You're the one trying to play us, brainiac."

"Man, that's bogus!" Evil complained.

"Sometimes you forget we got *you* in *our* pockets," Tyler explained. "It's not the other way around."

A defeated expression took shape on the Latino's face, as he reached in his pocket and produced a wad of one-hundred-dollar bills easily totaling over five grand. He then counted out five hundred dollars and placed it on the coffee table in front of Tyler.

"You're lucky I don't take that fat roll you got in your hand." Tyler said, as he scooped the money off the tabletop.

"C'mon, man!" Evil complained. "You gotta give me some sort of incentive for working with you!"

The look of anger that flickered to life in Tyler's eyes was all that was needed for Evil to know he had erred. Nevertheless, the violent detective proceeded to give the gangbanger a reply anyway. His Beretta came out of the holster in a flash as he jumped across the coffee table, grabbing the cocky little Latino by the neck. He then placed the barrel hard against Evil's temple as he spoke.

"How about I take you in for that double homicide we let you slide on?" Tyler said, through gritted teeth. "I'm sure your Spanish King brothers would be really eager to watch your back when they find out it was *you* that shot two of their boys to earn you this cushy gig!"

"How would you like to end up in the joint as a *neutron*?" Booker added, in order to heighten the leverage they had over him.

"Yeah, why don't you tell us some more stories about what happens to the convicts in the joint when they don't have a gang watching their back? You know, all the *Neutrons…* tell me what happens to them!" Tyler yelled, while his face grew red with rage.

"Alright! Alright!" Evil squealed. "I'm cool!"

Tyler thought for a moment that it would be easier to just shoot the little Latino and replace him with someone more complacent. They could easily manipulate a crime scene to look as if he had been shot in a drug deal gone bad. By shooting Evil with an unregistered gun they had picked off another dead gangbanger from another case, it would be impossible to trace the murder back to him and Booker. It's not as if they hadn't done it before and gotten away with it. In fact, Tyler and his most trusted anti-gang unit partners had been getting pretty good at tampering with crime scenes in order to cover their misdeeds. It was easy, since no one really questioned the death of a drug dealing gangster.

The dirty cop was seriously considering the idea. It was as if he could hear a nasty little voice inside his head urging him on. The notion teased him so much that he could actually feel his hand reaching for the unmarked gun that he kept in his ankle holster. It wasn't until his cell phone rang and broke his train of thought, that he discontinued the idea.

"Yeah?" He asked, after answering the cell phone and placing it to his ear. "We'll be right there."

"Who was that?" Booker inquired.

Tyler calmed down enough to return his gun to its holster. "The captain wants to see us." He answered. "Our new partner has arrived."

"Great." Booker said, in a less than eager tone. "Are we through here?"

"I think I got my point across." Tyler replied, looking at Evil as he visibly trembled.

"Good." Booker continued. "Let's bounce."

*   *   *   *   *

As the two crooked cops left the gangster's house, little did either of them realize that a creature of darkness was hitching a ride on the shoulder of Detective Lynch. It was this foul little creature that was whispering into Tyler's ear, urging him to kill the drug dealer. This dirty little imp has been the cause of much of Tyler's evil doings over the years, and will be for many more.

Chapter 4

The moisture on Ethan's palms was becoming unbearable. He didn't want to admit to himself that he was as nervous as he was, but after witnessing the glossy sheen of sweat on the inner surface of his hands, he finally concluded he was a bit tense. He discreetly dried the perspiration off on his pant legs, hoping his captain did not notice, and then continued to scan the many commendations decorating the office walls in order to pass the time until he met with his new partner.

It was not a fear of his duties that troubled Ethan, but it was more the anticipation of the rookie hazing he was sure he was going to get. Taking a bullet would be wonderful compared to the constant teasing and pranks that he had to endure when he first came on board as a patrolman. Still to this day some remnants of crusty tissue still caked the edges of his locker from when the guys filled it to the rim with wet toilet paper. The worst part about that prank was not the cleanup, as one might imagine, but it was the fact that they had not removed his civilian clothes from the locker before filling it up. Walking through the precinct in those squishy duds was a memory he did not want to relive any time soon.

"Relax kid." The burly police captain advised in his southern drawl, as he plucked a cigar box off his desk and offered one of the smokes to Ethan.

"No thank you, sir."

"Suit yourself," Captain Watkins replied, before taking one of the thick cigars out for himself and then placing the container back on the desktop. "But I've always found that these babies calm my nerves before a big press conference."

After saying so, the stocky man grabbed a decorative lighter off his desk that was in the shape of a small cannon and lit the cigar up, taking a few quick puffs to ensure that the red-hot tip remained aflame. It took only a few seconds for the dense cloud of smoke to reach Ethan's nostrils, and when it did, he could not help but twitch his nose in quiet disapproval. Just when the young man thought he could take the stench no longer, there was a knock on the door. Soon afterward, in walked Detective Tyler Lynch.

At first glance Ethan was unsure of what to make of Detective Lynch. Tyler was a lean young man with short cropped blonde hair, a clean-shaven face and a stern look of determination in his cold unfeeling eyes. It wasn't until Ethan took a closer inspection that he noticed the many tattoos around Tyler's forearms and neck that instantly made him look less like a cop and more like any of the random street thugs that they were intending to hunt down.

"You rang, Cap?" He asked, in a tone lacking the respect of one speaking to a superior officer.

"Yes I did." Captain Watkins replied, not seeming bothered in the least by the lax protocol. "Tyler, I want you to meet one of the newest members of your squad, Detective Ethan Brooks."

After the quick introduction Tyler turned to look at Ethan and the two men locked gazes for a brief moment. It seemed to take Tyler only a second to size Ethan up and then a lackluster gleam came over his eyes telling Ethan that he seemed unimpressed with him.

"'Sup, man?" Tyler asked halfheartedly, in his thuggish tone. "You ready to go bust some bad guys?"

"That's what they're paying me for." Ethan responded, as he eagerly stood from his seat.

"Take it easy on him Tyler." The captain said, as he took another puff of his cigar. "After all, it's his first day."

"You want me to babysit him or make him a streetwise detective, Cap?" Tyler asked, sternly.

"Work your magic, Merlin." Captain Watkins conceded. "Sorry kid, I tried to help. But on any count, welcome aboard."

"Ai'ght then." Tyler replied with a smirk. "Let's do this."

With that proclamation the two men left the captain to finish his foul-smelling stogie. Tyler walked through the precinct with a straight and steady pace all the while pointing out things of interest and sharing a little insight about everything he motioned to. Ethan did his best to keep up with him and was even able to catch a few words the speedy walker had to say. However, Ethan was unsure if the rude treatment was meant to make him a more effective detective or if Tyler just flat out didn't like him.

The pair of detectives finally came to a set of double doors that had the words 'Anti-Gang Task Force' stenciled in cheap black letters on its olive-colored surface. Tyler pushed both the doors wide open, testing the durability of each of their spring-loaded closer arms and then continued his quick stride until he came to a large open room filled with several benches, a dry erase board and a couple rows of metal

lockers. On the farthest bench from the two men sat one
Booker Briggs.

"Yo, Booker! Look alive! We got us a rookie on the
deck!" Tyler yelled, obnoxiously.

"Sup, man?" Booker greeted with a quick raise of his
head.

"Not much." Ethan responded, with a quick nod of his
own.

"This is the war room!" Tyler said loudly, spreading his
arms open wide to emphasize the point. "This is where we
meet to get briefed on some of the coldest gangsters in
town."

"Are you IAD?" Booker asked flatly, never removing his
eyes from Ethan's until he answered.

"Internal Affairs? Me?" Ethan stammered. "N-No. This is
my first stop since being out on patrol."

"C'mon Booker, man. Is that any way to treat the new
guy?" Tyler interjected before leaning in close to his
partner's ear. "I thought you were gonna be cool? Let me
handle this, ok?"

"He asks that to all the rookies." Tyler said to Ethan with
a smirk.

"So, what's our first order of business, chief?" Booker
asked Tyler.

"I thought you'd never ask." Tyler said, before tossing an
open file upon the bench in front of them. "This is Jimmy
Boose, a.k.a. "Pharaoh." He's as bad as they come, boys.
Pharaoh's a Gangster Apostle that runs a crack house down
on Blackstone Avenue. Just got out of the joint five days ago
after a seven-year bit for homicide."

"Who'd he off?" Booker asked in an uncaring tone, as he
flipped through the pages of the file.

"Shot his landlord right between the eyes when the old man served him an eviction notice for slingin' dope out of his apartment." Tyler answered.

"I can imagine he's going to try and do a lot worse to us, since we're delivering more than an eviction notice." Ethan chimed in.

"Smart boy." Tyler complimented, before tossing a folded-up paper on top of the file. "We are serving Pharaoh *our own* eviction notice."

Booker picked up the paper and unfolded it. "This is a search warrant. Are we positive we're gonna find anything?"

"Hey, Ethan, look over the file for a sec. I need to talk to Booker alone." Tyler said, as he pulled his partner aside.

Ethan hesitantly picked up the file and began skimming through the papers in order to give the men their privacy.

"I'm more than positive we're gonna find somethin'." The blonde-haired slickster answered with a wink, before pulling a kilo of crack out of his jacket pocket. "Pharaoh's cutting in on our business we have set up with Evil, so we have to get rid of him."

"Ai'ght. I'm down with that, but what about the golden boy?" Booker asked, referring to their newest member.

"Rookie detective gets capped serving high profile warrant…man, the story practically writes itself." Tyler replied. "We send junior through the front with the warrant and you and I come in through the back. If we're lucky, we can get rid of both of them at the same time."

"Yeah, yeah, I like the sound o' that." Booker agreed.

"Then it's back to business as usual."

"A'ight, then. Let's do this" Tyler said, as he slapped Booker on the shoulder and turned back to Ethan, who was still looking through the file. "Are you ready to get your feet wet, rookie?"

"Ready as I'll ever be." Ethan responded with determination.

"Then let's roll out!" Tyler announced, as they headed for the parking lot.

"Shouldn't I get my vest?" Ethan asked, referring to his Kevlar body armor.

"We have some in our car." Tyler answered.

"How come we're not going out through the motor pool?" Ethan inquired, as he hurried to keep up.

"Our car ain't from the motor pool." Booker interjected, as he pushed the exit door open that led to the parking lot and revealed the '69 Chevy Caprice to Ethan. "This is how the Anti-Gangbangers roll."

Ethan was momentarily taken aback by the classic automobile and stopped for a moment to admire it before climbing inside with his partners.

"Sweet ride." he gasped, with his eyes widened.

"Only thing better than eye googling it from the outside, is the ride you get from the back seat." Tyler said, as he fired up the smooth sounding engine.

"Really?" Ethan had to ask furrowing his brow at the comment.

"No, not really." Tyler admitted. "I just said that so you'd get in and we can be on our way."

"Right." Ethan acknowledged, as he climbed into the back seat.

After the door was shut behind him, Tyler punched the accelerator and the Chevy peeled out of the parking lot and headed West on State Street. As he drove, Tyler reached into the inside pocket of his jacket and produced a fat blunt rolled with marijuana. Without a second thought he placed the joint between his lips and lit it up, much to Ethan's surprise. After taking a few hits the blonde-haired thug passed the blunt to

Booker, who also took a few drags without so much as a care in the world. When Booker was satisfied, he then reached into Ethan's direction with the blunt pinched tightly within his fingers.

"No thanks, man." Ethan said, waving the joining away with his hand.

"Nope. Can't let ya slide, dog." Booker replied, not giving Ethan a chance to decline the narcotic. "It's part of the job description.

"Seriously?" The rookie asked, still not taking the joint from Booker.

"A lot of the work we do in our division is done undercover." Booker explained. "Imagine if I was some dope dealer and you were sent in to buy a bag of dope from me. I would be pretty suspicious of a guy buying narcotics from me if he wasn't intending to use them. Wouldn't you be?"

Ethan nodded his head at the logic.

"Any dope dealer would be." Booker added. "Then they'd pull out a pistol and blast you dead right then and there, no questions asked."

"What happens when we get dropped?" Ethan inquired, referring to the drug tests they get randomly.

"Captain's got our backs." Tyler interjected, as he turned the Caprice onto Kilburn Avenue. "We get the heads up two weeks in advance."

"Take the hit, dog." Booker said, in a firm tone.

Slowly, against his better judgment, Ethan removed the blunt from Booker's fingers and took a couple drags. The thick smoke burned his lungs and caused him to cough for several seconds, drawing laughter from his partners in the front seat. Ethan was no boy scout. He remembers smoking weed with his friends back in high school. But those days were only distant memories now. His lungs had long since healed themselves from those abusive times. With so little to gain and so much to lose, he would have never considered smoking the marijuana if it weren't for Booker explaining that his life could very well be threatened if he were to blow his cover while working covertly.

"That's it, rookie!" Tyler shouted. "Get you some!"

Ethan passed the blunt back to Booker and then slunk back in his seat, wondering if he had made the right career move.

*　　*　　*　　*　　*

When at last Hunter caught sight of the sturdy stone walls of the Illinois State Capitol Building, he knew his long journey to Springfield was at last at an end. Stepping out from the murky blackness of the portal in which the evil spirit used for traveling long distances, he placed each foot on the cobblestone courtyard and it was then that the demon was overcome with the feeling of uneasiness. There were some places that even he felt were too evil to tread, and standing at the doorway to Mistress Vixanna's base of operation was no exception.

Hunter stood speechless, immersing himself in the view for a long moment, while trying to maintain his composure.

"Are we not going to enter, master?" Dartamus asked, in a less than hopeful tone.

"Of course we are going to enter, buffoon!" Hunter snapped. "Do you really think we would have traveled all this way just to turn around and return back to our dreary existences? I am merely preparing myself for my meeting with Mistress Vixanna."

"Forgive me master." The deformed imp groaned, slumping his shoulders down in a defeated posture.

After a few more seconds of hesitation Hunter realized how futile his efforts were. No amount of grooming was going to ready him for the encounter with the current Principality of this region. Mistress Vixanna was a powerful demon with a wrathful tempter to match. His only course of action now, was to meet with the massive beast and state his case before he lost his nerve.

Without saying another word, Hunter moved toward the building, but instead of entering through the front doors, the demon directed his steps toward a side entrance used by maintenance staff. Seeing his master moving once more, Dartamus fell in line behind him dreading every footfall. The pair did not need to open the door once they arrived, but instead, their evil forms melted through the walls like water being absorbed by a sponge. Once inside the pair wafted their way into a section of the building that had been sealed off many years ago. The lack of human activity within the abandoned wing was what the evil creatures found most appealing. It was the perfect location in which to influence the lawmakers of the State, but yet remain secluded from the eyes of the guardian angels that were assigned to protect them.

When Hunter and his subordinate materialized on the opposite side of the two feet thick brick wall that divided the functioning portion of the building from the abandoned area, they stood in front of a doorway guarded by two savage, reptilian looking demons with long pikes firmly in their grasps. On their arrival the two guards crossed their pikes to bar them from entering into Mistress Vixanna's throne room.

"Ssstate your busssiness!" The larger fiend, standing on the left side of the doorway snapped in a snake-like tone.

"I am Hunter, wielder of the dual blades, and ravager of the northern cities of this region." The fair faced demon announced in a formal tone. "I seek an audience with Mistress Vixanna."

"Have you been sssummoned?" the large, reptilian looking demon asked, with a snarl.

"No." Hunter replied, honestly. "But we have traveled from afar to see her…"

"No sssummons, no entry!" The guard barked, cutting Hunter off in mid-sentence. "Missstress Vixanna has far more important matters to deal with than to wassste her time with the likesss of you!"

Hunter's hands slowly made their way to the hilts of his blades as he subtly entertained the thought of carving his way through the guards. He had no intention of undertaking the long journey back to his post without speaking with the Principality.

When the guards saw Hunter's threatening gesture, they immediately took a defensive posture, and soon the tense situation turned into a standoff. All sets of demonic eyes locked into an evil stare down, each waiting for the other to make a move. The situation only simmered down after there came a loud snapping sound from Mistress Vixanna's audience hall and then a headless demon corpse flew from the doorway, skidding to a stop at the feet of everyone in the group. Seconds later, the head to the cadaver came rolling through the entryway, where it landed by the body it had been attached to for centuries.

It became obvious to them all that Mistress Vixanna had become displeased with her last visitor, as the decapitated demon body within their midst provided evidence to that fact.

"Send him in…" Came the voice from the inner chamber that sounded like a mixture of hisses and growls.

After the order was issued, the guards returned to their previous attentive stance, and granted Hunter entry. As the white-haired demon confidently strode by, followed by Dartamus the guard that had given him all the trouble spread a sharp toothed smile across his face before saying some final words.

"Sssoon it will be your carcasss flaunted at our feet." He snarled, before the fallen demon's body dissolved to ash, marking its entry into the Abyss.

Hunter stopped his pace and casually looked into the guard's reptilian eyes before giving his retort. "If this meeting goes as well as I believe it will, then you only have a short time before your miserable existence is snuffed out by my hand."

"Enough!" Mistress Vixanna roared. **"If you seek audience with me, then step forward!"**

Hunter did as he was instructed, stepping into the dark domain of Mistress Vixanna's throne room with his servant Dartamus following from a somewhat safer distance. The temperature had grown noticeably colder, as the two could not see their breath when they exhaled. This happened whenever they were in Vixanna's presence. It was as if the demon was filled with such evil that it emanated off of her hideous form, sapping the space around her from whatever happiness or warmth it once had.

Once Hunter stepped into the pale lighting being cast down by the torches on either side of Vixanna's throne, he stooped into a low and gracious bow. Dartamus understood the formalities quite well and knew why Hunter chose to humble himself the way that he did when he visited with the creature. Still, the imp found the sight somewhat disturbing, since it was on the rarest of occasions that his master humbled himself in such a way. However, when Dartamus caught sight of Mistress Vixanna once again, the reason for Hunter's subservient behavior was brought back to remembrance.

Mistress Vixanna was an evil spirit of tremendous power that held an impressive rank within the demonic hierarchy. She was one of the many demons that chose to embrace a new form after her fall from grace; one that would not constantly remind her of her angelic heritage.

Before she was shunned by the Heavenly host, Vixanna had been one of the most beautiful Archangels that anyone had the good fortune of gazing upon. Her once shapely female torso was replaced with the scaly upper body of a hideous looking six-armed woman covered in boils and sores. Her head, that had once been covered with luscious golden tresses, was not covered with long, ebony-colored locks braided all the way down her curved spine. In her serpent-like orbs Vixanna held an evil gleam that teetered on the edge of anger and cruelty. When held within her mesmerizing stare she could entice a victim to do her bidding, or paralyze them with mind numbing fear. Just below the navel of the demon's muscular torso she resembled that of a giant snake. Her long serpent-like body laid roundabout in coils with each sleek scale eerily reflecting the room's lighting. On the tip of her lengthy tail she bore a rattler that emitted a threatening quivering sound as it vibrated, telling all within earshot that she was displeased. She was gigantic in size, towering over most of her subjects at a remarkable fifteen-foot height, not including the length of her unwound coils.

Her six arms moved ever so gracefully, as they each carried out separate tasks, none interfering with the other. One picked a grape from a collection of fruit by her side and placed it in her mouth, while another came behind and wiped away some of the juice that trickled down her smooth cheek. It seemed that every one of her limbs worked together in perfect unison, one complimenting the other. This never ceased to amaze Hunter, who often wondered what it would be like to face her in battle.

"Forgive me, Mistress Vixanna." Hunter said, in a soothing tone. "It was never my intent to cause you any displeasure."

"Hunter…" Vixanna cooed, when she at last realized whom it was in her audience hall her rattler noticeably growing silent. **"Come closer, my pet."**

As requested, Hunter stood upright and then strolled into the torchlight with the heels of his thigh high leather boots clicking off the marble flooring with every step.

"Hello Mistress…" Hunter purred.

"It truly is you." Vixanna said, in a tone that hinted of pleasure, if she could emit such a sound. **"What circumstance has brought you to me this day?"**

"My Mistress, it has become clear to me that our armies have been steadily repositioning themselves more and more eastward." Hunter began. "The movement of our troops has intrigued me. Is this a situation that I need to be concerned with?"

Vixanna did not respond immediately, but rather held her subject in her line of view for several seconds. **"What has spawned your sudden interest in the war?"**

At first, Hunter was unsure of how to answer the direct question. If he admitted to her that his current assignment is too dull, she may reassign him to an even less exciting project, and if he ever outright admitted that he had always lamented his decision in rebelling against God, she may very well launch his headless corpse into the hallway. However, the cunning demon knew exactly what he wanted to achieve from this meeting and had thought out the answer to the question before it had ever been uttered.

"My Mistress, it has always been my will to serve you." The silver-tongued devil began. "My current post has proven to be unfruitful and therefore supplied me with ample time in which to think. If there is even the slimmest glimmer of hope that we may win this war, I would like to be a key player in its orchestration."

"Your deadly talents have been missed, my pet." Vixana complimented, while stroking his chin with one of her large fingers. **"Your dual blades could have changed the outcome of several battles. I am pleased to hear of your sudden change in focus."**

"I only exist to please you, my Mistress." Hunter replied, before stooping into another gracious bow, while the torchlight reflected vividly off the colorful gemstones fastened in the hilt of his dagger.

"Of course." The enormous beast said, while slithering her coils around Hunter in an attempt to unnerve him. **"You say your current assignment has uncovered no new information? What age is the human you have been assigned to watch?"**

"Ethan Brooks is in his twenty-fourth year of life, Mistress." Hunter answered honestly, making sure to quote the name of the human he was assigned to.

"And God's purpose for his life has still not revealed itself?" She questioned, before finishing her circle around where Hunter stood.

"No, Mistress." The lavender-eyed demon replied. "He is married to a woman that bears the Seal of God, but that is as close to Christ as he has come."

"And what of his guardian, Cazzbein?" Vixanna inquired.

"The angel has frequented the human's home, but has not yet led him to God's plan." Hunter said, as he looked into Vixanna's cold, unfeeling eyes.

The enormous demon leaned down until her face was mere inches away from Hunter's, the drool from her maw dripping close to his well-polished footwear. She did this to test her servant's courage under pressure. When Vixanna saw that he did not so much as flinch at her grotesque appearance, she was convinced Hunter was telling her the truth and then slithered her way back onto her throne.

"You have been due for a promotion for some time now, Hunter, but you have always declined." Vixanna said, in an offhanded tone. **"If you really want to contribute your blades to the cause, then I have the perfect assignment for you."**

"Absolutely, My Mistress." Hunter replied, in a diplomatic voice.

"Lucifer is dividing his domains into seven major sections. We have been trying feverishly to spring the principality heading up this continent, but the angels have managed to thwart our efforts." Vixanna explained, while one of her multiple hands pulled a map of the world out from beside her throne, unrolled it, and pointed out several of the major sections. **"If you truly desire to be a key player in the war, you will accept the promotion to Captain, and lead an army comprised of thirteen legions into the abyss and escort Prince Larz into his section."**

"What will become of my current assignment?" Hunter asked, curiously. "It was my understanding that no one was better suited to defeat Cazzbein than I."

"Cazzbein has been a thorn in my side for far too long, and since your fighting styles are so similar, you are the best candidate to take him out." Vixanna agreed, stroking her chin with one of her many hands as she thought. **"But this new assignment is far more important at this time. Surely, you must have some subordinates that can spy on the human and keep you informed of his guardian angel's whereabouts."**

"Yes my Mistress. I can send Dartamus back in my stead and he can keep me posted of Cazzbein's movements." Hunter answered, drawing an evil eye from the little imp who had been trying to remain undetected from Mistress Vixanna during the course of the conversation.

"Dartamus!?" Vixanna exploded. **That worthless simpleton has still not met his end?"**

"No, Mistress." Hunter answered. "He is my most trusted servant. In fact, he has been with us this entire time."

"Oh, no…" The deformed imp moaned to himself.

"He has…?" The powerful demon asked, using one of her hands to reach for a brutal looking cat o'nine tails, as a gleam of wickedness sparked to life in her orbs. **"Where?"**

"Dartamus! Step Forward!" Hunter ordered.

It took several moments for Dartamus' twisted form to move into the torchlight, but as soon as he did, the shifty eyed demon heard a loud crack followed by searing pain racing down the left side of his torso. The stinging sensation was so severe that it brought him straight to his knees, while his dark, shadowy essence seeped out of several long gashes made from Vixanna's nasty scourge. With a sudden yank of the weapon's handle, she wrenched the sharp barbs tied to each of the nine leathery straps out of Dartamus' body, tearing several small chunks from his side.

"AAAHHHGG!!" The gnarled servant shrieked, while clutching his side in an attempt to relieve the pain.

"I have not soon forgotten your last visit, you bumbling swine!" Vixanna bellowed. **"Your lack of judgment cost me nearly a cohort of troops the night Ethan Brooks was born!"**

"Forgive me, Mistress!" Dartmus screamed, clutching his freshly made wound with crooked fingers. "I was not fit to lead such a large group!"

"You're not fit to exist!" Vixanna hissed, before snapping her cat o'nine tails across the imp's face.

"AAAHHHGG!!" Dartamus squealed, before collapsing to the ground from the agony.

Hunter watched the exhibition out of the corner of his eye and a brazen smirk took shape on his smooth features. Even though Dartamus was his closest comrade, seeing the twisted demon getting beaten brought a sensation of pleasure to the pale haired demon. Evil creatures of the Spiritual Realm possessed no sense of compassion. All they knew was pain, anger, and wrath.

The wicked scourging went on for several more minutes. Dartamus' screams had ceased long before. The deformed imp laid motionless in a pool of his own black essence on the shiny marble floor. Hunter began to wonder if Vixanna had only stopped her brutal treatment out of boredom. Nevertheless, for whatever reason, the beating had come to an end.

"I've changed my mind…" The evil Mistress growled after a moment of silence.

"Mistress…?" Hunter asked, needing some clarification.

"I hereby bestow upon you, the rank of Captain, with all the benefits and obligations that title holds…"

"Thank you, Mistress." Hunter replied, as he stood to attention.

"…But as for your first assignment, I have made a change…"

Hunter listened intently as Vixanna laid out her plan for his first mission under his new commission. The chat went on for several hours as the serpentine demon spelled out the details for the new captain. At first Hunter seemed less than enthusiastic, but the more Vixanna spoke, the brighter the twinkle of intrigue sparkled within his lavender eyes.

As the two demons conversed, Dartamus began to show a spark of life as his body began to stir on the ground. When he finally managed to open his swollen eyes, the imp saw Hunter standing over him with his arms crossed in front of his chest.

"I suppose I was wrong…" Hunter said in a nonchalant tone. "She did remember our last visit."

Dartamus was sure to hide the irritated expression that washed over his lacerated visage.

"Come, Dartamus," Hunter said, as he stepped toward the exit. "We have much work to do."

After struggling for a short time, the deformed demon managed to roll over and pluck himself from the floor. With a noticeable limp and many groans, Dartamus mustered the strength to follow after his master, elated to be leaving the confines of Mistress Vixanna's throne room far behind him. The shifty eyed servant was not pleased, however, when Hunter paused in the entryway and turned to ask Vixanna one final question.

"Mistress, with this title am I truly granted *all* the benefits the position holds?"

"Yes." The powerful demon responded, with a perplexed look on her hideous face.

"Wonderful." Hunter acknowledged, before unsheathing his saber and lopping off the head of the guard that had previously given him so much grief. The quick move was performed so fast that the guard did not have time to so much as flinch, as his headless corpse dissolved into nothingness.

"Well played, Hunter." The massive demon said, in as pleasant a tone as she could muster.

"That is the type of ruthlessness I desire from you."

"I do believe I am going to enjoy my new title." Hunter purred, as he slowly returned his saber to its sheath.

Chapter 5

Puko was incredibly bored with his assignment. The little demon was primarily used as a scout, and his job was to scan the skies high above the city of Rockford and bring back any information to the General of the region that involved guardian angel activity in the vicinity. As of late, he had not seen any of the Heavenly Host come through his area. He did not know if this was because none of the angels chose to travel through his sector, or if they were just smarter than he was, and capable of thwarting his detection. The latter was not hard to accomplish, due to the fact that the evil sprite was quite dim witted.

Puko's face looked like it had been scrunched up like a ball of paper as his beady, glowing yellow eyes shifted to and fro, staring at the sky, waiting for any sign of trouble. He had no nose to speak of, but rather two long, flat slits that served as his nostrils. The little demon's jagged teeth jutted out in all directions from under his tightly pierced lips, making it look as though a stick of dynamite had exploded in his mouth.

Nevertheless, even though Puko's features seemed somewhat comical, there was no mistaking he was a creature of pure evil. Just like all of his demonic brothers and sisters, Puko loathed humanity and desired nothing short of their decisive annihilation. Even if his current post seemed relatively boring, Puko knew he was doing his part to aid the army of malice in which he served.

Just as Puko was about to waft his way over to the other side of the tall building's rooftop that he utilized as his lookout, his fiendish gaze happened to catch a twinkle of light in the clouds. At first glance the sparkle of golden light seemed insignificant and not worth wasting his time on, but with nothing more pressing to draw his attention elsewhere, the demon continued to follow the little twinkle until it better came into focus. When the flicker of light emerged from the clouds Puko was better able to see and discern that it was two guardian angels streaking down to earth. But it wasn't until further scrutinizing that he made out the identity of one of the Heavenly spirits. It was then that a nasty toothed smile took shape over his wicked maw.

"Cazzbein…" Puko mouthed. "Mistress Vixanna will be very pleased to hear this news."

*　　*　　*　　*　　*

Ethan's breathing was beginning to quicken and his heart had noticeably started beating faster. He was already feeling some anxiety about serving the warrant and making his first official arrest on the new squad, but the hyper feelings he was having at this moment seemed unnatural. Large rings of sweat under his armpits had already soaked through his shirt and he could feel the perspiration forming again on the palms of his hands. After drying his palms once more on his pant legs, Ethan looked at the inner side of his hands and noticed the image seemed out of focus. He moved his hand around a bit and could see another image of his hand trailing the first. It then became aware to him that there had been something else in that blunt besides marijuana.

"How's our boy doing"? Tyler whispered to Booker.

Booker looked in the sack seat and saw Ethan staring at his hand. "Man, he's messed up! What'd you lace that blunt with?"

"Let's just say I put a little something extra in there for the rookie." Tyler replied with a grin, before turning the caprice onto Blackstone Avenue.

Shortly thereafter, the car came to a stop next to the curb and Tyler and Booker hopped out and headed to the trunk. Ethan slid his way to the door and slowly followed after them, still feeling the effects of the narcotic. Everything tingled to his touch and his mind was abuzz, as he struggled to focus. It took him a few seconds more than usual to make it to Tyler and Booker's position. Once he made it there he saw both the men strapping into their Kevlar body armor. Tyler tossed one of the vests to Ethan unexpectedly and he nearly dropped it.

"Get your vest on and check your radio to make sure it's working. We're going in quietly, so make sure the sound is turned down. It's only to be used to call for an ambulance, or for backup, which I don't think we'll need." Tyler explained. "We rely on hand signals, so we can go in as silent as possible."

"It's just going to be the three of us?" Ethan asked, while he slipped into his vest.

"The rest of the task force is busy with their own assignments. That's okay though, because we're cowboys, dog." Booker replied, double checking his firearm to make sure it was locked and loaded. "What do you think we need to do? Call half the precinct down for one guy?"

"We do the jobs nobody else can do." Tyler put in. "Before you showed up, it would have just been me and Booker pullin' off this gig. If you can't handle it, maybe you better go back to cuttin' parking tickets."

"I can handle it." Ethan responded, with determination.

"That's what we're about to find out." Booker replied, before shutting the trunk.

Tyler pointed out the house they were about to pull the raid on. It was a blue and white, two story, with a chain link fence surrounding the yard, setting unassumingly about a block up the street. Other than the lawn being overgrown it appeared to be as normal as the rest of the houses on the block.

"A'ight rookie, now's your time to shine." Tyler said, as he drew out his pistol. "Me and Booker are going through the back, you're taking the front."

"Keep an eye out for spotters too." Booker warned. "We don't want anybody tippin' this guy off that we're comin'."

Ethan nodded his head with confidence. Even though he was still feeling the effects of whatever Tyler had laced the marijuana with, he was still pretty excited about making the bust. Now, all he had to do was live through it.

*　　*　　*　　*　　*

Cazzbein finished his descent by landing ever so gracefully onto the rooftop of the house Ethan and his crew were about to invade. The guardian was followed closely by his muscular companion Gunther, who had already armed himself with his massive war hammer. Once on the roof, they both used their extraordinary vision to peer through the structure and gain some valuable information about what lay in wait for them inside. There were three human occupants in total, but what piqued the angels' interest more, were the six demon inhabitants that lurked about, invisible to the men.

"Do you see what I see my friend?" Cazzbein queried, as he slowly unsheathed his scimitars.

"Sport." the burly angel responded, with a sly grin, twisting his hands around the handle of his war hammer in anticipation.

"The scouts did well to inform me of this place, especially when my charge has business here." Cazzbein commented, as he ran two of his fingers down the edge of one of his scimitars, testing its sharpness. "Thank you for accompanying me on this venture, Gunthar."

"To be honest, my friend, I feel as if I owe you something for this opportunity in vanquishing some demon scum." The big angel uttered under his breath.

"Our primary goal is to protect the one known as Ethan Brooks." Cazzbein informed. "He will be approaching shortly from the west, just on the other side of those bushes. He and his group will be attempting to apprehend the one known as Jimmy Boose. His group will be trying to kill my charge."

"What is our plan?" Gunthar rightly asked.

"We have to cleanse the structure of any demons we find, so that they will not thwart us in our attempt to protect Ethan." Cazzbein hastily explained.

"Lead the way." Gunthar said, with the edge of determination in his voice.

After the statement, the two guardian angels plunged their way through the roof of the house carrying with them the element of surprise. Cazzbein drove a scimitar deep into the torso of the first devilish fiend he saw, instantly taking him out of the battle and sending him swirling into the Abyss. Likewise, Gunthar brought his hammer down with all his might on the backside of another one of the demon's heads, taking him out of the world of men and casting him into the Pit of Darkness after his comrade.

"We're under attack!" One of the remaining fiends screamed, as he unsheathed his longsword.

"What are we to do with the other members of Ethan's party?" Gunthar inquired, as he defended himself from a wicked looking dagger strike.

"They are of no consequence to us." Cazzbein replied, before sending another demon plummeting to his dismal end with a slash of his blade.

It was at that moment that the front door to the house crashed open under the weight of Ethan's boot.

"Police! Freeze!" He screamed, as he pointed his gun at the group of men in the living room. "Everyone down on the ground!"

The three men did not comply with Ethan's demands, as two of them bolted for the back door. Their exit was cut off though as Tyler kicked the door off the hinges and pointed his weapon at the fleeing suspects. In the spiritual realm, the last two demons Gunthar was battling knew that they were on the losing end of the battle, and took to the air, soaring through the ceiling in a desperate attempt to get away. Not willing to forfeit two additional swipes on his war hammer's handle, the burly angel took off after them.

The last remaining demon in the house knew that he was no match for the fabled Cazzbein and his fierce scimitars. With that in mind, he leapt toward Ethan in a desperate attempt to paralyze him with fear. If he were to succeed, the human would be unable to defend himself against any of the gangsters that may decide to open fire on him.

Ethan could tell by the photo in the file he looked at earlier, the last man in the living room was Jimmy Boose, a.k.a. Pharaoh. Jimmy Boose was a large, muscular black man with gangster tattoos lined up and down his powerful looking arms. The two men's eyes met during the tense moment and neither dared to look away. Then, without warning, Pharaoh went for the pistol he had tucked in the front waistline of his pants. After leveling the weapon in Ethan's direction, he squeezed the trigger and the weapon discharged, sending a bullet in the detective's direction. Ethan, likewise, fired a round from his gun with deadly intent in mind.

The next few events happened too fast for human comprehension.

Seeing what was transpiring, Cazzbein hurled the scimitar in his left hand at the demon about to attack Ethan. It sunk deep into his side, sending the beast veering off course. Then, with speed that only an other worldly being could achieve, Cazzbein grabbed Ethan's bullet out of the air and launched it at a different trajectory. The tiny projectile then crashed into the bullet fired from Pharaoh's gun and the momentum caused both intertwined bullets to get buried into the suspect's right shoulder, causing him to drop his weapon to the floor.

In the back of the house, Tyler had put his gun away and was busy putting the cuffs on one of the suspects. Booker was busy assisting his partner by making sure the last gangbanger never strayed from the sights of his pistol. However, when the two crooked cops heard the shots from within the house, they both took time to look at one another and flash an evil grin, pleased to think that at least one of their problems had been eliminated. It was at that brief moment that the last panicked thug realized Booker had taken his eyes off of him, and took off running back down the hallway in the direction of the front room in which he had just come.

"Hey get back here!" Tyler yelled angrily, before taking off after him. "Watch the one I got cuffed."

The fleeing suspect ran back in Ethan's direction. The young detective had already kicked the fallen pistol away from Pharaoh and was preoccupied with getting him into cuffs when the thug arrived. Ethan was out of range of the discarded weapon that was now laid at the gangster's feet that had just entered the room, and therefore was unable to stop him as he picked the gun up off the floor and turned to fire at Tyler who was coming up fast on his backside.

With Tyler's weapon already holstered, he was powerless to stop the gangbanger from firing. But before the thug could do so, Ethan launched himself into harm's way, tackling the armed man like a professional linebacker. The force of the blow was so great it carried both of them crashing through the drywall into the next room. With the suspect dazed and disoriented, it took little effort for Ethan to slap his second set of cuffs on him.

When Ethan was finished, he maneuvered his cuffed suspect back into the living room and threw him roughly to the ground, while Tyler stared at him with the look of disbelief on his face.

"What?" Ethan asked, after Tyler continued to gawk at him.

"That was cold, dog." He gasped.

"What'd I miss?" Booker asked, as he drug his thug to the living room and deposited him with the others.

"The rookie saved my life." Tyler said, in an astounded tone.

"It wasn't that big a deal…" Ethan replied, humbly.

"No, no, man! That dirtbag had me dead to rights and you saved me!" Tyler explained, in a grateful tone.

After saying so, Tyler walked out the front door to get some much needed air and was followed closely by Booker.

"So what happened, man?" Booker asked, when he finally caught up with him.

Tyler leaned up against the house with his hands wrapped around the back of his head, deep in thought. "I holstered my gun while I was cuffing our perp, so when I caught up to the one that took off running, he pulled a pistol on me. Brooks came out of nowhere and took the guy down. The rookie saved me, man."

"Don't go gettin' soft on me, dog." Booker advised.

"Have your forgot about the hustle we got goin' on with Evil?"

Tyler thought about it for a moment before giving an answer. "I ain't forgot nothin'."

"That's my boy." Booker said, with a smile. "Keep our eye on the prize. I wanna live off more than that dinky pension when I retire."

"Same here." Tyler agreed. "Now, all we have to do is live to see retirement."

"What kind of talk is that?" Booker asked. "I know what you need…"

"What's that?" Tyler inquired.

"Get that punk that tried to shoot you in a room all alone." Booker replied, as he lit a cigarette.

"You're the only one who understands me, Booker." Tyler mused, as he walked back in the house with the look of purpose on his face.

In the spiritual realm, Cazzbein was not quite finished with his end of things, as the humans were. He walked over slowly to where the last demon was writhing in pain on the ground and yanked his scimitar free of his hide showing no outward sign of emotion as he did so. The hideous creature looked up at the angel to see if there was any sign of pity in his azure eyes, but found none. Only fury could be found there.

"Today is the day that you receive your reward for turning against God Almighty!" He declared, before raising one scimitar high in the air and bringing it down upon the beast's neck without mercy.

With that unpleasantness out of the way, Cazzbein was filled with a sense of grim satisfaction. He turned to look upon Ethan, his newest charge, who was busy calling an ambulance for the suspect he had shot. Little did the human know that the simple words his wife had prayed over him that morning had opened a way for the angel to intervene and save his life.

The guardian could not help but shake his head at the thought, as he returned his scimitars to their sheaths.

"Such careless little creatures they are." He commented to himself, before spreading his wings and soaring through the ceiling of the structure to find his comrade.

"Alright, rookie, keep pressure on that wound until the paramedics get here, while me and Booker start the search." Tyler ordered, before he began rummaging through drawers and overturning tables.

"Yo, man!" What you lookin' for?" Pharaoh asked, in a tone that suggested both frustration and pain.

"You don't worry your pretty little head about it." Tyler shot back, before overturning a large decorative curio cabinet filled with porcelain figurines.

"Hey man! Watch what you're doin'!" Pharaoh screamed irritably.

"Sir, we have a search warrant." Ethan said, before unfolding the document for the injured gangster to see.

"Search warrant?" Pharaoh asked, angrily. "What are you guys expecting to find here?"

"You're under suspicion of distributing crack cocaine." Ethan explained, in a professional manner.

"Crack cocaine?" Pharaoh barked. "This is my momma's house! Ain't nobody slingin' no dope outta here!"

The very firm declaration made Ethan believe the thug was telling the truth. However, he knew crooks would say anything to get out of trouble. Ethan also knew that he was the rookie, and, therefore, had to follow his training officer's lead without question.

Several long minutes went by as Tyler and Booker continued their aggressive search. With every sound of glass being broken, Pharaoh would grind his teeth even more. Ethan strained his neck trying to catch a glimpse of what his partners were doing, since he had never officially been a part of a warrant search of a premises before.

"Someone call an ambulance?" A paramedic asked, while maneuvering a gurney through the mess Tyler was creating.

"Over here." Ethan acknowledged. "We have a gunshot wound to this man's right shoulder."

As the paramedics went about their business of strapping the muscular gangster to the gurney, Tyler took that moment to pull the kilo of crack cocaine out of his jacket pocket and walk back into the living room area.

"Today just isn't your day, Pharaoh." Tyler purred arrogantly, as he displayed the narcotics teasingly in his hand for the thug to see. "Found this stashed under the bathroom vanity."

"Man that ain't mine!" Pharaoh screamed. "You planted that, you dirty cop!"

"That's what they all say." Booker chimed in, before taking a drag off his cigarette.

"That ain't my dope!" Pharaoh yelled, as the paramedics wheeled him out the front door. "I ain't goin' back to the joint for this!"

"If not for this, how about attempted murder of a cop?" Tyler asked heatedly. "Either way, your future's not lookin' too bright."

Ethan watched as the gurney was loaded up into the ambulance. He could still not fight the feeling that Jimmy Boose was telling the truth. Even in his days out on patrol duty, Ethan had never run upon a crook that denied his charges with such passion. It didn't help matters any more to see Tyler and Booker smiling like a couple of grade-schoolers that had just tattled on another child on the playground.

"Hey rookie! Why don't ya pull the car up, while me and Booker look the place over for anything we might have missed?" Tyler asked, as he tossed the keys to the '69 Caprice to Ethan.

"Sure thing." He replied, after catching the keys and exiting through the front door.

The two crooked cops watched Ethan until he was out of sight and then Tyler grabbed the gangster that had tried to shoot him roughly by the throat.

"Take that one out on the porch." The blonde-haired detective growled, lustfully. "I'm gonna use this one to relieve a little tension."

"A'ight partner." Booker replied, before grabbing the other thug by the back of the neck and forcing him outside. "You heard the man."

Once Booker had left the room, Tyler began his assault of his prisoner. "You don't look so tough without a gun in your hand, do you, ya little weasel?" He asked, before slugging the thug deep in the diaphragm.

The gangster coughed uncontrollably after the unexpected move, as the wind in his lungs was forced out of his body.

"Yo, man, I wasn't gonna shoot you!" The gangbanger shrieked, in a failed attempt to defend himself. "I was just trying to scare you!"

"Oh, I see." Tyler said, sarcastically. "So I guess that makes everything alright? Well, I'll tell ya what, for kicks and giggles, why don't I just try and scare you to see how you like it."

Detective Lynch then grabbed the thug by the ear and proceeded to drag him into the kitchen area. Once there, he threw him down roughly in one of the chairs and then proceeded to turn on a waffle iron that was waiting on the kitchen counter. The hotter the waffle iron grew, the more the whites of the gangster's eyes became visible.

"Yo, man, what you fittin' to do?" He asked in a frantic tone.

"Don't worry, I'm only going to *scare* you." Tyler said, as he waved his opened hand over the hot metal surface. "Now, let me see those pistol wielding hands of yours."

Chapter 6

The Abyss. The prison for disobedient spirits was nothing more than an ominous bottomless pit surrounded by oceanic waters on all four sides. All demons in existence feared the primal prison deep, because it was specifically designed to hold and torment spirit forms. Never did Hunter believe he would be entering the foul, dark domain before the day of judgment, but here he was looming high above the smoldering gates with thirteen legions of the fiercest demon warriors he had ever witnessed backing his play.

The chasm they were about to insert themselves into resembled the mouth of a great volcano, complete with smoke and thick ash pouring out from far beyond their view. This was usually as close as any of the fiendish creatures dared to tread, lest wicked thoughts of their bleak future pierce their minds. However, scouts that managed to breach its unholy passageway and yet survive to tell the tale, sketched out a detailed map that pictured the dismal depths winding on for mile after desolate mile.

Even with the well drawn atlas firmly in hand, the whereabouts of Lars' location was still a mystery. This lack of information would therefore cost them when it came time to exit the dreadful confinement. Knowing this, Hunter felt fear for the first time since being cast out of the lustrous pearled gates of Heaven.

"The ranks are getting restless, Captain." Zaddik, Hunter's newly assigned chief officer, and by far the largest demon in the assemblage, drooled.

"Then we shall not keep them waiting." The white-haired demon replied, while pulling his gleaming blades from their sheathes.

"You must give them a word, Captain." Zaddik advised. Hunter furrowed his brow at the comment, clearly not understanding the sentiment.

"For courage." Zaddik added. "It inspires them, especially in a battle such as this."

The evil grin that Hunter flashed as his reply was all that was needed for Zaddik to understand his captain had grasped the purpose.

"Hear me!" Hunter screamed in a dramatic tone, as he turned to face his volatile army. "We are about to embark on a journey that will take us through the bowels of Hell itself! We will be met with heavy resistance, and I dare say most of your comrades will not return! But when we succeed…and we will succeed…our exploits will forever be remembered in infamy! Our names will be forever uttered off the lips of our demonic brothers and sisters as they sing them in war songs written for our glory! And…most importantly…Lucifer's army will be that much closer to winning the war for the Souls of Man! Remember your shame as you were cast out of the glorious gates of Heaven, carry it with you through this battle and let it strengthen you, for our day of triumph is at hand! Now, bring your wicked weapons to bear, and quench their thirst on the holy essence of our accursed kin, the guardian angels that turned their backsides to us and our aspirations! Brothers… Sisters…follow me through the gates of Hell, and let us bring home victory!"

Hunter's inspiring words whipped his warriors into a frenzy, as they returned their sentiments in the form of blood curdling screams. The spiritual world was shaken with their brief eruption of battle-ready war cries. Each and every warrior pounded their weapons against the old surface of their shields creating the sound of artificial thunder. The army's intensity fueled Hunter's vigor as he turned his attention back unto the gateway to the Abyss and was not surprised in the least to see the guardians of the region hard at work formulating a battle defensive.

Uriel, the most fanatical and pitiless of all of God's Archangels, had been called in from afar in an attempt to repel the hostile horde. Armed with his flaming longbow, the fiery red-haired Archangel took to the air, his piercing stare causing any enemy of the demon horde that looked his way to tremble in fear. His well armed battalion beneath his flight consisted of hundreds of the most stern warring angels he could amass in such a short time.

One of the warring angels in particular was Glistinia, the strawberry blonde guardian angel that had stood watch over Ethan Brooks' mother on the night of his birth. The fierce female angel was one of Uriel's most trusted comrades, and has aided him on many previous adventures. Like her larger companion, Glistinia was also armed with a fiery longbow that she used to take careful aim on Hunter, the captain of the throng of attacking demons and the leader of the party that ended Jody Brooks life in the world of man.

Fear did not exist in Glistinia's sparkling green orbs. The beautiful guardian had partaken in countless battles, and no demon she has ever engaged has survived to fight another day as they were now held captive below the gateway she now found herself protecting. Glistinia knew on this day, other demonic scum would share the same fate.

"WARRIORS!" Hunter screamed. "UNLEASH HELL!" After the vivid order was issued from Hunter's lips, the demonic legions plunged down upon the angelic defenders like a dark cloud attempting to blot out the sun. As soon as the army was set free Glistinia loosed three flaming arrows from her bow. The blazing projectiles sped toward Hunter's torso with deadly intent, craving the taste of the demon spawn.

However, with vision more keen than a hawk and nerves as calm as a gentle stream, Hunter swatted the arrows out of the air as easily as waving away gnats on a cool summer day. Spiraling his way downward in an attempt to confuse any more would be archer assassins, Hunter made first contact with the angelic line of defense. His razor-sharp blades sliced cleanly through every angel on which he took aim. At least nine of the Heavenly Host were cut down by his wicked assault, as he neared the gloomy entranceway to the abominable Abyss.

Hunter knew that angels could not be killed. They could, however, be injured badly enough that they could not continue fighting. Just as demons lose their precious shadowy essence when they are injured, angels also lose their glowing holy essence while wounded. When they are depleted of their costly life force, they need to be taken back to the Kingdom of Heaven, where they must rest and recuperate.

Flying at full speed, the white-haired demon looked over his shoulder to witness the devastation his handiwork had caused. A lustful smile spread across the smooth features of his visage when he saw the path of wounded angels strewn in his wake. Hunter was also pleased to see that his legions did not fare as badly as he had thought. After a thunderous collision caused by his warriors weapons colliding with the solid shields of the angelic defenders, a full legion of troops managed to break free and follow his lead toward the dismal gates.

So enthralled was he by the events of the battle that the newly made captain was nearly obliterated by an exploding arrow that struck the ground near his path of flight. Hunter had been so preoccupied with fighting his way to the rusted gateway that he had taken his eyes off the most dominant foe on the battlefield.

The Archangel Uriel.

The blast from the explosion was so intense that the demon was propelled away from the darkened entrance and sent crashing into a wall of jagged rocks. His flawless face was now marred from the blast and his backside was opened, seeping his dark, shadowy essence from many deep lacerations. Even with the suffering pain he felt throughout his body, the cunning demon still had enough frame of mind to leap away from his current position before another exploding arrow detonated the space where he had just occupied. That blast would have finished him for good if not for his quick actions. He knew then and there that a change in strategy was needed if they were going to pull off a victory.

"Zaddik!" Hunter cried, at the top of his voice.

"Yes, Captain." The large demon responded from the other side of the gateway, as he wounded another angel with the jagged spikes of his morning star.

"Send two legions to distract our large adversary!" Hunter ordered, just before dodging another exploding arrow. "Or we will be annihilated on these rocks!"

"We cannot afford to sacrifice such a large number of troops for a diversion, Captain!" Zaddik replied, as another angel stepped forward to replace the fallen comrade the big demon had just downed.

"We cannot afford *not* to!" Hunter screamed.

After the exchange of words, Zaddik took hold of the signaling device he had strapped around his neck that resembled a large ram's horn and let loose with three successive bellowing blasts. Instantly the remaining demons on the field of battle turned their attention toward him. Zaddik then used a few quick hand signals to instruct the warriors of the new orders, and within moments two legions broke off their attack with the front line of angels, taking to flight.

The swarm of demonic warriors charged toward Uriel and surrounded him on all fronts, causing the mighty Archangel to discontinue the use of his longbow, and unsheathe his flaming longsword.

The distraction served its purpose.

"Zaddik!" Hunter called to his chief officer. "You and I must take advantage of this opportunity, while Uriel is unable to bombard us with arrows!"

"What of the legion that managed to break through the line with us, Captain?" the burly demon asked, while clubbing two more attacking angels with his morning star. "They will be decimated trying to keep the guardian angels off our tail!"

"Leave them! They are of no concern to me!" Hunter spat, evilly. "Our mission is to free Lars!"

Zaddik nodded his head before falling in line behind Hunter. The two demons then closed the gap between them and the foreboding gateway as quickly as they could, as the battle raged on behind them. When they at last arrived, they pushed one of the giant gates open until just enough room had presented itself for them to squeeze through.

Once their feet had touched down on the scorched soil of the loathsome place which was the Abyss, they wondered why they had fought so hard to enter. The darkness was so thick it was as if trying to walk through a tangible object, while the screams of their tormented brothers and sisters echoed in their ears, drowning out the ability to think.

"T-This place is dreadful, Captain…" Zaddik stammered.

"I concur…" Hunter acknowledged, timidly. "The sooner we find Lars, the sooner we may leave."

"You're not seriously going to continue?" Zaddik asked with the edge of fear in his tone.

"Of course." Hunter replied, the sound of courage no longer detectable in his own voice. "If we leave now, Mistress Vixanna will lop off our heads and we will end up here as prisoners ourselves."

Zaddik could not argue with the knowledge. So, with nothing to lose, the pair of demons set forth on their quest, as the weight of their burden bore down upon them with every heavy footfall.

*   *   *   *   *

The ride away from the scene of the raid was a quiet one. As soon as Ethan caught sight of the prisoner with the freshly made burn marks on each of his hands climbing into the back of the paddy wagon, he knew exactly what had transpired while he was out fetching the car. It also did little to soothe his anger when his partners did nothing to hide the fact that they had beaten the man and just didn't want the rookie around to be a witness.

"You're just about as quiet as a hooker in church, rookie." Tyler finally said, breaking the silence.

"I'm just sorry I missed all the action." Ethan replied, in a flat tone.

"What're you talkin' about?" Booker asked, pointedly. "You were in the thick of all the action."

"Well, I don't remember any of the prisoners tripping onto a piping hot waffle iron." Ethan shot back. "Must have missed that part."

After the young detective spoke his mind, he could feel the car veering right and then come to a stop next to the curb. Obviously, he had gotten underneath Tyler's skin with his comment.

"Listen up, rookie!" Tyler snapped, after throwing the car in park and then turning around in his seat to look into Ethan's eyes. "You can't always be a goodie two shoes out here! These are the streets, and you have to play by the streets rules or you're not going to last very long out here! Now, me and Booker got a certain way we like to roll out here, and if you don't like it, maybe you should go back to patrol duty!"

Ethan was momentarily stunned by his training officer's words and did not have a reply forthwith. All Ethan could think about was all the hard work he had put in to get here, and there was no way he was going to take a step back now.

"Look, rookie, I was forced to bring you into the mix." Tyler admitted. "Now, you saved my butt back there. I can't deny that. So, I can bring you into the game slowly, or not at all. The choice is up to you."

"I'm not going anywhere." Ehtan answered, with finality.

"Alright, then." Tyler replied. "But you have to accept the way we do things without question or get out."

"Fine." Ethan conceded.

"Good." Tyler responded, with a slight grin, before turning to Booker. "Now that we are all straight up in here, let's introduce junior to some of our contacts."

"Tasha?" Booker inquired, with a hopeful tone in his voice.

"Partner, you just read my mind." Tyler answered, before putting the car back in drive and pulling away from the curb.

"Don't we have to interrogate the suspects?" Ethan rightly asked.

"Not yet." Tyler replied. "I wanna wait for all the bullets to come back from forensics before we question them. Let 'em sweat it out in holding for now."

"As soon as we get the 411 from the lab, them boys won't be able to deny a thing." Booker put in.

"Right now, I need to pay Tasha a visit." Tyler said, as he turned the car onto North Court Street, and parked in front of an apartment building that looked fairly decent considering the part of town they were in. "Tasha's a prostitute by trade, that we throw a little cash at whenever she gives us valuable intel. Right now we owe her a little bit of money for the info she gave us on Pharaoh."

"Let's go." Booker cooed excitedly, before exiting the vehicle.

Ethan and Tyler followed their partner's lead and climbed out of the Caprice. After following the sidewalk up to the front door, Tyler pressed the buzzer for apartment 304. A few moments passed and then a charming female voice with what sounded like a Latino accent answered the call.

"Yeah...?"

"Open up, babe, it's me." Tyler replied, casually.

Ethan was quick to note the pet name that his blonde haired partner used to address the woman. It was clear to him that Tyler had a somewhat casual relationship with her. How casual was still yet to be determined.

"Come on up." The woman said, before the buzzer sounded, unlatching the electronic lock.

Once they were allowed access, the three men stepped inside and walked several feet before entering an elevator.

Tyler pushed the button for the third floor, as Ethan inspected the lobby. The young detective was still impressed with how refined and clean the building was. He knew that the city had been making some good deals with contractors and property owners in the area, in an attempt to improve the living conditions on some of the low-level parts of town. The concept was to fix the area up enough to raise the property value, so that property owners could ask more for rent. If the regular riff raff could not afford the cost of living in the area, then they would be forced to move elsewhere, subsequently lowering crime, such as drug dealing and prostitution. Ethan could not help but smirk at the thought of how the latter seemed to have been unaffected, such as in Tasha's case. The rise in the cost of living only served in creating a higher classed hooker.

When they had at last reached the third floor, the elevator doors opened and the men exited. They then took a sharp left and walked until the apartment numbers reached 304. Tyler gave a few knocks, the door opened wide, and it was then that Ethan figured out why Booker had been so eager to come here.

Tasha was beautiful. She was not at all like the prostitutes Ethan was used to hauling into the station house for solicitation when he used to be out on patrol. She had a clean and classy look about her. The woman stood only five feet four inches tall and had a tanned complexion to her smooth skin, leading Ethan to believe even further that she had some Latino heritage about her. Her light auburn locks had been highlighted with blonde streaks, and possessed delicate curls that ended just down the center of her petite spine. She eyed the men, Ethan in particular, for a long moment with her stunning brown orbs before stepping aside and allowing them entry.

"What's up, Tasha?" Tyler asked in a cocky tone, before giving the woman a flat handed smack on her bottom. "Haven't heard from you for a while."

"I've Just been busy." She replied, in a meek sounding tone.

"Yeah, I guess turnin' tricks all day can be a bit time consuming." Tyler replied, without any concern for the woman's feelings. He then plopped himself onto her couch making himself right at home. "Oh, before I forget, Ethan, this is Tasha, one of our street contacts. Tasha, this is Ethan, our rookie."

"Hello." Ethan greeted, before extending a hand for a shake.

It had been quite some time that Tasha had been spoken to in a respectful manner. So stunned was she with the man's courteous behavior that she said nothing right away. Unsure if the young man was a dirty cop, as the other two, Tasha did not outright welcome the newcomer. Eventually, though, she did take hold of his hand and give it a halfhearted shake, more for formalities than any other reason.

"So how much did we make?" Booker asked, lustily.

"Fifteen hundred." Tasha answered, hesitantly. "I kept your money separate from mine."

"Keep it." Tyler said, before she had time to turn and retrieve the money. "Your info on Pharaoh was dead on. You've earned it."

"Man, Tyler!" Booker barked. "That's seven large of *my* money you're dealin' with play'a."

"Come on, Booker! We'll earn that back in less than a week." Tyler argued. "Let her have this."

"A'ight." Booker conceded. "But if I can't have my Benjamin's, at least let me sample some of our product."

After saying so, Booker wrapped his arms around Tasha's slim waist and pulled her in close to him. Ethan could tell by the woman's demeanor she wanted no part of what he was about to do. When Booker started kissing Tasha on her neck the woman put her hands between him and herself, but did not push away due to fear of what he might do. Judging from the woman's apprehensive behavior, Ethan knew she had been put in this situation before. When he reached the point where he could take the scene no longer, Ethan took a step forward so that he could intervene on the woman's behalf. However, his gallantry was not needed. Before he could take another stride, a tender voice could be heard from the other side of the apartment.

"Momma…?"

"Please…stop." Tasha finally worked up the courage to say. "Not in front of Nina."

Soon after Tasha had spoken, a skinny little girl of about four years of age with the most innocent big brown eyes Ethan had ever seen, walked into the room to stand with the men.

"Come on!" Booker snapped. "Can't you get a babysitter or somethin'? We just let you keep fifteen G's, surely you can afford one!"

"Alright, alright." Tasha replied, before squirming out of Booker's grasp. "I will take her to my sister's apartment down the hall."

"You know, you really don't have to do that.' Ethan interjected.

"Says who?" Booker shot back in a frustrated tone.

Tasha knew what the men were capable of due to the fact that she had witnessed the carnage their violent tempers had caused first hand. She did not want to see their wrathful anger come to a boil tonight as it had in the past. She could tell Ethan was just trying to help. Maybe there were some good guys left out there in the world and she had just not seen one in so long that she had forgotten about them. In order to save herself and the newly met stranger with the good heart, she acted quickly.

"No, that's alright." She replied, with a wink. "It's my job after all."

"Come on, rookie." Tyler said, after climbing off the couch and heading past Ethan to the door. "Let's give these two some privacy."

Against his better judgment, Ethan followed Tyler out of the door, leaving Booker to conduct his foul business. After the elevator ride back to the ground level, the pair walked quietly down to where their '69 Chevy Caprice was parked. Ethan leaned up against the door of the car and looked up at Tasha's window, wondering if there was anything he could have done differently to defuse the situation, so that the young woman would not have to go through with what she was enduring at this moment.

After about thirty minutes had passed, Booker strutted out of the building with a smug smile on his face. Ethan did his best not to punch the man square in the mouth, as they all climbed into the Caprice. As the engine fired up and the car pulled away, Ethan could not help but think that he had become a police officer in order to put people away such as these two. The fact that they were considered officers of the law sickened him. Maybe one day, he would get to do the one thing his heart wanted him to do. After all, the world would be a better place if he did.

Chapter 7

Hunter stopped for a moment and knelt down, rubbing a hand through the scorched ground. Zaddik, his newly appointed chief officer, and he had been traveling through the wretched Abyss for what felt to be days. Truth be known, it may have only been a few minutes, since time in the eternal land of the damned held no merit.

The wounds to his face and back caused by Uriel's arrows were fully restored, due to the accelerated healing abilities possessed by all the spiritual beings. Not so much as a scar remained on his flawless visage as he stood to his feet and surveyed the area.

For the first time since the two demons entered the dismal terrain the pathway opened into a great cavern, the ceiling of which stretched so far above their heads that it disappeared out of the range of even their extraordinary vision. Water raged down on all sides of a naturally made rocky bridge, drowning out all other sound. The structure was in the shape of a large cross, obviously meant to remind those that tread here of the consequences of their decision not to follow Christ. This section was the first area they had seen where the light actually penetrated the darkness, allowing them a brief glimpse of the atrocious domain. It was as if the scenery was only made visible to shed despair on all those that set foot in the horrible place.

"Despicable…" Hunter groaned aloud to himself, when he caught a glimpse of the cross shaped formation.

The white-haired demon then gestured to Zaddik for the pair to continue, and slowly the two moved forward until the walls swallowed them up once again. After the two had reached a point where the sound of the rampant waters and tortured screams of their imprisoned kin had subsided enough for them to hear again, Hunter spoke.

"That is as far as the map goes, and still we have yet to locate Lars or any of our fallen comrades." He groaned.

"The map has been pointless anyhow." Zaddik complained. "The whole time we have been here we have traveled in a straight line."

"We are getting closer, though." Hunter said, with the faint sound of hope in his voice. "The screams are getting louder."

"Then let ups continue." Zaddik urged. "The sooner we free Lars, the sooner we can leave this foul place behind us."

"Agreed." Hunter acknowledged, before tearing the map in two and letting it fall to the ground.

After the brief conversation, the pair moved onward. Every ten paces or so an ear-splitting shriek, much louder than the rest of the screams, would echo off the rocky walls, sending chills down the demons spines. Fear was a sensation that was uncommon to the creatures. Nevertheless, as they traveled through the mysterious terrain that was created specifically for punishing evil spirits, they could not help but feel terror rising within them the further they tread.

When they had taken several more strides both demons noticed a severe rise in temperature. It was the first time since their creation that either of them had felt the sensation of heat. Normally, spiritual creatures felt nothing in particular. They felt the sting of an angelic weapon when wounded by one in battle. They felt a surge in power and influence when feeding off the fear being drawn from their human victims. They also felt uncontrollable agony when commanded to do something under the authority of the Lord Jesus Christ. Nevertheless, common everyday sensations, such as warmth or chill had never been felt before unless traveling through the abyss or standing in the presence of Mistress Vixanna.

"Do you feel that captain?" Zaddik asked, looking at his hands, wondering what the feeling was that had just come over him.

"Yes, I feel it too." Hunter answered, but not at all surprised by the sensation.

"What is it?" The burly demon inquired.

"It is the heat of hellfire." Hunter replied. "And it will get far worse before we reach our goal, I assure you."

As the two conversed, they could feel their feet sinking into the warm soil. The intense heat was now affecting the ground on which they walked.

"What's happening?" Zaddik queried, watching his boots as they seeped into the heated dirt.

"The warmth is causing the ground to break apart under our weight." Hunter answered, lifting one foot off the ground to inspect his highly polished footwear. "We must take to flight from here on."

Just as he had said, so he did. Hunter started flying further down the tunnel, and Zaddik quickly followed suit. The further they flew, the hotter the area around them grew.

Up ahead the white-haired demon saw an intense light and could make out the crackle of a roaring fire.

"We are nearly there!" He screamed, elevating his voice over the screams and burning fire.

After the announcement, the ground beneath them disappeared as the cave opened up into an enormous pit of flame. They immediately ceased their forward progress and hovered above the inferno, inspecting their new found surroundings in fearful awe.

The roof of the pit appeared to be made out of a thick sheen of clear rock, through which the floor of the Kingdom of Heaven could be seen. No doubt the view was meant for added torment to those that found themselves forever trapped within the unquenchable flame of hellfire. The tortured souls would then be able to witness first hand all of God's children that they had wronged in their lifetime, receiving their eternal rewards, while their own souls were scorched for all eternity.

Suspended from the bottom of the ceiling, the two demons could see thousands of their demonic brothers and sisters hanging by sharp hooks that had been pierced through their tongues. Their wings had been burned to a cinder by the incredible heat, so that they had no choice but to dangle out of range of the fire below by the hook in their tongues or fall to the flame beneath them to roast.

"What manner of punishment is this?" Zaddik pondered, aloud.

"They have been hung by their blasphemous tongues." Hunter answered. "The day of judgment has not yet come, so they have yet to taste the flame."

"Look!" Zaddik interrupted, pointing to a large demon half the size of a football field chained to the side of the cavern with his wrists in fetters.

"Lars!" Hunter gasped, after finally catching sight of the object of his quest. "At last, we can free him and get-"

"Captain Your wings?" Zaddik screamed, after witnessing the smoke beginning to rise from Hunter's feathers.

"The heat is consuming them!" Hunter yelled.

"Mine too!" Zaddik shrieked.

"Quickly, we must get as far from this flame as we can!" Hunter advised, before soaring back in the direction they had just come.

When they at last arrived in a cooler area, their wings instantly began to restore themselves. Every singed feather grew back to its original form without so much as a blemish remaining.

"That explains how our kin are unable to leave." Hunter said, more for his own ears to hear than Zaddik's. "The heat is so intense that it devours their wings, and the ground breaks apart when one tries to stand upon it."

"So how are we going to free Lars?" The large demon inquired.

"You may not have noticed, Zaddik," Hunter began, turning to look his comrade in the eyes. "But many of those imprisoned spirits hanging by their tongues back there, were members of our thirteen legions."

"I did not have the time to ponder…" Zaddik replied.

"We will have to free them, two at a time." Hunter explained. "You take one and I take one. We will bring them back here, so that they can heal. Their assistance will be needed when we loose Lars from the fetters, and to fight our way back out of the Abyss."

"I understand, Captain." Zaddik acknowledged. "Lead the way."

$$* \quad * \quad * \quad * \quad *$$

No matter how fast the demon flew, the guardian angel inevitably seemed to be gaining on him. Darting to and fro through the trees only served in slowing his momentum, so the twisted imp quickly changed tactics and decided to soar straight through them instead. The evil spirit had been grievously wounded, as a trail of his dark essence leaked out of numerous lacerations inflicted by the fierce fighting angel of war.

The demon was merely sent on a simple scouting mission. The assignment was not supposed to be that dangerous, as scouting missions rarely were. Unfortunately, the emissary had been misinformed on this occasion and was unaware that this particular home was wholly protected by the most intense sword bearer the spiritual realm had ever known.

Suddenly, the fleeing demon caught a glimpse of hope. In his mad dash the nasty fiend had become disoriented and did not immediately realize he was flying toward friendly territory. There was a high-ranking wiccan, a witch serving false gods, living nearby, and her home was infested with dark spirits. If he could survive for a few moments more, he could reach her dwelling and find allies to aid him in this battle.

Veering his flight westward, the demon headed in the direction of the witch's home. When he spotted her townhouse mere yards away, the evil spirit felt a sensation he had not felt in centuries.

He felt hope.

The moment was short lived though. For when the hell spawn was about to streak through the walls of the wiccan's home, the pursuing angel launched his weapon through the air. The dangerously, razor sharp tip of the scimitar sunk deep into the demon's backside, emerging from the center of his chest. The blow was fatal, sending the doomed imp straight to the ground. The demon managed to struggle himself to his knees just as the guardian angel wrenched his scimitar free from his back.

"You shall be rewarded with an eternity in The Lake of Fire for your services, fiend." Cazzbein growled, before cleanly lopping the demon's head off.

After the headless corpse fell to the ground, Cazzbein utilized its black coat to wipe the sticky, dark essence off his scimitar's blade. As he did so, the angel watched as the demon's body dissolved into ash, as it undertook the long journey to the Abyss. While he tarried, Cazzbein felt the ever-growing presence of evil closing in upon him.

When he finally looked up from his cleaning, Cazzbein witnessed at least thirty evil spirits rising from the wiccan's house. Their faces twisted into angry, jagged toothed scowls as they prepared to unleash their displeasure upon the angel that had just eliminated one of their brothers.

Even in the overwhelming show of numbers Cazzbein showed no sign of fear, as he unsheathed his other scimitar, preparing for the forthcoming battle. After all, he served God Almighty; and his God was not the spirit of fear.

Just as he had sized up the competition and waited for the first demon to make its move, they mysteriously began to withdraw back into the witch's home. Thinking them to be cowards, the guardian angel returned his weapons to their sheaths and prepared to leave. The thought crossed his mind of taking the fight to them and vanquishing the demons from the wiccans home. But after further debating the issue, he realized it was the witch that welcomed the hellish devils into her home to aid her in her foul, unnatural magic, so she deserved whatever torment they gave her. After he turned to leave, Cazzbein figured out the reason for the demon's sudden change in courage. Standing behind him, at an impressive thirty feet in height, was Michael, the Archangel predestined to defeat Lucifer in the final battle of the War for the Souls of Man.

Michael was by far the most handsome angel to ever grace the golden streets of the glorious Kingdom of Heaven. His thick blonde mane flowed past his perfectly rounded shoulders, ending midway down the backside of his brilliantly crafted golden chest plate. Strapped loosely around his trim waist was the greatsword foreordained to deal the final blow to Lucifer that would end the Prince of Darkness's reign of terror on humanity.

Michael looked at Cazzbein with his piercing blue eye, as the expression of concern was clearly displayed on the masculine features of his unblemished visage. Cazzbein could tell merely from the sound of silence that filled the air, the Archangel carried with him the weight of a distressing message. Michael was the Field Commander of the vast angelic Army of God, so for Cazzbein to receive a visit from him personally, proved to the angel how urgent the circumstances that brought him must be.

"Sir?" Cazzbein asked in a respectful tone, as he stood to attention.

"Be at ease, Cazzbein." Michael said, placing a soothing hand on his shoulder.

"Yes, sir." The obedient guardian acknowledged.

"Cazzbein, how fares your current assignment?" the powerful Archangel queried.

"It goes well, sir." Cazzbein replied, honestly.

"You are watching over Ethan Brooks, are you not?" Michael asked solemnly.

"That is correct, sir." Cazzbein replied, honestly.

"Has your charge come to accept Jesus Christ as his Savior?" The huge Archangel inquired.

"Not yet, I'm afraid." Cazzbein responded, as he looked to the ground. "But he is in good company. His wife is a servant of God."

"That is fortunate news," Michael said, turning his gaze toward the nighttime sky. "But being joined in wedlock to a Christian will not earn him a seat at The Great Feast."

"True." Cazzbein admitted. "And God's purpose has yet to reveal itself."

"Actually, it has." Michael corrected. "However, it has just scratched the surface. It will further come into focus as time goes on."

"It has?" Cazzbein asked, in an astonished tone.

"That is neither here, nor there, Cazzbein." The Archangel replied grimly. "For the reason I have called tonight is for a far greater purpose."

"My talents are at your disposal, Commander." Cazzbein said, with the sound of cold determination in his voice.

"As always, you are one of my bravest guardians." Michael admitted, as he looked Cazzbein over with a satisfied gaze.

"What is the mission?" The angel asked.

"Your old nemesis, Hunter, with the assistance of thirteen legions of demon warriors, handpicked by Mistress Vixanna herself, have dealt Uriel's small contingent of angels a surprising blow." Michael said, in a regrettable tone.

"Impossible…" Cazzbein gasped.

"So we thought." The Field Commander responded, before crossing his massive arms across his chest. "The attack came as a total surprise. Uriel did his best to gather enough angels to create a defensive in such a short amount of time. Nevertheless, his efforts were not good enough."

"What was their target?" Cazzbein queried.

"The Abyss." Michael answered in a no-nonsense intonation.

"What?" the fierce sword bearer asked. "Why? What could they possibly hope to obtain by such a foolhardy venture?"

"As always, the army of darkness operates in the shadows," Michael replied. "But as you know, there are some very powerful evil spirits imprisoned down there that must stay confined at all costs. If they were to be freed, the shift in power could be significant."

Cazzbein thought of the consequences for a moment before saying a word. When he finally realized the severity of the threat, he was eager to get started.

"We must stop them." He said, with the edge of determination in his voice.

"I am glad to hear you say that.' Michael sighed, with relief. "However, it will be a daunting task, considering many of our best warring angels were wounded in the initial battle."

"What do you ask of me, Commander?' Cazzbein inquired.

"Your enthusiasm is only overshadowed by your bravery, my brother." Michael complemented. "I need for you to gather a small band of your most trustworthy companions, and enter the Abyss. Once there, deal with Hunter and whatever demons he has with him."

"I will fight to the last drop of my essence, Commander." Cazzbein said, through gritted teeth.

"I know you will." Michael replied, in a flattering tone.

"You are the one warring angel best suited to deal with Hunter. What I am saying, my friend, is that your sword-bearing skills are called upon."

*   *   *   *   *

After leaving Tasha's apartment building, Tyler drove his crew back to the station house. When he stopped the car in front of the entrance instead of pulling into a stall, Ethan knew something was up.

"Ain't you comin' in, dog?" Booker asked.

"Nah, nah, you go ahead." Tyler replied. "I'll see ya in the morning."

"Ai'ght then," Booker said, before getting out of the car. "I'll bounce."

As Ethan began climbing out of the car from the back seat, Tyler grabbed hold of his arm.

"Not yet, rookie." Tyler said, as he lit a cigarette with his free hand. "Climb up front. I wanna have a talk with you."

"Okay…" Ehtan said, after a lengthy pause, as his mind could not help but think the worst.

As soon as Ethan was seated up front Tyler drove away, leaving the station house behind them. Ethan had no idea what the slickster was up to, so he dared not say a word. Instead, he waited for Tyler to initiate the conversation, since, after all, it was him that wanted to talk.

The drive was a short one. In fact, Tyler simply drove across the street into a five story parking garage. Once he had reached the top level, Tyler then drove to the furthest corner of the structure and placed the car in park.

"Come on, get out." Tyler said, as he climbed out of the car. Tyler stopped at the corner of the facility, he placed his foot upon the cement wall and looked out at the city.

Ethan hesitantly followed his team leader, still not knowing what to expect. When Ethan at last made it to his side, he saw why Tyler chose to come here.

The cityscape was spectacular. From this section of the parking garage one could see the Faust Landmark three miles down East State Street, while several city blocks in the other direction, The Metro Center dominated the landscape. The view was breathtaking. From several stories above the world, everything seemed serene. Ethan could not help but think, the peace and quiet was most likely the reason Tyler chose this location in which to speak with him.

"What's up?" Ethan finally worked up the courage to ask.

"Well, rookie, I just thought I'd bring you up here for a little chit chat." Tyler answered, before taking a drag off his cigarette. "After rolling around with the street scum all day, I like to come up here and unwind."

"You picked a good location." Ethan admitted, staring down at the tiny people on the sidewalk far below.

"Listen, Brooks," Tyler began. "The real reason I brought you up here is to talk to you about our crew."

Ethan did not interrupt. He also could not help but notice Tyler used his last name to address him, instead of calling him rookie. Maybe that meant that he actually made an impression on his training officer.

"You did good out there today." Tyler acknowledged. "You really saved my butt. I have to tell ya, me and Booker are a pretty tight set. You have to be if you're gonna do the type of work we do. You gotta be able to trust the guys that have your back. Ya feel me?"

"Yeah…I agree." Ethan answered, not sure of where Tyler was going with the conversation.

"It's just that, I'm about to expose you to a whole new world, and I have to know you're ready for it." Tyler continued. "You're gonna see some things that really turn your stomach and make you wanna puke, but we have to remain professionals and do our jobs."

"I'm listening." Ethan said, after Tyler paused to hear his reply.

"I guess what I'm tryin' to tell you is, in order for me and Booker to trust *you*, then you gotta get a little dirt on yourself."

"What do you mean?" Ehtan asked, unclear if he was hearing Tyler correctly.

"I mean…Me and Booker got a lot of irons in the fire, and we need to know we can trust you." Tyler added, before flicking his cigarette butt off the roof of the structure.

"Of course you can trust me." Ethan said, still unsure of the nature of the discussion.

"Well, anyone can say they can be trusted. But in order for us to truly trust you, you have to stop being so uptight. You can't go gettin' all bent out of shape when you see one of us bending the rules a little." Tyler explained, looking at Ethan to see if what he was saying was sinking in at all. "You have to start workin' the streets and come up with a hustle of your own, so that we know you're one of us."

"Are you telling me to break the law?" Ethan asked, flatly.

"Cops don't rat out other cops." Tyler said, with a scowl.

"Otherwise people begin to think they are working for Internal Affairs and they wind up catchin' a bullet in the back one day when they're serving a high stakes warrant. Capeesh?"

"Yeah…I get it." Ehtan answered, looking Tyler in the eyes to let him know he did not appreciate the threat.

"Over 15,000 man-years of incarceration time have been handed down by Illinois State judges due to my crew's investigations." Tyler explained. "Our record is impeccable. The captain grants us a wide berth, so long as we don't mess up. He knows what we're up against out here and he knows what we have to do to get the job done. If you want to do some good, this is the place to do it. So, if you're going to be a part of this unit, you have to be in all the way or not at all. Understand?"

"Yeah. I understand." Ethan replied, in a firm tone.

"Good. Well…Go on home. Get some rest. And I'll see you in the morning." Tyler said, in an overly pleasant sounding tone, before climbing back into the car and driving away.

Ethan watched as the '69 Caprice drove off down the ramp of the parking garage to the lower level. As he walked to the elevator, the young detective could not help but wonder what to do about his quandary.

One thing Tyler said was truthful. Cops don't squeal on other cops unless they want to be ostracized. Ethan now thought he made the wrong career move by joining the anti-gang task force. All he ever wanted to do since childhood was to become an officer of the law, so that he could better serve the community. Now, Ethan wondered if even the police were too deeply corrupted for him to be able to fight crime.

What good would it do to lock criminals up, when you're working side by side with crooks on a daily basis? Does it make a difference that they had badges, and other street thugs don't" He wondered, as he reached the elevator and pressed the call button. The answers to his many questions did not immediately arrive, as did the elevator.

Once inside, Ethan pressed the button that would bring him to the first level, where he had parked his car earlier that day. The ride to the ground level took no time at all. When the doors opened up, he could see his older model sedan waiting for him in the very first stall. As he walked toward his vehicle, Ethan peered across the parking garage and out the wide opened archways to East State Street, where he saw a patrolman issuing a speeding ticket to a person behind the wheel of a fancy sports car.

The scene awoke memories in Ethan's mind of his own days out on patrol duty. He could not help but notice the irritated expression on the officer's face as he had to ask the pedestrian several times to turn the radio down. Ethan remembered numerous times he had similar experiences, and how he had to restrain himself from pulling the inconsiderate jerk out of the car and physically reprimanding them. He did not miss those days.

That is one area of his new position he did like. Certain areas of physicality could be overlooked. There were other perks to his job he also liked. For one, he wouldn't miss the old "blues" he had to wear to work every day. Sitting in a hot patrol car on a blistering summer day would not be missed either. Always being under a microscope in the eyes of the public could, for the most part, be forgotten, since he no longer stood out from the rest of the community in his uniform.

Maybe there were more benefits to working with the anti-gang task force than he thought. He could still do a lot of good. Tyler did warn him that he would see some things that would turn his stomach, he just needed to remain professional. Even if that meant turning a blind eye to his new partners' wrongdoings. He was the new guy after all. It's possible that's just the way things were done when working undercover. As long as he didn't allow himself to get drawn into their "dirt" he should be alright.

Hopefully…

Chapter 8

Ethan had been awake for the last half an hour, staring lovingly at his sleeping wife. He could not resist the sight of Becky as she slumbered peacefully with her face scrunched up in the soft comforts of her pillow, and her long, blonde hair mussed like a model doing a photoshoot at the beach.

Becky was asleep when he got home from work the night before, so he hadn't had the chance to tell her about anything that had happened on his first day, and he wondered if that was for the best, all things considered.

It wasn't until the alarm clock's annoying buzzer went off that Ethan tore himself away from his thoughts. As easily as he could, the young detective reached behind his back and hit the off button. After doing so, he then rolled himself out of bed trying to cause as little disruption as he could. A part of Ethan wanted Becky to wake up, so that he could get one of her encouraging pick-me-up speeches that she was good for. However, after further debating the issue, Ethan decided it was best to let the woman sleep, so that she would not urge him into telling her about the details of his vicious first day.

Utilizing the greatest stealth he could manage, Ethan crept quietly through the dark to the closet using only his memory to guide him while doing his best not to turn on the light. It wasn't until he whacked his toe on the dresser that he realized his wife had rearranged the bedroom furniture the day before.

"Ouch!" Ethan yelped, as he grabbed his big toe in his hand and squeezed it tightly in a failed effort to stop the throbbing pain.

"Ethan?" Becky asked, in a groggy tone.

"Yeah?" He answered.

"Be careful, She continued. "I moved the furniture around in here."

"I got that." Ethan replied, in a somewhat sarcastic intonation. "I was trying not to wake you…"

"No, no, that's okay. I wanted to get up and hear about your day." Becky said, as she stretched her body to its limits and then climbed out of bed. "Let me get the coffee started, and then I'm all ears."

Ethan started laying his clothes out on the bed, as his wife trotted by. When he had finished, he joined her in the kitchen, where he saw his favorite cup sitting on the table next to the morning paper. After the coffeemaker was done brewing, Becky filled Ethan's cup to the rim, and then her own, before sitting down in the seat next to him, anxious to hear how her husband liked his new position.

"So…how was your first day?" She asked, before taking a sip of her java.

"Brutal." Ethan replied honestly, as he flipped through the paper.

"Seriously?" Becky asked, putting her cup back on the table, so she could give her husband her full attention.

"Yeah, but I'm sure it'll get better." He responded, scanning through the local news section.

"Well, what did you do?" Becky prodded. "Tell me what was so bad."

Ethan took a sip of his coffee before answering his wife. He didn't want to go into great detail, otherwise she would worry herself sick every time he went to work.

"First off, the guys I work with are kind of irritating." He said, doing his best to gloss over the main issues.

"Maybe you just need to get to know them better." Becky responded, hoping to lend a little moral support.

"Maybe…" Ethan said absently, as his eyes caught the story of the Anti-Gang Task Force's drug bust on Jimmy Boose.

"What else was so bad?" Becky inquired, continuing to dig for answers.

Now that his wife was awake and asking so many of the questions he really didn't want to tell her the answers to, Ethan wished he could go back in time and warn himself about the dresser being moved. If he could do that, Becky would still be sleeping peacefully, he would not have to be evading so many of her questions, and his big toe would possibly not lose its nail.

"You know…why don't I just leave my work at the office." Ehtan replied, strategically, as he tried to bury the article about the drug bust and the violent shootout under some sale ads. "How was your day?"

"Wow!" Becky gasped. "Your day must have been really awful for you to ask about *my* day."

"It's not that, Becky." Ethan said, in the most comforting voice he could conjure, as he placed his hand on top of hers. "It's that my new position is pretty dangerous, and I don't want you to worry."

Becky could tell by the look in Ethan's eyes that he was telling her the truth. Maybe it would be for the best if she did not know too much about what goes on when her husband is working. She remembers how she did not sleep through the entire first year after Ethan began his career as a patrolman. The young woman could only imagine what goes on now that he is working undercover with some of the most dangerous men alive.

"Okay." Becky answered, squeezing Ethan's hand. While the two held hands and stared into each other's eyes, the phone rang, tearing them away from the touching moment.

"I'll get it." Ethan said as he stood to his feet and walked over to the phone hanging on the wall. "Hello?"

"Brooks?" Tyler's voice asked from the other end.

"Yeah."

"We need you to get down to Rockford Memorial A.S.A.P." Tyler stated flatly.

"I'll be there as soon as I can." Ethan responded, before he heard the dial tone on the other end of the line.

"Does this mean what I think it means?" Becky queried.

"Yeah," Ethan moaned. "The start of another beautiful day."

*   *   *   *   *

The rocky terrain just outside the rusted gates of the Abyss was still littered with the wounded warring angels from the previous battle when Cazzbein and Gunthar arrived. The two angels swooped down and set foot on a jagged landing overlooking the grotesque scene. The pair were sickened at what they saw, but what was far worse, were the cries of pain wafting up to their ears as they took in the sight.

"Horrific…" Was the only word to come out of Gunthar's mouth, as he stood motionless by his comrade's side.

"Hunter will pay with his very existence." Cazzbein spat. "However, before we let our emotions get the better of us, we must focus on our current assignment. Otherwise, the demon horde will use our feelings as a weapon against us."

Before Gunthar could reply, Anthony, the youthful looking messenger angel, and Glistinia, the strawberry blond bow slinger, landed quietly next to the pair. The expressions on their faces mirrored those of their partners as they were equally appalled.

"Well met, brothers." Glistinia greeted.

"Salutations to you as well, Glistinia and Anthony." Cazzbein replied, turning to face his allies.

"After scouring the battlefield, I have found Glistinia and delivered her to you, per your request." Anthony said, in a satisfied tone. "Now, if my services are no longer needed-"

"Actually…" Cazzbein said, subtly, before pulling a small, golden chest plate from the ground. "My orders were to get a band of able-bodied angels together to keep Hunter and all other demons from escaping the Abyss. And you, my friend, are currently more able-bodied than the warring angels strewn about the field beneath us."

Anthony's reaction was an unexpected one. Gunthar thought the angel would come up with an excuse to be somewhere else or try to shy away from the request. But to the group's amazement, Anthony seemed to be overtaken with a sensation of pleasure by the invitation.

"Really?" The rosy cheeked angel asked, in an astonished tone. "I have waited for this moment my entire existence, but every time I think I will be joining the troops in battle, I am called away elsewhere. Now, I can finally prove to everyone I am not just some errand angel."

"What better way to confirm you are not just a messenger than to wet that mace of yours on the hides of those traitorous demons." Gunthar said, firmly, as he gave the smaller angel a heavy handed pat on the back.

"As I will." Anthony replied, eagerly taking the breastplate from Cazzbein's hand.

"What is the plan?" Glistinia wisely asked.

"We are going into the Abyss to stop Hunter." Cazzbein answered, in a no-nonsense manner.

"Just the four of us?" Glistinia queried, with a raised brow.

"That is correct."

"Do we even know how many demons accompany Hunter?" The lovely angel felt the need to inquire.

"Most of the thirteen legions that were under Hunter's command were cut down in the battle." Cazzbein replied, as he turned to look into the female's green eyes. "The reports I have been given say that Hunter's party is very small, and that is if he travels with anyone at all."

"Personally, I hope the dog travels with a large horde." Gunthar put in, before pulling his mighty war hammer into view. "That many more gashes to adorn my shaft with."

"Wow!" Anthony gasped, after catching a glimpse of all the scratches Gunthar had made on his weapon to represent the total number of demons he had personally sent to the Abyss. "What is your current tally?"

"Over seven thousand, the last time I counted." The big angel replied, proudly. "Looks like you could use a few for your mace." He remarked, after seeing how little the weapon had been used.

"I shall start a count today." Anthony said, with purpose.

"I am not afraid of battle." Glistinia remarked. "I have vanquished many demons from the world of man myself. However, I am no fool either. We may not be able to be killed, but we most certainly can be captured by our enemies if the numbers are too great for us to manage."

The female's comment silenced the group for a moment, as they pondered the thought. Each of them had felt the sting of loss, as they had all known a comrade that had been captured in battle. Some demon warriors can be seen in battle fighting while wearing their enemies primary wing feathers as trophies. With that in mind, the horrors they must be enduring at the hands of the evil demonic forces can only be imagined, as they are nearly never reclaimed.

"I have trust in our abilities." Cazzbein reassured them.

"As do I." Anthony replied, resting his mace over his shoulder. "Why, Cazzbein himself dispatched a full legion by himself in the Battle at Heaven's Gate."

"There is no question we are a force to be reckoned with," Glistinia pressed. "However, if Hunter is successful in releasing a mere fraction of the demons imprisoned down there, then we will find ourselves outnumbered beyond even our wildest imaginations."

"Truer words have never been spoken." Cazzbein agreed. "That is why we must plunge ourselves through those gates below us with haste, so that we can stop him from fulfilling his goal."

"I am ready." Gunthar said, flexing his muscles as he twisted the shaft of his hammer tightly in his hands.

"The sooner the better, I say." Anthony added.

"Since I cannot convince any of you to hearken your ears to the voice of reason," Glistinia said with a slight grin, as she slung her bow from around her shoulder. "Then I shall loose my arrows for our cause."

Cazzbein merely flashed the group a satisfied smile, for he was genuinely pleased at what he saw. If he were to scour the entire universe, he would not be able to find three more noble companions in which he would entrust his freedom. The angel knew his trust was well placed, nonetheless, he couldn't help but feel a bit of anxiousness. Soon, he would be engaging the most dangerous adversary he had ever fought while doing so in the bowels of hell itself.

*　　*　　*　　*　　*

As soon as Ethan pushed open the solid oak door that led to Pharaoh's hospital room he knew something was wrong. To what level, though, he could not tell. Both Tyler and Booker were standing at the end of the gangster's bed with arms crossed over their chests, giving no outward impression of their intentions. Out of the three of them, Tyler was the only one that wore a perplexed expression on his face.

"There's our boy, dog!" Booker howled, before giving Ethan a firm slap on the shoulder. "The cowboy!"

"What?" Was the only word that the young detective could manage.

"Of all my years on the force, I've never seen anything like it and I've seen some pretty messed up stuff…" Tyler said, shaking his head in disbelief.

"I don't understand." Ethan admitted, not sure if this was just another one of his partners' mind games.

"Where did you learn to shoot a pistol like that, Buffalo Bill?" Tyler continued, before tossing a plastic baggy on Pharaoh's bed by the gangster's feet.

Ethan picked the baggy up and twirled it around in his hand to get a better look at its contents. Inside was what appeared to be a small, mangled ball of metal. But at closer inspection, Ethan could tell by the slight discoloration between the metals that it was actually two pieces of metal intertwined with one another.

"What is it?" He asked, when he couldn't figure it out.

"That's what the surgeon pulled out of pharaoh's shoulder." Tyler replied, looking at Ethan for a reaction.

"*This* is my bullet?" He asked, in a puzzled tone.

"Actually, that's yours *and* Pharaoh's bullets." Tyler corrected, keeping an eye on the rookie in order to witness a physical change in his emotions.

"I still don't get it." Ethan said, further admitting his ignorance.

"C'mon, dog!" Booker interjected, before snatching the bag out of Ethan's hand. "Quit your playin." You shot Pharaoh's bullet out of the air, and took him out in the process."

"Wha-...No…I mean…if I did it was purely coincidental. Ethan said, struggling to find the words.

"Didn't I tell you, Booker? The rookie's got eyes like a hawk and a heart like a lamb." Tyler said, with a snicker.

"I'm telling you, I didn't…I couldn't have made that shot intentionally." Ehtan continued. "No one could have."

"Nobody but you, apparently." Tyler said, jokingly.

"Actually, Detective Brooks is correct." An unfamiliar man's voice cut in. "Not without a little help."

When the room full of detectives turned to see who had interrupted their fun, they saw a pair of figures they had never seen before; a male and a female to be exact.

The man, whom they all suspected had been the one to make the comment, stood around six feet two inches tall, with sandy blonde hair streaked with gray and a thick mustache speckled with a hint of white. His eyes held a cold steel blue pigment and looked as if they were staring a hole right through anyone unfortunate enough to be trapped within their gaze.

The female, on the other hand, was a very attractive woman with dark, chocolate-colored tresses that just graced the edge of her shoulders. She possessed deep brown orbs that were far more warm and inviting than her colleague's, yet they still managed to maintain the same seriousness that her partner's did.

"I don't believe we've had the pleasure." Tyler said, opening a way for introductions to be made.

"I'm Special Agent Steven Cutler and this is my partner Special Agent Sarah Flaherty." The man replied, as the pair flashed their FBI credentials.

"Federal agents?" Booker asked, in a surprised tone. "What else did Pharaoh get busted for that we didn't know about?"

"Pharaoh?" Agent Cutler asked, not understanding who Detective Briggs was referring to.

"We're not here for the drug peddler." Agent Flaherty responded.

"Oh no…we'd actually like to ask Detective Brooks some questions if he doesn't mind." Agent Cutler said, after figuring out who they were addressing as Pharaoh.

"Um…sure…I guess that's alright." Ethan answered.

"Good." Agent Cutler said, his face never changing its serious exterior. "May we step out into the hall?"

"Yeah…that's fine with me." Ethan replied, before stepping past the two FBI agents and into the hallway.

After Ethan and the two agents exited the room, Booker turned to his partner of more than ten years and gave him a dirty look. Tyler could tell by the scowl that Booker was thinking the same thing as he was.

"What do you think that's all about?" Booker asked, suspiciously.

"I don't know, but I don't like it." Tyler admitted, moving closer to the door in hopes of catching a bit of the conversation.

"I'll tell ya what it is. Your boy's turning on us." Booker said, angrily.

"You don't know that. You're just being paranoid." Tyler replied. "Besides, Brooks got nothin' on us."

"Are you kiddin'? Man, on his first day alone, he knows about Tasha, he knows we smoke dope on the job, *and* he knows we planted that kilo on Pharaoh so we can keep our business running smooth with Evil." Booker said, heatedly.

Tyler flew across the room and seized Booker roughly by his shirt collar, shoving him up against the wall as he did so.

"Watch your mouth!" He growled. "Did you forget the banger we set up is in the room with us?"

"Relax, man…" Booker said, while getting his partner to loosen his grip on his collar. "He's so heavily sedated from surgery he can't even open his eyelids."

"You'd better hope so." Tyler said, through tight lips, before backing away. "Besides, the rookie doesn't know anything about the gig we got goin' with Evil."

"What…?" Booker asked, "I thought that's what you were talkin' with him about last night."

"Nah, nah. I didn't feel the need to bring it up just yet." Tyler answered. "Besides that, everything we're doin' wouldn't merit the Feds getting involved."

"Well, then how do you explain them showing up?" Booker inquired.

Tyler thought about it for a moment before giving his response. "Maybe it has nothin' to do with us."

Out in the hallway Ethan's mind was wondering the same thing as his partners. And just like his partners, he could not figure out what the unexpected visit was all about. Neither did it escape the young detective's attention that Agent Cutler held within his hand a file labeled, "Ethan Brooks." This did not sit well with the young detective, due to the fact that no one ever wanted the FBI to have a file on them.

"Detective Brooks, you're probably wondering why we wanted to meet with you today." Agent Cutler began.

"Well, I'd be lying if I said I wasn't." Ethan admitted.

"That's natural." Agent Flaherty remarked, in a disarming tone.

"To get right down to business, detective, the FBI's been keeping a file on you since your very…how shall we say…*unusual* arrival into the world." Agent Cutler continued.

"Unusual?" Ethan inquired, this being the first time anyone has referred to his birth in such a way.

"Agent Cutler and I investigate cases that suggest a trace of paranormal phenomena." Agent Flaherty stated flatly.

"Para-what?" Ethan questioned.

"Paranormal phenomena." Agent Cutler answered, his face managing to maintain its somber demeanor. "Cases that are, more or less, unable to be explained by scientific means."

You mean like, ghosts and goblins?" Ethan queried, trying not to sound too disrespectful.

"Ghosts, goblins, UFO's, aliens…" Agent Flaherty began.

"So, what does this have to do with me?" Ethan rightly asked.

"The FBI database red flags any police reports or news stories that contain unexplained phenomena. The night of your birth held just such aspects." Agent Flaherty continued.

"Such as?" Ethan asked, still clueless as to where the agents were heading.

Agent Cutler opened the file in his hand and retrieved an 8x10 photograph and handed it to Ethan. "The night you were born, a garbage truck's air lines to its brakes unexplainably ruptured, as did the emergency braking system, causing the rig to run out of control in the direction of your mother. However, for some reason none of the investigators on the scene could figure out how it came to a standstill, leaving no marks on the pavement to suggest the brakes ever came into play. The photo you are looking at was taken of the front end of the truck."

Ethan examined the photo for a moment. It was the first time he had ever seen the wreckage of the truck before, even after hearing about his miraculous birth all his life. He was still unsure of what it was he was supposed to be seeing in the photo, other than a mangled heap of twisted metal.

"You know, I've heard about all this before, but I have never actually seen any proof to substantiate the death of my mother until now." He said, as a tear began to form in his eye. "But I still don't understand what I'm supposed to be looking for here."

"If you cast your view just above the grill of the semi, and just below where the windshield used to be, you should be able to make out the shape of…" Agent Flaherty said, pointing out the area she was talking about with a ballpoint pen.

"A hand…" Ethan gasped, after finally seeing the image with his own eyes.

"A fairly *large* hand impression." Agent Cutler added.

"That can't be…? Can it?" Ethan asked, the question made for his own ears as much as for the federal agents.

"I've learned a long time ago with this job, everything must be considered." Agent Flaherty commented.

"So, why are you guys just now bringing this up?" Ethan felt the need to know.

"To be honest, Detective Brooks," Agent Cutler began to answer. "We wouldn't have had need to bring it up at all, if an additional red flag had not alerted us to another instance in your life."

"What was it this time?" Ehtan wondered aloud.

"It was your amazing marksmanship skills." Agent Flaherty answered.

"Even you would have to admit, shooting a bullet out of midair takes some pretty disciplined concentration." agent Cutler pressed.

"More like an immense amount of luck." Ethan reasoned.

"Kind of like the immense amount of luck needed to stop a runaway semi?" Agent Flaherty countered.

"You can't possibly be suggesting I had something to do with the semi incident?" Ethan asked, in a more aggressive tone. "I wasn't even born yet."

"Detective Brooks, are you familiar with an ancient artifact known as the Spear of Destiny?" agent cutler asked, changing the subject without warning.

"Can't say that I am." Ethan responded.

"In the Gospel of John of The Holy Bible, John writes that Christ's side was pierced by a spearhead from one of the Roman soldiers at the Crucifixion. According to legend, it is rumored that whoever possesses this spear will rule the world. It may have been this rumor that led nineteen-year-old Adolf Hitler to the lance in 1908. It was said that Hitler considered the spear to be the very source of his ambitions to conquer the world. Thirty years later, Hitler arrived in Vienna to oversee the annexation of Austria. He also witnessed the transfer of the Hapsburg Crown Jewel collection, which included the Spear of Destiny, from Vienna to Nuremberg. Once the spear was safely settled in Germany, Hitler declared that his war for world conquest could begin in earnest."

"What are you saying?" Ethan asked, pointedly. "You think I'm going to try and take over the world?"

"Let's just say, the FBI considers matters of the occult to be a serious issue." Agent Flaherty answered. "And when someone has as many *coincidences* in their life as you do, we can't afford to take it lightly."

"We have to squash World War III before it gets started." Agent Cutler added.

"I assure you, I'm just a normal man." Ethan replied, before handing the photo back to Agent Cutler.

"So was Hitler." The agent countered.

"Even if you are just a normal man, Detective Brooks, we still think you are going to play a major role in the happenings of the world." Agent Flaherty said, giving no indication that she was in any way joking. "Whether that role be for good or evil is yet to be determined."

"I can't believe what I'm hearing." Ethan muttered, shaking his head in bewilderment. "I'm telling you, I have no aspects of world domination."

"Sometimes our path is chosen for us, Detective Brooks." Agent Cutler said, in a straightforward manner.

"If you see any more strange things happen, please give us a call." agent Flaherty informed, while handing Ethan a business card with her number on it.

"Well, I can tell you this meeting was pretty *strange.* Does that count?" Ethan asked, sarcastically.

"No." agent Cutler said, in his customary serious tone.

"We'll be in touch, Detective Brooks." Agent Flaherty added, before the pair turned to leave.

Ethan kept an eye on the two agents until they were swallowed up in the crowd of people further down the hallway. He could not help but think to himself how this had to be the strangest morning of his life as he turned and reentered the room where he had left his partners.

"What was that all about, rookie?" Tyler asked, once the young detective was standing in their midst.

"I really don't know." Ethan replied, honestly, before slipping Agent Flaherty's card into his pocket.

"It must have been somethin'," Booker interjected. "They had you out there awhile."

"They were asking me questions about my birth…" Ethan answered in a baffled tone.

"Your birth?" Tyler asked, the sound of relief in his voice. "What'd you do, smuggle a ton of cocaine in through your mama's womb?"

"I wish it was that simple." Ethan replied. "But it's far more complicated than that."

"Well, you know how I hate complications." Tyler said, satisfied that the meeting had nothing to do with Booker or himself. "Let's get rollin'."

After the three men left to start their busy day, the door to the room closed behind them with a click, as the door latch secured itself into place. Once the room had emptied, Jimmy Boose, the gangster known as Pharaoh, opened his eyes. He had been awake the entire time, unknown to the men. The only question now was what to do with the newfound information he had just overheard…

Chapter 9

When the heel of Anthony's boot sunk into the loose soil on the other side of the gates that lead to the Abyss, only one word came to mind.

"Interesting." He said, before lifting his foot from the ground and inspecting the sole.

"What?" Gunthar asked, in an irritable tone, quickly becoming aggravated with his little friend's constant remarks.

"It's not at all what I expected." the cheerful angel replied.

"What did you expect?" Fire and Brimstone?" The burly angel queried. "That is further up ahead, I would wager."

"Now that you mention it, I'm not at all sure what I expected." Anthony answered, with a smile, while wiggling the toe of his sneaker further into the dirt.

"How far do you think it goes?" Glistinia asked Cazzbein, referring to the tunnel lying before them.

"I do believe it goes on forever." Cazzbein answered, grimly. "It is the *Bottomless* Pit after all."

Without another word, Glistinia plucked an arrow from her quiver and notched it in her bow. After doing so, the projectile glowed brightly with a Holy light, illuminating their bleak surroundings like an artificial sun. With nothing more than a subtle loosening of her slender fingers from the taut string, the arrow went sailing down the tunnel like a rocket, only to be swallowed up by the darkness several hundred yards away.

"That was not reassuring." Cazzbein said, in jest.

"Be that as it may, shall we continue?" Gunthar asked, eager to commence with the fighting.

"As you wish, my friend." Cazzbein answered, before stepping away from the gates.

They had not walked far before the light became completely smothered by blackness. Once the lighting was choked out, Cazzbein unsheathed one of his scimitars and held it high in hand, using the weapon's Holy essence to pierce the unnatural darkness. The black obscurity was conceived to be dense enough to overpower even these creatures' extraordinary vision; nowhere in existence could a darker place be found. The angels tried to put the gloominess in the back of their thoughts as they trudged forward, because they knew the land in which they tread was truly a cursed domain, devised to punish Satan and his fallen army. With that in mind, the group could not be more grateful for their decision to fight for God Almighty.

After walking for what seemed a short eternity, the companions came to the section of the cavern that opened up into the area where the raging water poured down on all sides of a cross-shaped bridge.

"Marvelous…" Cazzbein gasped, when he caught sight of the cross. It had been the only sign of hope since they had entered the domain.

Before they progressed upon the naturally made structure, Cazzbein signaled for the group to stop so that they could converse before the falling water absorbed all sound.

"I think it best we lay out our strategy before continuing." Cazzbein said, flatly. "Once we begin crossing the bridge we will be unable to communicate if we find ourselves engaged."

"Such as now?" Anthony asked, pointing a slim finger behind the group, causing them to turn their attention to the other side of the canyon.

Before they were fully prepared, hundreds of demons poured out of the opening from the opposite side of the bridge, soaring overhead like enormous bats. Their terrifying screeches erupted throughout the open cavern drowning out even the sound of the ferocious falling water.

Glistinia loosed a successive volley of arrows, firing three of the charged missiles at a time toward the advancing minions. Each arrow found its mark, sinking deep into demon flesh, landing squarely in the center of each fiend's torso.

Not one to be shown up, Gunthar unleashed several merciless hammer swings that connected with demon cranium. Four of the monstrous creatures thudded to the ground as he took them well out of the battle with his wide arcing strikes.

Even Anthony was faring well. The smaller angel worked his mace with deadly skill, smashing two demons directly between their beady red eyes, where they then spun blindly down into the cavern below.

Leading the way, Cazzbein went to work weaving his scimitars with fluent potency, creating an impenetrable field of razor-sharp lashes. Nearly twenty of the advancing demons were cut down before he realized a very real truth.

"They are not attacking…" He mouthed to himself, before ceasing his assault.

"Why are you stopping?" Glistinia asked, before firing off another set of charged arrows.

"They are not fighting back. They are merely fleeing! The fear of this place has sapped their will to fight!" Cazzbein screamed. "Gunthar! Anthony! Keep the fiends from escaping!"

"What of me?" Glistinia rightly asked.

"You and I will head off further down the passageway and confront Hunter!" Cazzbein replied, before slashing another demon out of the air. "We must stop him from freeing any more of these monsters, lest we find ourselves fighting the same demons over and over again!"

"Agreed!" The strawberry blonde angel yelled, before falling behind her leader.

Once she was by his side, the two ventured forth, leaving Gunthar and Anthony to protect the tunnel that led outward from the fleeing demons. It took them little time, as they had only stepped halfway down the cross shaped bridge before they spied their goal. At the end of the bridge, Hunter, the snowy haired demon stood confidently, weapons already in hand.

Cazzbein placed his mouth close to Glistinia's ear, so that she could understand him amongst all the turmoil that surrounded them. "Keep the underlings off of me!" he said plainly. "I will deal with him!"

With that grim order issued, Glistinia began her devastating missile assault once more, as Cazzbein stepped toward Hunter, twirling his scimitars around his fingers to test their balance as he walked. Once he had made it to the end of the bridge where Hunter stood, the sound of the crashing water and fleeing demons was quietened just enough for the two spiritual beings to converse.

"We meet again." Hunter remarked, with a malicious grin, as his leathery wings burst open wide with excitement.

"So we have." Cazzbein replied, expanding his wings to their limits, so as to display his dominance.

"This time we will have a decisive outcome." Hunter drooled, the edge of anticipation clearly evident in his voice.

"I agree." Cazzbein responded, with determination.

The two spiritual beings stared at one another for a brief moment, each sizing the other up while formulating their first moves. Always the aggressor, Hunter charged in first, his saber's sharp point aimed squarely at Cazzbein's exposed neckline. With little effort, the angel swatted the attack away with his left scimitar and then wisely followed up with a thrust from the blade in his right hand, directed toward the demon's midsection. Matching the angel's speed, Hunter deflected the scimitar away with his dagger, while thrusting his saber inward from a new trajectory, targeting his enemy's ribs. The attack was easily slapped away with an adept scimitar and countered once more. The dazzling display of swordsmanship continued for several long minutes without disruption as the mortal enemies parried each other's attack routines time and time again.

With more than a few tricks up his sleeve, Hunter began flailing his enormous bat-like wings with powerful flaps that sent dirt from the spiritual land into Cazzbein's sparkling blue orbs, temporarily blinding him. The angel had no choice but to back away from the fight, as he desperately rubbed his eyes, trying to restore his vision.

Seeing his foe at a disadvantage, Hunter swung his saber in for a killing strike aimed at his enemy's head. However, even though he could not see, Cazzbein was able to hear the blade whistling its way toward him and raised his left arm, hoping to block the attack with the scimitar in that hand. When he felt the sting of the razor-sharp edge cutting into his forearm, he realized it was not his weapon that had opposed the strike, but his own limb. Fortunately, though, the act of desperation was able to save him and buy just enough time to regain a portion of his sight. Through watery eyes he could see his glowing essence trickling down the gold-plated armguard he wore about his forearm. To his dissatisfaction, the sabers slash cut into his appendage merely an inch above the protective gear, drawing a shrill laugh from his opponent.

"First strike belongs to *me*, this time!" Hunter cackled, as he rushed in with another flurry of jabs and slashes.

"So it does…" The angel said softly, managing to block every successive attack.

Cazzbein could tell Hunter was overflowing with confidence as the demon came at him with a shower of blade tips. Wisely, the angel used this to his advantage. He parried all but one of the attacks away with no problem. The last thrust, though, the guardian spun gracefully out of harm's way, causing Hunter to stumble off balance under the weight of his own forward momentum. After the demon staggered by, Cazzbein pulled both his scimitars back in preparation. When Hunter turned to face the angel he was met with two scimitar thrusts quickly making their way toward his midsection.

Frantically, the demon raised his weapons for a block, quickly having to change his strategy from offense to defense. His weapons barely managed to deflect the deadly tips of his enemy's weapons from surely ending the duel, but were not able to keep the sharp edges of the angel's brilliantly crafted blades from slashing either side of his torso as they passed by. Now, it was his dark essence that poured out of fresh wounds.

The pain was nearly unbearable, as Hunter bit his lower lip in anguish, causing him to cease his assault and once again step back into a defensive posture.

This time it was Cazzbein that set the pace. The angel sprang upon his prey with a wild sparkle in his eyes, coming in with his scimitars at nearly impossible angles for the demon to fend off. Never had the demon seen a more poetic showing of swordplay. The needle-sharp points of the guardian's weapons were getting harder and harder for him to fend off as they came within fractions of an inch of his body. Hunter knew it would be only a matter of time before the blades penetrated his defenses and ended his blight on the world of man. The demon was nearly about to resign himself to his fate when he saw something further down the tunnel that caused a sharp toothed grin to spread across his fair features.

Paying the creature's sudden change in demeanor no mind, Cazzbein pressed on, sensing that his victory was well in hand. However, when he pulled back his right scimitar for what was sure to be the finishing blow, that's when the battle took a turn for the worse. As soon as his arm was fully retracted, the angel felt something extremely heavy wrap itself around his shoulder and waistline, stopping him in mid swing as it squeezed him like a vice. Without another thought, he felt himself being hurled off his feet as he was flung back into the wall of the cavern with enough force to cause him to drop the scimitar he was about to end the duel with.

"Lars…" Hunter gasped, with wide eyed bliss, after realizing he had just been saved from certain doom.

The massive demon towered over the guardian like a bright red skyscraper covered in thick scales. His yellowish, snakelike eyes scanned the cavern briefly, gathering visual information of the battle raging on around him. When the chief Prince had finished sizing up his opponents, his serpentine tail twitched with excitement, causing the sharp barbs at the end to emit a dim glow.

He was not impressed.

After his centuries long imprisonment within the flames of Hell, Lars dared anyone to stand in the way of his freedom, welcoming their efforts with an insatiable thirst.

"Gunthar! Anthony! We have *big* trouble!" Glistinia yelled, before loosening several charged arrow shots at the monstrosity.

"A chief Prince!" Gunthar screamed, after catching sight of the enormous creature emerging from the cavern.

"Anthony! These minor underlings are of no consequence! We must ensure that we keep that *thing* from ever leaving this domain!"

"Truer words have never been spoken!" The smaller angel responded, positively.

The trio of guardians hastily made their way down the cross-shaped bridge, hoping to get to Cazzbein before the chief Prince could deal out any more punishment. Nevertheless, their efforts would not come in time, for when they had only reached the center point, Lars slammed a massive fist down on Cazzbein's chest, crushing the angel. Then, as if that had not been enough of a display of brutality, the chief Prince plucked the guardian from the ground by his beautiful, white feathered wings, where he then tore them from his backside.

With a shriek of agonizing pain Cazzbein crashed face first into the cavern's floor and then tumbled off the side of the bridge. The angel's companions had no choice but to watch as he disappeared into the mists of the raging water several hundred feet below.

"Cazzbein!" Gunthar cried out, after seeing his old friend abused at the hands of the massive demon. "I must go after him!"

"No!" Glistinia shouted, as she grabbed the large angel by the shoulder. "We must deal with Lars first! Cazzbein would want it that way!"

A moment of hesitation was all it took for Gunthar to realize Glistinia was right.

"Use some of that anger to defeat this fiend!" The female continued.

"Agreed!" Gunthar answered, as he raised his war hammer in preparation.

As they turned to consider the beast, Lars let loose a ferocious roar that made the whole cavern rumble beneath their feet. The display of supremacy may have disheartened the angels had it been performed before they had seen their precious friend beaten so mercilessly. Nevertheless, the thunderous bellow may well have fallen on deaf ears, for it only served to fuel the angels hearts with venom.

With fierce war cries of their own, the three warring angels charged in with intentions of malice in mind.

Glistinia took to the air, where she pelted the large demon with round after round of glowing arrows. The charged projectiles sunk deep into the chief Prince's scaly hide and then exploded into balls of radiant Holy energy. While on the ground, Gunthar and Anthony swung their bludgeoning weapons in perfect timing, as they targeted a single large scale that was larger than both of their frames combined, hitting it time and time again. They worked the same area vigorously, trying to remove the scale and expose the vulnerable flesh underneath. Unfortunately, the assault only seemed to cause the gigantic demon a moment of discomfort.

With nothing more than a simple swat, Lars crumpled Anthony up against the cavern's wall, taking him out of the battle entirely. After doing so, the enormous demon turned his attention toward Gunthar. Exhibiting unnatural speed for a creature his size, Lars quickly spun around, sending the barbs on the end of his tail in the hammer wielding angel's direction.

Three of the sharp tips sunk deep into Gunthar's chest, sending jolts of pain throughout his muscular frame, before the force of Lars' huge tail sent him crashing into another section of the unforgiving stone walls. Once the weight of the demon's tail was lifted off of him, Gunthar crumpled to the ground showing no signs of movement.

It was then that another succession of exploding arrows buried themselves into Lar's backside, reminding him of the final angel in the battle. Turning to consider the strawberry blonde guardian, Lars could see that she had already notched her bow for another round.

The shots would never come.

With centuries worth of pent-up anger, Lars curled his twisted fingers into a tight fist and lashed out at the bow slinging angel. The large knuckles landed squarely upon the guardian's leather chest plate, sending her sailing into the stone wall on the opposite side of the bridge. Her broken body then collapsed to the ground in a small heap, rendering her incoherent.

Pleased with his display of domination, the chief Prince of demons strode confidently across the bridge, unopposed from that moment on. The other recently freed underlings swarmed behind him, making sure to stay out of his way, lest they incur his wrath.

Hunter, who had been surprisingly quiet during the onslaught, returned the dagger with the colorfully jeweled hilt back to its scabbard. Before he did likewise to his saber, he ran his tongue down the length of its blade, savoring the taste of his arch enemy's essence. It was still warm, and surprisingly sweet. When he was satisfied, the white-haired demon slid the elegant weapon back into its home and then walked over to the edge of the bridge, where he peered down into the raging waters below.

This was not how he wanted their rivalry to end. Nevertheless, a victory was a victory. The demon also knew, had Lars not intervened, it may well have been him swinging by the end of his tongue above the unrelenting flames of the Abyss.

At least I am rid of you." Hunter said to himself, before sliding a stone off the side of the bridge with the toe of his highly polished boot.

The stone descended for several hundred meters before it came into contact with a solid surface. It then rebounded off the rocky crag of the cavern's walls, following a zig zagging pattern as it hopped off several other large stones, before skidding to a stop next to the broken frame of a marred guardian angel.

After Cazzbein was brutally beaten and then cast over the side of the bridge by Lars, he crashed off numerous jagged rocks before landing face down upon the mossy boulder in which he now laid motionless. His glowing, Holy essence poured out of countless open wounds and now gathered in puddles next to his ravaged physique. The guardian could feel the healing effects of his body beginning to repair some of the damage that had been done, but the process would take much time. For now, anyway, he was completely vulnerable.

Among all the cuts and bruises that plagued his body with pain, the angel felt a sharp pinch in his neck that caused him the most discomfort at that moment. Since the displeasure was merely being caused by the awkward angle in which his head was positioned on the rough stone that served as his resting place, Cazzbein knew this pain, at least, he could do something about.

Using what strength he had left, the guardian managed to rotate his head toward his right shoulder, relieving himself from the ache that he had been feeling. After doing so, he caught a glimpse of something he knew would not bode well for him. It was the dirty, pale foot of a fallen angel.

The child of darkness stood silent for a short time before tapping the tip of his sword on the rock's mossy surface in order to gain the angel's full attention. When he was sure Cazzbein was well aware of his presence, he knelt down and looked into the guardian's shimmering blue orbs.

"Remember me?" Vermillion teased, with a rotten toothed grin.

Cazzbein could only grunt his reply, but had the words been audible, they would not be pleasing to the demon's ears.

"I have been waiting a short while for you to tread foot through my domain." Vermillion said with a scowl, before unwrapping the scarf from around his crooked neck. The covering had been used to cover a small scar that was upon the demon's esophagus area. The same spot where Cazzbein had rested the tips of his scimitars years ago, the night Scott died in that dirty tavern. "Now I have the opportunity to return the gesture, my old friend."

Knowing the creature meant him ill will, Cazzbein still could not help but think of his charge, Ethan. For the time being, the human would have to do without his protection. At this moment, Cazzbein was weak and unarmed, as his scimitars laid somewhere upon the bridge far above him. Powerless to fend off his captor, the angel resigned himself to his current fate and could only watch as Vermillion roughly seized him by his ankle and drug him further off into the darkness.

Chapter 10

Leaving crooks alone to sweat it out in the interrogation room may not sound like the most effective way to break a case wide open. However, when you look at it from the bad guys point of view, the downtime was actually quite torturous. Trapped within the small, confined space with nothing to eat or drink for hours at a time eventually took its toll on a person's physical body, while the instant fear of the unknown and sleep deprivation was more than enough to test one's mental prowess.

Detectives also found that it was a valuable tool in which to size the suspects up. Staring at the crooks through the two-way mirrors helped the interrogators to plot out their interviewing tactics before they ever entered the room. Tyler knew from years of experience, the one that sweated the most under the bright lights was usually the one that was going to give up the most information. With that in mind, he wanted to make sure Ethan was nowhere near the crook that was going to accidentally cough up any evidence about the drugs being planted.

"This doesn't make a whole lot of sense to me, dog." Booker admitted to Tyler after he pulled him aside.

"What doesn't?" His partner asked.

"Why are we interrogating these clowns?" Detective Briggs inquired. "It's not like they're gonna tell us where the drugs came from, since we were the ones that planted it on Pharaoh. And three cops can testify in open court that that thug pulled a pistol on you. It's a done deal, so why the charade?"

"Relax, Booker." Tyler said, coolly. "This is all for formality purposes. I just need to put down in our report that we interrogated the perps and they didn't talk."

"Aren't you a little worried one of them will say somethin' that might cause us to draw some heat?"

"Just do what I say, and we'll be fine.' Tyler advised.

"The guy in room one looks like he's about ready to spill his guts to somebody, so you go in there and talk with him. Make sure he says as little as possible. In the meantime, I take the rookie with me into room two and teach him some interrogation techniques because that guy looks as cool as a cucumber and shouldn't say anything that will turn any unwanted attention our way."

"What about his hands?" Booker asked, referring to the grill marks that Tyler burned into his skin.

'I'm sure he'll say something about it, but I don't care." Tyler admitted. "We have to bring junior into the mix with us, so eventually he has to learn the job can get a little gritty at times. If he has a problem with it, we cut him loose."

"If you say so." Booker replied, as he headed to the door leading into interrogation room one.

"Hey!" Tyler shouted, getting Booker to stop and look at him. "Be cool."

Detective Briggs nodded his head in agreement and then entered the room to begin his interrogation.

"Hey, Brooks!" Tyler shouted to Ethan, who had been sitting in the next room the whole time. "Look alive! I want to teach you some interrogation techniques."

"Alright." Ethan replied, as he made his way to Tyler's side. "I'm all ears."

"First…you want to sit out here and analyze the suspect for a few minutes and get a feel for what you're in for." Detective Lynch advised, as he crossed his arms and leaned up against the wall, staring at the perp sitting all alone in the small room. "Ideally, what you want to see is your man squirming around in his chair, licking his lips, and a lot of sweat on his brow."

"Signs of nervousness." Ethan responded, sizing the perp up while reviewing a file of known information about him.

"Absolutely." Tyler complimented. "But as you can see, our man is given' us no indication that he is feelin' apprehensive at all. He's cool, composed, and maybe even a little angry."

From the file, Ethan learned that the suspect's name was Frank Harris. A.K.A. 'Big Thirsty.' He was a Gangster Apostle with a known history of selling dope and gang activity. He had a stocky build and wore his hair up in braided piggy tails, apparently thinking the style made him look tough.

"So, what do we do in this case?" Ehtan rightly asked.

"This is when I like to rattle their cage and get into their heads. You know, use some of that anger to our advantage. For instance, the first thing I'm gonna do is make fun of that stupid hair style." Tyler answered. "It's all about presence too. The entire room is designed to give the suspect a sense of helplessness. See how he's made to sit in the chair across the table from us, and how our side of the room has the light switch, the door, the two-sided viewing glass. Everything that is *of* control is in *our* control."

"Yeah…" Ethan replied, hanging off his trainer's every word.

"We want to get in his face, close the distance between him and the room's only exit, giving him the sensation that the walls are closing in around him. Another tactic is to try and play him and his partner against each other, make one of them believe the other ratted him out. You'll also see that I like to talk down to the tough guys. It gets under their skin and irritates them, makin' them speak out in anger, and a lot of times they end up sayin' somethin' about the case they wish they could take back. But since we already read him his rights, anything he says in that room is fair game. So, once he starts confessing to stuff, we begin slowly backing away, giving him his personal space back. This then gives the suspect the sensation that he is getting a huge weight lifted off his shoulders by confessing to us.'

Ethan nodded his head in acknowledgment, never taking his eyes off the suspect in the other room.

"You ready for this?" Tyler asked.

"Absolutely." Ethan responded, eagerly.

"Let's do this." Tyler said, as he flung the interrogation room door open. "Wake up, Pippy Longstockings!"

"Yo, man, I don't want to be alone with this guy!" Frank said, as his eyes opened wide. "This guy's crazy!"

"Well, you're not going to be alone with him." Ethan chimed in, as he shut the door. "That's why I'm here."

Just as Tyler had coached him, Ethan moved in and sat on the table, crowding the suspect's personal space. Tyler, on the other hand, chose an even more direct route. He marched straight into the room and placed the flats of his palms on the stainless-steel table top, leaning over mere inches from the crook's face.

"Nasty burn marks." Detective Lynch pressed, trying to shake the suspect up. "What'd you do, have a nasty waffle iron accident?"

"You know what happened, cracker!" Frank yelled, as he leaned himself back in his chair, balancing himself on two legs. "Y'all did this! Police brutality! But who's gonna believe me, right?"

"I don't know what you're talking about." Tyler lied, before kicking the legs of the chair out from underneath the gangbanger, causing him to crash to the ground. "Looks to me like you're just accident prone."

Ethan shook his head slightly, not agreeing with his training officer's tactics, but going along with it, so as not to cause any friction.

"You're bogus, man!" Frank screamed, as he jumped off the ground.

"Sit down!" Tyler growled, with authority.

Frank gave the detective an evil scowl, as the thought of retaliation crossed his mind.

"SIT DOWN!" Tyler yelled, even louder than before, letting the suspect know who was in charge.

Seeing no immediate solution presenting itself that would get him out of the room, the thug wisely took his seat.

"So, Big Thirsty, how'd you get your name?" Ethan asked, offhandedly, trying to keep the thug off guard.

"I got it 'cause I'm good at makin' that paper." Frank answered, in his customary cocky manner.

"Well, your homies should have called you Little Schoolgirl, because you look like a dork with those antennas sticking out of your head." Tyler interjected.

"Man, why am I here?" Frank asked, growing tired of the insults.

"How about attempted murder of a cop during a raid for starters, or did that slip your mind?" Tyler continued to press.

"That was in self-defense!" The thug yelled. "That raid was bogus! You didn't have no right to be there! We weren't even slingin' no dope!"

"Well, that kilo of crack cocaine we found at the residence says otherwise." Ethan chimed in.

"That dope was planted!" Frank screamed. "That wasn't even Pharaoh's crib! He never did business outta his mama's house!"

"People change." Tyler countered, with a smug expression on his face.

"But the times don't!" Frank reasoned. "Pharaoh had only been outta the joint a couple of days! There ain't no way he'd had enough time to score a kilo of dope in that short amount of time!"

The thug's sound logic was enough to spark Ethan's interest, causing the rookie to furrow his brow at Tyler as he connected the dots in his head.

Tyler was quick to catch Detective Brooks' sudden change in facial expressions, and quickly changed his line of questioning.

"Regardless, if it was your dope, Pharaoh's dope, or Pharaoh's mama's dope, that doesn't change the fact that you tried to kill me, you piece of dirt!" Tyler growled, as he noticeably became more aggressive. "And I'll see to it you spend the rest of your natural life playing basketball in Statesville unless you testify against your homie."

"Man, I ain't sayin' a word against Pharaoh!" Big Thirsty yelled, firmly. "That dope was planted!"

"You sound pretty confident about that." Tyler shot back, as he stood upright and made his way behind the suspect, leaning in close to his ear. "Let's hope your partners are as team oriented as you are. But considering you have a lot more at stake here than they do, I'd say it's let's make a deal time."

"What do you mean?" Frank asked, as the sound of concern came into his voice.

"Well, let's think about it. You and Pharaoh are both goin' down for attempted murder of a police officer. You and Pharaoh are also goin' down for distribution of crack cocaine. But the third member of your crew, your boy in the next room, is only carryin' a distribution charge. I'm sure that little weasel will be more willing to cooperate since we can get his charges reduced. He might even get off with nothin' more than probation. It all depends on how I write up the paperwork."

Ethan could tell Frank's mind was working overtime as he weighed the alternatives out in his mind. The seeds Tyler was planting in his mind were beginning to take root.

"What are you wantin' me to do?" Frank conceded.

"Brooks, why don't you step out for a minute and give me a chance to talk one on one with Big Thirsty here." Tyler said, after taking a seat across from the suspect.

"...Sure…" Ethan replied, reluctantly, before he left the room.

Once out in the hallway, the young detective stared at the two men in the small interrogation room and wondered what was being said that was so secretive that he was made to leave. Both Pharaoh and Big Thirsty seemed adamant about the drugs being planted on the premises. And considering some of the tactics he'd already witnessed his partners using in order to get the job done, it would not surprise him if that turned out to be true.

Ethan turned up the wall mounted speaker that enabled outsiders to hear the interrogations as they were in progress. Unfortunately, Tyler must have anticipated the move, as the two men were conversing in whispers. Obviously, whatever was being said was not meant for his rookie ears.

"Smart move, Big Thirsty." Tyler said softly.

"Why are you whisperin'?" Frank asked, in a perplexed tone.

"In order for this deal to work, we can't let my partner hear." Tyler answered, honestly, while motioning toward the two-way mirror.

"So, what am I supposed to do?" Frank asked, in a hushed voice.

"You agree to roll on your boys, and testify in open court that Pharaoh was slingin' dope out of his mama's house, and I'll personally see to it that your paperwork gets lost in the shuffle.' Tyler offered, strategically.

"I thought you said your boys were gonna testify against me." Big Thirsty said, in a concerned tone. "How you gonna get them to forget what they saw?"

"Just remember, those are *my* boys." Tyler continued, adding emphasis to the word my. "If you sign the confession, I could get 'em to testify that they saw you selling girl scout cookies or any other story I see fit."

"There's only one problem." Frank said, as he thought the scenario through. "I'm not a snitch."

"Alright…" Tyler said, as he stood from his seat and walked toward the door. "I'll make sure to send you a postcard from the great outdoors."

"Wait!" Big Thirsty yelled, just as Tyler's hand grasped the doorknob.

"What's in it for you if I go through with this?" The desperate thug asked.

Tyler turned loose on the knob and then returned to his seat after he realized the meeting was not yet over.

"I'm not gonna lay all my cards out on the table for the likes of someone like you." Tyler said, as he glared at the gangster. "But let's just say, I get you off the hook on this one, and I keep you in my pocket for favors to be named later."

"Either way, my future ain't lookin' too bright." Big Thirsty groaned.

"It'll be a lot brighter than it would be behind razor wire." Tyler reasoned.

"How many times have you cut deals like this before?" The thug asked curiously.

"You'd be surprised how many of your fellow gangbangers I have on my payroll." Tyler cooed, as he slid the confession form across the table. "Now sign."

Against his better judgment, but seeing no other alternative presenting itself at that moment, Big Thirsty took the pen from Tyler's hand and signed the confession in the allocated spot.

"Welcome to the crew." The crooked cop said with a grin, before scooping the papers off the table and heading out the door.

Once he was in the hallway, Ethan turned to consider him, curious as to what kind of dirty deal had just been conducted.

"So, did you get the confession?"

"I got something better than that." Tyler said, not looking Ethan in the eyes.

"What could be better than getting a would-be cop killer off the streets?" Ethan queried.

"We got ourselves a confidential informant on all the deals being done by the Gangster Apostles." Tyler replied, with a white toothed smile, as he fanned the confession form in front of the rookie.

"I don't get it." Ethan admitted. "How is knowing all the moves of the Gangster Apostles in Statesville going to help us out?"

"Oh, Big Thirsty's not going to prison." Tyler corrected. "Which is why me, you, and Booker need to rewrite our statements, so they all match."

"What do you mean he's not going to prison?" Ethan asked, with a firmness in his tone. "He tried to kill a cop."

"That's how the game's played, *rookie*." Tyler barked, making sure to stress the fact that Ethan was still new to the squad.

Before Ethan had a chance to respond, the door to Interrogation room 2 opened and out walked Booker. He knew by the looks on his partners faces that something was amiss and was quick to interject himself.

"What's up, dogs?" He asked.

"Junior here doesn't understand the importance of valuable CI's. He thinks we should send Big Thirsty away for the rest of his natural life instead of tappin' into him for info on the GA's." Tyler answered, not sure how Booker would respond to the news since hearing about it for the first time.

"Yeah…that's how we have to roll sometimes, Brooks." Booker said, as Tyler caught the hesitation in his voice.

"So, you're okay with recanting your original statement?" Ethan asked.

"Well…if Tyler says that's what we gotta do, then we gotta do it." Booker answered with the same reluctance in his tone as before. "He's the commanding officer. He knows more than you and me about what's goin' on. If he sees somethin' in the grander scheme of things that we don't, just roll with it."

Dartamus, the evil little imp that had been temporarily placed in charge of keeping tabs on Cazzbein's charge, hearkened his ears at the comment. This could be his opportunity to start Ethan down the path of ruin. Before the human had time to give his reply, the plump little demon eagerly hopped up on his shoulders and murmured words to his subconscious that would test the human's will to do the right thing.

"This isn't worth the battle…" The demon drooled. "Just go along with it…"

Ethan eyed his partners suspiciously for a moment, unsure of what to think. They were both higher ranking officers than he was, and had worked the streets longer than he had been on the force. If this was the way they had to operate to keep blood from flowing through the streets, then maybe he should follow their lead.

"Alright." Ethan conceded, after a short battle of wills. "Whatever you want, it's fine with me."

"Good…" Tyler said, with relief. "I'll fill out the reports later and then give them to you and Booker to sign. In the meantime, tell me how the talk with your scumbag went."

"Better than expected." Booker answered, with a smile. "Turns out, Pharaoh had his nose turned in a different direction."

"What do ya mean?" Tyler asked, with a raised eyebrow.

"Peewee told me that Pharaoh was gettin' into the arms race." Booker replied. "The little snitch even dropped the name of their supplier."

"A kilo of dope *and* some firepower…." Ethan interjected sarcastically. "I guess Pharaoh had a lot of cash on his commissary when he got released from Statesville."

Tyler rolled his eyes at the snide comment and then continued his talk with Booker.

"Sounds to me like Pharaoh got dreams of expandin' his territory while he was locked up. He was armin' his boys for a war." Tyler calculated. "What's the name?"

"This cat's big time…" Booker began. "He's a legal arms dealer that owns a gun shop on Broadway. His name's Bobby Lister."

"Got the address?" Tyler asked.

"Right here in my hot little hand." Booker replied, waving the paperwork teasingly.

"Let's ride out and pay Bobby's shop a visit." Tyler said anxiously.

*   *   *   *   *

The pungent stench of death was thick in Vermillion's dark domain, as Cazzbein hung shackled by his wrists from the ceiling of his small cell. All about the angel was blackness, as the only form of light being emitted came from the glowing essence of his own body now trickling to the ground. His numerous wounds that he had earned after a brief encounter with Lars, the Chief Prince of demons, would have healed long ago, had the demonic underlings guarding him not continually opened them every hour. Even his once gorgeous, white feathered wings were not allowed to grow back, as the evil imps cut them off whenever they began to protrude from his muscular back.

He was indeed their prisoner.

For the time being, Cazzbein would have to reside himself to the unpleasant treatment Vermillion had to offer him. His glowing essence still ran freely from the gaping wounds, weakening him to the point that escape was not an option. Cazzbein knew the fiends would only punish him to the brink of his spiritual body's tolerance. Anything beyond what his form could endure and the angel would disperse into nothingness, and then regenerate into Heaven where his body would then fully heal, allowing him to fight once more. Cazzbein knew the demon horde would never allow that scenario to play out. As long as they held him captive, he was not a threat.

What tortured the angel more than the abusive handling, was not knowing if his friends shared similar fates as he, and now occupied cells alongside him, or if they were still out there someplace planning his rescue. Being an eternal creature was not always a benefit, when one's current position was so abysmal.

The door to his cell squeaked loudly as it had done every hour for the length of his imprisonment. The angel knew the sound well, as it marked yet another round of abuse. When Cazzbein had first arrived at the dreadful domain his resolve had been steadfast. Now, though, the guardian could feel his determination pouring from his body as steadily as his glowing essence.

"Ah, I see you are still with us." A familiar voice said, in a taunting tone.

It was then that the light of a glowing torch illuminated the evil visage of his captor, Vermillion. In the demon's hand opposite the torch, the fiend held a wicked looking dagger close to Cazzbein's face, displaying the weapon as if it were some sort of prize. However, when the demon witnessed how much essence covered the floor of the cell, he slowly lowered the dagger out of sight.

"A pity you have been depleted of so much of your precious essence, angel. I have half a mind not to torture you this hour. After all, we don't want you to heal so quickly from those old wounds, now do we?" Vermillion drooled, as he considered the Holy creature.

Without warning, Cazzbein felt the dagger's deadly sharp point sink deep into his abdomen, making a new laceration while causing him to cry out in pain. The angel's scream returned only the sound of several demons' laughter. Nowhere in this domain would he find a friend.

Vermillion's serpent-like eyes took in the exhibition with a sickening pleasure. He then wrenched the blade free of the guardian's torso as roughly as he could, so that Cazzbein would whimper even more for his delight. A rotten toothed smile then graced the demon's pale face, as he was genuinely pleased with his handiwork.

"Get comfortable guardian." Vermillion cooed. "I will see to it that you spend the remaining time until Judgement Day here in my friendly abode.

The dismal realm of the forgotten was then filled with the sound of a shrill cackle, the resonance of which spread even more despair through Cazzbein's already faltering heart.

Chapter 11

The noontime sun blazed in through the passenger side window of the '69 Caprice, drowning Booker with its intense heat, and giving him the sensation of what it would be like to be cooked alive in the scorching flames of a baker's oven. The unpleasant sensation caused him more than a little discomfort, as he fidgeted around uncomfortably in his seat. Performing stakeouts in the summertime heat was no one's ideal way to spend a Tuesday afternoon. Unfortunately, they were an essential part of the job and had to be done no matter who disliked it.

"Hey dog, can't we find some shade to park in? I'm gettin' blacker by the minute in this sun." Booker whined, as he fanned himself off with an old takeout menu from a Chinese restaurant.

"Sorry partner." Tyler answered, while looking through a pair of binoculars. "This is the only spot I could find in all this lunch time traffic where I could keep an eye on our boy."

"How's the rookie doin'? Booker asked, hoping for some action soon that would give him the opportunity to leave the vehicle.

"I'm not sure..." Tyler replied. "So far all he's done is a lot of standin' around."

"Why do I get the feelin' we're wasting our time?" Booker complained.

"Probably, because your brain cells are bein' slow cooked in your head right now." Tyler mused, trying to lighten the mood. "Hold on! I think we got somethin'?"

"Our perp's on the move." Ethan's voice came over the radio.

"Time to roll." Tyler said, as he started the car's engine.

A few seconds later a white Malibu drove past their position heading South. Tyler hesitated for a moment and then slowly pulled the Caprice out behind the perp, so as not to tip him off. Normally, he would not have cared about being detected, but since the downtown area was now full of pedestrians rushing around to get lunch, Tyler decided to follow the car until they reached a less crowded area in which to make the stop.

When the Malibu finally turned into a quiet neighborhood on Cunningham Street, Booker hit the wailer and turned on the dash mounted red and blues. The Malibu drove about two blocks up the road and looked as though it was about to make a run for it. Nevertheless, for whatever reason, the driver decided pulling the car over was the best solution.

"Get out of the car, now!" Tyler screamed, after jumping out of the Caprice and drawing his firearm.

On the passenger side of the car, Booker eagerly followed suit, making sure to keep the sights of his firearm trained on the driver.

Before long, the Malibu's car door opened up and a muscular black man with gangster tattoos up and down his arms stepped out with his hands in the air.

"Yo, man, what'd I do?" The man asked, with a disgruntled expression on his face.

"Get on your knees and cross your legs behind your back!" Tyler ordered, making sure to point the barrel of his weapon at the perp's center mass.

The man eyed them evilly for a moment, and then wisely fell to his knees and intertwined his ankles behind his back. As soon as he was in the requested posture, the detectives knew he would have a difficult time running away, so they began to approach him, weapons still drawn. When they had come within range, Booker took the perp by the wrists and began slapping the handcuffs on him.

"Am I under arrest?" the man asked, after Booker had finished restraining his arms.

"Well, that all depends on you, now doesn't it, homie?"

"What do ya mean?" He asked, while Booker retrieved his wallet and handed it to Tyler.

The crooked cop opened the black, leather wallet and removed the man's Illinois State ID card and briefly scanned it for information.

"What? No driver's license, *Sean Grooves*?" Tyler inquired, making sure to emphasize the perp's name after he had found it.

"Don't you know it's against the law to operate a motor vehicle in Illinois without a state issued driver's license, Sean?" Booker asked, as he began the search of the man's Malibu.

"Hey! Don't you need a warrant to do that?" The man hastily inquired.

"Nah, Nah. We have probable cause." Tyler lied, just as Booker popped the trunk.

"Well, well, well…look what we got here, partner." Detective Briggs said, in a cynical intonation.

"What'd you find?" Tyler asked, as he patted the suspect down for weapons.

"Got ourselves a big ol' duffle bag full of semi-automatics." Booker answered, while continuing to rifle through the bag.

"Well, ya got me beat." Tyler said, mockingly. "All I found on him was this Remington 9 mm."

It was at that moment Ethan pulled up in a confiscated minivan they had signed out for use with the sting they were conducting. The young detective exited the vehicle and made it to Tyler's side, pleased with how he had executed his part in the operation.

"How'd I do?" He asked, fishing for a compliment.

"You did good, but I wouldn't give you an Oscar." Tyler said, smoothly. "Get over yourself."

"So, what are we gonna do about these semi-automatics, Sean?" Booker asked, before depositing the green duffle bag next to the suspect.

"I ain't never seen those guns before in my life." Sean replied, while avoiding eye contact with the detectives.

"That really doesn't matter, Sean." Tyler responded, as he knelt down to eye level with the suspect. "We have three detectives that said we pulled them out of your car."

"Since you're denying possession, I guess it's safe to say, you don't have registration for any of 'em. Booker chimed in.

"And if we start matching up serial numbers, I'm sure we'll discover they've all been stolen, right Sean?" Tyler pressed on.

"I wanna see my public defender." The suspect said, firmly.

"Whoa, homie! You're jumping the gun here. I never said you were under arrest." Tyler replied, strategically.

Ethan understood the deceptive tactic well. If they never placed the suspect under arrest, they would never have to read him his rights, and if they never read him his rights, the suspect would never be granted the right to legal counsel. Therefore, they could question Sean all day and his precious rights would never be violated.

"So, what do y'all want then?" Sean asked, in a thuggish manner.

"That's some nice ink you got there." Tyler said, offhandedly, dismissing the suspect's question as if it had never been asked.

"Them look like GA tats to me, partner." Booker added.

"You know, we just arrested a Gangster Apostle recently, didn't we?" The blonde-haired detective said, in a mocking tone. "Ever heard of a GA named Pharaoh?"

The suspect never answered. Instead, he stared down at the ground, doing his best to ignore the detective.

"Name must be slippin' your mind, huh?" Booker asked, with the sound of irritation rising in his voice.

"Speaking of slipping…let me make sure those cuffs don't slip off your wrists. Sometimes officers tend to put them on a little loose." Tyler said, before moving behind the suspect and cinching the handcuffs up as tight as the thug's wrists would allow.

"AAAHHH??" Sean howled in pain. "Alright, man! That's enough?"

Ethan watched his training officer punish the suspect and surprisingly he had no reaction. He could not explain his own feelings at that moment. Maybe he had been seeing this sort of treatment too often, and had slowly been becoming callous to it. However, it seemed like something more was taking place. It was as if he was actually beginning to enjoy seeing the unmanageable suspect getting what he deserved. He could hear his inner voice filling his mind with thoughts of control. In times past it had always frustrated the young detective whenever a suspect resisted the authority his badge had given him, and now he had the power to do something about it.

"This treatment is necessary." Dartamus whispered in Ethan's ear. "He was going to use those guns to bring harm to someone, so it's only right that he gets the same treatment in return. It's the only kind of treatment these animals understand."

Ethan could not understand his own thought process, but for some unexplainable reason an irresistible grin formed on his lips.

"Now, how's that memory of yours?" Tyler said directly into the thug's ear. "Is it gettin' any clearer?"

"Yeah, I know Pharaoh!" Sean yelled. "I also know how you dirty cops set 'em up too!"

"That doesn't ring any bells to me…" Booker lied. "How about you, partner?"

"Sounds like the same load of garbage I hear every day from these clowns," Tyler answered. "Maybe this concept is new to you dimwits, but you can't sell narcotics on the streets. It's illegal. It always has been and it always will be. It's not like they came up with the law overnight."

"He didn't have no dope!" Sean argued.

"Get up!" Tyler ordered, as he roughly pulled the suspect from the ground by his shackled arms. He then maneuvered him over to the car and slammed his face onto the hood with authority. "You'll speak when we tell you to speak!"

"A'ight, man!" Sean yelped. "Chill!"

"Now, tell me what these guns were gonna get used for or I'll see to it you're sharing a cellblock with every *rival* gang member Rockford has to offer!" Tyler threatened, angrily.

"You wouldn't last through the night." Booker warned.

"A'ight! A'ight!" Sean shrieked. "I'm just the delivery boy! The cat you wanna chat with is Silky!"

"Silky?" Ethan asked, trying to keep up.

"Silky's one of Pharaoh's lieutenants." Booker quickly explained. "He must be tryin' to make a move up the food chain."

"Where can I find Silky?" Tyler asked through gritted teeth, as he twisted Sean's arms back in an unnatural position.

"AAAHHH!" The thug screamed even louder than before.

"He hangs out down at Mr. C's!" That restaurant down on West State Street! He ain't never without muscle though! You won't be able to get near him!"

"You don't worry your pretty little head about that." Tyler replied, as he began removing the cuffs from the gangster.

"Wait…you lettin' me go?" Sean asked, not sure how to feel about the sudden turn of events.

"Yup." Tyler answered, walking back to his '69 Caprice.

"But they'll kill me when they find out I talked!" The thug shouted, not sounding near as tough as he did at the beginning of the conversation.

"I guess you should have thought about that before you hitched your wagon to the wrong horse." Tyler said, with no emotion.

"Welcome to the gangbanger way of life, dog." Booker put in, before climbing into the passenger seat.

Ethan slowly made his way back to the minivan he had driven to the scene. As the young detective drove past Sean Grooves, who was still leaning up against his own vehicle with a blank stare on his face, he knew he would never see the man again. His GA buddies would surely end his life, and make the process slow and painful when they did. Such was their way. Ethan made a memory note of Sean's features, because in a few days he knew the thug's body would most likely wind up in some back alley or under an overpass waiting for the police to conduct a murder investigation on. Already his second day in his new position and Ethan was beginning to see how the game was played. Lock up the heavy hitters to pad your jacket with the commendations, and let the gangbangers sort out the low-level members for you. It was a dirty way to do business, but it seemed to work.

*   *   *   *   *

Hunter's white toothed smile could be seen long before he ever stepped foot into Mistress Vixanna's audience chamber. Even after the customary chill from her evil form sapped the warmth out of the room and the condensation could once more be seen exiting through his pearly white teeth with every breath, his emotions remained unchanged. The ivory haired demon knew that he had fulfilled every objective to his assignment flawlessly, and therefore had no need to feel apprehensive when in his mistress' presence. He was, for this moment, a hero among his brotherhood and he would stand before them as such.

After Hunter felt the subtle embrace of the room's dim torch lighting caressing his form, he stopped and waited for Vixanna to consider him. He didn't have to wait long.

As soon as Vixanna caught sight of her minion, she arose from her throne, and motioned for all the hundreds of high-ranking demons throughout the audience hall to stand at attention, as an unnerving silence soon followed. The quiet was soon replaced by thunderous applause led by none other than Vixanna herself.

The praise continued for several long moments before the six-armed demon began to hush the crowd. Once the room returned to its normal tempo, Vixanna addressed the horde of amassed demons like a mother speaking to her offspring.

"Behold! Our brother has returned to us unscathed!" The demon said, with as much enthusiasm as her animal-like voice could fathom. **"Hunter, the angel slayer, has witnessed first-hand the depths of the bottomless pit, and survived to tell the tale!"**

With that dramatic proclamation, the demonic throng once more erupted into a thunderous ovation. Hunter turned his head ever so slightly and took in the scene with gushing pride, as few fallen angels ever had the satisfaction of being labeled a hero of the eternal War for the Souls of Man. This was indeed his finest moment and he would bask in its glory as long as was allowed.

"Now, my brothers and sisters, due to the efforts of this brave demon, we may continue on to phase two of our master's plan!" Vixanna shouted, with pleasure. **"While I speak, the chief prince, Lars, is on his way to fulfilling his portion of the great scheme, and then God Almighty's reign will be that much closer to its end!"**

After Vixanna's defiant words, the massive gathering of demons exploded into cheers so loud that slight tremors could be registered on the Richter scales in the world of men. Hearing the massive demon's speech encouraged the minions to believe the long war would soon be over, and possibly, if all the portions of the intricate plot unfolded as it was meant to, they may not all spend eternity in the Lake of Fire, as was foretold.

"Now go, my children, and mark all the most vile and despicable humans you can, for the great battle is nearly upon us!"

As ordered, the evil spirits took to flight. The sight of which was like witnessing an eclipse, as their dark forms blotted out the sun with their numbers. Shrieking like frenzied beasts, the demons set off to satisfy their mistress, their goal clearly in mind. They could not afford anything to stand in their way, for they knew their eternal existences depended upon their success.

"What of me, my mistress?" Hunter asked, after the audience hall was emptied.

Mistress Vixanna once more turned her serpent-like gaze toward the snowy haired demon, and then slowly took her seat. Hunter noticed that her stare did not contain as much venom as it did on his original visit, and her six arms were not moving in the frantic manner in which they once had. Instead, the arch demon's eyes beheld him with concern, while her limbs flowed with what could only be described as a guarded grace, as they carried out separate tasks in unison.

"You have done well, my pet." The monstrosity cooed.

"Thank you, my mistress." Hunter said, graciously, as he bent into a low, respectful bow.

"No one had foreseen your success, not even our master." Vixanna complimented, before one of her limbs brought a glass of wine to her lips for her to sip.

"Just doing my part for the war effort, my mistress." The white-haired demon replied, with poise.

"It is more than that, my pet!" Vixanna growled, with the tone of hostility rising ever so slightly in her grating voice. **"Your actions have caught the eye of Lucifer himself."**

"Mistress?" Hunter asked, his voice suggesting that he did not fully comprehend.

"You are dangerous." She responded, in a point-blank manner. **"That mission was suicidal at best. I was merely hoping to be rid of you, as I grew weary of your contempt for this war. And now, word of your exploits have reached the master's ears. What am I to do with you?"**

"Nothing." Hunter answered, in an arrogant intonation. For the first time since the conversion began, the ivory-haired demon understood Vixanna's motives. She had meant to send him to his doom. Unfortunately for her, the capable sword bearer not only survived, but had gained enough heroic renown to capture the attention of both his, *and* Vixanna's master.

"What did you say?" The powerful demon hissed.

"You will do nothing." Hunter growled back, defiantly. "For if you act out of jealousy, Lucifer will see that as a sign of weakness on your part. Surely, he would not desire for his troops to be led by such a weakling as that! He may even replace you with someone like…me."

"Know your place!" Vixanna shrieked, as she grabbed hold of her wicked scourge and cracked it several times for emphasis. **"For the moment you are still under my command!"**

"Ha! The fact that you did not whip me to shreds just now proves my words are true!" Hunter gloated. "If the master hears of me being punished, it will surely be your head! You no longer have the means in which to hold me under your thumb any longer!"

Vixanna lifted the table next to her throne high above her head and then flung it into a nearby wall, causing the sturdy piece of furniture to break into pieces under the power of her wrath.

"Silence!" The outraged demon bellowed, her voice echoing off the room's towering ceiling.

Hunter merely rested his hands on the hilts of his weapons, satisfied with the conversation's turn of events. His relaxed posture only served to make Vixanna all the more angry. It was then, seeing her servant's hands resting on his *dual blades*, that she remembered a card she had yet to play.

"Tell me, my pet," Vixanna began, her voice noticeably calmer than it was just moments before. **"How did you defeat Cazzbein so easily?"**

The arrogant expression that Hunter had been wearing was quickly replaced with one of shock, as he was stricken dumbfounded. Vixanna smiled within herself, because she knew her clever maneuver had struck a nerve. She had finally found a way to bring her overconfident servant back under her control.

"I told you Cazzbein would prove no match for me." Hunter replied, strategically dancing around the question.

"That is not what I heard." The demon purred, as her six hands performed insulting gestures simultaneously.

"Lars spins a different tale."

"The angel was defeated." Hunter said, flatly. "How that goal was accomplished is of little consequence."

"**'Tis a pity.**" Vixanna said, smoothly, luring her prey in with every word.

"What is?" Hunter asked, taking the bait.

"**'Tis a pity we will never know which of you is the better sword bearer.**"

Hunter had no reply forthcoming, but the scowl he bore on his visage was all that was needed for Vixanna to know she had succeeded in bringing her arrogant servant down a notch or two.

"**I am through with you…**" Vixanna said, in a dismissive tone. **Leave my throne room.**"

Hunter did not leave immediately. Instead, the white-haired demon subtly entertained the thought of lunging at the grotesque beast and carving her into many segments of useful snake skinned products. At that particular moment, a nice pair of boots would be much more useful than her enormous frame.

Swallowing his pride, Hunter turned on his heels and exited the audience chamber, leaving Vixanna behind. The meeting was not a complete failure, since he had learned their leader had taken note of him. However, the ivory-haired demon knew he would never gain the respect he deserved from his comrades unless he dealt with Cazzbein once and for all.

Chapter 12

Michael stood speechless for a long moment in the belly of the Abyss, surveying the carnage. Nothing could have prepared the mighty Archangel for the massacre he beheld with his own sparkling blue eyes. Lars had swept through the group of angels like a wrecking ball. Truly, his small band of trustworthy guardians were never meant to face the chief Prince in battle. The golden-haired Archangel was hoping Cazzbein and his group would have caught up with Hunter before he and his evil horde ever had a chance at freeing the powerful demon. Unfortunately, as he witnessed his warring angels' broken forms on the ground, he soon discovered that was not the case.

Never was the Abyss illuminated in such a fashion as it was while being graced with the presence of the noble being. His Holy essence produced such a penetrating glow that it lit up the entire surroundings as if the sun itself had just appeared.

The powerful angel had not been searching long before he happened upon Anthony's crumpled up frame. The sight of the little angel in such shambles pricked Michael's heart.

Given enough time, he knew Antyony's spiritual body would heal itself fully. Nevertheless, time was not on their side.

Michael bent down and placed a large hand on the small angel's shoulder and uttered a simple word.

"Arise."

At the sound of the Archangel's request, Anthony could feel his body contorting back to its original form. All the damage sustained at the hands of Lars was healed within seconds, as the little angel stood to his feet fully restored.

"Oh, Commander…" Anthony said, having enough wits about him to address Michael by his title. "I can explain…"

"There is no need for explanations, my friend." Michael replied, in a comforting tone. "I have another assignment for you that requires great haste."

"Surely, Commander." Anthony said, standing at attention. "I assure you, I shall not fail…this time."

"You did not fail, Anthony." The wise Archangel confirmed, in his deep, caring voice. "You were merely overwhelmed. This fight was never meant to take place. Had I the angels to spare, the outcome would have been entirely different."

"As you say, Commander." Anthony said, hanging off of every word.

"I need for you to deliver a message to our prayer warrior in the field," Michael continued, as he handed the messenger a rolled-up scroll that he had pinched between his belt and waist. "Give this message to the human, Joe Horton."

"Consider it done, Commander." Anthony replied, before unrolling the scroll and reading its contents.

Michael scanned the cavern while his messenger took in his new assignment. All the angels that he had commissioned for the failed mission were accounted for, save one. A perplexed expression then overtook the handsome angel's features.

"Anthony…where is Cazzbein?" He asked, in a concerned tone.

The inquiry caused Anthony to take his nose out of the scroll long enough for him to search his surroundings.

"I truly do not know, sir." The messenger replied, honestly. "I only remember Lars attacking him over there, near the opening on the other side of the bridge."

Michael stood to his feet and strode over to the area that Anthony had indicated. The Archangel then furrowed his brow at the evidence he beheld. To his horror, he saw Cazzbein's brilliantly crafted scimitars laying in the dirt, but the angel was nowhere to be found. Michael knew that all warring angels considered their weapons to be extensions of their own bodies, and Cazzbein was no exception. To see his scimitars abandoned in such a way was a clear indication their owner was in danger.

"He's been taken!" Michael said, with urgency.

"What!?" Anthony gasped, before rolling up his scroll.

Both the angels understood the immediate action that needed to be taken if they were ever going to see their friend once more. Usually, once an angel was taken, they were never seen or heard from again. All angels have lost comrades to the horrors of the deep; it was the closest experience the spiritual beings could use to relate to death.

"We must go after him!" Anthony said, boldly.

"No, my friend." Michael replied, with sincerity in his voice. "Your mission is far too important. Go now, I urge you."

"What of Cazzbein?" The messenger rightly asked.

"I know he is a close friend to you," Michael began, in a somber intonation. "But you will have to leave the rescue up to Gunthar, Glistinia, and myself. We will find our brother in arms, I assure you.”

Anthony disliked the fact that he would not be included in the search efforts, but he understood his superior officer’s reasoning. The only thought that kept him from conducting the rescue himself was knowing Michael, the mightiest of the Archangels, was leading the efforts first hand. With that thought firmly in mind, Anthony gritted his teeth, and with a nod of his head, the messenger then took to flight to deliver Michael’s message.

Once Anthony had disappeared further down the cavern, Michael raised his right hand toward Glistinia, while his left hand he positioned in Gunthar’s direction.

“ARISE!!” The Archangel demanded, as his powerful voice shook the cavern walls.

The two broken angels heard the command even in their current condition. As soon as the solitary word was uttered, the power of the Archangel’s decree could be felt surging through their bodies like a jolt of life-giving energy. The angels could feel every joining in their spiritual forms snapping back into their proper positions. When the entire process had finished, the two guardians pulled themselves off the ground fully revived.

“No time for idle chit chat.” Michael warned. “Cazzbein has been taken captive. We must find him before his trail grows cold.”

*　　*　　*　　*　　*

As soon as the door flung open and the bell hanging
around the spring-loaded closer arm announced the entry of
Detective Tyler Lynch and his crew, the owner knew there
would be trouble. Without saying a word, the cook behind
the counter dressed in a white, grease-stained T-shirt headed
in the opposite direction when he saw the men making a
straight line to the back of the restaurant where Silky and his
gang hung out.

Silky seemed to show little care as the determined men
approached him, but the four muscular thugs surrounding
him definitely showed concern. Each of them stood from
their seats, and crossed their arms in front of their massive
chests, waiting for the strangers to make the first move.

"Gentlemen, gentlemen, to what do I owe this unexpected
visimitation?" Silky asked, in an extremely arrogant fashion.

Ethan was very unimpressed with the scrawny little thug.
Quickly sizing the slender gangbanger up, Ethan could swear
he must have stood only five-feet four inches tall, and that
was if he wore thick soled shoes. If he were soaking wet,
Silky may have tipped the scales at a whopping one hundred
and fifteen pounds. He was dressed in a white tank top, a
faded pair of blue jeans and a gray baseball cap that he wore
with the bill turned backwards. There was nothing
remarkable about him at all except for the way he tried to
sound educated when he spoke, but even that did not work
for him, due to the fact that he constantly mispronounced
words and often used them in the wrong context.

"I hear you're openin' up a gun shop, Silky." Tyler
answered in a straightforward tone, as he took a seat across
from the thug.

"I don't have the simplisitist idea what you are referring to, officer." Silky lied, before folding his arms and sinking back into his chair, nonchalantly.

"You might wanna take this a little more seriously." Booker warned.

"Well, well, well, do my eyes deceit me?" Silky asked himself, not catching the fact that he meant to say deceive. "Booker Briggs, you still kickin' it with these cats?"

"It's where the real money is." Booker replied, sternly. "I don't never seem to be low on the dough either." Silky countered, as he pulled a thick roll of twenty dollar bills out of his pocket with a hand covered with gold rings. "I'd have to say I'm doing pretty satisfactionary myself."

Tyler grew tired of the arrogance oozing off the cheap thug. He roughly snatched the money out of Silky's hand and slid it into his own pocket. "Thank you, Silky drawers. My funds were gettin' a little low."

"Hey you can't just-just…" Silky stammered.

"Looks like I just did." Tyler retorted, with a scowl.

It was then that one of Silky's bodyguards decided to intervene. He leaned over and placed his hands on the edge of the tabletop, glaring into Tyler's eyes as he spoke.

"Don't think you can come up in here and disrespect my boss like that, pig."

Tyler knew when he took the lead position of the Anti-Gang Task Force that he could not afford to show fear. It was part of the job description. The no nonsense detective figured out at an early age that when you stood up to thugs like these they normally backed down, and on those rare occasions where they didn't, the dirty cop would simply put a bullet through them and tamper with the crime scene to make it look as if he acted in self-defense.

Tyler saw that the brutish thug had placed too much of his weight on the table as he leaned in. A simple lesson in physics was all that was needed to get his point across to the gangster. Tyler kicked the thug's right ankle out from underneath him with such force, that he came crashing down hard, causing his jaw to smack the tabletop with such velocity he nearly lost his entire bottom row of front teeth.

The move was extremely effective in teaching the gangster some manners, but it also spawned the remaining bodyguards to reach for their pistols. However, the three officers were the quicker, and had their well-trained hands aiming their weapons at the gangsters before they ever pulled their guns from their waistbands.

"Whoa Whoa! Gentlemen, please!" Silky shouted. "This ain't no way to conduction a meeting!"

"It's conduct, you idiot!" Tyler said, before smacking the cocky gangbanger on the nose with his drawn gun. "If you're going to try and sound smart, you should at least have a fourth-grade reading level!"

"A'ight! A'ight!" Silky shouted, as he pinched his nose. Seeing the situation beginning to escalate, the gangster decided to take a different approach with the officers. "Boys, put your pistols away, and go hang outside. Let me talk to these fine men for a minute."

"Oh, it's a little more complicated than that, *homie*." Tyler growled. "I came to take you *downtown* for a chat."

"Y'all ain't takin' Silky anywhere." One of the bodyguards interjected.

Tyler stood from the table and grabbed Silky roughly by his shirt collar, yanking him to a standing position, while placing the barrel of his Berretta firmly against the bodyguard's forehead.

"You want bloodshed, well I say it begins with you."
Tyler barked, angrily.

Ethan's mind was racing. He had not been in the new
division a full week, and already he was about to be in his
second shootout. The young man began to wonder if he was
going to make it home to see Becky or if this was how his
life would end. It was then that Ethan remembered the reason
he wanted to join the Anti-Gang Task Force to begin with.
He wanted to clean up the streets of creeps such as this, and
he knew the Anti-Gang Task Force was the best place to
make that happen.

With that thought, the young detective found his courage
and everything seemed to become clearer to him. Ethan now
understood why Tyler conducted himself in the way he did. It
was because he had to.

The thug looked into Tyler's eyes and saw only hatred for
his kind. He knew the detective would sooner gun him down
than look at him a second longer. With better judgment
overshadowing his pride, the bodyguard slowly released the
hammer on his weapon and put the gun back into the
waistband of his pants.

"Smartest move you made all day." Tyler said, in an evil
tone. "Now, if you boys don't have any more objections,
we'll be on our way.

With that said, the three men backed out of the restaurant
with their weapons still drawn and Silky securely in their
possession. When they felt they had reached a safe enough
distance, they holstered their weapons and made their way to
their vehicles.

"Hey Booker, why don't you take Silky down to the
station." Tyler said, before slipping the cuffs on their prisoner
and placing him in the back of the minivan Ehtan had driven

to the restaurant in. "Let him sweat it out for a minute. I want to take the rookie on a solo run."

Booker stared at Tyler for a moment, wondering what was going through the man's head, just as he did on many previous occasions. Booker submitted though, realizing his partner was far too complicated to figure out. With that thought realized, he conceded and did as Tyler said.

"I'll need the keys." he said to Ethan, as he held his hand out.

Ethan was as confused as Booker with the sudden change up, but decided it must be for training purposes. He slid his hand into his pocket, produced the minivan's keys and handed them to Booker.

"You're riding shotgun, rookie." Tyler said, plainly, as he climbed behind the wheel of his '69 Caprice Classic and waited for Ethan.

Once Ethan had settled into the passenger seat the two set off to whatever destination Tyler had in mind.

"You know, Brooks, you're really coming along nicely." The blonde-haired slickster admitted.

"Thanks." Ethan said, gratefully.

"That's why I wanted to ride with you today." Tyler continued. "I want you to get to know me a little better, so you have an understanding of what makes me tick."

"Alright." Ethan replied, not knowing if getting to know Tyler better would be a good thing or a bad thing.

It was about that time Tyler pulled the car into the Van Mildre Nursing home parking lot. When the vehicle came to a stop, Tyler looked at Ethan with a serious expression on his face. "Come on. I want you to meet someone."

Ethan followed Tyler through the front entryway and down several long winding hallways. When they finally arrived at room 194 Tyler opened the heavy wooden door and stepped inside. The room's sole occupant was a young woman that Ethan determined must have been in her mid-teens. The young detective noted that she had the same tone to her blonde hair as Tyler, but after further examination, Ethan recognized several other distinctive characteristics as his training officer. In fact, other than being female the only other defining feature that separated the two were the numerous machines the woman was hooked up to that kept her alive.

"Brooks, I want you to meet my baby girl, Emily." Tyler said, in a much friendlier tone than Ethan had ever heard him use before.

"Your daughter." Ethan mouthed aloud, in an intonation that suggested he finally understood.

"Yeah, Brooks, I spawned some offspring," Tyler joked.

"What happened?" The young detective asked, while motioning to the life support machines.

"She was caught in a drive-by shooting." Tyler answered, sincerely. "She was datin' some thug wannabe when his posse was shot up by rival gang members.

"I'm sorry…" Ethan said, when no other words came to mind.

"Hey, whatcha gonna do, right?" Tyler replied, as nonchalantly as he could manage. "Emily was the only family I ever had…Her mother didn't give a squat about her…I raised her on my own. She was a good kid, but started hanging out with some loser with a slick tongue and a nice car. I could tell right away he was bad news, but she didn't listen to me…had to find out on her own."

"Everyone's like that when they're young." Ethan said, in a comforting tone.

"Yea, I know." Tyler answered, his eyes getting watery. "Our department put their best detectives on the case, but since it was gang related, and we didn't have an Anti-Gang Task Force at the time to deal with their type of violence, they didn't want to risk their lives by getting too involved. So, since no one was talkin', it turned into a cold case, due to lack of evidence. That just didn't sit right with me. I mean, why should my daughter be turned into a vegetable just because some gangbanger doesn't know how to aim a gun? It was about that time I started doing some investigatin' on my own. I roughed up her boyfriend pretty bad to get him to cough up the name of the gang that shot her. After I found out what gang did the shootin', I went out and found one of the little punks and beat him senseless until I got all the names of the shooters. From there I did what the police were unable to do."

"What happened?" Ethan asked, hanging off of every word.

"Let's just say I made them regret the day they ever joined a gang." Tyler answered, vaguely. "What I'm really tryin' to say Brooks, is that I know you have a good heart, and you're doin' your best to play by the rules. That's great! Don't get me wrong. But before you stick up for the rights of every scumbag gangbanger that got his hands on a gun, think about the rights of the decent people just tryin' to make it through life the best way they can. These dirtballs we put away every day are animals. I don't even consider them part of the human race. I think of them as human waste."

"I can definitely see why." Ehtan admitted, after hearing Tyler's story.

"Today, for instance," Tyler continued. "If Silky and his crew would have got a hold of those guns, they would have shot up the town like the old west days. If that were to happen a lot of civilians could have gotten killed. We took oaths to protect people from trash like him."

"You're right." Ehtan answered.

"Now, I know you can fight…and I know you can shoot," Tyler went on. "So, I'm happy to know you got my back in a pinch. But what I really want to know is…Can you play by the same rules as these animals we put in cages on a daily basis?"

"I'll try harder." Ethan answered, after a moment's thought.

"That's not good enough…" Tyler said, shaking his head. "Brooks…I need to know…can you unleash hell?"

Dartamus watched the entire conversation with great interest. A pleased smile spread across the shriveled features on his face when he discovered the discussion was heading in the direction he desired. If all went well, the pudgy, little demon knew he could then begin phase two of his plan to bring Ethan down the road to ruin.

Moving in close to Ethan's ear, Dartamus whispered the soothing words he wanted to take root within the human's heart. "You took on an oath to protect and serve, because you wanted to clean up the streets. Now you have that opportunity. Tyler knows more than anyone how to get the job done, so follow his lead."

Ethan gave the request some serious thought. He even looked at Emily who was struggling to hold on to life for added emphasis. And then, he gave his most heartfelt reply.

"I *will* unleash hell."

Chapter 13

Tyler wanted to spend the rest of the day in some serious one-on-one training with the newest member of the Anti-Gang Task Force. He took Ethan deep into gangland, exposing the rookie to the hardcore killing zones. The task was simple enough. Tyler wanted the rookie to become callous to the everyday situations they could be dealing with, and the only way that could be achieved, was to drag Ethan straight through the cesspool of scum head on.

Detective Lynch started out small. He drove Ethan to a few back-alley walls that had been 'tagged' by numerous gangs. He explained the difference in the colors, symbols and letters that were used, taking time to point out which 'tags' belonged to which gangs. Ethan, as always, listened eagerly.

"This might look like nothing more than a bunch of senseless graffiti to you now, rookie," He said, in a straightforward tone. "But this is like a roadmap. It will let you know who's turf you're stomping around in. Multiple 'tags' means you're in a hot zone where several gangs are fighting over the same turf."

"What does that mean?" Ethan asked, pointing out the car window to the letters 'ACGAN' that someone had spray painted around a six-pointed star surrounded by pitchforks.

"That's actually gangbanger code." Tyler explained. "That simple little layout of letters tells me we are deep in Gangster Apostle territory."

"How can you tell?" Ethan rightly inquired.

"Well, whenever you see the letter 'A' in the front of these 'tags,' that means 'Almighty,' and the letter 'N' trailing the 'A,' that means 'Nation.' Tyler enlightened. "Of course, by now you know the 'GA' stands for Gangster Apostles. So, what we got so far is, The 'Almighty Gangster Apostle Nation'."

"What about the 'C'?" Ethan questioned.

"Whatever letter appears there usually stands for whatever 'set' or 'crew' left the tag." Tyler continued. "My guess is here, the 'C' most likely stands for Central Avenue."

"I never knew all that gibberish actually stood for something." Ethan admitted. "I just thought it was sprayed that way because gangbangers didn't know how to spell."

"I wish it was that simple." Tyler said, as he drove the car a bit further down the alley to check out another tag. "Do you see this one?

"Yeah." Ethan answered, after looking at some graffiti of several pitchforks with curved ends sprayed over the letters 'VRK'.

"What do you think that stands for?" Tyler asked, quizzing his student.

"That's easy." Ethan replied, thinking he knew the answer. "Vice Royals."

"You would think so, wouldn't you?" Tyler inquired.

"Actually, the Vice Royals use the Shepherd canes as one of their symbols, and the Gangster Apostles use pitchforks.

At the bottom of these pitchforks, you see they are curved. This means, whoever sprayed this, purposely sprayed their rivals' symbols upside down, showing disrespect. And the 'K' on the end of the 'VR' means killers. So, this is in fact, a slap in the face to the Vice Royals nation, because it says, Vice Royal Killers. Obviously, the Gangster Apostles have a turf war brewing with the Vice Royals in this area."

"Wow." Ethan responded. "I guess this is trickier than I thought."

"It takes time." Tyler replied, as he pulled the car out of the alley. "Now, let's go do something more exciting."

"What do you have in mind?" Ehtan asked, excited about the new knowledge he was picking up.

"You know how the police department makes money off of fines and drug busts in order to fund their operations?" Tyler questioned.

"Yeah…" Ethan replied, unsure of where his training partner was going with the question.

"Well, we have to do that too." Tyler said, nonchalantly. "Only, we can't let anyone know about it."

Ehtan grew noticeably quiet after the revelation, giving Tyler the impression that he had reservations about the idea.

"Listen, Brooks, you can't go around being a choir boy in this line of work." Tyler stated flatly. "These scumbag gangbangers are making a fortune off of selling dope to civilians, destroying their lives in the process. We need to take that money away from them and ruin whatever cushy little gig they have set up. If we happen to supplement our incomes in the process, so be it."

"Listen, I know a lot of guys on the force take money on the side for many different reasons, but I just don't feel comfortable doing it." Ethan said, honestly.

It was then that Tyler pulled the car over to the side of the road, and placed it into park.

"Brooks, there's at least nine other men on the Anti-Gang Task Force, and they're all padding their pockets. There could be a tenth guy, if you play your cards right, but the other guys won't trust you if you don't play by *our* rules."

"It's not that I don't want to, because, man, I could use the money." Ethan explained. "But I have a wife. I don't want to do anything that's going to get me into trouble. I like having a clean conscience and sleeping at night."

"Brooks, I've been doing this for years. Everyone on the squad has, and none of them, including me, has been in trouble over it." Tyler continued. "And I'll tell you something else, if anyone decided to rat on us, they'd regret the day they ever did."

"I don't know…" Ethan groaned.

"Brooks! It's not an option." Tyler barked. "Either you fall in line and do like the rest of us, or you're out. No questions asked."

As always Dartamus, the cruel spirit of darkness, saw an opportunity and sprang into action. "This is the chance of a lifetime!" the stumpy demon drooled into the human's ear, as spittle dripped from his chin. "You can rid the streets of crime ridden filth and earn some extra money for the family you plan on making with Becky."

Ehtan considered the ultimatum that had been unceremoniously presented to him. It was not just losing his new position that spurred his decision. It was, once again, that little nagging voice in his head that started making sense. He and Becky had been talking about having children one day, and if they were going to be able to afford the additional expenses, they would need more income. After a light contemplation, Ethan conceded to his weaker side with a nod of his head. "Alright. What do you want me to do?"

"That's my boy!" Tyler said, with a flicker of excitement in his voice.

After the brief conversion, Tyler shifted the Caprice into drive and sped off down South Central Avenue, taking them further into gangland.

*　　*　　*　　*　　*

The shackles were beginning to cut deep into Cazzbein's wrists, as the angel rested his entire weight upon them, drained of nearly all consciousness. The last purging of his essence was far more exhausting than any of the previous sessions had been. The guardian could only believe that the taxing effects were due to the numerous unhealed wounds covering his bruised and battered body. His demon captors never allowed his cuts to fully mend before they entered his cell and reopened them, oftentimes making new ones before leaving him alone to drain of his precious Holy essence.

The ordeal had been grueling to say the least.

Nevertheless, with no way of escape revealing itself, Cazzbein found himself helpless, and growing weaker by the hour. The angel had been drained of such an enormous amount of essence, that he could no longer maintain his Holy glow to light his small cell, and now hung limply in complete darkness. If escape had been an option when he was first brought to this dismal place, it was surely a fleeting thought now.

Cazzbein could again feel the nubs that had once been his beautiful swan like wings beginning to grow back. This had been a frustrating dance for him. The wings would get to the point of growth that they would cause him discomfort, and then Vermillion would enter his cell just long enough to lop them off once more and gloat.

The guardian decided this time would be different.

Concentrating with all his might, Cazzbein focused on the healing of his wings. He could then feel them beginning to grow. To what end, the angel did not know. It was possible he did so just to prove his defiance to his captors. It mattered little. If he could at least manage to grow his wings to where they no longer caused him pain, he would feel that he won a small battle.

Cazzbein's ears twitched slightly when he heard a tiny popping noise come from over his shoulders. It was working. He stretched the limbs as far as he could and it felt as if the wings had grown an entire foot in length during the short amount of time. The pain also subsided a bit, as he could feel the first feather begin to grow. The angel managed a slight smile at the thought. For the first time since being taken captive, the angel experienced a sensation he had nearly forgotten. He felt happiness.

It was at that moment the door to his cell flew open without warning. There, Vermillion, the malnourished looking demon, stood with his gruesome cleaver protruding from his boney hand. "I figured as much." He said with a dry cackle. "It is about this time in an angel's imprisonment when they begin to give up hope."

Cazzbein could feel what little optimism he had been feeling sink away to oblivion, for he realized another draining session was upon him. The dim spark of enthusiasm that had begun to show in his clear blue orbs, slowly faded to nothingness with every step the demon drew near to him. After Vermillion stepped past his line of vision, the angel felt the all-familiar cut of the dark spirit's cleaver as it severed his freshly grown limbs to nubs once more.

"Ahh! This one had a feather on it." Vermillion said, smugly as he waved the sheared off limb in front of Cazzbein's face. "You will learn your place, guardian or I shall enjoy teaching it to you."

Cazzbein let his head hang back down in a defeated manner, no longer having the strength to spit insults at the demon.

"You are not nearly as arrogant as you were all those years ago back in that barroom, are you?" Vermillion cooed. "Scott sends his regards, guardian. He has settled into his eternal damnation as your precious Ethan shall. All in due time. I hear he has a new spirit watching over him now. However, this spirit is one of darkness. Just something for you to think about while you are in my care."

Slowly, the door to the tiny cell closed, leaving the angel in darkness once again. As hard as Cazzbein tried to not let the demon's words trouble him, they did. He could not help but feel he let Scott down all those years ago. The charge he had been sent to protect just before Ethan, was now swimming in a lake of eternal flame. Even though Cazzbein protected the human sufficiently from physical harm, the angel, with all his efforts, could not bring the man to Christ. And now, due to his inability to stop Hunter from freeing Lars, his current charge, Ethan, was now in danger of the same fate.

With nothing but his wounds to keep him company, Cazzbein slunk back on his shackles and hoped his friends would not give up on him.

* * * * *

Both Gunthar and Glistinia could tell by the look on Michael's chiseled features, the mighty Archangel was beginning to feel the effects of frustration. Their search efforts thus far had proven unfruitful, even after encountering countless hidden enclaves of demonic forces that had to be dealt with. Hundreds of glowing eyes peered at the group of angels from behind tall rock formations as they passed by, none of which daring to lock blades with the Archangel foretold to defeat Lucifer in the final battle. Nevertheless, all of the monstrous figures could not help but wonder what great circumstance had brought the angelic beings to their unholy domain.

The hunt did not go well until Gunthar caught something out of the corner of his eye that urged a closer inspection. After kneeling down on one knee, the powerful angel saw a trail winding its way back beyond the cavern's walls. It looked as if someone had tried to cover the trail up by whisking dirt over the signs of a struggle.

"I have found a trail!" Gunthar yelled, drawing the attention of his comrades.

After the pair of angels made it to Gunthar's location, Glistinia caught sight of a path made from an angel's freshly spilled essence.

"I do believe we are on the right track." She said, while pointing out her findings.

"Good work." Michael complimented. "We must be on guard from this point on. There is no way of telling how many minions will be guarding him."

"Agreed." Gunthar said, as he pulled his war hammer off his shoulder.

As the group followed the trail of angel essence, they discovered the glowing liquid appeared to be getting more vivid and moist than it had been, indicating that they were getting closer to finding their fallen comrade. The trail of angel blood led them to a rusty looking steel door, so thick that one could only assume it was not only meant to keep someone out, but to also keep someone in.

"Prepare yourselves." Michael commanded, as he unsheathed his greatsword.

Gunthar and Glistinia followed the Archangel's lead and quickly took a defensive posture, waiting for him to make the next move. They didn't have to wait long. With a tremendous burst of speed, Michael surged his way toward the sealed entryway like a blur. After lowering his shoulder, the Archangel crashed into the thick steel door with as much force as two locomotives meeting head on at breakneck speeds.

As impenetrable as the door was meant to be, it proved little effort for Michael, as the powerful Archangel's assault ripped it off its strong hinges. After the thick steel panel slammed to the ground, the trio was greeted by the surprised glares of hundreds of dark spirits. When the initial shock wore off, the evil minions scattered to arm themselves with cruel weapons of war, letting the angels know the prisoners of their facility would not be given up without a fierce fight.

"Let's show these creatures what true companionship is!" Michael roared, before the three of them leapt into battle.

Chapter 14

Elmer Fisk was a small-time defense lawyer who didn't mind taking on the cases no one else wanted to get their hands dirty with. It didn't bother the little man's conscience in the least to protect the occasional murderer, rapist, or even a pedophile or two, so long as his retainer was paid in full. So, needless to say, when Jimmy Boose, a.k.a. Pharaoh contacted him with his case against the Winnebago County Police Department, the sleaze-ball attorney wasted no time jumping into his cheap suit and bowtie before making a beeline to the hospital to see his newest client.

The bald little man had a horrible reputation with everyone at the courthouse for his ability to get the most loathsome and depraved criminals off the hook with legal loopholes. That is why it was no surprise to the officer guarding Jimmy Boose's door to see Elmer approaching him while trying to cover up his bald head with the few scraps of hair he had yet remaining.

"Officer, I'd like to see my client please." The dirty lawyer said, in his screechy voice.

The guard briefly scanned Elmer's credentials and then stepped aside while a disgusted expression washed over his face.

"Everyone is entitled to legal counsel, officer." Elmer said, after catching the man's less than jubilant countenance.

"Whatever helps you sleep at night, Fisk."

"I actually sleep quite well, thank you, on a big mound of money.' The sordid little man replied, before stepping inside his client's hospital room.

"I see y'all got my message." Pharaoh said, in a pained voice, as he managed himself into a seated position.

"Police corruption is a serious accusation, Mr. Boose." Elmer replied, flatly. "If this case can be proved, we could stand to make a lot of money by suing the city."

"Call me Pharaoh." The gangster said, offhandedly.

"I can't do that." Elmer answered in a formal tone. "We want to appear respectable in front of the judge, so we need to practice proper etiquette even when we are alone. I will call you Jimmy or Mr. Boose."

"A'ight." Jimmy replied, contently, after a quick consideration.

"Now, you say you overheard the detectives involved in your arrest admit to planting the contraband on you?" Elmer inquired, relentlessly.

"That's what I done told your secretary on the phone." Jimmy answered.

"I just want to make sure I get all the facts, Jimmy." Elmer replied, before taking a seat next to his client's bed. "So, tell me, where did this conversation take place?"

"About three feet away from where you sittin'." Jimmy answered, as he pointed to the exact location in the room.

"That's odd…" The creepy attorney thought aloud. "I wonder why they would have felt comfortable enough to carry on that conversation while you were in the room?"

"'Cause they thought I was knocked out from the drugs the doctor used when he took that slug outta my arm, that's why." Jimmy responded, with frustration beginning to grow in his voice.

"I see…" Elmer continued. "And were you feeling any effects from the painkillers they gave you?"

"They didn't give me no painkillers!" Jimmy yelled, in an angry tone. "They didn't want to waste any of their precious drugs on some dope slingin' wannabe cop killer, so they let me feel every bit of the pain!"

"Easy, Jimmy." Elmer said, trying to calm his client down. "I still need to ask you some questions."

"Ask away. I ain't goin' nowhere." The gangbanger said, in a much calmer intonation.

"Were there any witnesses in the room at the time the detectives were having this conversation? Maybe a nurse or doctor, perhaps?"

"Nah. Nah. Them cops is dumb, but they ain't stupid" They made sure it was just the two of 'em!" Jimmy replied.

"I see…" Elmer said, absently. "Wait! I thought you said there were three detectives that arrested you?"

"There was. One of 'em was a rookie. You could tell."

"How could you tell?" Elmer pressed.

"'Cause the two slick talkin' ones kept calling him rookie for one thing, and then they kept sending him away on mini missions at my mama's house, so he wouldn't see 'em plantain' that dope on me. And when they was here they made sure he was outta the room when they was talkin'." Jimmy replied, in his typical thuggish manner.

"That's it!" Elmer said, excitedly. "He's our way in!"

"Whatcha mean?" Jimmy had to ask, due to the fact that his wits were not near as fast as his attorney's.

"The rookie!" Elmer answered. "They knew what they were doing was wrong, so they hid their law-breaking tactics from him! It's possible they may not have corrupted him yet!"

"So what's that mean for me?" Jimmy inquired, as always thinking of his own angle.

"It means, if we can turn him against his buddies, we might have a case." Elmer said, in a hopeful tone.

"You mean I gotta stake my life on a cop's word?" Jimmy queried, angrily. "Man, ain't no dirty cop gonna throw his life away over a gangbanger. Are you new to this lawyer thang?"

"It's not as hard as you think it is, Jimmy." Elmer replied, with a wink. "I have at least one friend that works in the Internal Affairs Division. If there's anybody that can get under this kid's skin, it's him."

Jimmy stared at the attorney with a less than enthusiastic look on his face.

"Don't worry, Jimmy." Elmer said, in an attempt to gain his client's trust. "Let me view the arrest report and make a few phone calls. I can make you a rich man...*legally.*

   *   *   *   *   *

Booker was beginning to get bored. He couldn't remember the last time he was made to hang out around the station house and wait. What made matters worse was the fact that Tyler never made it clear to him if he and the rookie were coming back anytime soon. The passing time was beginning to wear on him just as it was on Silky who was still seated in Interrogation Room #1 waiting to be questioned.

Booker glanced at the clock on the wall and discovered that both he and Silky had missed lunch. Depriving suspects of a meal or two was a tactic used to get a perp to talk, but it was no way to treat a detective. Booker had a feeling his partner would come marching straight through the doors and wonder where he was if he were to sneak out for a quick bite. That was just his luck after all. So, against his stomach's strong urging for nourishment, Booker folded his arms, leaned irritably against the wall, and waited.

On more than one occasion since being told to babysit, Detective Briggs wondered if he should be getting worried. The image of Tyler grabbing him roughly by his shirt collar while they were in Pharaoh's hospital room replayed over and over again in his mind. His partner's actions did not sit well with him in the least.

Another thought that plagued Booker's mind was the rookie's miraculous shooting ability and the fact that he saved Tyler's life with some impressive grappling skills. The rookie was beginning to show him up. Detective Briggs now wondered if Tyler was grooming the rookie to take his place.

In an attempt to dismiss the tormenting thoughts, Booker took hold of his cell phone and called his partner.

"Hello." Tyler's voice greeted on the other end of the call.

"What's up, dog?" Booker said, in his most pleasant tone.

"What do you want me to do with Silky?"

"Is he giving you trouble?" Tyler asked, sarcastically.

"No, but-" Booker began, before he was cut off.

"Then why can't he just sit there for a while?" Tyler inquired, not understanding the dilemma.

"It's just that I ain't ate lunch-" Booker tried to explain.

"You don't have to ask permission to eat." Tyler said, pointedly. "Go get some lunch."

"A'ight then." Booker replied, the sound of pleasantness quickly disappearing from his voice.

"Hey Booker, wait!" Tyler said, trying to catch his partner before he hung up. "Have you checked those guns into evidence yet?"

"Nah, I still got 'em in the van." Booker answered. "Why?"

"I want you to do the old 'Slide-N-Grab' on ol' Silky." Tyler replied.

"By myself?" Booker asked. "We ain't never pulled a solo performance on that move before."

"I got faith in you." Tyler responded, before disconnecting the phone call.

Booker returned his phone to its case on his belt and then stared at Silky through the two-way glass.

"The ol' 'Slide-N-Grab,' huh?" Booker said aloud to himself. "A'ight."

With that thought firmly in mind, Booker went out to the parking lot and opened the back door to the van where the illegal guns were stored. He briefly rifled through the duffle bag until he found the perfect pistol in which he would use during the interrogation. It was a stainless-steel Smith & Wesson .357 Magnum, with a highly polished wooden handle.

"That's the one, baby." Booker purred, before slipping the gun into the back side of his pants waistline, and covering it up with his shirt tail. Minutes later, Booker entered the interrogation room with his tired suspect.

"Look alive, Silky!" Detective Briggs yelled, before slamming his hand on the table.

"Brother, why do you wanna treat me so disrespectfully?" Silky moaned.

"What are you gripin' about?" Booker queried.

"Y'all apprehended me before breakfast, and now deny me lunch too?" Silky whined.

"So, what are you tryin' to say?" Booker asked, as he took his seat on the other side of the table.

"I'm tellin' you, I want a cheeseburger." The arrogant thug said, before sinking back into his chair and crossing his arms.

"Later." Booker replied, as he reached around his back and took hold of the Smith & Wesson. "But first tell me where you got this."

After saying so, Booker pulled the gun from his waistband and slid it across the table with enough momentum that Silky would either have to catch it or let it hit him and fall to the floor. Just as expected, the skinny thug panicked, and grabbed the .357 Magnum by the handle before it had a chance to slide off the tabletop.

"Man, I ain't never seen this pistol before in my life!" Silky shouted, before tossing it back on the table.

"Well, it's got your fingerprints all over it." Booker said, calmly, before plucking the gun off the table top with a handkerchief.

"MAN, THAT'S BOGUS!!" Silky screamed loudly.

"Yeah, right." Booker cooed with a smile. "That's what they all say."

"I ain't gonna just sit here and take that! Y'all saw what he did!" Silky yelled at the camera mounted in the corner of the room. "This ain't legal!"

"No. But it's justice." Booker said, evenly, as he looked deep into the thug's eyes. "Oh, and just so you know, since this wasn't a formal interrogation, I took the liberty of unplugging the camera. So, as far as a jury is concerned, your prints got on that Smith & Wesson when you purchased a duffle bag full of illegal weapons."

"Whoa, partner!" Silky said, in a much calmer tone than before. "Come on now, what do you want from ol' Silky? Women? Money? I can cut you in on a big ol' piece of the pie. Set you up for life. What do ya say?"

"I say, a big-time collar like you, I wouldn't let slide for all the money in Rocktown." Booker said, evilly, before exiting the room.

After leaving the thug alone, Booker turned and looked through the two-way glass to see how his guest was getting along. Gone was the appearance of arrogance. The detective couldn't help but smile, because he knew the tactic that had worked hundreds of times in previous cases had just worked again.

"The ol' 'Slide-N-Grab saves the day once again." Booker said aloud to himself, before strutting off to a much deserved lunch.

*   *   *   *   *

"Alright Brooks, here's the plan." Tyler said, before pulling the Caprice to the curb about a block ahead of a group of gangbangers. "I'm gonna fly up on these bangers and you're gonna jump out. The one that runs, is the one that's guilty."

"Guilty of what?" Ethan asked, sincerely.

"Of something." Tyler replied, nonchalantly. "It doesn't matter. I just want to show you how we can have a little fun."

With that said, Detective Lynch slammed the accelerator down and peeled off down the road. When he came within twenty feet of the men, Tyler slowed the car down, allowing Ethan to jump out and take chase. Just as the blonde haired slickster predicted, one of the thugs bolted, tearing off down a back alley.

"Hey! stop! Police! Stop running!" Ethan yelled. "Give me a break, man, I'm not a track star!"

Tyler had danced this dance at least a thousand times, and knew exactly what to do. Never stopping the Caprice, he circled around the block while Ethan stayed hot on the perp's heels. When their suspect came within a few feet of the end of the alley, Tyler screeched his car to a halt, blocking the man's exit. Unable to stop his momentum, the thug slammed into the side of the Caprice hard, bringing the chase to an end.

"What are you running for?" Ethan asked, heatedly, as he roughly grabbed the banger by the shoulder and threw him down on the hood of the car. "Didn't you hear me screaming for you to stop?"

"Man, what y'all want with me anyway?" the white banger asked, while assuming the arrest position.

"You sure act awfully suspicious for somebody that doesn't know what they did wrong." Tyler said, as he exited the car and made his way over to the perp's side.

"Well, y'all must want somethin' or ya wouldn't be hasslin' me!" The thug replied, as Ethan turned him around.

"You got that right." Tyler admitted, while holding his hand out. "Give me the bank roll."

"Come on dog, I've been out here workin' all day!" The gangster yelled.

"Peddlin' dope isn't considered working." Tyler growled. "Now hand it over."

"This ain't right, dog." The thug said, as he reached in his pocket and produced a fat roll of twenty-dollar bills that he then slapped into Tyler's waiting hand.

"Dope too." Detective Lynch added, fanning his fingers greedily.

"Man, come on Tyler!" Pharaoh's gonna have my hide!"

"What do they call you?" Ethan asked, not letting it slip his attention that the perp called Tyler by his first name.

"Why don't you ask your boy here?" The banger said, as he fetched the drugs from his pocket and gave them to Tyler. "Y'all the Po Po. I gotta do your job for ya?"

"His name's Shifty." Tyler answered. "He's one of the local GA's that sling dope this far down South Central."

"Man, this ain't right, Tyler." Shifty repeated. "This is the third time this month you done took my stash."

"Kind of makes you think he doesn't want you dealing dope on his streets, huh?" Ethan asked, sarcastically, growing tired of dealing with morons like this on a daily basis.

"They never learn." Tyler said, while he counted his fresh stack of money.

"My crew's gonna think I'm stealin' from 'em if ya keep takin' my stuff." Shifty complained.

"Apparently you haven't heard the news, so I'll enlighten you." Tyler began. "I busted Pharaoh the other day and Silky's sitting it out in the cooler. They got too much on their plate at the moment to be given' you any thought. So, you got no worries for the time being anyway. Now run along."

"You serious?" Shifty asked, truly not knowing if the detective was playing with him or not. "You're cuttin' me loose?"

"I'd get going if I were you, before he changes his mind." Ethan warned.

"Y'all don't have to tell me twice!" Shifty said, before bolting away from the detectives.

"Ehtan watched as the thug quickly disappeared into the scenery, wondering what the point to all that was.

"Why didn't we bring him in?" He finally worked up the courage to ask.

"We're out for the big-time collars," Tyler explained. "Let the flatfoots deal with the small timers."

"How do we explain the evidence then?" Ehtan queried.

"We don't *explain* it. We *split* it." Tyler answered, as he held out half the money for Ethan to take.

"I don't know…" The young detective said, tentatively, still struggling with his conscience.

"See, this is exactly what I'm talkin' about, Brooks." Tyler said. "You're gonna have to loosen up if you're gonna be on my crew."

Ehtan did not reply. He merely stared at the five hundred dollars Tyler was offering him, as his mind worked overtime, locked within a battle of morals.

"What are you so worried about?" Tyler said, in an irritable tone, as he slid the money into the inside pocket of Ethan's jacket. "Nobody but me is ever going to know about it."

Ethan watched as Tyler walked back around to the driver's side of the car. Part of him was pleased that he did not take the money. However, the other part of him felt like a coward for allowing Tyler to stash the money on him anyway. For better or worse he still had the thick roll of twenties resting in his pocket.

"It's okay." Dartamus' voice cooed in his ear. "He is your superior officer. If he says it's alright, then it's alright."

For whatever reason, Ehtan suddenly felt at ease. It was as if the words calmed him and allowed him to settle the debate he was having with his conscience only moments ago.

Ethan felt as though he was suddenly warped to an alternative universe where the rules no longer applied. Throughout his many years as a patrolman, he was always taught never to take bribes or falsify reports. But now, here his training officer was teaching him that that sort of behavior was necessary in order for him to be trusted. With a frustrated shake of his head, Ethan climbed into the passenger seat of the '69 Caprice and decided he would deal with what to do with the money at a later date.

Chapter 15

As soon as Tyler pulled the Caprice onto North Court Street, Ethan figured out exactly where they were headed. His suspicions were soon made reality when the car stopped in front of Tasha's apartment building. He had not seen the prostitute or her daughter, Nina, since his first day on the Anti-Gang Task Force. Nevertheless, the thought of Nina being exposed to her mother's harsh living style had crossed Ethan's mind on more than one occasion.

"Well, come on Brooks." Tyler said, when he saw Ethan staring blankly at the outside of the building. "You're not gonna just sit here in the car, are you?"

"No, I'm coming." Ethan answered, before climbing out of the vehicle.

As they walked up to the entryway, the detectives spotted a drug dealer peddling his stock, while holding the security door ajar. When they came within range of the man, Tyler flashed his badge after taking hold of the door.

"Beat it. This is my neighborhood." He said, without slowing his pace.

Wisely, the dealer took off in the other direction and never looked back. Minutes later the two arrived at Tasha's apartment. Tyler knocked on the door a few times and then they heard the expected reply from the other side.

"Who is it?" Tasha asked, in her thick Spanish accent.

"It's me and Brooks Tasha, open up." Tyler ordered.

Within seconds the locked clicked, followed by the door being opened. Once done, there stood the lovely Latino woman with a swollen left eye. It didn't take being a detective for both the men to know she had been smacked around by someone.

"Geez! What happened?" Tyler asked, taking the woman's face into his hands for a closer inspection.

"One of the guys got a little rough." Tasha said, nonchalantly.

"What's his name?" Tyler asked, with hostility rising in his voice.

"I don't know what his name was." Tasha replied. "They're all John to me."

"Is Nina alright?" Ethan inquired."

"Why wouldn't she be?" Tasha asked, before taking a hit off her crack pipe. "She wasn't the one getting hit."

The woman's answer turned Ethan's stomach. Seeing some strange man slapping your mother around would be enough to scar any child. Any nurturing mother would have come to that conclusion and changed their profession as a result.

"The next time this happens, call me." Tyler said, in a tone that sounded more like he was talking to a piece of property than another human being.

"Alright. I will." Tasha replied, before taking another deep inhale of her poison. "So, did you bring me anything?"

"Of course." Tyler answered, as he pulled a plastic bag of crack cocaine out of his inside jacket pocket and then held it out for Tasha to take. "Do you have anything for me?"

"Another fifteen hundred." Tasha replied, as she pulled the money out of an old coffee can.

"Mama?" Came Nina's voice.

"Hey kiddo!" Tyler said, in a halfhearted tone. "How have you been?"

Nina did not respond to Tyler's greeting. Instead, she ran to her mother and hid behind her timidly.

"Nina! Go to your room and let mama talk. Tasha scolded.

"I can take her off your hands." Ethan offered. "I think there's some cartoons on TV."

"Do you want to watch cartoons with Detective Brooks, Nina?" Tasha asked.

At first the girl was apprehensive. But after looking into the young detective's deep blue eyes, she found a quality she had never seen before.

Nina found kindness.

After that new realization, the girl could not refuse. Gingerly, Nina stepped over to Ethan's side and took him by the hand. Afterward, she led him into the living room to watch the cartoons he had promised her.

"I want to know what this creep looked like." Tyler demanded, as he took the wad of money from Tasha's hand and replaced it with the bag of narcotics. "If we let one guy get away with it, then they'll all think they can."

"I don't remember…" Tasha said, irritably, while she loaded up her pipe with the dope Tyler had brought her. "It's not important."

"I just want to handle this the right way." Tyler urged.

"You already said to call you if it happens again." Tasha commented, while she blew the nasty smoke out of her mouth. "And I said I would."

"Well, just so we're clear," Tyler began. "If this jerk comes back again, you let me know."

While Tyler and Tasha talked in the kitchen, Nina was getting better acquainted with Ethan in the living room. As promised, Ethan found some cartoons on the television for them to watch, and as soon as Nina saw that she could trust him, she began to open up.

The girl, who had been starved for attention, broke out her favorite dolls and coloring books, taking time to tell a brief description of each toy she showed to the detective. Ethan could tell the girl had not had a playmate in quite some time, so he listened intently as Nina told her tales.

Nevertheless, being the productive detective that he was, Ethan saw the opportunity as a way to question the other witness that had seen Tasha getting abused.

"Nina?" He asked softly. "What happened to your mama's eye?"

"A man hit her." Nina replied, honestly, as she continued playing with her dolls.

"Do you remember what the man looked like?" Ethan queried, in a tone that sounded as if he were trying to coax a skittish deer to come to him.

"He was shoooort…and had white hair over his ears…but was bald on top of his head." Nina explained, in a childish manner.

"Do you remember anything about his face?" Ethan continued to question.

"He looked like this…" Nina replied, as she scrunched up her face in a mean looking scowl.

Ethan couldn't help but snicker to himself, because he knew the girl was trying to tell him the man was angry.

"I mean did he have a mustache or anything? Maybe a scar or something?" He asked, wanting to get as much helpful information as he could from the only one talking about the incident.

"He had really bushy hair above his eyes." Nina answered, mimicking what she had described with her hands.

"You mean he had really bushy eyebrows?"

"Yeah, the hair above his eyes." She repeated."

Ethan leaned in close to the girl's ear for his next question, so as to make it seem as if it was supposed to be their little secret.

"You wouldn't happen to know his name, would you?" He whispered.

"Ummm, mama kept yelling, Bob stop! You're hurting me, Bob! You can't take her, Bob!" Nina replied, before taking hold of a book and plopping herself down on the couch with her new friend. "Read this to me!"

Ethan could tell the child had grown tired of his game of twenty questions. He was pleased that her attention span had held out just long enough for him to obtain enough information about the man that abused her mother. In order to show Nina that he was appreciative of her cooperation, Ethan took the book from Nina's hands, and decided to reward her by reading her the story.

As he read the book to Nina, the girl's last answer to his question continued to replay in his mind.

Who was this Bob guy trying to take? He thought. *Was the man angry at Tasha for not letting him take Nina?*

The unanswered questions dug at the detective. He tried to hide his anger from Nina as he continued to read her the story, but it took every fiber of his being. Ethan decided right then and there that this Bob character needed to be found and questioned. It's entirely possible this was not just a random John smacking around a prostitute. This could have been the tip of something far more sickening.

"Sorry to break up your little play date, Brooks, but we have to roll." Tyler interrupted.

"Well, Nina, looks like I have to go." Ethan said, coolly.

"But save my spot, alright?"

"Alriiight…BROOKS!" Nina responded, saying his name for the first time.

"Looks like you made a friend." Tyler mused, as Ethan climbed off the couch.

"Yeah, she's a good kid." Ethan said.

"Brooks! Brooks! Brooks! Brooks! Brooks!" Nina yelled, as she ran around the coffee table excitedly.

"Alright, let's go." Tyler said, in a restless tone. "We had a long day today."

Ethan could not agree more, as he followed Tyler out of the apartment and down to the car. Tyler could tell Ethan had something on his mind, due to the fact that he was so quiet. However, he did not question him until they were inside the Caprice.

"Listen, Brooks, I know by now when you clam up like that you have somethin' to say, so spill it." Tyler sighed. "Is it my relationship with Tasha?"

"No…although I would like to know how that all came about…but no." Ethan replied. "It was something that Nina told me."

"What was it?" Tyler inquired, wondering what a small child could have possibly said that was so troubling.

"The guy that roughed up Tasha is named Bob." Ethan answered. "I think he may have been trying to abduct Nina."

"Wha-what makes you think that?" Tyler asked, his interest peaked.

"Nina said Tasha was screaming for Bob to stop hitting her, and that he could not take *her*." Ethan replied, making sure to emphasize the word. "I'm assuming he was talking about Nina."

Tyler sat motionless for a moment as he thought. "It may be nothin', but just in case, I'll have some of my beat cop buddies investigate."

"I thought we could check it out." Ethan urged.

"Seriously Brooks, I'm touched you want to help out Tasha's kid, but this is really a job for the blue shirts." Tyler replied with a sigh, referring to uniformed officers. "We've taken some big-time players off the board the last few days, and kept a gang war from starting up. That's what *we* do."

The expression on Ethan's face gave away what was on his mind. He couldn't believe Tyler wanted to leave this up to some uniformed officers to handle, when they could just as easily take care of the matter in less than an hour.

"Now, let's get back to the station house and call it a day." Tyler said, before he shifted the Caprice into gear and drove away.

*　　*　　*　　*　　*

David Grimes pushed his chair under his desk, eager to head home after a long day. The life of an Internal Affairs

Detective was a lonely one, so needless to say, going home was a more pleasurable experience for him than it was for most officers. When you were considered a 'rat cop' no one on the force wanted to hold a conversation with you unless they were telling you how despicable you were for not abiding by the same unwritten code as everyone else. That code being, 'Don't snitch on fellow cops.'

Detective Grimes headed up a high-profile investigation several years ago that brought down several dirty cops in the Rockford Police Department. That was his first case, and the reason he found himself ostracized among his coworkers. David often wondered if the police would ever show up at his address if he or his family were in danger, or if the officers on duty would consider his death a righteous kill. Even though the thought kept him up at night, Detective Grimes felt he was doing the right thing by ridding society of the same manner of lawlessness that ran rampant through the streets; the same manner of lawlessness he took an oath to fight. To the people of low moral fiber, having a badge was too much power to maintain being uncorrupted.

I was never liked much even before I took the job at IAD. David thought to himself, as he strode to the elevator.

When the elevator finally came, Detective Grimes stepped inside and pressed the button that would take him to the lobby. After the stainless-steel doors slowly closed, David found himself alone, listening to the typical melody of modern-day elevator music. The melody had the same effect on him today as it had on several occasions in the past, causing David to let loose a long yawn.

Within less than a minute, the elevator stopped, the doors opened wide, and there he stood on the ground floor of the newly built Justice Center. As he walked to the exit, he noticed the maintenance staff labeling the directory. He could not help but snicker to himself when he caught the new name of his division.

The Office of Professional Standards.

Yeah, like changing the name is going to make cops tolerate the division any better. The detective mused to himself, as he walked out of the building.

As soon as he stepped foot into the parking lot, David could feel the weight of someone's stare upon him. When he turned to see who was eyeing him, he was not surprised in the least to see the shady little defense attorney, Elmer Fisk.

"What can I do for you, Fisk?" David asked, in a tone that suggested he was not fond of the lawyer.

"I have a case for you." Fisk said, as he leaned casually up against someone's car.

"What is it this time?" David asked, sarcastically. "You want me to investigate the mayor for corruption?"

"No, no, no. "It's even bigger than that." Elmer replied, as he pulled himself off the automobile and stepped closer to the detective. "Detectives Tyler Lynch and Booker Briggs."

David could not disguise the look of interest that washed over his face. The two detectives of whom Fisk mentioned had been a point of interest to him for some time now. Unfortunately, due to the fact that they were such highly decorated officers, David was told by his superiors to give them space to work.

"Do you know how many police brutality cases cross my desk with those two names on them?" David asked. "This better be good."

"It is." Fisk replied, with a lustful smile. "My client, Jimmy Boose, claims to have heard them arguing in his hospital room about planting narcotics on the premises where he was arrested."

"Soooo, you're telling me, that an x-con that just got out of prison for murder, is claiming he was *innocent* of new drug charges brought up against him?" Detective Grimes asked, with cynicism dripping from every word. "That's unheard of."

"It's true." Fisk said, confidently.

"Do you have proof of this?" David asked, with a heavy sigh.

"Not yet." Fisk answered. "But I think I know how we can get it."

"How?"

"Jimmy told me that our two honored detectives are training a rookie." Fisk explained. "He said they kept sending him away when they planted the contraband and whenever they talked about it."

David ran his fingers through his thick brown hair as he thought.

"So." He eventually replied.

"Don't you see it?" Fisk urged. "If they're having to work closely with this rookie, and yet hiding all their illegal deeds from him…"

"…then they haven't corrupted him yet." David said, absently finishing the attorney's sentence.

"Well? Fisk asked, wondering if the detective fully understood.

"What's this rookie's name?" David finally asked.

*   *   *   *   *

Ethan lumbered through the front door of his home, physically drained after a hard day's work. He barely had the energy to plop his frame into his favorite lounge chair and kick off his shoes. The young detective reached for the television remote as quietly as possible, so as not to disturb his wife who was busy cooking dinner in the next room. Nevertheless, once the television came to life, his covert efforts were proven futile.

"Ethan, is that you?" She called, once she heard the commotion coming from the living room.

Ethan could not help but roll his eyes at the sound of her voice. He could not recall ever having done that before, but for some unexplainable reason his wife's tender voice had the same effect on him as hearing someone running their fingernails across the surface of a chalkboard.

"What does she want?" Dartamus drooled in his ear. "Doesn't she know you worked all day and want some alone time?"

"Yeah." Ethan replied to his wife, in a short, snappy tone.

"I'm making your favorite dish." Becky said, her own intonation suggesting a follow up response was forthcoming.

"That's good." Ethan responded, listlessly.

"Anything good on the news?" She asked, as she began setting the table.

"No." He answered, just as the story of his miraculous shot came on the tube, causing him to quickly shut the television off.

"What was that story about?" Becky asked, in mock curiosity.

"Nothing important." Ethan lied, trying, as always, to shield his wife from the dangers of his profession.

"Sounds like they were about to talk about that 'Miracle shot' *again*." Becky said, emphasizing the fact that she had already heard about the shooting her husband was involved in.

"Oh, so you've heard?" Ethan asked.

"Yeah." Becky replied. "So, were you ever going to tell me?"

"No." Ethan replied, honestly.

"Why not?" She felt the need to ask. "It's one thing to hear that your husband was in a shootout, but to hear the only reason he's not dead is because he actually shot the guy's bullet out of the air? I mean, come on Ethan, that's a pretty big deal."

Ethan did not immediately respond to his wife's angry statement, as he measured his words carefully.

"I told you it was a dangerous job." He growled, with the sound of finality in his voice.

In all their years of living together Becky had never heard Ethan take such a tone with her before. He was either extremely exhausted or the job was beginning to wear him down. Whatever the reason, she could tell by her husband's dismissive intonation he did not have it within himself to get wrapped up in an argument.

"Well, dinner's ready." She said, changing the subject.

Ethan carried himself into the dining room and sat down heavily in his chair. Even the delicious aroma of the thick, black angus steak adorning his plate next to the seasoned vegetables and rice pilaf did little to excite him. Showing little emotion, Ethan plucked his fork and knife off the table and went to work carving his meal, as Becky watched in silence. After a long moment, she finally worked up the courage to speak.

"Is there anything you want to talk about?"

Ethan let his fork clang down on his plate and then stared at his wife.

"What do you want to know, Becky?" He barked.

Becky had never seen her husband act this way before. His tense movements and angry tone was putting her on edge.

"I-I just want to talk…" She replied, nervously.

"You want to know about my day." Ethan said, flatly.

"Only if you want to talk about it." Becky responded.

"She's prying!" Dartamus screamed into Ethan's ear. "Why won't she just leave you alone?"

Ethan could feel his heart beginning to pump, as his breathing grew noticeably faster. He had never experienced such frustration. He felt like a wild animal trapped in a corner that was ready to pounce. He could feel himself about to explode into anger.

"Why won't you just drop it?" He yelled.

Becky was taken aback with his very loud response. For the first time since she had known Ethan, Becky was scared he might strike her. It wasn't until her own guardian angel wafted encouragement into her ear that she continued speaking without fear.

"Your husband *needs* to talk." The angel said, gently.

"Ethan…I get the feeling you need to talk about your day, even though you may not feel like it." The woman replied, in a tender tone. "The Bible says, 'A soft answer turneth away wrath: but grievous words stir up anger.'" (Proverbs 15:1 KJV)

As soon as Becky spoke the words of God, Dartamus' ears began to burn as if they had been set aflame. The devious little imp screeched in horror, as he clamped his hands over his ear holes, unable to perform his duties of stirring up anger within his human captive. As he fell to the ground in severe pain, he turned to look at Becky and saw the Seal of God glowing brightly on her forehead. The bright light from the authenticating signet singed his eyes, causing him even more discomfort.

The angel crossed his powerful arms across his chest as he stared at the demon with the look of contempt etched within his chiseled features.

"This home is wholly protected." He announced, plainly. "You must leave."

Dartamus was in no condition to debate the issue, as he felt as if he had just been bathed in hellfire. Barely able to stand, the evil minion blindly stumbled his way through the walls of the house until he felt as though he had reached a comfortable distance. With every footfall that brought him further away from the home, Dartamus could feel the pain subsiding. Wisely, he decided, since the home of Becky Brooks was protected from him and his kind, he would have to continue his quest to bring Ethan down the road to ruin whenever the human was outside the confines of his abode.

Back within the house, Ethan suddenly felt as if a huge weight had been lifted from his shoulders. His heart returned to its regular rhythmic pumping, and his breathing slowed. For whatever reason, Becky's words had soothed him. Maybe talking with her would help him make some sense of the feelings he had been having as of late.

"I don't know what's going on with me anymore…" He finally said.

"What do you mean?" Becky asked, as she took her husband's hand.

"It's this job…" Ethan admitted. "I feel like I'm constantly having to…to… compromise who I am."

Becky listened intently, genuinely trying to understand what Ethan was saying.

"How so?" She asked.

Ethan looked into his wife's clear blue eyes and could not resist sharing his thoughts with her, even if it meant exposing her to the gritty nature of his chosen profession, and in turn cause her to worry whenever he left for work each day.

"There are things I have to do at work in order to perform my duties…effectively." He said, after choosing the correct words.

"Like what?" Becky inquired, beginning to understand. "Nothing illegal I hope."

"Nothing that would get me arrested, but might get me fired." Ethan admitted.

"Well stop it!" Becky scolded.

"As if it's that easy." Ethan snapped. "I worked hard to get this promotion, and I want to keep it. I just wish things didn't have to be the way they are."

Ethan could tell by the look on Becky's face that she did not grasp what he was telling her. And how could she? She doesn't know about the inner workings of the Police Force, and how hard you have to fight against your morals in order to fit in.

"Is it peer pressure you're talking about?" Becky queried, trying to put herself in her husband's situation.

"Something like that." Ethan answered, sinking back in his chair out of frustration.

"Is this promotion really worth losing your job over?" Becky asked.

"I can do a lot of good as a detective." Ethan replied. "It's just…I have to do a lot of looking the other way, if you know what I mean."

"Oh, Ethan." Becky said, sympathetically. "You need Jesus."

"What?" Ethan said, in a stunned tone. He always knew his wife's faith meant a lot to her, but she never actually came out and spoke to him about it before.

"You need Jesus." She repeated.

"How's that going to help?" Ethan asked. "I already have enough rules I have to abide by, and you want to give me more?"

"Is that all you think being a Christian is?" Becky inquired. "Just a bunch of rules?"

"I don't know." Ethan answered. "I guess I never really thought about it before.

"You do believe in God, right?"

"I guess so…" Ethan said.

"Well, what do you think happens to you when you die?" Becky pressed, hoping she was getting through to him.

"I have no idea." He answered. "I try not to think about it."

"Well, I know where I'm going when I die!" Becky said, with a smile. "Don't you want to be there in Heaven with me? Isn't your eternity too important to gamble with?"

"Really, Becky, I love you and I know you're into the whole church thing. In fact, your moral convictions were one of the things that attracted me to you. But I'm just not in the mood to hear about it right now." He replied, sternly.

Becky hesitated before her next response, as she chose her words carefully.

"I won't push my love for Christ on you, Ethan Brooks," Becky began. "But you almost got shot yesterday. If your own death doesn't make you wonder about the hereafter and make you want to change, I don't know what it's going to take."

Ethan looked at his wife as she rose from the table. He had never seen her speak of anything so passionately before.

He hoped he didn't offend her by dismissing the subject so carelessly.

"You can stop me from talking to you, Ethan." She said, as tears welled in her eyes. "But you can't stop me from praying for you.

Chapter 16

The cityscape sped by Anthony with incredible velocity as he raced to his destination. Michael, the Field Commander of Angels, had personally departed unto the youthful looking guardian a message that needed to be delivered with haste. Never one to displease, Anthony took on the responsibility without hesitation.

Delivering important messages was Anthony's main obligation in the Army of the Lord. The angel knew the reason he was best suited for the job is because his smaller size enabled him to travel much faster than his more muscular brother and sisters. Every second mattered in the war, so it was vital that the lines of communication stay unbroken. When a human was feeling discouraged or downtrodden, it was a message from the Lord that uplifted their spirits and encouraged them to battle on. If the angel was delayed for any amount of time, that could cause a human to fall into deep depression and drift away from God forever. Anthony was determined not to have that scenario play out on his watch.

Another important purpose for delivering messages quickly was troop movement. Many battles were lost simply due to the fact that the messenger angel in charge of delivering the orders for the repositioning of troops had been captured or delayed. The forces of darkness that ravaged the land of man carry out their evil deeds under a veil of secrecy, and their malicious actions are beyond normal comprehension, so it is nearly impossible to anticipate where or when they will decide to strike. The Heavenly Hosts depend heavily on the reports of their scouts in order to figure out what the demonic spirits are planning. One or two evil minions may slip by undetected, but a mass of many legions was going to raise some attention.

Anthony's rate of speed was beyond comprehension. His current trajectory was taking him through a dilapidated building that looked as though it had been abandoned for quite some time. Never slowing his pace, the messenger flew through the bricked surface as if it were constructed of nothing more than air and then reemerged out the other side unhindered. It was a maneuver the angel had performed millions of times, and would quite possibly do a million more before the War for the Souls of Man came to its conclusion. However, on this occasion, two ravenous spirits of darkness happened to be lurking through the forsaken building and took notice of the message bearer. Unknown to Anthony, the two demons soared after him in silence, so as not to raise alarm.

The scrawny looking spirits of malice tucked their arms behind their backs to gain momentum. If they were ever going to have the chance at catching the angel they would need every advantage possible. With every flap of their bat-like wings the angel slowly came within range. The hem of his flowing white robe was mere inches from their grasp.

Silently, the minions unsheathed their jagged swords, as they hoped to end the forthcoming battle quickly.

Indeed, the battle would be swift.

Just as the demons filthy paws were about to grab his garment, Anthony pulled his silver mace from his belt and delivered a crushing blow to the face of one of the demons. The impact was so severe the evil spirit was momentarily blinded by his own mashed visage. It spiraled uncontrollably back to the earth, its ambition to fight squashed as badly as its facial construction.

The second demon had thought the prey was going to go down quietly. When it discovered that was not to be the case, it settled in for a long fight. Nevertheless, its efforts were unnecessary.

Anthony had grown confident in his fighting skills since his first taste of battle back in the Abyss. Fearlessly, he took the battle to the demon. He swung the mace over his head in a wide arcing sweep where it landed squarely upon the minion's noggin with a sickening crunch. Afterward, the demon found himself plummeting to earth as his counterpart did a moment ago. The entire fight had taken a fraction of a second in the human time frame, and soon Anthony was on his way once more.

A few moments later, Anthony found himself swallowed up by the city, as tall buildings now surrounded him on all sides. It was then that he recognized his destination. Seeing the apartment building where his contact lived, Anthony swooped downward, gaining speed as he did so. After plunging himself through the wall of the structure, he emerged in a living quarter occupied by one Joe Horton.

The human was on his knees at the foot of his bed, deep in prayer. In fact, this was where Joe spent most of his day, unless called upon. Anthony could not help but notice how differently the human looked since the first time he had delivered a message to the man twenty-four years ago at the night of Ethan Brooks birth.

Long gone was the man's youthful exterior, as the color white now speckled his jet-black hair. The signs of experience also showed vividly in the form of wrinkles around the man's deep-set eyes. Also gone were the man's selfish ambitions, as he had fully dedicated his life to serving God.

The angel watched the human curiously as he prayed. Anthony could never fully grasp the effects of aging, since he himself remained as youthful looking as he did since the day of his creation. The messenger just knew it had something to do with the slow decay of the fleshy encasing that enveloped the spirit of man. Why God decided to cover these creatures souls in such a way remained a mystery to the angel, as it did for a countless millennium. Nevertheless, Anthony knew the Lord had a purpose for all things, and it was not his place to ponder.

Joe's magnificent eyes seemed to glow intensely even from behind their eyelids. The human had been given a miraculous gift at an early point in his life. Joe was granted with the ability to see within the world of the spiritual realm. And on this day, that gift was needed.

"Good afternoon brother." Anthony said, casually.

At the sound of the guardian's unexpected voice, Joe nearly jumped out of his skin, as he leapt several feet away. Even though his amazing vision gave him the capability to behold both divine and demonic creatures firsthand, it always startled Joe when the spiritual beings popped in unannounced.

"Oh, Anthony! You scared me!" Joe gasped, as he clutched his chest. "We have to work on a better system for when you visit me or my life will be cut short by many years." The angel merely looked at the human, not understanding his complaint.

"I have a message for you from Michael, Field Commander of Angels." Anthony announced, professionally.

Joe pulled himself off the floor and stood before Anthony. Joe was nearly six feet tall and yet seemed dwarfed by the angel that towered over him by nearly a foot and a half.

"Are you sure you are one of the smaller angels, my friend?" Joe asked, remembering a previous conversation the two had had in the past.

"Yes, quite sure." Anthony replied, not comprehending the concept of small talk.

"Marvelous." Joe said, as he shook his head in amazement. "What is your message my friend?"

"You are to meet with Ethan Brooks, and reveal his purpose." Anthony replied, in a matter-of-fact tone.

"Ethan Brooks? Why does that name sound so familiar?" Joe asked aloud, as he pondered the name. "Oh! That's the name of that detective that fired the miracle shot! His name has been all over the news the past couple of days!"

"He is also the son of Jody Brooks." Anthony said, flatly.

"Jody Brooks." Joe said, absently. "That is a name I haven't heard in about twenty years."

"Twenty-four years, one month, four days, three hours, twenty-five minutes and thirty-two seconds to be exact." Anthony answered, a plain tone.

Joe looked at his friend with his continuously radiant eyes. He knew the angel was not trying to be a smart-aleck with his very precise retort, but it was just his way. Joe figured that all the angels had to keep a very accurate recording of the happenings of man, and that must be why Anthony knew that bit of information so precisely.

"So, the infant survived." Joe said, more for his own ears than for his friend's. "I was worried, since his birth came under such dangerous circumstances. If it had not been for my disbelief. I would not have hesitated, and then I would have gotten there sooner and warned that young woman of what was about to happen."

"Miss Brooks is with the Lord now." Anthony said, in a reassuring voice, as he watched the human stroll to the refrigerator. "It was her time. Nothing you could have told her would have changed that. Your mission was to save the child."

"Still, I did not arrive in time to do that either." He replied, as he opened the door to the refrigerator to see nothing more than the half-eaten fish dinner from the night before. "God's grace is sufficient for me."

"That was your first mission Joe." Anthony said, in a calming tone. "You have responded sufficiently on every request thereafter."

"I won't let you down, my friend." Joe replied, as he closed the door to the refrigerator and again considered the angel. "What is Ethan Brooks' purpose?"

A broad smile spread across Anthony's handsome face as he began to give Joe the answer.

*   *   *   *   *

BZZZZZZ!

BZZZZZZ!

"Ethan! Wake up!" Becky said, prodding her husband's back with her elbow in a halfhearted attempt at waking him. "Your cell phone's vibrating!"

"Wha-?" He replied, in a groggy tone, while only able to open one eye. "It's three a.m. Who would be calling me at this time?"

The young detective reached for the vibrating contraption and took hold of it just before it pulsated off his nightstand and onto the floor. After managing to focus his eyes, he was not at all surprised to see Tyler's name on the caller ID display.

"Hello?"

"Brooks! It's Tyler!" Detective Lynch said, in a hasty tone.

"What's up?" Ethan barely had time to ask before Tyler started in again.

"That dirtball roughed up Tasha again." He said, angrily. "And this time he took the kid."

"Nina?" Ethan gasped, "No!"

"I'm sorry I didn't listen to you earlier." Tyler said. "But this time Tasha gave us the guy's full name. I want you to go with me to pick him up."

"Yeah, sure!" Ethan responded with urgency. "Do you want me to meet you at the station?"

"Nah nah. I already got the arrest warrant. I want you to meet me at his address." Tyler answered. "It's 817 Acorn."

"Got it!" Ethan said. "Give me half an hour!"

"A'ight." Tyler replied, before ending the call.

"What's going on?" Becky rightly asked, after hearing the earnestness in his voice.

"A little girl of one of our street contacts was kidnapped."
Ethan replied, as he hopped out of bed and began throwing
some clothes on.

"Oh! That's awful!" Becky said, in a shocked tone.

"I know." Ethan responded. "That's why I have to hurry
up and get to his place before he does something stupid."

"Be careful." Becky advised, with a sad look in her eyes.

"I will." Ethan said, before rushing out of the bedroom.

"I love you…" Becky said to the emptiness.

*　　*　　*　　*　　*

The drive took less time than Ethan had anticipated. Both
Tyler and Booker were already on the scene when he arrived.
He pulled his car alongside theirs and placed it into park, but
before he had time to climb out, Tyler met him at his door
and motioned for him to roll down his window.

"I just wanted to warn you about somethin'." He said
seriously. "I know this is an emotional time for all of us,
since this is someone we all know, but don't go too crazy in
there. I want this scumbag to pay. So, everything has to be
done by the book on this one, so that he can't get off on a
technicality."

"Alright." Ethan agreed.

With that confirmation, the trio headed to the door of the
blue, two-story house. After they had reached the porch,

Tyler pounded on the door with enough force to wake the neighborhood.

"Robert Dudley! Open up! We have an arrest warrant!" Tyler screamed, moments before he kicked the door off the hinges.

Once the door was no longer an obstacle, the detectives rushed in with guns drawn. They then took off in separate directions, clearing each room before advancing to the next. Ethan was beginning to get discouraged after they had searched the entire lower level and still had not found Nina or the suspect. It wasn't until he heard Booker's announcement that his mood began to change.

"He's over here!" Booker yelled, as he leveled the sights of his gun on the perp.

Ethan rushed in the direction where he had heard Booker's voice and ended up in the kitchen. He saw Detective Briggs pulling the suspect out of the stairwell that led to the basement. He looked exactly as Nina had described him.

"Robert Dudley, you are under arrest." Tyler said, before reading him his Miranda rights.

"Where's Nina?" Ethan asked, with hostility.

Tyler and Booker nearly didn't recognize the rookie's voice, due to the venom that soaked every word.

"Yeah, scumbag! Booker growled. "Where's the girl?"

"What are you talking about?" Bob asked, with a feigned perplexity.

"Don't play that 'I don't know what you're talking about' game with us!" Ethan snapped. "Where's Nina?"

Tyler had never seen Ethan react with such anger. He liked it. It was as if he had accidentally stumbled upon the young man's weakness. That weakness being, protecting those that could not protect themselves. The slickster decided to tuck this tasty bit of information into the recesses of his complex mind for a later date.

When Ethan saw the suspect was not talking, he pushed past him and headed toward the basement.

"Nina!" He screamed. When the detective heard no reply, he feared the worst.

"He killed her." Dartamus spat in his ear. "He snuffed the little girl out like she was yesterday's garbage."

"No!" Ethan yelled, trying to get the thoughts out of his head.

Ethan searched the basement thoroughly but found no sign of Nina. He made his way back upstairs where he was met by Booker who had a displeased look on his face.

"Upstairs is clean." Detective Briggs said. "How did you do?"

"Nothing downstairs either." Ethan groaned.

"Let's get him back to the station and interrogate him." Tyler said. "He'll tell us what we want to know."

"That will take too long! Dartamus screeched into Ethan's ear. "Why not interrogate him here, where there are no witnesses!"

Ethan shook his head at the thought. He agreed with Tyler. In order for this creep to get the time he deserved they would have to perform every procedure right down to the letter. Knowing this, Ethan seized Bob roughly by his arm and drug him to the door.

"Hey! You can't treat me like this!" He yelled. "I have rights! You haven't even told me what this is all about!"

Ethan spun Bob around and shoved him up against the front door. "How about roughing up Tasha Mendes for starters, and possible kidnapping?"

"I don't know what you're talking about." Bob said, with an arrogant grin.

Ethan looked into the suspect's eyes and saw no sign of remorse for his deeds. He could feel his anger growing inside just as it had with Becky at the dinner table. Only this time, the target of his wrath deserved a good pummeling. He could feel his hand curling up into a tight fist, as the thought of beating the information out of Bob raced through his mind.

From across the room, Tyler could see Ehtan was losing his cool. Wisely, he quickly intervened and stepped between them before the rookie did something they would all regret.

"Hey Booker, why don't you take our little dirt bag to the car?" Tyler asked, as he pulled Ethan off to the side. "Easy rookie, he's only tryin' to provoke you."

"Well, he's doing a good job." Ethan growled.

"I ain't never seen you like this before, Brooks." Tyler said, as he slapped a reassuring hand on Ethan's shoulder. "I like it."

"You've finally earned his approval." Dartamus cooed, causing a pleasant smile to take shape on Ethan's face.

"Thanks." the young detective said. "But I'm not going to be happy until Nina is found."

"None of us will be." Tyler confirmed. "That's why we have to break him as fast as we can. There's no tellin' what condition we are going to find her in."

*   *   *   *   *

Michael cut through three demons at a time with every swipe of his mighty greatsword, while Gunthar and Glistinia dispersed of the underlings struggling to flee the Archangel's wrath. The evil minions' defenses did little to do anything more than slow the trio down as they carved their way through the foreboding structure with ease. Along the way the rescuers would open every cell they passed by, freeing as many captured comrades they could find. Many of the guardians they released had not been seen for centuries and were in too bad of shape to join in with the fighting, so they were ordered to return back to the gates of Heaven and heal.

The rescuing angels relentlessly pressed forward. They had successfully cleared the entire level before they discovered a winding stairwell leading to a lower section. With nothing standing in their way, the guardians made their way into the depths of the lower dungeon.

"Hideous." Gunthar commented, as he gestured to a room full of medieval looking instruments of torture.

"Let us find our brother and leave this dreadful place." Michael said, before pushing forward.

After they had passed through the chamber there was only one door remaining. Gunthar reached for the handle and flung the door wide open. There they found their friend, Cazzbein, shackled to the ceiling of the tiny cell by his wrists.

He looked almost unrecognizable. The angel's lean body was covered in open cuts, and his glowing essence trickled steadily from the wounds before gathering in puddles on the ground.

"Cazzbein!" Gunthar cried, genuinely pleased to see his friend again.

"Stand back." Glistinia advised, as she took aim on Cazzbein's restraints.

After she had a clear shot, the angel let loose an arrow from her bow and clipped his shackles clean off. Cazzbein's weakened body then collapsed into Gunthar's waiting arms.

"Ver- Ver-..." Cazzbein muttered.

"He is trying to tell us something." Gunthar said, tilting his friend's head back so that he could talk.

"Vermillion..." He at last managed.

"That traitorous dog!" Gunthar spat. "He is the one responsible for this!"

"I did not see Vermillion during the assault." Glistinia said, as she rubbed her chin in thought.

"He must yet remain in the structure." Gunthar replied, with a twinkle of battle lust in his eyes.

"I want you and Glistinia to scour the structure until you have found him." Michael ordered. "Do not destroy him though. Just make sure that fiend does not escape."

With that command issued, Gunthar and Glistinia bolted out of the cell to find the demon responsible for their friend's condition. Michael looked down at Cazzbein with pity, as the angel slumped over revealing the stumps where his gorgeous wings had once been attached. The mighty Archangel knelt down and looked into his comrade's eyes before issuing a simple command that revived the angel.

"Cazzbein, arise and be healed."

Once Cazzbein heard his commander's words enter his ears, the healing process began. Like a twig budding from a tree, the main bones of his wings sprouted from his torso. He could feel the hollow shafts stretching forth from the main bone with new life and then suddenly shimmer with brilliant light as each and every fine strand grew in, completing the growth of every lost feather. The angel's numerous lacerations instantly sealed themselves, no longer allowing his precious essence to spill out. In a matter of seconds Cazzbein was once again whole.

The guardian slowly stood to his feet, still a bit weak. However, once he had reached an upright position, a wave of strength flowed over his body like the warming beams of a springtime sun.

"AAAHHH!" Cazzbein screamed, as he stretched his wings to their full extension. "I feel invigorated!"

"Good." Michael replied, with a smile. "Because your charge needs you."

"Ethan…" Cazzbein said softly. "Is he in danger?"

"The human is not in any imminent danger, no." Michael assured. "But he is the victim of spiritual attack. I fear if you do not intervene soon, he may slip so far into evil that the effects will have long term influences over him."

"I just need my scimitars." Cazzbein said, with determination. "Vermillion must have them."

"Fear not, my friend. They are in my possession." Michael responded, as he held the weapons out for Cazzbein to take. "Gunthar and Glistinia are in pursuit of your captor as we speak."

In the upper level, the scrawny demon was about to make his escape. He could see the destroyed remains of his thick doors scattered about the entryway. He could not help but wonder why his minions did not lower the gates to further secure the portal. The thought was of no consequence at the moment, however, as Vermillion made a dash for the exit.

"Vermillion!" Gunthar roared. "Stand and fight!"

The pale looking demon merely stopped long enough to flash his enemies an evil grin and then once again raced toward his escape. Seeing their enemy about to get away, Glistinia launched an exploding arrow at the large chain used to hold the gate open." Once it connected, the entryway was showered with a dazzling display of sparks and then the heavy gate slammed shut about a foot in front of the fleeing demon.

"No! Vermillion cried, as he wrapped his boney fingers around the rusted bars and tried with all his might to make it budge.

"Your luck has run dry, fiend." Gunthar spat, as he slowly approached the frightened demon.

"Please! Show mercy!" Vermillion groveled, falling to his knees.

"The same mercy you have shown our brothers and sisters, so you will be shown." Glistinia said, flatly.

"Stand back!" Vermillion warned, as he grabbed his cleaver and waved it about in order to keep the angels at bay.

"I believe he belongs to me!" Came a familiar voice from behind Gunthar and Glistinia.

The two angels stood aside so that the doomed demon could see who had spoken. There with his wings flapping with wild intensity stood a fully healed Cazzbein. The angel stalked the demon with every footfall.

"Stand and fight, villain." Cazzbein said, plainly.

Seeing what his partner had in mind, Gunthar kicked a longsword over to Vermillion that had been left behind from one of the demons they had been defeated earlier, so that the two could combat one another, each armed with dual blades. The weapon came to a stop at Vermillion's knees. The scrawny demon hesitantly plucked the blade from the ground, and then stood to his feet. The angels were not going to let him survive this ordeal, so he figured he might as well go down fighting.

"W-we don't have to do this old friend…" Vermillion stammered.

"Old friend?" Cazzbein asked, in a hostile tone. "Ha! You showed me no such pleasantries while I was in your care that would suggest we are friends, you blasphemous worm!"

"I was merely performing the duties that were assigned to me…" Vermillion explained, as he held both longsword and cleaver out in his shaky hands. "It is just that this blasted war is hell!"

"You are about to learn a new definition of hell, I assure you." Cazzbein said, with venom.

Sensing his nemesis could not be persuaded with words, Vermillion rushed in with the longsword already pulled back for a strike. When he came within range, the demon plunged his blade forward aimed at Cazzbein's torso. With nothing more than a fluid movement, Cazzbein deflected the strike with the scimitar in his left hand and then slashed a clean line through Vermillion's neck with the blade in his right.

The entire battle took less than a second. A clang echoed through the entryway as the demon's sword and cleaver fell to the ground. It was then followed with Vermillion's body falling to the left and his head falling to the right. Silence then followed, as Cazzbein returned his scimitars to their scabbards. And then, as expected, Vermillion's form transformed into a pile of ash as he was transported into the depths of the Lake of Fire.

Afterward Cazzbein turned his attention to his rescuers.

"Thank you, everyone." he said, with the deepest sincerity. "Never has anyone had such companions that would risk all to save them from such a horrible fate. Truly, I am blessed to be able to call all of you my friends."

At first, no one responded. They all knew he had suffered an angel's version of hell at the hands of the demonic horde. But then, Gunthar stepped forward with a broad smile spread across his masculine face.

"You would have done the same for any of us." The big angel said, as he slapped a heavy hand on Cazzbein's shoulder.

"Anthony would have been here as well," Michael assured. "Unfortunately, I had to send him on an assignment that involves your charge, Ethan Brooks. The only way I could get him to accept the mission was to assure him I would come here in his stead."

"Bless him." Cazzbein whispered. "Speaking of which, I must return to my duties."

"I want both of you to accompany him." Michael said to Gunthar and Glistinia. "The demon army is shifting their forces. With the freeing of Lars, we think Lucifer is planning to draw the world of man into another dark era. It is crucial that Ethan Brooks learn his true purpose in the grand scheme of life."

"Glory!" Cazzbein proclaimed.

"It is imperative this assignment be completed successfully." Michael added. "That is why the Lord chose the four of you for this mission."

"Four?" Glistinia asked, seeing that there were only three of them standing before the Archangel.

"Yes." Michael answered. "Anthony will also be accompanying you. Each of you possess a special talent that the other does not. And each of your special talents compliments the talents of your companions. Anthony possesses speed that the rest of you cannot achieve. Gunthar possesses brute strength that is unrivaled among angels. Glistinia possesses deadly accuracy with her bow that brings a desperately needed ranged attack to the group. While Cazzbein is the finest sword bearer the spiritual realm has ever beheld."

Cazzbein turned to consider his friends. Michael had never spoken truer words. Each of them did bring a special ability to the group that none of the others could achieve on their own. Truly the Lord knew what he was doing when he brought them all together.

"Now that your mission has been assigned, I must return to Heaven. Remember, protect Ethan Brooks with every fiber of your being." Michael said, before taking to flight and leaving the group standing in the entryway of the empty fortress.

"There is no time to waste." Cazzbein said, firmly.

"A call to arms then." Gunthar suggested, as he held his big arm out for the others to grasp.

Cazzbein clasped his hand over the big angel's wrist, followed by Glistinia taking hold of his. Once they had assumed the position, the three let loose with a hearty proclamation that filled them with the urge for battle.

"FOR THE GLORY OF THE LORD!"

Chapter 17

Becky had her hands full with a basket of laundry when someone unexpectedly rang the doorbell. She plopped the basket down in the living room next to the couch and then headed to the front door to see who it was. Peeking out around the curtains, Becky saw a man she had never seen before. He had neatly combed, dark brown hair that he wore parted to the right, and also possessed a strong, prominent jaw line. Judging by his dark gray trench coat Becky could tell nothing of the man's intentions, nor who he represented.

Hesitantly, Becky opened the door. As soon as the stranger saw that he had her attention, he pulled his badge out from underneath the trench coat and identified himself.

"Good morning, Mrs. Brooks. I am Detective David Grimes from the Office of Professional Standards." He said, casually. "I'd like to ask you a few questions, if I may."

"The office of what?" Becky asked, not familiar with the name.

"It's actually better known by its previous name, the Internal Affairs Department." David replied. "May I come in?"

What have you done Ethan? Becky thought to herself. "Ethan isn't here." She responded. "And I don't know when he will be back."

"Actually, it's better if we talk without him." David answered. "May I?"

Seeing that she had nothing to hide, and not wanting to appear as if she did, Becky let the man come in.

"What is this about?" She rightly asked.

"Well, Becky…may I call you Becky?" David inquired.

After Becky nodded her approval David continued.

"Well Becky, I don't want to worry you," He said, trying to put the woman at ease. "But I was just curious to know how your husband has been settling into his new assignment?"

"Fine, I suppose." Becky answered. She knew from speaking with Ethan that detectives from the Internal Affairs Department were no friend to the regular police, so she wisely volunteered no more information than she had to.

"Because, it has come to my attention that he has been placed under the command of a couple of pretty unsavory training officers." David said, plainly. "In fact, I have a stack of complaints up to my chin sitting on my desk back at the office ranging anywhere from excessive force to racketeering."

Becky did not give a verbal response. Nevertheless, she didn't need to. She recalled earlier conversions with her husband where he had told her about the dirty cops he had been assigned to work with. She inadvertently broke eye contact with the detective when he had brought mention to the men. The subtle change in demeanor was all Detective Grimes needed to realize he had hit the nail directly on the head. Wisely, he continued with his line of questioning.

In his experience, David had learned that it's best not to go after the suspects directly, but instead, make the family and friends of the suspect squirm until they cough up a valuable piece of information.

"He's told you something, hasn't he?" The detective pressed.

"Ethan doesn't talk about his job much." Becky replied, as honestly as she could. "He doesn't want me to worry."

"Ah, I see." David said. "Well, that's a good rule to live by, I guess. It's a dangerous career after all. If you don't want your wife to worry about you, it would be best not to tell her every detail of your job. It would also be a good rule to live by if you were a dirty cop and didn't want your wife to accidentally slip up and incriminate you."

"What are you implying?" Becky asked, in an angry tone.

"Oh, come on Mrs. Brooks. You know exactly what I'm getting at." David countered, firmly. "Ethan's done something and you're protecting him."

"That's a lie!" Becky yelled. "I think you should leave."

"Well, alright." David said, before slowly turning toward the door. "But I should warn you before I go. If Ethan has done something illegal and happens to tell you about it, you could be brought in on charges for obstruction of justice. On the other hand, if you happen to remember anything or happen to see something from this point on that you would like to tell me about, I'll leave you my card so you can get in touch with me."

Becky took the business card from the detective's hand and then motioned for him to step through the portal.

"Oh, just one more thing…" David said, in a disarming tone. "Do you happen to have a number where I could reach you in case I have any more questions?"

Becky eyed the detective suspiciously before answering.

"It would help to have a number, so that I don't have to pop in unexpectedly." He continued.

Becky could not argue with the sound reasoning. "I have a cell phone number, but I don't have anything to write it down with."

"Allow me." David responded, as he pulled a silver shafted pen from his pocket along with a piece of paper.

Becky hesitantly took the pen and paper, then scribbled her number down for the detective. She then handed them back when she had finished.

"Oh, you can keep the pen." David said as he folded the paper up and slipped it back into his pocket. "Compliments of the Winnebago County Sheriff's Department."

Becky laid the pen down on the table by the front door and again motioned for David to leave. Once he was through the portal, she closed the door and locked the deadbolt behind him. She leaned up against the door for a long moment, as she regained her wits. As much as she hated to admit it, the brief conversation with the detective terrified her. She looked at her hands and could see them visibly trembling.

Have these dirty cops talked Ethan into doing something illegal? Becky thought to herself. *And if so, has she involuntarily become a co-conspirator to a crime?*

She shook her head to clear the thoughts from her mind. In an attempt to forget about the discussion, Becky walked back to the couch where she had left the basket of clothes. She began checking the pockets for anything she didn't want going through the washer. It was a routine she had practiced ever since she accidentally put Ethan's wallet though the washer years ago. The process was going along smoothly until she picked up one of Ethan's jackets. When Becky dove her hand into the inside pocket, she felt something unusual. She pulled it out, and couldn't believe her eyes. In her hand she held a roll of twenty-dollar bills that looked to be over a few hundred dollars.

"Oh, Ethan…" She gasped to herself. "What have you done?"

Detective Grimes sat out in his car for a moment before driving away from the Brook's residence. He couldn't help but smile to himself when he thought about how perfectly he had planted the seed in the mind of Becky Brooks.

"It's only a matter of time now…" He said, before slowly driving away.

*   *   *   *   *

"Where is she?" Tyler screamed into Bob's face, as he slammed his open hand on the stainless-steel tabletop.

"Who?" The greasy looking suspect asked, with an arrogant grin on his face.

Ethan had been watching the whole interrogation through the two-way mirror for the last two hours, and was beginning to get as frustrated as both Tyler and Booker, who were actually performing the questioning. Tyler wanted the rookie detective to "sit this one out," since his emotions were obviously getting the better of him. However, "sitting it out" was causing Ethan to grow even angrier. Nina Mendes was the *only* positive thing to happen to him since making detective. If he couldn't manage to keep the child out of harm's way, Ethan wondered what good it was for him to become a detective in the first place.

"Nina Mendes, you piece of dirt!" Booker repeated for the fifth time since the interrogation started.

"Never heard of her." Bob lied, as he leaned back in his seat in order to put distance between himself and the angry detectives.

Tyler kicked the legs out from underneath Bob's chair, which caused him to fall backwards and hit the back of his head on the wall behind him. Tyler regretted the fact that he was letting this creep get the better of him, but at the same time, it brought him so much pleasure to see the creep in pain.

"Police brutality! Police brutality!" Bob screamed, after he pulled himself off the ground. "I need some help in here!"

Tyler rushed the suspect, grabbing him roughly by the shirt collar, and then rammed him into the wall.

"You have no idea what police brutality is." Tyler growled. "But I'd be willin' to show it to you."

"He's going to blow it and this creep is going to walk!" Dartamus screamed into Ethan's ear. "You know what you have to do!"

It was at that moment the interrogation room's intercom crackled to life.

"Detective Lynch, can I see you for a moment?" Ethan asked.

Tyler could not help but feel a little irritated when he heard the rookie beckoning him. If Ethan had anything to say about his interrogation skills, he was going to get a taste of the punishment Bob was about to feel.

The door flew open hard and Tyler stepped into the hallway. He could tell by the look on Ethan's face, the rookie was chewing at the bit and wanted to get involved. Maybe that wasn't such a bad thing, since he himself was growing angrier with every passing minute.

"What is it, rookie?" Tyler asked, in an irritated tone. "I'm about to break this guy!"

"Really?" Ehtan asked. "Because from out here, it looks like he's really pushing your last nerve. And don't forget, Nina is still out there somewhere. We still don't know what condition she's in. Every second counts."

"Yeah, well…do you have any better ideas than what I'm already doing?" Tyler asked.

"Actually, I do." Ethan replied. "Cut him loose."

"No! No! No!" Tyler answered. "We cut him loose now and the first thing he's gonna do is kill Nina and dump her body."

"You said you wanted to be able to trust me. You said you wanted me to get some dirt on myself." Ethan reminded Tyler. "If you let me handle this investigation from her on out, I will let you have all the dirt you're looking for."

"And if you're wrong?" Tyler inquired.

"If I can't get Bob to tell us where Nina is…" Ethan began. "Then I'll resign."

"What?" Tyler had to ask, not believing his ears.

"You heard me right.' Ethan responded. "If I can't get him to tell us where Nina is, then I will resign. To tell you the truth, if I can't get this done, then I don't even want to be a cop anymore."

Tyler looked into Ethan's eyes and knew that he was serious. The rookie hadn't had a very good time slipping into his new position, but Tyler noticed as of late he showed a lot of potential. Either scenario worked out well for him. The rookie either found the girl and solved the case, or he didn't find her and quit, leaving Booker and himself to continue their underhanded deeds.

"Alright, rookie. If that's the way you want it." Tyler agreed. "Just tell me what you need."

After a brief conversation, Ethan headed downstairs to the motor pool to sign out the undercover police van that they had used when they picked up Silky, while Tyler reentered the interrogation room.

"Well…today must be your lucky day." Tyler said, in a mock tone. "Someone just paid your bail."

"What?!" Booker asked, heatedly. "He hasn't even been-"

With a wave of his hand, Tyler motioned for Booker not to finish his sentence. Picking up on the cue, Booker bit his tongue.

"Who paid my bail?" Bob asked, buying into the lie. "Was it Tasha?"

"I don't know." Tyler fibbed. "They don't tell us that information."

"Well, I can't say I'm sorry to be leaving." Bob said, haughtily, as he stood to his feet and pushed the chair under the table. "It's been real…it's been fun…it just hasn't been real fun."

"Ha! Ha! Ha! Tyler laughed in a fake intonation. "Well, Bob, hopefully this will all get worked out."

"I'm sure it will." Bob said, as he made his way out of the room, leaving the two detectives alone.

"Do you mind tellin' me what that was all about?" Booker had to ask before he spontaneously combusted.

"The rookie says he has a plan." Tyler answered.

"You're leavin' this case up to the rookie?" Booker inquired, with the look of disbelief displayed on his face.

"I am, since he told me he would either find the kid or quit the force." Tyler replied, as he took a seat and folded his hands behind his head.

When Tyler saw the scowl on Booker's face suddenly turn into a white toothed smile, he knew his partner was pleased with his decision.

Back downstairs, Ethan pulled the undercover police van out of the motor pool and onto Winnebago Avenue. He knew Bob would be exiting the building soon and that preparation time was limited. Quickly, he drove the van over to his car and hopped out. Ethan then ran to the trunk of his car and opened it up. Searching the trunk as fast as he could, the young man eventually found the belongings he was searching for. The objects of his interest were a black ski mask, some overalls, and a winter coat that he used when clearing snow off the driveway of his home, and a simple roll of duct tape.

"You know what you have to do." Dartamus whispered into his ear, egging him on.

Ethan hastily tucked the ski mask into the back pocket of his jeans, grabbed the other articles of clothing, and then ran back to the driver's side of the van. He then speedily drove the van onto East State Street and waited for Bob to exit the front of the building.

Ethan had a feeling Bob would be taking a bus home, since he was brought to the station house compliments of the Winnebago County Sheriff's Department. Now, it was merely a matter of waiting.

Within a time span of about five minutes Ethan saw his target emerging from the police station. During that time, Ethan had already managed to climb into the overalls and winter coat, so as to hide the outfit that Bob had already seen him wearing earlier that night. Just as he suspected, Bob turned in the direction of the bus stop. He then slowly drove about half a block ahead of Bob and shifted the van into park. Once done, Ethan jumped into the back and quickly slipped the ski mask over his head. After doing so, Ethan placed the roll of duct tape underneath the back of the driver's seat, so that he could reach it in a hurry whenever it was needed. When he had finished his hasty preparations, the young detective cracked the sliding side door just enough so that he could keep an eye on Bob's position. When the suspect was within a few feet of Ehtan's location, he sprung into action, and leapt out of the van's sliding door like a paratrooper dropping behind enemy lines.

"Hold it right there, scumbag!" Ethan yelled, before grabbing Bob by his neck with both hands and flinging him into the van.

Ethan tossed Bob with such velocity his face crashed into the sheet metal on the opposite side of the van. He then climbed in behind the greasy suspect, closed the door, and reached for the duct tape. Bob was in such a surprised state of mind that he barely put up a fight. By the time he realized what was transpiring, Ethan already had his wrists and ankles bound together with the multi-functional duct tape.

"Wh-what are you doing?" Bob stammered.

Ethan did not respond. Instead, he went about his business of binding Bob's wrists to a steel ring that was welded to the floor of the van used for securing unruly criminals.

"Wh-who a-are you?" Bob asked, in a concerned tone.

"I'm a friend of Nina Mendes, you piece of human filth." Ethan answered, in an eerily calm tone. "And I'm going to find out what you did with her."

"You can't do this!" Bob screamed, in a panicky voice.

"Give me one good reason why." Ethan demanded.

"Aren't you a cop?" Bob rightly assumed, since he had left the interrogation room only moments before.

"I never said anything about being a cop." Ethan responded, before slipping a piece of duct tape over Bob's mouth. "Now shut up until I ask you to speak again."

Ehtan could see the fear dancing wildly in Bob's eyes. It was the fear of someone who had no choice but to relinquish their well-being into the hands of someone who meant to do them great harm. Ethan wondered if Nina shared that look when Bob had abducted her. Whether she did or whether she did not was of no consequence, because Ehtan was going to find out where she was in a matter of moments.

Ethan climbed back into the driver's seat and pulled away from the curb. The entire snatching took only a few minutes, and was performed so fast that it raised no attention from anyone passing by, much to his relief. He drove Bob south for several long miles. They eventually came to a run-down baseball diamond near the Rock River that hadn't been used for many years. The airport was only a few miles away and occasionally the area would be drowned out by the sound of a jet taking off. Ethan figured this would be as good a place as any to perform *his* interrogation, since there was nobody around for miles. Even if someone did happen by, the sound from the aircraft would drown out any screams Bob was about to make.

Ethan shifted the van into park and then climbed into the back with his captive. He was pleased to see Bob's arrogant expression had been replaced with nervous beads of perspiration rolling down his bald head. The sensation of fear would help in heightening Bob's senses, and therefore get him to feel everything Ethan was about to do to him that much more. Ethan welcomed this. Since Bob was not trained to resist torture, he should give him the information he needed quickly.

Slow and methodically, Ethan pulled a brown paper bag from the passenger seat and then set it between him and his prisoner. He unwrapped the top and then dove his hand inside to produce its contents. The first tool to emerge was a simple nutcracker. He made sure Bob got a good look at the utensil and then placed it on the floor of the van. Next Ethan pulled out a rusty pair of pliers and placed them on the floor of the van next to the nutcracker. After doing so, he then removed a pocket knife with a three-inch blade. Ethan was hoping the interrogation would not last long enough for him to have to use the knife. In fact, he was not even sure how far he was willing to go to get the answers from Bob. Ethan's heart was already working overtime with the feelings of both fear and anger. The only thought that kept him going at this point was the thought of getting Nina home safely.

Ethan reached for the strip of tape covering Bob's face and ripped it off, tearing bits of stubble out of his captive's face as he did. Once his mouth was uncovered Bob screamed like a terrified school girl.

"HHEEEELLLP! SOMEBODY HHEEEELLLP!"

"Scream all you want." Ehtan said, in a relaxed tone. "There's nobody around for miles to hear you."

When his captor made no attempt to silence him, Bob had no choice but to believe him. He then discontinued his initial thought and began struggling against his restraints, trying feverishly to put distance between him and the masked stranger. Nevertheless, the duct tape held firm.

"Wh-what do you w-want from me?" Bob asked, in a pitiful voice.

"I already told you what I want." Ethan responded, in a cold tone lacking any feeling. He then plucked the nutcracker off the floor of the van and held it out for Bob to get a good look at. "Nina Mendes. Where is she?"

An innocent man would have responded with, *"Who?"* or *"I don't know what you're talking about."* But when Bob grew silent, Ethan knew his helpless guest was trying to think of an appropriate lie that would aid him in getting out of the predicament he now found himself in.

"He's going to lie to you!" Dartamus yelled, fueling Ethan's anger. "You know what you have to do!"

"Wrong answer." Ethan growled at his captive, before quickly slipping one of his fingers into the nut cracking device.

As Ethan squeezed the two ends of the tool together, a sickening crunch filled the van's cargo area, as Bob's index finger was broken in two.

"AAAAHHHH?" Bob shrieked. "Wait! Stop! Please!"

"I'm only going to ask you *nine* more times, and then I'm going to get angry and crank it up a notch." Ethan growled. "Where is Nina Mendes?"

Once again Bob did not answer. It was not because he was trying to be brave, but rather self-preservation that caused him to remain silent. He didn't know what his captor would do to him after revealing that he indeed had anything to do with the girl's disappearance. However, the silence only served to fuel Ethan's anger all the more, so once again, Ethan put the nutcracker to use on Bob's fingers. This time it was the middle digit that was snapped in two with a nauseating crack.

"AAAAHHHH?" Bob screamed, before banging his own head time and time again into the wall of the van.

Ethan wondered if the reason he did this was to distract his mind from the throbbing pain in his hand or if he was merely trying to knock himself unconscious. Either scenario mattered little to him though as he slid Bob's ring finger into the device for another round.

"Wait!" Bob shouted.

"Are you going to tell me what I want to know?" Ehtan growled, through the mouth hole of the ski mask. "Because I can keep this up all night."

"I'll tell you where the girl is!" Bob said anxiously. "Just promise me you won't turn me in to the cops!"

Ethan gave his response in the form of yet another broken finger. Only this time, he proceeded to pluck the rusty pair of pliers off the floor and twist Bob's nose from side to side. The man's snout snapped in two under the pressure, causing a stream of crimson to flow forth from both nostrils.

"What are you doing?!" Bob yelled. "I said I would tell you where she is!"

"You don't get to make demands of me! Ethan scolded.

"Such arrogance!" Dartamus shrieked. "Kill him!" Without realizing what he was doing, Ethan tossed the pliers to the ground and quickly picked up the knife. His anger was getting the best of him. In the heat of the moment Ethan had forgotten right from wrong. And more importantly, he had forgotten who he was.

"Wait! I'll tell you!" Bob yelled, hysterically. "The girl is being kept in my basement! There's a hidden storage area behind the far wall! Just please stop!"

Ethan had the tip of the knife held less than an inch away from Bob's left eye. He had no memory of taking hold of the weapon, nor did he know what he had intended to do with it. He was grateful, however, that the tactic was enough to frighten Bob into talking. With the unpleasantness at an end, Ethan began slowly moving the knife away. It wasn't until the salivating demon on his shoulder began urging him on once more that he stopped.

"Wait! You have to kill him!" Dartamus ordered. "You can't risk him discovering who you are! KILL HIM!"

The evil thoughts made sense to him. He couldn't let Bob go after this. How was he going to explain Bob's condition to Tyler and Booker? His mind was a jumble of mixed emotions and his heart was pumping so fast that he could hear it in his ears. The plan had been thrown together so hastily that Ethan had not thought of an appropriate exit strategy. Maybe killing Bob was the best solution.

Slowly, Ethan began moving the knife toward Bob again.

"What are you doing?!" Bob asked, frantically. "I told you where she is! You have no reason to do this!"

"Yes…" Dartamus cooed. "Do it…"

The negative energy created from Bob and Ethan's fear was so exhilarating the little imp was in ecstasy. In fact, he was so consumed with evil bliss that he hadn't realized another spiritual being had entered the van behind him. With one fluid motion Cazzbein, Ethan's rightful guardian, had brought both his scimitars down in an arcing swoop that sheared the demon's wings clean off.

"AAAHHHH!" The pudgy demon yelped, as he fell back through the fan's wall in agony. When Dartamus finally regained his thoughts, he saw Cazzbein standing over him with scimitars in hand. The filthy little spirit was wise enough to know he was nowhere near the caliber of fighter as the angel was, so he made no move to unsheathe his own blade. Wisely, he bolted from the area as fast as his chubby, little legs could carry him never looking back.

"Shall we make chase?" Gunthar inquired, war hammer already in his powerful grasp.

"No." Cazzbein replied, as he sheathed his blades. "I want Hunter to know I am free once more."

With that settled, Cazzbein dove back through the van's wall to aid his charge. Leaning in close, the angel whispered soothing words into Ethan's ear that he knew would calm him.

"There's no need to continue." The angel said, softly. "You have Becky to think of."

As if a switch had suddenly been flipped on in his head, Ethan moved the knife away. The voice of reason had returned to him. His pulse slowly returned to normal, and his feelings of anger had unexplainably fled. The young man still did not know what he was going to do about his current circumstance, but he did know he need not make it any worse.

Ethan tossed the knife back into the brown paper bag, and proceeded to pick up the other objects he had used to extract the information from his prisoner. He then tossed the utensils into the passenger seat of the van and placed a new piece of duct tape over Bob's mouth. After doing so, he climbed back into the driver's seat and drove back to Bob's house.

Ethan made sure to drive the van into the garage so that the neighbors would not see him unloading Bob out of the side door. He then directed Bob to the basement so that he could personally show him where Nina was being hidden.

"Where is she?" Ethan demanded.

"S-she's behind that wall." Bob stuttered.

Ethan used the rest of the roll of duct tape to bind Bob's arms around one of the supporting pillars in the basement. When he was sure Bob could not escape, Ethan ran to the area where his prisoner had indicated. There had been some shelving that had recently been hung on a newly made wall. Nobody would have been able to see this no matter how thorough an inspection had been conducted. If Ethan hadn't known exactly where to look, he would have easily missed it as well.

Hastily, Ethan tore the shelving and drywall down. On the other side there was a dark, shallow cubbyhole. He quickly pulled a flashlight from his pocket and clicked it on. When he discovered the storage area's contents, he finally breathed a sigh of relief.

There Nina was, hunkered down in the furthest corner. The child was dirty and shaken, but other than a few scrapes, she was relatively unscathed. Apparently, Ethan and his partners had jumped on the call fast enough to where Bob had no time to harm her.

Ethan lifted the girl to her feet and walked her into the lighting of the basement. When the child's eyes had adjusted to the brightness, she looked at her rescuer. Even the confines of the ski mask could not hide the kindness in Ethan's blue eyes. When a gentle smile formed on her dirty little face, Ethan could tell Nina knew who he was. Before she had time to speak, he placed a finger over her month to silence her. "This is another one of our secrets." He said, in a calming tone.

When the child nodded her agreement Ethan breathed another sigh of relief. It was at that moment Ehtan did something he had never done before.

He thanked God.

*   *   *   *   *

Unknown to the humans and the angelic guardians, the entire scene had taken place under the watchful eye of Nefareus, one of Mistress Vixanna's many scouts. As silent as death itself, the demon wafted away from the area to give his mistress an account of what he had just witnessed. With any luck, a reward would be in his future.

*   *   *   *   *

After Ethan had freed Nina, he had no other choice but to call his partners back to the crime scene. When Tyler and Booker made their way through the back door, they saw Ethan and Nina sitting at the kitchen table. Tyler was wise enough to figure out that the rookie had done something underhanded in order to find the child just by seeing the discarded ski mask laying on the table.

"What happened, Brooks?" He asked, plainly.

"I found the girl." Ethan replied evasively.

"Looks like ya used a little old school justice to do it." Booker added, after picking up the ski mask from the table and displaying it for the group to see.

"Well, I got a little dirt on me now." Ethan responded.

"Maybe more than a little." Tyler said, as he took the ski mask from Booker's hand.

"Do you think you can cover for me?" Ethan asked, hopefully.

Tyler spun the ski mask around in his hand as he thought.
When the rookie first joined his team he wanted nothing
more than to send him packing. However, as of late, Ethan
has proven himself to be a valuable member. Now that the
rookie has done something that needs covering up, Tyler
believes he can be a trusted partner as well.

"How bad is it?" Tyler finally asked.

*   *   *   *   *

Beads of nervous perspiration ran down Bob's bald head
as the jailor scooped up the morning paper, grabbed his ring
of keys and then began leading him from the booking area to
his cell block. His already sore and broken fingers throbbed
with a great deal of pain after being aggravated once more by
the officer in charge of his fingerprinting. His broken snout
had been roughly set back into place and taped into a splint,
causing dark bags to appear under his eyes from the soreness.
Add those aspects to the orange jumpsuit that was two sizes
too small, and at the present, Bob was quite a miserable sight
to behold.

The jailor fumbled around with his key ring for a moment
until he found the key he was searching for. After doing so,
he unlocked the barred door and slid it open where he was
met by twenty rough looking inmates.

"Good morning, everyone!" The jailor shouted loudly,
before plopping the morning paper down on the day room

table. "I just wanted to let you fellas know you can all sleep easy tonight, since we finally caught that kidnapper!"

"Kidnapper?" One of the meanest looking inmates asked, in an angry tone.

"Oh yeah!" The jailor bellowed. "It's all right there on the front pages of the paper."

The convicts all gathered around the paper to get a look at what the jailor was referring to. There on the front page was a huge color photo of Bob's mugshot, complete with his broken nose.

"Oh, and before I forget." The jailor continued, as he nudged Bob into the room. "Here's the newest addition to your cell block."

It took no time at all for the convicts to figure out what the guard was hinting around about. The jailor could not outright tell the prisoners to make life miserable for Bob, since he was bound by law to guarantee the safety of all the men in his care. Nevertheless, the message was received loud and clear. Once the barred door slammed shut behind Bob, the convicts slowly gathered around the newest inmate. It was then that Bob realized what it meant to do hard time.

Chapter 18

Hunter worked his blades with utter precision as he sparred with four of the best warriors his legion had to offer. Truth be told, he toyed with the foursome and could have easily ended the contest at any moment had he any other matter to occupy his time with.

One demon came at him with a high thrust aimed at his neck while another attacked simultaneously from his right flank with a slashing attack directed toward his ribs. It took little effort for Hunter to parry the blade away from his ribs with his saber before eluding the sword tip aimed at his neck by stepping slightly to the side. After doing so, the crafty demon wrapped the attacker's arm up within his own before he had time to pull away, and then unceremoniously flung him to the ground where he landed with tremendous impact.

Before the other two minions had time to begin their attack Hunter went on the offensive. The pale-haired demon bolted toward the pair with blinding speed and then fell to his knees, letting his momentum carry his chiseled frame between them. As he passed by, he gashed deep lines through their exposed knees that caused them to collapse into one another, consequently taking them out of the mock battle.

"This is the best my legion has to offer?" Hunter scoffed, as he returned to his feet.

With every successful attack routine he performed scenes of his battle with Cazzbein taunted him. The ivory-haired sword bearer knew he would not improve his skills unless he had a more worthy opponent, and that thought frustrated him to no end. If the opportunity ever presented itself again that he may face his archrival in swordplay, he wanted his skills to be as sharp as his blades. Hunter knew that goal would be unobtainable with the low caliber opponents he faced at this moment.

"Master!" A familiar voice cried, causing Hunter to turn his concern away from his brooding.

When he turned to see who had called for him, Hunter saw his faithful servant Dartamus running toward him. The fact that the imp chose to run rather than fly did not escape his attention.

"Why do you dare bother me while I spar?" Hunter growled.

"A thousand pardons my master!" Dartamus begged. "But you ordered me to summon you if Cazzbein made his presence known to me!"

A white toothed smile then overtook Hunter's sharp features. Before saying another word to the imp, he turned his concern again to his four sparring partners.

"On guard!" He commanded, causing them to raise their weapons for another wave of swordplay.

Once they were at the ready Hunter began his assault. With fierce determination ablaze within his eyes he sprinted toward them. Not wanting to be taken by surprise, the group swung their weapons in every direction. Hunter knew their attacks were simply executed out of desperation.

As if seeing their weapons coming at him in slow motion, Hunter weaved around each of their blades, often missing their deadly, razor-sharp edges by less than an inch. Once he successfully eluded their swords, he countered with a slash to whatever appendage presented itself. The massacre that followed looked like helpless chunks of meat being diced to pieces in a blender.

When the onslaught was complete, Hunter stood within the middle of the group's battered bodies, wholly victorious.

"Is that wise, master?" Dartamus queried. "They are, after all, the best in the legion.

"They will heal." Hunter said, firmly, as he wiped the essence from his serrated dagger on one of the fallen opponent's robes. "Where are your wings?"

"Trophies for our enemy." Dartamus replied, as he hung his head in defeat.

"I gather Cazzbein is at Ethan Brooks' side once more?" Hunter asked, as he sheathed his blades and walked over to stand before his minion.

"Yes, my master." Dartamus answered. "I had nearly influenced the human to commit murder before the guardian appeared."

"So, the human has started down the path to ruin, then?" Hunter inquired, as he thought.

"I fear my work will be for naught, however, now that Cazzbein has returned." The pudgy imp was sure to put in.

"The angel will soon be taken care of!" Hunter snarled. "We shall soon partake in the battle to end all battles!"

"Yes, my master." Dartamus replied, as he backed away from the hostile demon. The plump, little imp had never seen Hunter so consumed by an adversary in all the thousands of years he had been in service to him. The sight of which was terrifying.

"How soon before you are prepared to accompany me?" Hunter asked, with purpose.

"I should be healed within the hour." Dartamus replied. "Are you sure you want to join me on this venture?"

"Absolutely." Hunter answered. "I shall need for you to keep an accurate account of our duel. If I defeat Cazzbein, I want victory ballads to be written in my honor, so that my acclaim shall ring loudly in the ears of our brothers and sisters. Likewise, shall I fall to his blades, I desire for everyone to know I at least had the courage to challenge the guardian in battle."

"You shall not fall, my master." Dartamus said. "For if you are in need of aid, I can lend you a hand."

"No!" Hunter replied, heatedly. "I desire no aid! I want nothing to sully our duel! There shall be no excuses as to-"

"Captain!" Came the call from an unknown demon that suddenly burst onto the scene, cutting Hunter off in mid-sentence.

"Impudent whelp! Is this how you regard your superior?" Hunter spat with venom. "I should have you flogged for interrupting me!"

"I am here under the authority of Mistress Vixanna." The demon responded, showing little concern for Hunter's threat. "By her orders, I am not to be harmed."

"Vixanna sends you on a fool's errand, buffoon!" Hunter shot back angrily, before unsheathing his saber and placing the tip against the rude demon's throat. "For if you persist in testing my patience, I shall send your head back as a gift for our mistress!"

The demon weighed his options carefully before continuing. When better judgment at last overshadowed his pride, he refrained from displaying any more arrogance.

"Forgive me captain." The demon finally apologized. "Mistress Vixanna summons you to her chambers."

"Off with you before I lose my temper." Hunter spat, returning his saber to its sheath.

The demon wasted little time in exiting Hunter's domain, thankful to have his head still attached.

"Vixanna toys with me." The ivory-haired demon snarled. "How dare she give lackeys the authority for which to harass me."

"Whatever could she want now?" Dartamus queried.

"My end, no doubt." Hunter replied.

"Why would she want to harm the only demon to survive the bowels of the Abyss?" Dartamus had to ask. "You are a hero to the demonic army."

"That is reason within itself." Hunter answered.

"I know I am of little intellect compared to the likes of you, master." Dartamus began. "But I have to admit, I do not follow."

Hunter stepped away from his servant as he gathered his words.

"Vixanna openly revealed her true intentions for my last quest, after everyone had cleared her throne room from my celebration gathering, Dartamus." Hunter responded, while holding his head up high. "She never meant for me to survive."

"Why would she want that? The little imp asked, truly perplexed.

"Don't you see?" Hunter snapped. "Now that I have proven myself to be so valuable, my exploits have reached the ears of the prince of darkness himself. She is now feeling threatened by my prominence."

"She is truly a fiend!" Dartamus retorted. "I suppose one would have to be in order to hold her position as long as she has."

"Yes." Hunter replied. "We could learn from her."

"Nevertheless, we still do not know why she has summoned you." Dartamus said, plainly.

"Whatever the reason…" Hunter began, as he turned to face his servant. "I can assure you it will not be pleasant."

*   *   *   *   *

After Ethan had explained by what means he was able to locate Nina, Tyler and Booker agreed to cover for him. Since Bob did not know who his abductor had been, they all three put their heads together and concocted a story that would best explain the situation without getting any of them in trouble. Tyler and Booker both had alibis that could be corroborated by half the Winnebago County Sheriff's Department, since they never left the station house after releasing Bob. The only aspect of their story that could not be explained away with ease was Ethan's whereabouts.

At first, Tyler suggested telling everyone that Ethan was never called in. However, they all knew Bob would squeal about Ethan being at the scene at the time of his arrest, so that explanation would simply not do. Not to mention the fact that Ethan's phone records would show that he got the call, and his name was on the vehicle sign out sheet for the police van.

Tyler then argued that even though Ehtan was called in, that still did not mean he was the one that interrogated Bob. It did not help matters that Bob was roughed up in a van moments after Ethan logged one out through the motor pool. Tyler agreed to put in his report that he sent Ethan home after the arrest, but for that story to truly work they would have to make the vehicle logout sheet disappear. For that to happen, each of them would have to work together as a team.

"We all know what we have to do." Tyler said, with determination, as he watched the officer behind the desk of the motor pool cage carefully. "We'll only have one chance at this.

"What happens if we get caught?" Ethan asked, nervously.

"That's not an option." Tyler shot back. "Now, is everybody ready?"

"Ready as I'll ever be." Booker answered.

"Same here." Ethan responded.

"Alright, let's do this." Tyler said, before handing Ethan a large Styrofoam cup filled with steaming hot coffee.

Like a well-trained thespian, Ethan headed up to the motor pool cage with hot beverage in hand. Once he got to the counter, he set the coffee down and rang the buzzer that would call for the officer in charge to help him.

"Yeah?" The officer asked, in an irritated intonation.

Ethan welcomed the man's snotty attitude. It would help to ease his conscience for what he and his crew were about to do to the man.

"I'm here to log van #23 back in." Ethan replied.

"Here ya go." The officer said, as he flung a clipboard onto the counter and slid it through the opening in the cage.

As Ethan signed his name onto the sheet, Booker walked up behind him right on cue. Ethan finished his business and walked away from the counter, intentionally leaving his coffee behind. Once he had left, Booker asked for the sign out sheet for which the officer attending the desk responded by sliding him the same clipboard he had previously given Ethan. While Booker feigned the act of signing his name to the sheet, Tyler strode up to Booker's side right on time.

"The rookie told me you started another fight with him today." Tyler lied, with a stone-cold expression on his face.

"What of it?" Booker asked, in a rehearsed angry tone.

"What is it with you and him?" Tyler snapped back.

"I told you I don't like him!" Booker played along.

"Well, why don't you start a fight with me?" Tyler asked, as he moved to push Booker. As he did so, Tyler made sure he knocked the Styrofoam cup full of coffee all over the logout sheet and counter.

"Now look what ya did!" Booker barked, as he grabbed the sheet from the clipboard and began cleaning up the mess with it.

"Hey! What are you two doing?" The officer behind the cage asked heatedly. "I need that sheet for my records!"

"Oh man! I'm sorry!" Booker apologized, doing his best not to laugh from the charade.

"Here, give me that!" Tyler said, before snatching the paper away from Booker's hand, trying as hard as he could to crumple it up. After doing so, he faked trying to straighten it back out again on the counter. While he did, the wet paper easily tore in two.

"Give that document to me, detective! Right now!" The officer screamed, while he held his hand through the opening in the cage.

Tyler handed the two soggy pieces of paper back to the officer, making sure both pieces were unreadable before relinquishing it. The officer took them from Tyler and spread them out on the table where they tore into yet another piece.

"Just great!" The man yelled. "Now this is just useless wads of trash! What is it with you two? Why don't you take your fight outside and leave me alone?"

"Sorry, man." Booker said, in mock sympathy.

"Yeah, man, I'm sorry too." Tyler added. "We'll get out of here and leave you to your business."

As soon as the two rounded the corner and were out of the man's view, they busted out into insane laughter. They continued laughing until they reached the parking lot area where Ethan waited anxiously.

"I take it everything went alright?" He asked hopefully.

"Rookie, you got nothing to worry about." Tyler replied, between laughs. "Unless he goes around the entire precinct and gets everybody that originally signed that list to sign a new one, you're off the hook."

"That's awesome." Ethan said, with a sigh.

"I don't know, rookie, if the police force doesn't suit ya, maybe you should go to Hollywood and be a star." Booker joked.

"Hey now, I think we all should be nominated for an Oscar after that performance." Tyler interjected.

"What about the phone records?" Ethan felt the need to ask.

Once Tyler's snickering died down, he gave his response.

"There's really no way of getting a hold of the phone records without exposing you." He answered. "We'll just have to roll the dice your name won't come up in the investigation."

"Bob's already seen ya, rookie." Booker added. "It ain't like ya can go back in time and change that. The phone records are unimportant."

"You're right." Ethan conceded. "Thanks guys."

"No problem." Tyler said, as he slapped a hand on Ethan's back. "But just remember, now that we stuck our necks out for you, when the time comes, you have to get our backs too. We're a team. And a team protects its members."

"You got it." Ethan replied. Although his words sounded convincing, the rookie detective's mind was filled with dread at the thought of keeping all of Tyler and Booker's secrets silent. His new allies have inevitably tied his hands. "What's next?"

"I don't know about you, rookie, but we're heading home." Tyler answered.

"That sounds like music to my ears." Booker put in. "I only got about two hours of sleep before I got the call."

"Actually, that does sound good." Ethan admitted. "I guess I'll see you guys tomorrow."

After Ehtan made it to his car, he rotated the key in the ignition and sat in the driver's seat while the engine idled. As he waited in the automobile, Ethan could not help but feel an overwhelming sense of relief come over him. He saved a young girl's life this day, and from the outcome, may have very well altered the rest of her life, due to the fact that Nina was taken into the care of Child Services. Taking her out of the dangers of her mother's filthy world will forever change Nina's life for the better. When he finally embraced his satisfaction, Ethan shifted the car into drive and drove home.

*   *   *   *   *

Becky ran to the living room and hastily took a seat in the easy chair facing the front door when she heard Ethan's car pull into the driveway. She dreaded the expected confrontation she was about to have with her husband, but knew it was necessary in order to keep him from falling further into trouble to the point that he would not be able to get out.

Becky wondered what sort of position she should be sitting in when Ethan first laid eyes on her. She didn't want to come across as being a controlling old nag, so she leaned back in her chair and crossed her legs casually, hoping the posture would put him at ease. The woman knew her husband had a weakness for her curvaceous lower limbs, so she pulled her skirt hem above her tanned knees and prayed they would lull him into a decent mood. When the door at last opened, Becky jumped. Obviously, she was more nervous than even she cared to admit.

"Becky…" Ethan stopped in mid-sentence when he saw five hundred dollars spread out on the coffee table in front of his wife. "What's this?"

"That's what I'd like to know." Becky responded, in a calm tone.

"Well, where did you get it?" He asked, as he closed the door and took a seat on the couch.

"I pulled it out of the inside pocket of your jacket." The woman replied, in an intonation that suggested she searched for answers.

"Oh, no." Ethan at last responded, when he remembered the money Tyler had taken off Shifty, the Gangster Apostle they had shook down in the alley the day before.

"So, you remember now?" Becky asked.

"Yes, I remember." Ethan answered, as he began scooping the money off of the tabletop. He had meant to be rid of the money by now, but with all the excitement of the past few days, he had found himself too distracted.

"So, where did this money come from?" Becky pressed.

Ethan stopped what he was doing and eyed his wife for a moment. She had never urged him to speak about his job before, and the request took the young man by surprise.

"You know I don't like to talk about the job, because I don't want to-"

"-because you don't want to *worry* me?" Becky said, in a sarcastic tone, finishing her husband's sentence. "It's too late for that."

"What do you mean?" Ethan rightly inquired.

Becky placed the business card she had received from the Internal Affairs detective on the coffee table and slid it over to Ethan.

"A friend of yours came to visit me yesterday." She answered, as her eyes welled with tears. "I wanted to gather my thoughts before asking you about it. That is why I didn't bring it up after you came home from work last night. Now tell me where this money came from, Ethan."

Ethan plucked the card off the table and read it quietly to himself. It was then that he realized why his wife was so concerned. He let the card fall back onto the table as he thought for a reply that would put his wife at ease.

"It was money that Tyler took off a street thug." The man answered, honestly. "He demanded I take it."

"Oh, come on, Ehtan!" Becky snapped. "You just took drug money from some dope dealer like you were his supplier?"

"No!" Ethan shot back. "It's not like that! Tyler wanted me to take it, and I told him I wouldn't."

"Then how did this money get into your jacket?" Becky queried in a heated tone.

"I told him I didn't want the money, and he told me I had to take it before he and Booker could trust me! And then he slid it into my pocket!" Ethan answered, truthfully.

Becky could tell by the sincerity in her husband's voice he spoke the truth.

"I meant to get rid of it before bringing it home by filing it into evidence, but this job has me flying around by the seat of my pants at times, and I forgot about it." Ethan went on to explain.

"You do know this was an illegal act, don't you?" Becky said, as she took Ethan's hand within her own.

"You don't understand…" Ethan replied. "I have to depend on these guys with my life. If they didn't trust me and wanted me dead, all they would have to do is send me into a drug house to get shot up. The gangsters would do their dirty work for them and they would walk away like nothing ever happened."

Becky understood her husband's dilemma and gave him a hug.

"There is a way out, you know." She said, when the thought suddenly occurred to her.

"What?" Ethan asked.

"You can work with this detective to bring Tyler and Booker down." The woman replied, as she moved away from Ethan's embrace and slid the card closer to him.

"No! No way! Ethan shouted. "I worked hard to get to where I'm at! If I turn on a couple of fellow cops, my career is over!"

"It sounds like these cops you are protecting are worse than the criminals you lock up on a daily basis!" Becky responded, matching Ethan's volume. "You'd be doing the world a lot of good ridding the streets of them!"

Ethan grew silent for a moment as he seriously gave the idea some thought.

"I can't do it." He at last replied.

"Then you will probably go to jail with them." Becky added, as she plopped back into her seat. "Because this detective isn't going to stop. I would suggest turning on them before they serve *you* up to him." If they would be willing to get you killed, what's to say they wouldn't set you up for this detective to take down?"

Ethan did not immediately respond, as the weight of his wife's words hit him hard. She had never made more sense than she did with that one simple statement. Tyler and Booker would turn on him at the drop of a hat. They held no loyalty to anyone but themselves.

"Just think about what I've said." Becky advised, before kissing Ethan on the cheek. "Let me know what you decide. "I think that's only fair. And in the meantime, I want you to come with me to church this Sunday."

Ethan watched in silence as his wife walked into the kitchen. When she was gone, he picked the business card off the table once more and looked it over as the pros and cons of contacting the detective bounced around in his head.

"This could not have come at a worse time..." He muttered to himself, as he reflected on the brutal interrogation he had just given Bob. Afterward, he slipped the card into his pants pocket and followed after his wife.

On the table by the front door there sat a silver shafted pen given to Becky by the Internal Affairs detective. The writing contraption seemed innocent enough as it lay there on the table oblivious to the conversation that had just taken place in its presence. However, at closer inspection, one would see that it was not merely a simple writing tool. But in fact, it was a sophisticated miniature microphone used for eavesdropping. The pen had not been given to Becky out of generosity. It had been shrewdly planted in the residence for the sake of conducting an investigation by gathering some much needed information.

Out in the street in front of the home there sat a van with vinyl lettering on the side that read, 'Joe's Plumbing.' It was not a plumber's vehicle though, because a plumber would have no use for the state-of-the-art surveillance equipment located in its cargo compartment. Seated in one of the chairs behind the control panel was Detective David Grimes of the Internal Affairs Department.

A satisfied smile spread across the detective's face when he overheard the conversation take place between the young married couple. He fully understood the dilemma Ethan Brooks found himself in. It was not David's intent to get the young man hurt. However, using Ethan's uncertainty against him was one of David's specialties. As an Internal Affairs detective, David knew the best way to get an unwilling participant to cooperate was to turn his allies against him. In this case, Ethan's greatest ally was his wife, Becky.

"The trap has been set boys." David said to his crew. "It's only a matter of time now."

Chapter 19

Hunter once again caught sight of the vine covered walls of the Illinois State Capitol building. His last visit was less than pleasurable. Even though it should have been a moment of his greatest triumph, it turned into an opportunity for Vixanna to reveal her contempt for him. Such was the way of the demonic hierarchy. Thoughts of pleasure were a fleeting hope that were last felt behind the strong walls of the Kingdom of Heaven. Even though he dreaded the visit with every fiber of his being, the journey was a necessary one, since his presence was requested by his master, Mistress Vixanna.

Hunter passed through the abandoned wing and stepped foot into a long-forgotten courtyard. The demon could see hundreds of human servants within the dark enclosure occupying the area in spirit form. They were slaves, brought to this stronghold through séances and black perverted magic involving the summoning of demons. They were here in the spirit by their own free will, each devoting their lives and identities to Mistress Vixanna for whatever little gains she had offered them. Yet even though they voluntarily communed with evil spirits, they still could not see the ultimate price they would all soon pay if they did not immediately cease their wrongdoings. That price being an eternity of suffering by means of the Lake of Fire prepared for the devil and his fallen angels.

Hunter found their presence to be revolting. After all, while a human still possesses even one breath of life in their fleshly bodies, they still withheld the chance at having their lives redeemed by Jesus Christ. Then they could bask in all the glory of God's kingdom as he himself once had. If given the opportunity, Hunter would gladly choose a different path so that he would not have to face an eternity of suffering. But since his fate was forever sealed, and he was doomed to face an eternity of fire and brimstone, he vowed to do his part to make God suffer too. The only way he and his kin saw that they could achieve this, was by taking as many of God's beloved humans with them to hell when they go.

Human slaves were quite a lucrative commodity. After all, some jobs could only be carried out by creatures in the flesh. Most humans were slaves already without ever realizing or admitting it. Slaves to their own sins and carnal desires. They were the everyday common men and women of the world that gave into their temptations on a regular basis, and whose only thoughts were of themselves. These slaves were very helpful in making the lives of Christians unpleasant with their subtleties; such as butting in line at a restaurant, cutting someone off on the road while driving, or carrying on a cell phone conversation in a movie theater during the feature presentation.

Then…there were *other* slaves. Slaves that gave in to greed, lust, adultery, and even fear. These were slaves that could be manipulated into carrying out such atrocities as robbery, battery, or even murder.

For example, if a slave were to be enticed into a mainstream drug induced lifestyle, he or she could be persuaded into committing robbery to supply their habit with a source of income in which to feed their addiction. And if a slave were seduced into having an adulterous affair behind their spouse's back, and he or she were going to be exposed of their infidelity, fear may drive them to murder whoever was about to do the whistle blowing.

But the slaves housed at Vixanna's keep were a different sort of breed altogether. These were slaves that knowingly and outright had given up their freedom to serve Mistress Vixanna. They were slaves who were fooled into believing that if they sold themselves into servitude to the demon, the powers of darkness would make their lives more pleasurable. And they believed her lies to the end. So much in fact, that they would die if they thought the act would gain her approval.

Fools to the end. Hunter thought, as he made his way to a winding staircase that took him to the second level.

Once the demon stood upon the mid level of Vixanna's stronghold, he found himself in the throne room of his master. He was surprised to see that he was not the only henchman that had been summoned to this meeting, as there were a handful of his devilish kin surrounding his mistress. Lars being one and Nefareus, a scout. His talents were best utilized for the collecting of information. Something told Hunter that Nefareus' presence here this day was no accident. Most likely the demon had brought Mistress Vixanna some intelligence that spawned this gathering.

"At last. The final member of our assemblage has arrived." Mistress Vixanna hissed.

"Had I known my absence was causing my mistress any distress, I would not have tarried." Hunter purred sarcastically, as he stooped into a low bow, immediately drawing a look of disdain from Vixanna.

"May we begin, Mistress?" Nefareus dared to ask, drawing an evil glare from the demon and causing her rattler to vibrate unpleasantly.

"I have already rewarded you for your information, Nefareus!" Vixanna growled. **"But don't test me! I run the affairs of this keep, not you!"**

"Forgive me mistress." Nefareus was quick to reply, lowering his head in submission.

"Our loyal brother, Nefareus, has brought news that will interest you." She continued, while placing a consoling hand on the scout's shoulder, that told him it was safe to lift his head again. **"It seems that your arch nemesis, Cazzbein, has been spotted at the human, Ethan Brooks' side once more."**

"I am aware of the guardian's presence, Vixanna." Hunter said arrogantly, purposely not addressing the demon as mistress. "My servant, Dartamus, has already made me privy to such information."

"Have his wings healed nicely?" Vixanna laughed.

"He is whole once more." Hunter replied, not missing the insult.

"Cazzbein is more than a capable fighter." Lars said casually. "To be pierced by his blades is no reason for shame. For no demon has been able to penetrate his defenses in a duel."

"I have been wounded by the guardian we know as Cazzbein." Hunter put in. "But not without leaving a mark of my own on his fair skinned hide."

Hunter's comment brought about looks of good esteem from his colleagues as they all knew full well what a tall task it must have been to injure the fierce warring angel.

"Impressive." Lars said, in a smooth tone that suggested pleasure.

"And I am not afraid to face him again." Hunter added, hoping his mistress would send him on the quest to kill his arch enemy.

"No." Vixanna shot back with a smile, knowing where the minion was headed with the comment. **"You have proven yourself incapable of dealing with the guardian. Cazzbein shall indeed be dealt with, but we will approach the matter using our minds, not our emotions. You have let this rivalry become too personal and have not used strategy when dealing with him. We already know where our enemy is, and we can use this to our advantage. We will now destroy him with our numbers and overwhelming might."**

Hunter could tell by the expression on Lars' reptilian face the arch demon could not deny the reasoning in Vixanna's words, but it did little in taking the sting away. Hunter wanted to end Cazzbein's existence by his own sword tip. Satisfaction would not be met unless combat took place fairly in a one-on-one duel to the end. He must know who is the better between them or risk being haunted with that question for all eternity.

"If I may, my mistress," Nefareus interjected. "There is still the matter of the human…"

"Human?" Hunter asked, curiously.

"We are not positive about your claims, Nefareus." Vixanna replied pointing her index finger at him from one of her many hands.

"Human?" Hunter asked again, with a little more emphasis.

"Nefareus claims the human Joe Horton has been contacted by the messenger angel, Anthony." Lars replied, after he saw that Vixanna was ignoring Hunter's question. "We believe Ethan Brooks is dangerously close to realizing God's purpose for his life. And if Joe Horton has been brought in to aid him, we believe Ethan Brooks will play a pivotal role in God's army. This we cannot allow."

"That is why we have brought in some assurance." The mistress added, waving a hand to usher someone in the antechamber.

From a side entrance three unknown figures quietly emerged. They stepped across the large room utilizing great stealth as they added their numbers to the horde. Even for creatures of the spiritual realm their silence was most extraordinary.

"Rippers…" Hunter muttered under his breath, with disgust.

Rippers were nothing more than assassins. The thought of bringing in common killers such as these to dispose of Cazzbein brought a wave of revulsion over Hunter. He would not let the assassins soil the rivalry between himself and the noble angel, if at all possible.

"I would like to introduce the three most skilled Rippers known to our kind. Jinx…Sinjj…and their leader…Mara Di'Vour." Vixanna announced, causing each of the assassins to bow once their name was announced.

Sinjj was one of the largest demons in the room, third only to Mistress Vixanna and Lars of course. He stood nearly eight feet in height, and had large powerful muscles bulging out from under his black chainmail armor. The giant black feathered wings jutting out from his massive back looked as though they had been plucked off a vulture's body and merged with his own. His face was smooth and fair all the way down to his rugged jawline, while his long blonde locks resembled that of the hair of the Vikings that ravaged the seas of a long-ago age. Grasped tightly in his right hand was a wicked looking mace with sharp spikes sticking out from all angles. A dark trail of soot followed the weapon wherever it moved, making it appear as if an intense fire burned from within.

Jinx was quite mysterious. His shoulders were stooped and his posture was poor. His scrawny body and pale skin made him look as though he were malnourished and sickly, while his balding head was half covered with stringy black hair making him appear older than anyone in the room, even though everyone was the same age. He had two leathery bat-like wings poking out from his long black cloak adding an even more demonic dimension to his already hellish exterior. Sheathed about his thin waist were two long daggers, each complete with highly jeweled hilts, while a bandoleer of silver throwing knives was slung around one of his bony shoulders.

The ill looking demon noticed Hunter eyeing the decorative facade of his weapons and quickly flashed him a sharp toothed grin that caused the fuming demon to scowl even more evilly than he had already been since the assassins entered the room.

Mara Di'Vour was in a class all her own. The leader of the Rippers was a beautiful female with shoulder length, stark white hair just gracing the edge of her gleaming lavender eyes. She was garbed in a tight-fitting black robe that dangled at her ankles and clung firmly to her curvaceous figure with two slits rising up to thigh level so as to show off her shapely legs.

Her ebony-colored wings resembled those of a raven, with the tip of every primary feather pierced with a golden ring. Hunter recognized the act for what it was. Each ring was crafted from the weapon of a guardian angel that she had slain in battle. It was a way to openly flaunt her captures, while being able to intimidate any future enemies she may encounter.

Obviously Mara Di'Vour is a force to be reckoned with. Hunter thought, as he spied the dangerous looking pair of sabers strapped around either side of her petite waist.

"They shall accompany you on your journey." Vixanna declared. **"I want that angel captured, first and foremost. After he is imprisoned, we can continue leading the human down the road to ruin."**

"I really don't think it necessary to involve these, Rippers my mistress." Hunter urged, hoping the powerful demon would reconsider.

"This human would not be alive today, if you and your crew had not failed to dispose of him at the time of his birth." Mara Di'Vour unexpectedly chimed in.

"For your information, his mother was sealed by God, and was wholly under his protection!" Hunter shouted defensively, in a heated tone. "That mission was a failure from the beginning!"

Seeing his leader being talked down to by Hunter caused Sinjj to instinctively step between them.

"You'd do well to watch your tone." The muscular demon warned in an even tone, while bringing his smoldering mace up to Hunter's face to emphasize his statement.

"How dare you!" Hunter rebuked him angrily. His saber was out and deflecting the mace to the side before the larger demon knew what had happened. "You need a lesson in manners, so you will know your place!"

The two demons withheld each other in a scornful gaze for several tense moments. Everything else in the room no longer held any importance to the pair as they both refused to back down from one another. Suddenly, without warning, a loud crack exploded within the throne room, followed by a stinging burn so intense that it brought the two demons to their knees.

Hunter knew full well what had caused the searing pain, due to the fact that he had felt it on several occasions over his long existence. He looked down at his left hip and saw a sharp, flaming nail attached to a leather strap buried within his torso. When he traced the strap back to its source, he was not surprised to see that it was one of the nine burning lashes of Vixanna's malicious scourge. The weapon was by far the cruelest instrument of torture Hunter had the misfortune of falling victim to. It consisted of nothing more than nine straps of leather each bound to barbaric looking nails that were always aflame with a mystical fire, attached to a handle firmly within her savage grasp.

"Enough!" Mistress Vixanna shouted, slamming three of her fists down on the arms of her throne in disgust. **"There will be no more discussion on the matter! I want that guardian taken care of once and for all. We will deal with the human once the angel is out of the way. Am I making myself clear on the matter?"**

Everyone in the throne room replied with a resounding "Yes, mistress." After taking a cautious step back from the angered demon.

Seeing that her illustration of power had once again brought a measure of order back to the meeting, Mistress Vixanna released Hunter and Sinjj from their excruciating agony. With nothing more than a telepathic command, each nail tore itself loose from their bodies and made its way back to Vixanna's side.

Hunter rubbed the new wound in an attempt to work out the numbness. When a tingling sensation began to overtake the injury, he knew he would soon be regaining feeling once again. He returned his saber to its scabbard and then hoisted himself to his feet, making sure he was standing before Sinjj could pick himself off the floor, so he could prove to the larger demon which one of them had the stronger resiliency.

The act did not go unnoticed to Sinjj, as he struggled to regain his footing.

"Mistress Vixanna," Hunter said, in his most soothing tone. "If I may have a word with you in private?"

The angered demon narrowed her eyes to slits as she regarded the henchman.

"Your request is denied."

Vixanna's reply angered Hunter so deeply that he could not hide the expression of rage that quickly overtook his visage.

"You have your orders everyone." Vixanna said, with finality. **"Now be off."**

With those final words the meeting was at an end. All the demons turned and walked toward the exit except for Hunter. He paused for a moment as if there were something he intended to say, while the look of fury still graced his fair features. But when he caught sight of Vixanna deliberately twirling her fingers through the leather straps of her wicked scourge, the words quickly faded. With nothing further for him to do, the demon spun on his heels to follow the rest of his kin out of the throne room.

Chapter 20

Ethan fidgeted uncomfortably in his suit as he sat next to Becky in one of the furthest seats from the pulpit. It had been quite some time since he had attended church, often appearing only because his foster parents forced him to go when he was a child. Although the hard wooden pews had been replaced with soft, cushiony seats, they were still set very close to one another and caused him to inadvertently rub elbows with his neighbors. Nevertheless, Ethan decided that if it would help put his wife's mind at ease about current events, he would attend.

The young man couldn't help but look through the window to the cold December day just outside, as the church slowly filled up with its congregation. A flake of snow descended to the ground, followed by yet another. It looked as though there was going to be a white Christmas this year.

"Who do we have here, Becky?" Came an unfamiliar voice that tore Ethan from his daydreaming.

"This is my husband, Ethan." Becky replied.

Ethan turned to see an older gentleman dressed in a fine, tan suit with specks of gray within his jet-black hair. He had no other outstanding features to speak of other than his clear blue eyes that glowed with a clarity Ethan had never witnessed before. The pleasant stranger extended his hand to give Ehtan a friendly greeting while an inviting smile adorned his face.

"Ethan, this is Pastor Joe Horton." Becky said, finishing the introduction.

"Good morning, Ethan." Pastor Horton greeted. "I was beginning to wonder when Becky would bring you here for us to meet."

"Good morning, pastor." Ethan returned the sentiment, and shook the man's hand warmly. "I've heard good things about your church, so I thought I would come and experience them for myself."

'We're glad to have you." Pastor Horton replied. "We won't disappoint."

"I'm so glad you came, Ethan." Becky said, after the preacher walked away.

'I know you are, hon." Ethan responded, as he took hold of her hand. "Maybe this is what I need."

Lurking within the shadows of the overhang just above the entrance to The Spirit Led Church, Dartamus spied the situation with eyes of cruelty. After watching Ethan's conversation with the good pastor, the dark spirit slithered his way down the wall utilizing the nearest shadows for cover. The minion moved skillfully through the dark, shaded areas of the church until he made his way to where Nefareus and his master Hunter waited impatiently.

"The situation is worse than we had originally feared." The sniveling little demon groaned. "The boy has been befriended by Joe Horton."

Evil creatures of the spiritual realm were quite familiar with all of God's servants. Any servants of God Almighty that interfered with the dealings of their dark world by winning souls for their most hated enemy were considered a threat, especially when they knew how to use the word of God to cast out evil spirits and teach others to do the same.

Pastor Joe Horton was a powerful warrior for God, and had exorcized countless demons while he walked the earth. The demonic forces would have destroyed him long ago had they been able too. However, since he was sealed by God and full of the Holy Spirit, there was little the powers of darkness could do, other than watch as the good pastor continued to hinder their evil deeds.

"This is no chance encounter, be assured." Hunter remarked to his two companions.

"What do you mean?" Nefareus inquired, his dark eyes scanning Hunter's visage for an explanation.

"I sense this is why the messenger angel contacted Joe Horton." Hunter answered. "He aims to teach Ethan Brooks the art of exorcism."

"But exorcism can only be conducted by a child of God." Nefareus commented. "Ethan Brooks is yet unsaved and bears not the seal of God."

"We must act quickly if we are to keep the human from asking for Christ's gift of eternal life." Hunter spat, the title of God's Son bringing distaste to his mouth.

"Aren't we going to wait for Mara Di'Vour and her Rippers?" Nefareus wisely inquired.

"I've seen neither hide nor hair of those assassins since we departed from Vixanna's keep." Hunter replied, with a tone of contempt. "But make no mistake, her and her band of cutthroats are around here somewhere."

"What is our next move, master?" Dartamus dared to ask, fearing the consequences of interrupting the two more powerful demons.

Hunter flashed his servant an evil eye to let him know the interjection was not welcomed, and then proceeded to answer.

"First and foremost, we must make certain Ethan Brooks does not ask forgiveness of his sins. For if he does our mission will have utterly failed. I dread what dire consequences await us at Mistress Vixanna's many hands if that were to happen."

The logical reasoning caused Dartamus and Nefareus to nod their heads in agreement.

"We must also be mindful to stay out of sight. Pastor Horton has the ability to see within our world, so if we are discovered by him, he will vanquish us with one of his prayers." Hunter added. "I want the two of you to distract Ethan Brooks from hearing the sermon as much as possible. If we can keep him ignorant on the matter, he will not know how to ask for forgiveness."

"What will you be doing during all this?" Nefareus asked, as he rubbed a pale hand down his sharp chin.

The evil spirit shot Nefareus a wicked grin before answering.

"My name is not Hunter by some mere twist of fate, Nefareus." He replied with a smile. "I will be trying to locate our enemy, Cazzbein. And when I find him…we will see once and for all which one of us is the better sword bearer."

"I thought the Rippers were summoned to dispose of Cazzbein." Nefareus commented, as he eyed Hunter suspiciously.

"Do you see them?" Hunter asked, in an over dramatic tone. "It appears to me as if they want to work alone. But I will not sit back idly and watch as that burdensome guardian angel meddles in our affairs!"

"I see." Nefareus answered, seeing through his cohort's feigned anger. He knew Hunter must be planning something a little less discreet for their enemy. Personally, it mattered little to him if Cazzbein met his end via the hands of the Rippers, or the tips of Hunter's saber and serrated dagger, so long as the angel was dealt with.

"Now…let us be about our business." Hunter said with finality, as he took to the air under the power of his darkened wings, being mindful to stay within the shadows.

Nefareus watched as Hunter flew out of sight and then slowly turned his attention to Dartamus. "I hope your master's lust for Cazzbein's demise does not doom us all."

*　　*　　*　　*　　*

The church seemed alive with a pleasant spirit, as everyone went about their business with broad smiles spread across their faces. While the interior was pleasant to the eye, the most notable feature was the twelve-foot hand sculpted wooden image of Jesus on the cross displayed directly behind the baptistery.

Ethan was awestruck by the craftsmanship of the church's tall arched ceilings, which stretched high above the forest green padded seats and matching wall to wall carpeting. Both the first and second levels of the sanctuary were circular in design, so as to get the best acoustics from the sound system. Extending out of the upper level was a modest sized area set aside for the audio, video, and lighting equipment, where everything from microphones to spotlights were run by the touch of a button. Ehtan took in the beauty of the room with a boyish fascination, never knowing in the least bit that he himself was being closely observed by the denizens of darkness.

Nefareus and Dartamus hid themselves within the shadows being cast from the opposite side of the lighting equipment high in the rafters. From their vantage point they could see the congregation in its entirety. However, they were not looking merely upon the flesh. Instead, they bore their extraordinary gazes upon the souls of the church members. After this was done, they could see which of the humans' souls were pure and clean, and which ones were covered in sin.

If a human was unrepentant, their soul would appear scarred and filthy, because sin still clung to the spirit like a cancerous growth, eating away at them until their conscience was as hard as a deadened artery. However, if a human was repentant, meaning they did not only ask for forgiveness of their sins, but also turned away from their iniquities altogether, their souls would appear clean, and healed, glistening as white as a new fallen snow.

Unrepentant souls were quite useful to the creatures of darkness. In addition to being easy to commune with, they could also be manipulated and used as pawns, therefore being continuous thorns in the sides of Christians.

"There!" Nefareus hissed with pleasure, while pointing out the object of his excitement. "The fat one in the third row. She is mine." He said, rubbing his hands together with anticipation. "Who do you choose?"

"I have something else in mind." Dartamus answered, before diving off the platform they had been sharing.

Nefareus watched as his ally soared his way down toward Ethan's position, wisely becoming one with the human's own shadow, so as to keep out of sight. Afterward, Nefareus himself dove off the narrow structure and headed for his fattened victim.

When the lights began to dim within the sanctuary, the band choir director made a few hand gestures to the choir, which was their cue to begin singing the song, "I'll fly away."

Everyone in the congregation stood to their feet, some clapping their hands with the beat, while others held their hands up in praise. Ethan found the charismatic show a little intimidating at first, but after the song played a few more verses, he could not help himself, and started tapping his hands on the back of the seat in front of him with perfect rhythm.

Watching Ethan enjoy the music made Dartamus restless. Invisible to everyone else in the church, the demon stood behind the young man and whispered subtle suggestions into his ear.

"What are you doing?" the evil spirit asked, craftily. "There are people staring at you."

The comment was successful in making Ethan self-conscious. He peered out the corner of his eye suspiciously, and although there was no one looking in his direction, he could not shake the feeling that they were. Without realizing it, his hands had stopped keeping rhythm, and a feigned, uninterested expression came over his face.

Vanity had won.

Soon afterward, the song had finished and everyone was asked to be seated. It was then that the robust woman seated in front of Ethan turned her attention toward him.

"Well, I didn't know we had a new member in our midst!" She said, with an exaggerated smile. "Let me come keep you company."

Without being invited, the woman worked her way back a row to sit next to Ethan. She miscalculated where she was intending to place her rump and nearly squashed him had he not hastily moved to the side. She sat down with a crash and let loose a heavy sigh, as if just moving those few steps had taken every ounce of energy from her body.

"I'm sister Hardy." She announced, holding her plump hand out to be shaken.

"I'm Ethan." He answered, returning the gesture with a firm handshake.

"You know, Ethan, your wife tells me that you are a police detective. I just wanted to let you know I heard that Tommy Higgins over there sells drugs to children." The gossipmonger said in a matter-of-fact tone, even though she didn't know for sure.

The unconfirmed remark caused a mischievous grin to form on Nefareus's lips. His little rumormonger was doing better than he expected. Just a few more twisted half-truths needed to be spewed from her gossiping mouth and Ethan would be left wondering what kind of church he had stumbled his way into.

Peering out from behind the flawlessly sculpted statue of Jesus on the cross, Cazzbein kept a close eye on his charge. The angel was well aware of the battle being waged around Ethan even though the young human was not. The angel knew he could vanquish the two demons with little effort, but he wanted to tactfully remove Sister Hardy from the scene without making his presence known to the evil spirits.

It was then that an idea formed in the guardian's mind. With great haste the angel made a straight line through the walls of the church, passing through wood, drywall, and even concrete without effort, until he was finally hovering above the parking lot outside. He then located Sister Hardy's car and flew toward its back end. Reaching inside the transmission, Cazzbein took the vehicle out of gear, where it then proceeded to roll slowly back in the direction of the entrance, blocking cars from coming in. Satisfied with his handiwork, the angel then made a direct path back inside, where he would wait for the seeds of his efforts to flourish.

Once inside, Cazzbein watched Ethan and sister Margaret carefully. The woman was still hard at work spewing misinformation with her gossiping tongue. However, that was soon about to change.

As if on cue, one of the ushers ran down the aisle stopping at Sister Margaret's side. He then muttered something into her ear that caused the large woman to exit the church in a hurry.

Mission accomplished. The angel thought with a smile. Once Sister Margret left the pew, Nefareus stood in the walkway already searching for another puppet. Little did the demon know, Cazzbein was not going to allow him the opportunity.

With lightning quick speed, the sentry soared down the aisle where he unceremoniously delivered an elbow to Nefareuos's nose. In the spiritual realm a sickening crack could be heard that caught the attention of more than one evil spirit, as Nefareus's body thudded to the ground.

"Hunter!" Dartamus shrieked. "Cazzbein is down here!" Up in the sound booth a lustful smile crossed Hunter's visage. At last, his nemesis had revealed himself. Unsheathing his saber and serrated dagger, Huner plunged himself into the mix without heeding any concern for his own well-being.

Knowing what was coming next, Cazzbein unleashed his scimitars from their scabbards and braced himself for the expected impact. Both combatants' weapons met hard with a metallic crash and a shower of sparks.

Hunter was enthralled in the battle. He pressed onward, the tips of his weapons coming in at Cazzbein from impossible angles. But, somehow, the guardian angel managed to send the razor-sharp edges of his enemy's blades bouncing harmlessly away before they had a chance to do any damage.

Even though Cazzbein fought for his own well-being, he found the skirmish more irritating than anything else, because it took his attention away from his charge, Ethan. Between parrying Hunter's blades, Cazzbein managed to look in Ethan's direction and was disgusted to see Dartamus whispering more poisonous remarks into the human's ear.

By this time, he had figured out Hunter's attack routine, and was now ready to make his first offensive move. When the demon came in for another round, Cazzbein immediately deflected both weapons and then gave his enemy a sharp kick to the chin.

The attack came out of nowhere. It had been well placed and delivered with incredible power. Hunter fell to his backside hard, seeing stars as he did so. The angel knew his chance was slim, but that it must be taken.

With reflexes as quick as a beam of light, Cazzbein made a mad dash toward the fiendish little devil, Dartamus, and knocked him to the ground with a solid fist to his jaw. Dartamus tumbled over a few times and then came to rest in a heap a few feet away. By this time the preacher was ready to deliver the message God had placed on his heart.

"You must pay attention to the sermon, Ethan." The angel said softly into the young man's ear, in a tone that heeded both encouragement and urgency. Cazzbein noticed that once his message was given, Ethan indeed straightened up in his seat and began paying attention.

The small words of sustenance were all the angel had time to speak before Hunter was upon him again. By this time, Nefareus had recovered and found himself another puppet in which to distract Ethan with. It was Tommy Higgins, the one that Sister Margret had accused of dealing drugs. The demon moved in close to the man's ear, stroking his chin with a filthy hand like a master rubbing the fur of a pet feline.

"Sister Margaret has been spreading rumors about you again." He said, in a subtle tone. "She told the newcomer you were a drug dealer."

*   *   *   *   *

After Ethan started paying close attention to the words Pastor Horton was speaking, he began feeling a stirring within his soul. It was a restlessness that he had never felt before. It was as if there was something more to life than just merely existing, and he wanted to be a part of it.

"Did our God not create *everything?* As it says in Isaiah 45:7, "I form the light, and create darkness: I make peace, and create evil: I the Lord do all these things."

"We are to love everyone, not just the people that are good to us, because God has created us all, and given all the chance at repentance."

"Just as Jesus said in Matthew 5:44 - 45, "But I say unto you, love your enemies, bless them that curse you, do good to them that hate you, and pray for them which despitefully use you; that ye may be the children of your Father which is in heaven: for he maketh his sun to rise on the evil and the good, and sendeth rain on the just and on the unjust." Pastor Horton spoke the words passionately. "Brothers and sisters, hear me! There are going to be people in your life that test you, but be mindful in how you handle them!"

The sermon hit Ethan like an arrow through the heart. He felt as if the preacher was speaking directly to him, and knew the words were meant for the relationship between Tyler, Booker, and himself. But it was Pastor Horton's final statement that struck the biggest chord of all.

"I once heard a story of a man that was disgusted with the evil that engulfed the world. So repulsed with the corruption and greed that surrounded him that he cried out to God and asked, 'Why won't you send someone to do something about these wrongdoings?' And God answered him in a still small voice and said, 'I did send someone…I sent *you*.'"

Ethan was hanging off of every word at this point, and then came a tap on his shoulder. When he turned to see who it was, he was a little surprised to see Tommy Higgins standing in the aisle with a smug look upon his face.

"I'm sorry to bother you, but I couldn't help but notice Sister Margret was speaking to you earlier." Tommy said, in a hushed tone.

If the man had come a few moments earlier, Ethan may have indulged him with conversation. However, Ethan was enjoying the sermon far too much to be disturbed now, and was almost shocked at the words coming out of his own mouth.

"Whatever it is, it can wait." He replied firmly. "I'm listening to the preacher right now, as you should be."

The snippy response seemed to stun Tommy, as the expression on his face suddenly transformed from self-assuredness, to anger. "I just wanted to clear something up-."

"I don't care." Ethan replied, with finality. The answer seemed to infuriate Tommy, but not near as much as it enraged Nefareus, who had been feeding the words into the man's ear the entire time.

"I'll see you after the sermon then." Tommy scoffed, before returning to his seat.

The comment did little to derail Ethan from the message. As Tommy walked away, the pianist began playing the slow melody, 'Just as I am,' which began the invitational. As the music played, Joe Horton spoke words of encouragement to any ear that needed it.

"With every head bowed and eye closed…if there is anyone here who does not know if they would go to heaven if the Lord came back today, please raise your hand…I want to pray for you."

A few people throughout the congregation raised their hands, and when Pastor Horton saw them, he immediately said, "thank you." Ehtan knew he was not saved either. He knew he would not be taken up in the clouds if the rapture took place today. Not only that, his mother was not here with him today because an unexpected accident claimed her life. Where would he end up if the same fate overtook him?

The preacher continued, "Hell is filled with good people who squandered their lives and never gave themselves over to Christ. Don't be one of them…"

Hell? Ethan thought. The possibility never crossed his mind that he would end up in that dreadful place. He was a good person after all, and just assumed all good people went to Heaven. Before he realized it, his trembling hand slowly raised into the air as if by its own accord. So subtly did the movement happen that he almost thought it hadn't been made. But when the preacher responded with a loud, "thank you," it was confirmed that he had indeed raised his hand and wanted confirmation on whether or not he was going to Heaven. As promised, Pastor Horton said a little prayer under his breath for everyone who raised their hands. It was a short, quiet, little prayer, but one that held great influence.

*   *   *   *   *

In the spiritual realm the savage battle was still being waged. Cazzbein was hard pressed battling Hunter, while simultaneously trying to keep the other evil minions from distracting Ethan. Nevertheless, his efforts were paying off.

Suddenly, a faint call came to him. It was soft at first, barely able to be deciphered, but a call nonetheless. Someone was praying for his charge, and Christ was passing that message on to him!

In the midst of the skirmish the words became louder, until finally they grew so overpowering that they could not be ignored, even if he had wanted to ignore them.

Somewhere within himself an unseen force renewed his vigor, and he fought with both passion and urgency.

*   *   *   *   *

"We are going to sing a few lines from the hymnal, and if you raised your hand and want to know for certain that you will go to Heaven, won't you please meet me here at the altar?" Pastor Horton urged.

In unison the congregation began singing the words to the slow tune the pianist was playing. "Just as I am…without one plea…"

The words tugged at Ethan's heart…

"Jesus, the living Son of God, died on an old rugged cross to give you the opportunity to know you would go to Heaven…don't turn Him away…" Pastor Horton continued.

Ehtan's hands began to sweat…"

"It was no coincidence that, whoever you are, you chose to come here to the Spirit Led Church, in Rockford, Illinois, on this very day, to hear this very message…"

Ethan's heart was pounding in his chest, as a battle waged within him. He wanted to step out into the aisle and run frantically to the altar, but for some reason that could only be explained as fear, he stayed where he was, clutching his sweaty hands into the back of the seat in front of him.

*   *   *   *   *

Back within the spiritual realm Cazzbein fought vitally to reach Ethan. He looked at his charge and was sickened to see Dartamus standing on the young man's shoulders in order to keep him from stepping out into the aisle. It was crucial that the evil spirit be dealt with this instance. If Ethan was held up even a moment too long the invitation would be over, and the human would go home never experiencing the gift of Christ. Furthermore, who was to say the human would ever feel a calling this strong again in his lifetime?

Cazzbein knew he needed both scimitars to effectively battle Hunter, but Ethan's eternal soul was far more important. Risking all, the angel launched one of the blades in Dartamus' direction. The hilt smacked the demon in the head, knocking him off the Ethan's shoulders.

"Ethan go!" The angel screamed frantically. "This may be your only chance!"

*   *   *   *   *

It was at that moment Ethan felt a great weight lifted off his shoulders. He heard the music with more clarity, and the message spoke to his heart with more precision.

"Won't you come, friend?" Pastor Horton said, in a somber tone. "This may be your last chance…"

With nothing more holding him back, Ethan stepped out into the aisle. His actions caught the eyes of everyone in the congregation, especially Becky. The young man didn't seem to mind though, because he needed to make things right between him and his Maker. Ethan's legs carried him with purpose as he strode up to the altar. When he arrived, Pastor Horton was there to meet him just as he had said.

"What can I do for you, Ethan?" The preacher asked, already knowing the answer.

Ethan's clear blue eyes quickly filled up with tears as he replied in a desperate tone, "I want to be saved."

*　　*　　*　　*　　*

Seeing his enemy distracted, Hunter lunged at Cazzbein with his saber aimed at his back. Anticipating the attack, the angel tried to spin out of the way, but was unable to fully get out of range of the deadly weapon. The saber cut a deep gash down his side, causing much of his essence to pour from the wound.

"First blood is mine once more, guardian!" Hunter spat, evilly.

The pain was overwhelming. Cazzbein fell to one knee, holding the lesion with one hand, while groping for the scimitar he had thrown at Dartamus with the other. His hand was only a few inches away when a foot kicked the weapon out of his limits.

He looked up expecting to see Hunter, but was amazed to see another demon standing over him. It was Mara Di'Vour, the leader of the Rippers assigned to capture him. A malicious gleam twinkled in her orbs, when she realized how simple her task had now become.

Raising her saber high in the air for the incapacitating blow, Cazzbein could only stare in disbelief, waiting with dignity for her hit to render him unconscious. He knew the demons would not be giving him a killing blow, because he would just emerge again within the gates of Heaven to heal. However, if they took him captive, that would be far worse, due to the fact that the time he spent away from Ethan would be destructive to the human's life. That fate was not what the Lord had intended, however, as a rescuer came to his aid in the form of his most hated enemy.

"No!" Hunter screamed, as he sent his serrated dagger hurling through the air toward Mara.

Hunter's weapon collided with Mara's saber, giving Cazzbein just enough time to roll toward his discarded scimitar.

"He is mine! I will not have you soil our rivalry with your unnecessary assistance!" Especially when I have done all the work thus far!"

Cazzbein plucked his weapon from the ground just in time to see Rippers, Sinjj and Jinx, flying toward him. In his weakened state, the angel wondered how he was going to survive, or even *if* he would survive. He stood to his feet defiantly, scimitars in each hand, waiting to tackle the challenge with determination.

However, that was not to be.

A blinding light exploded within the sanctuary so intense that it expelled all the demons from the church with incredible influence. Cazzbein had seen this light before, and was overcome with praise at its sudden appearance, as he stood in the church aisle absorbing its healing power. He turned his azure orbs upon the altar, and a white toothed smile overcame his flawless features when he saw Ethan kneeling in prayer.

Pastor Horton looked into Ethan's moist eyes after having led him in the prayer of forgiveness, and a smile spread across his lips as well.

"Ethan Brooks," The pastor said, in a calm tone. "You are saved."

Chapter 21

Crack!

The familiar sound of Mistress Vixanna's hideous scourge being put to work could be heard rising from the darkest sections of her stronghold's torture chamber. Low level demons with no real significance, scurried in all directions when they heard the dreadful sound in which they were all too well acquainted. Their many faces flinched in unison as they winced in imaginary pain, due to the fact that they knew full well the amount of suffering the helpless victim was being exposed to.

Crack!

The sound came again. It was every bit as loud and ferocious as it had been when it was first heard an hour ago. And the steady, rhythmic pattern gave no evidence it would be stopping any time soon.

Crack!

Once more the vicious symphony sliced through the late-night air, echoing off of the damp stone walls until it finally died out somewhere deep within the structure. Like all foul creatures of darkness, the underling's self-preservation told them to be thankful it was another tortured soul being abused, and not *their* backsides being torn to pieces by the wicked scourge.

"Please Mistress, I beg you! I cannot take any more!" Hunter pleaded in anguish, his back torn to shreds by the malicious device.

The six-armed demon narrowed her eyes to slits as she considered her victim. She subtly entertained the thought of beating the minion till his demise, but then wisely reconsidered.

"Not only did you fail to defeat the guardian angel once you interfered…but you hindered Mara Di'Vour from doing so as well!" Vixanna screamed, more for her own ears to hear than Hunter's. **"And to make matters worse, you allowed the human to receive the Seal of God."**

Hunter dared not defend himself, lest he welcome more of his master's angry torment. Instead, he wisely remained silent, bound to the whipping block as his precious life essence ran freely from the tears in his back.

"By all rights I should kill you." Vixanna said, in a matter-of-fact tone. **"But…I am going to spare you."**

"Thank you, Mistress!" Hunter exclaimed.

"Do not thank me." She replied coldly. **"If it were not for the fact that you are the best suited henchman in my crew to deal with Cazzbein, I would slay you without a second thought."**

"That's it?" Mara Di'Vour asked, in an irritated tone. Her and her colleagues, Sinjj and Jinx had been standing nearby enjoying the show alongside Nefarius and Dartamus, who had previously received similar treatment at the hands of their angry master.

"Are you questioning my judgment?" Mistress Vixanna asked, turning her evil gaze toward the Ripper.

"No, Mistress." Mara answered, her eyes wisely turning to the ground in submission. "Forgive me."

"I thought not." Vixanna responded, slithering her snake-like body to the other side of the whipping block so she could look upon Hunter's face. **"I should be thanking you. After all, you fell neatly into the trap I had set for you. Lucifer no longer looks upon you with favor, and my position is once again secure. You have now realized how I managed to remain Principality of this region as long as I have."**

Hunter glared into the arch demon's eyes with contempt, because he knew she was correct. It took much effort, but somehow, he managed to hold his tongue.

"If you want your duel with this angel so badly, then you shall have it." The demon growled. **"You are already dead in my eyes, so I might as well use you for what little value you have. If you can defeat Cazzbein, you will have regained your worth, but if you fail and are killed at his hands, it will mean little to me. Do you understand?"**

"Yes Mistress…I thank you for your mercy…" Hunter replied faintly, the words bringing distaste to his mouth.

"As for you two…" Vixanna began, slithering past Hunter to consider Nefarius and Dartamus, who were lying on the floor of the torture chamber after having received their brutal scourging.

"Did Joe Horton see you?"

The two weakened demons turned to face one another, each fearing the answer they would inevitably have to give, but not knowing which one was going to give it.

"Answer me!" Vixanna growled, while raising her scourge in a threatening manner.

"We do not know, Mistress." Nefarius finally answered. "If he did see us, he did not let that knowledge be known to us."

"Mission accomplished." Vixanna said, with sarcasm dripping off every word.

"What would you have us do, Mistress?" Dartamus asked, in a pitiful tone.

"That is why you two will never be anything more than the inferior subordinates that you are, because you lack vision." Vixanna replied, rubbing a finger from one of her many hands across her chin as she thought. **"We will do what we must to salvage this mess."**

"What is our next move?" Mara Di'Vour asked, hesitantly.

Vixanna furrowed her brow at the Ripper, and did not immediately answer the question. Even though she was staring directly at the Ripper, Mara could tell her thoughts were elsewhere.

"We torture the human."

"What?" Mara asked, in an astonished tone."

"We torture him." Vixanna said, evilly. **"God has an important plan for this human. We can already trace his family lineage back to creation, and therefore know what flaws he possesses. We will use these weaknesses to destroy the human's testimony, so that he is unable to lead others to Christ."**

Mara grinned maliciously as she nodded her head in agreement.

"There is no doubt Ethan Brooks will turn on his partners, now that he has the Holy Spirit to guide

him down the path of righteousness." Vixanna continued. **"So, we will use the humans Tyler Lynch and Booker Briggs to aid us in torturing the new born Christian."**

"What is my role, Mistress?" Mara queried, eagerly.

"As for you and your Rippers…" The powerful demon said, as she used one of her free hands to untie Hunter's wrists from the whipping block. **"Find that troublesome angel and bring him to me…alive."**

*   *   *   *   *

Cazzbein watched his charge as he prepared himself for work, just as he had watched almost every day of the human's life since his conception. However, on this particular morning, something troubled the angel deeply. Truly, he was pleased that Ethan had come to know the Lord, nevertheless, there was something gnawing at the angel to the point that he knew he needed to act.

Glistinia wafted to her friend's side and could not dismiss the feeling he had something deeply troubling within his thoughts.

"What troubles you, friend?" She asked, politely.

"After our skirmish in the chapel yesterday, a thought occurred to me." He answered, somberly.

"Pray tell." Glistinia urged.

"I fear it will never end." Cazzbein said, with the sound of seriousness in his tone.

"What will not end?" She queried.

"The constant attacks on the human's well-being."

"I fear you are correct." Glistinia agreed.

"If only I could find the source of these attacks," Cazzbein began. "Then I could crush it at its source."

Glistinia looked at her friend with her soft, green eyes and could not help but think he truly did not know who had been sending the attacks against Ethan.

"Are you telling me you don't know who the Principality of this region is?" she dared to ask, fearing she would upset her friend even more than he already was.

"No. I do not." Cazzbein answered, plainly. "I only know that Hunter appears to be within the lot."

"Cazzbein," Glistinia said, as she took her friend's hand within her own. "It is the archdemon, Mistress Vixanna."

"Vixanna!" He declared with his own lips.

"Yes." Glistinia acknowledged. "She is the one responsible for the death of Ethan's mother at the night of his birth and she was a constant thorn in the life of my charge, Jody Brooks."

"How do you know this?" Cazzbein asked.

"Well, a long time ago, the great warring angel, Jubiel thought as you do." Glistinia went on to explain. "She went in search of the archdemon, to put an end to its constant tormenting of her charge. However, she was lost to us. The arch demon defeated her."

"I see." Cazzbein replied, grimly.

"The path you seek is far too treacherous." Glistinia warned. "And that is even if the path to the she-demon would ever present itself, since her location is unknown to us."

"Then how did Jubiel find her way?" Cazzbein had to know.

"She happened upon a portal." Glistinia replied. "That is the only way to get there."

The answer did not sit well with the angel. He knew that the appearance of such a portal is greater than the odds of lightning striking three times in the same place.

"Please put such notions from your thoughts, my friend." Glistinia said, with sincerity. "I would hate to lose you to Vixanna as well."

*   *   *   *   *

Ethan sat in his car on Monday morning just outside the newly built Justice Center, where the Office of Professional Standards was located. Since his spiritual transformation the day before, Ethan saw the world in a whole new light. The young detective seemed to be filled with a new found courage that he had never felt before. Ethan now wondered why he had ever compromised his beliefs just to protect his thuggish partners.

Never again. The young man determined.

If protecting criminals just because they had a badge was an unwritten rule among the police, then maybe that unwritten rule needed to be broken.

Even though Ethan was courageous enough to break the code of silence that all police officers were bound to, he could not shake the feeling of nervousness that he was feeling. Sitting in his car outside the IAD office made him feel extremely exposed. He wanted to make sure the detective that contacted Becky was in his office before he ever stepped foot inside the building. In order to do this, Ethan reached into his pocket and pulled out the business card that Detective David Grimes left with his wife. Slowly, he punched the numbers into his cell phone and waited for a response.

"Detective Grimes." Came the answer on the other end of the line.

"Um-yes, um…this is Detective Ethan Brooks…" He said, nervously. "You left this number with my wife and wanted me to call."

"Oh, yes." Detective Grimes replied. "This is an unexpected surprise. To what do I owe this pleasure?"

"My wife told me you had an open file on detectives Tyler Lynch and Booker Briggs." Ethan said, casually. "You just needed a witness to come forth to strengthen your case."

"Your wife told you correctly." Detective Grimes replied, in a hopeful tone. "Are you volunteering for the task?"

"I might be interested in helping your investigation on one condition." Ehtan responded, shrewdly.

"What's the condition?" David inquired.

"I'll need immunity."

There was a pause as Detective Grimes considered the demand.

"Why would you need immunity, Detective Brooks?" David felt the need to ask.

"Well, in order to gain the trust of my partners, I had to do some things I'm not particularly proud of." Ethan replied honestly. "And a lot of times I had to look the other direction while those same partners conducted illegal activities. But I did these things only because I feared for my safety."

David gave the request some serious thought before he gave Ethan his answer. He had been trying to take Tyler Lynch and Booker Briggs down for so long that the request seemed insignificant in the grand scheme of things.

"No problem." David said. "Why don't you stop by the office and we can talk about all this in more depth."

"Actually, I'm already here." Ethan replied. "I'm in the parking lot."

"I understand." David said, not sounding the least bit surprised. "You don't want to risk any of your fellow officers seeing you walk into my office."

"Right." The young detective answered honestly.

"I completely understand." David replied. "I tell you what, call your partners and tell them you're running a little late, then meet me at the Hollywood Diner on 11th Street in twenty minutes. We can talk more once we get there."

"I can do that." He answered., with the sound of relief in his voice.

Ethan did just as Detective Grimes instructed and met him at the Hollywood Diner on 11th Street. He made sure to park his car in one of the furthest stalls from the street, so none of the patrol officers would see it if they happened to drive by. Once inside, he saw a man waving him over to a booth in the back of the room. As he approached the booth, Ethan noticed the detective was not alone.

"Detective Brooks?" David asked, when he was within earshot.

"Detective grimes, I presume?" Ethan responded, before taking a seat. "Who is this?"

"I'm sorry, Ethan, this is one of my tech guys. His name is Doug." David answered. "I didn't have time to explain it to you over our brief conversation earlier."

"I just thought we'd be meeting alone." Ethan rightly said.

"Technically, we are." David answered. "I want you to know, everyone that works at the Office of Professional Standards has a rigorous background check, and they are extremely trustworthy. So, anything you say here will never leave this table."

After Detective Grimes had said his disclaimer speech, Doug placed a digital recorder on the table between the men.

"Then what's that for?" Ethan inquired, pointing at the device.

"Well, you mentioned you needed immunity in order to testify against your partners," Detective Grimes began. "So, I called the District Attorney's Office and had them get the paperwork drawn up and faxed over. Since you are a public employee, you already have a certain amount of immunity that would allow you to testify in open court without incriminating yourself, but in order for it to work effectively, we will have to conduct what's called a Garrity interview."

So, you want me to spill my guts?" Ethan inquired, looking at the recorder uneasily.

"That's how it works." David acknowledged. "I ask you some questions and you give me the answers."

Ethan weighed out the circumstances in his mind before giving his response. He knew that if the recording of this meeting ever happened to fall into the wrong hands, he and his wife would be dead. The risk did not seem worth the reward.

"You know, I don't feel too comfortable with all this." He said, before standing to his feet. "I need some more time to think about everything."

"Before you go," Detective Grimes said, as he pulled a photograph of a gang member out of a tan folder and then placed it on the table for Ethan to see. "Do you know this man?"

Ethan picked up the photo off the table and examined it for a moment. It was Shifty, the drug dealer that Tyler shook down for his money and product a few days ago. It was also the same drug dealer's money that found its way into Ethan's jacket when Tyler wouldn't take no for an answer.

"Yeah, I know him." Ethan answered, before placing the photo back down on the table. "His name's Shifty."

"Well, he might go as Shifty to all of his Gangster Apostle buddies out on the street, but his real name is Eddie Hines." Detective Grimes replied, in a matter-of-fact tone. "I guess when you boys in the Anti-Gang task Force shake 'em down out on the street, you don't bother getting their real name."

"What's that supposed to mean?" Ethan asked, angrily.

"Well, it's just that Eddie was picked up the other night for a narcotics bust, and he had some interesting things to say about you and Detective Lynch."

"Like what?" Ethan queried.

"Something about you two stripping him of his narcotics and money." David answered, as he read from a paper within his tan file. Detective Grimes did not inform Ethan that he actually coerced the gangbanger to talk due to the Intel he gathered from the hidden microphone hidden in the young detective's house. "You know, the funny thing is, when I checked the evidence room's log in sheet, there was no mention of this. Care to explain?"

"Are you trying to threaten me?" Ethan asked, with hostility growing in his voice. "After I came here to try and help you?"

"You listen, and listen real good," Detective Grimes said in a firm tone, as he also stood to his feet and looked Ethan in his eyes. "I don't care if you help us because you feel like it or because I have to twist your arm into it. Either way, I'm going to get your testimony. All this immunity business, I was just doing that as a courtesy to you."

Ethan stared at the Internal affairs detective for a long moment with no comment forthcoming. It would appear as if the detective had backed him into a corner.

"So what do you want?" Ethan finally asked, when no other option presented itself.

"First of all, sit down." We're making a scene." David ordered.

When the men returned to their seats, Detective Grimes continued.

"I want to know all the illegal activities that Detective Tyler Lynch and Detective Booker Briggs have been involved in. Especially everything you know about Jimmy Boose's arrest. You might remember him better as Pharaoh." He answered. "All this business with Shifty is small potatoes. I'm after the bigger, juicier stuff. You give me your testimony in court, and I'll give you my word, anything with your name attached to it disappears."

"How do I know I can trust you?" Ethan felt the need to ask.

"You can't." David answered, honestly. "But I *can* swear to you, that if you *don't* help me, I won't only drag your name through the mud, but also your wife's. After the District Attorney tears her apart in the courtroom, she'll regret the day she ever met you."

"Leave my wife out of this!" Ethan growled.

"Well, that's really up to you now…isn't it?" David said, with an arrogant smile.

*   *   *   *   *

After the conversation at the Hollywood Diner was concluded, Ethan drove across town to the Morning Glory Restaurant where Tyler liked to conduct the morning meetings. He looked through his snow pelted windshield at his partners sitting in a booth within the restaurant. They had no idea what was about to befall them, and he aimed to keep it that way as long as he could. Both Tyler and Booker were as dangerous, if not more so, than the thugs they took an oath to rid the streets of. If they knew the young detective was working with Internal Affairs to put them in jail with the crooks they personally helped arrest, Ethan knew they would not hesitate to kill him.

Detective Grimes was successful in getting Ethan to tell them a great many details about a great number of cases. If the Garrity Immunity worked the way he hoped, none of his involvement in the investigations would ever come back to haunt him. It did give Ethan a little sense of relief when he realized his involvement was pretty minimal to begin with. Nevertheless, before ending the meeting, Detective Grimes' tech man fitted Ethan with a wire, so that they could record any future underhanded deals that took place.

Ethan made sure to regain his composure before exiting his car. He knew it was vital for him to act as cool as he could if he were going to be able to help IAD take the two crooked cops down. When the winter time chill hit his exposed face, he knew remaining cool in the Northern temperature was not going to be a problem.

When he entered the restaurant, he noticed Tyler was busy chatting away on his cell phone.

"Hey Brooks! Over here! The crooked cop announced, when he saw Ethan standing in the entryway. "Yeah, I got to let you go. He just got here."

"What's up guys?" Ethan asked, as he slid into the seat next to Booker.

"Thanks to your investigative skill, you'll be happy to know your buddy, Bob, is facing a fourteen-year prison bit." Tyler answered, while holding his glass of orange juice in the air for a toast.

"Not only that," Booker interjected. "But I heard he made a few new *friends* down in C-block. My buddy Danny works down there as a correctional officer, and he told me ol' Bob's face was swollen, 'cause he *fell* in the shower."

Ethan could not help but notice Booker emphasized the words 'friend' and 'fell' in his comment. He understood the meaning loud and clear. Obviously, some of the inmates took offense to Bob's abduction of a little girl and proceeded to let him know about it by roughing him up a little.

"Now *that's* a way to solve a case." Tyler added, before taking a sip of his OJ. "I don't know how you did it, Brooks, but Bob was as talkative as a kid on a sugar high when we brought him back to the station house."

"Just doing my job." Ethan said, in a less than enthusiastic tone.

"You see that, Booker?" Tyler asked. "I told you he could be one of us."

Booker gave his agreement with a nod of his head, as he put a cigarette in his mouth for an after breakfast menthol.

"And that's why I think it's time to bring him in on some of our hustles."

"Yeah, he's earned his way in, dog." Booker concurred, before blowing smoke out of his mouth. "I agree."

"Hustles?" Ethan asked, unsure of the true nature of what the two men were referring to, but having somewhat of an idea.

"We're not going to talk about it here." Tyler said, as he plucked his bill off the table and scanned it for the total. "You'll learn a lot faster with some *hands-on experience,* rather than me just telling you about it."

"Time to meet Evil?" Booker asked, referring to the drug dealer they had under their thumb.

"Time to meet Evil." Tyler acknowledged, as he threw his money for the bill on the table. "Let's roll."

"So, are we going to do any *actual* police work today?" Ethan inquired.

"What do you mean, *actual* police work?" Tyler asked, feeling a little offended by the question.

"Well, I mean, we still haven't busted that gun dealer for selling those semi-automatics to Silky, right?"

"I gave all that info to some uniformed buddies of mine and they already took care of it." Tyler answered, as the three of them scooted out of the booth and headed for the exit. "Sometimes you have to throw your friends a bone every now and again."

"It'll help get the homies you like to work with a promotion." Booker put in.

"That makes sense." Ehtan replied, as the three men stepped out into the cold winter air once more.

"Follow me and Booker to Evil's place, where we can do some *actual* police work." Tyler said, sarcastically.

Ethan did as he was instructed, following Tyler and Booker as they drove to the drug dealer's home in the '69 Caprice. The drive took less than fifteen minutes, taking them from the relatively quiet neighborhoods of Loves Park to the hotspots of Westside Rockford. When the charcoal gray colored muscle car came to a stop in front of a large house on Winnebago Street that had been sectioned off into several apartments, Ethan knew they had reached their destination.

The three men exited their vehicles and made their way up the sidewalk to the run-down looking residence. After they arrived, Tyler proceeded to knock on the door so hard Ethan thought it would fall off the hinges.

"Hey Evil, open up!" Tyler yelled.

"Hold on, dog!" Came an erratic sounding voice from the other side of the door.

A few moments later the door opened up a crack and a short Latino, highly strung out on some powerful narcotics, stared at them with a blank look on his face.

"Is this a bad time?" Booker asked, as they watched the gangster twitching uncontrollably.

"It doesn't matter if it is or if it isn't." Tyler said, rudely, before pushing his way into Evil's apartment.

Once inside, the men saw a young woman sitting on the couch who was in the same, if not worse condition than the Latino. Obviously, Evil had been entertaining a guest before the men came calling.

"Hit the bricks, sister!" Tyler barked, as he threw the woman's coat atop of her. "We got business to discuss, so you need to bounce."

The woman received the message loud and clear and then proceeded to run out the door as soon as she caught sight of their badges.

"Man! What are you doin' runnin' off my company?!" Evil shouted.

"Shut up and sit down!" Tyler yelled back, equaling the Latino's volume.

"What's up, Dog?" Evil felt the need to ask, as he took a seat on the couch.

"Nothing's up." Tyler answered, while sitting in a chair across from the drug dealer.

"So, why'd you run my woman off?"

"I just wanted to introduce you to Brooks, our new partner." Tyler replied, as he motioned for Ethan to step forward. "He's the one I told you about."

Ethan couldn't help but feel as though he was on display, due to the fact that he was. Evil looked him over pretty hard with his shifty eyes. When his face twisted up with an expression of dissatisfaction, Ethan knew something was wrong.

"So, this is the snitch, eh, dog!?" Evil yelled, before jumping from his seat and pulling a pistol out of the waistband of his pants, pointing it in Ethan's face.

Looking down the barrel of Evil's gun, Ethan knew his partners had just fed him to the wolves.

Chapter 22

Little Angela stretched her arms to their absolute limits, but the container that held the homemade chocolate chip cookies she was reaching for still eluded her tiny fingers. Nevertheless, the child of six years had a steadfast determination and would not cease until her goal was achieved.

Moving to the table, she maneuvered one of the chairs onto the slick linoleum, and then pushed it flush against the kitchen counter. After brushing her long auburn bangs from her eyes, the child then climbed atop the seat, where she could then reach the object of her desire without any further hindrance.

She flipped the top of the cow shaped cookie jar open, and it made the prerecorded "mooing" sound the girl loved to hear so much. However, this evening the animated noise brought little pleasure to Angela. The aroma of the tasty treats was every bit as tantalizing as the day her mother pulled them from the oven, but the girl did not allow herself the pleasure of giving in to her desires. Instead, she took a

plate from the dish drainer next to the sink and gathered a
small stack of morsels for her grandmother.

Once she had gathered the last of the cookies, Angela
removed a glass from the cupboard and hopped off the chair.
The girl then took the plate of treats and the empty glass to
the kitchen table, and headed to the refrigerator. She pulled
out the carton of milk and filled the glass to the rim, spilling
a few drops on the table as she did so. The girl was going to
clean the mess up, but not before she brought her
grandmother the late-night snack.

Angela picked the plate of cookies up with one tiny hand
and took the glass of milk in the other, then headed out of the
kitchen. Her little bare feet pitter pattered their way off the
hardwood flooring as she made her way down the long
hallway that led to her grandmother's bedroom. Once there,
she slowly walked to her grandmother's bedside and set the
treat down on the old woman's nightstand.

"Grandma, I brought you some cookies and milk."
Angela said softly. "I know how much you like them."

The child's grandmother turned her head in the direction
of Angela's voice. Her eyes were glassed over and she barely
looked coherent enough to even know who the child was.

"What are you doing, sweetie?" Angela's mother asked
from the hallway.

"I brought grandma some cookies, because I know they
make her feel good." The child replied, in a deeply sincere
tone.

Angela's mother stooped down on one knee so she could
look into her daughter's eyes, while trying to fight the tears
from welling up within her own.

"Grandma's not feeling well enough to eat, hon." She
told the girl, in her most comforting voice. "But it was very
nice of you to think of her.

"What am I going to do with these cookies then?" The girl asked, holding the plate of morsels up for her mother to get a better look.

"Go ahead and eat them yourself at the kitchen table."

"But what can I do for grandma?" Angela asked, genuinely.

The concerned mother stood to her feet and looked at the woman that had given birth to her, lying in bed drawing in labored gasps of air.

"Pray." She said, the words barely audible.

Perched upon the backboard of the grandmother's bed like a vulture awaiting its next meal, a monstrous looking demon watched the females from the spiritual realm. His mission was simple. He was to keep the old woman sick, so the rest of the family members would lose faith in God. So far, his labors have been working, but after hearing the last words the mother had spoken, he began to grow concerned.

He narrowed his grotesque, bulbous eyes to slits as he watched the little girl leave the room. His sickly yellow orbs lacked pupils, but he still took the scene in with picture perfect clarity. His hatred for the humans was unrestrained, as he brought to their home nothing but pain and misery. He would not allow the old woman to recover from her illness if at all possible.

Angela entered the kitchen and then set her plate and glass on the table. She had not forgotten about the small spill she had left from pouring the milk, so she retrieved a napkin from the counter and thoroughly wiped the mess away. After doing so, she climbed into the chair and folded her tiny hands together, holding them up to her forehead.

"Dear God, thank you for these cookies and the milk. I thought my grandma would like them, but Mama says she's too sick to eat. Can you please make grandma feel better? I miss our trips to the park. In Jesus' Name I pray, Amen.

With that said, Angela took her first bite from one of the cookies. Before her taste buds could absorb the flavor, a cool sensation ran down her spine, causing each hair to stand straight up as it did so.

"Angela." A soothing voice called from behind. When the girl turned to see who it was that had called to her, she knocked over her glass of milk, making an even bigger mess than the one she had just cleaned up. She was frozen in place with awe once she saw who the voice belonged to.

It was a handsome angel. His shimmering body seemed to absorb the very lighting from the room, as he stood before her with arms spread wide.

"Fear not, child." He said, rubbing a comforting hand down the girl's soft cheek.

"Who *are* you?" She asked in amazement, not able to take her eyes off the gorgeous creature or even blink.

"My name is Anthony." He replied, gently. "And I come bearing good news. The Lord has heard your prayer and the prayers of your mother. Your grandmother will be healed soon. Do not lose faith."

"Thank you!" The girl proclaimed. "Oh, thank you very much!"

"Angela?" Her mother called, while walking to the kitchen. "Who are you talking to?"

As soon as the angel heard the mother's voice he faded from sight, but was still standing within their presence.

"Mama! The most wonderful thing just happened!" The child screamed excitedly.

"What?" Her mother asked, watching her daughter's eyes growing wider with every second.

"I said a prayer just like you told me to, and an angel came to tell me grandma was going to be alright!"

Her mother didn't quite know what to say. She believed in prayer, and knew that God could heal, but had never been a part of a miracle that she knew of.

"That's wonderful news." She answered, not sure of what else to say. In her heart she wanted to believe, and with nothing left to lose, that is exactly what she chose to do.

After bringing the message he was sent to deliver, Anthony floated his way upward, passing through the ceiling as if it was made of thin air. Once he was out within the nighttime air, the messenger set his sights toward the sky. He wasn't asked to come to the domain of man very often, but when he was, Anthony wanted to fulfill his assignment to satisfaction and then return to the Kingdom of Heaven.

As the angel spread his wings and took to flight, something took hold of his flowing white robe and roughly tugged him down to the roof of the house. When he regained his bearings, Anthony turned to see who or what had grabbed him out of the air. A sense of dread overcame him when he looked into the eyes of the deadliest creatures of darkness he had ever seen.

"Mara Di'Vour…" He gasped.

"That's right, messenger." the demon growled. "My Rippers and I have been scouring the earth for the first sight of you. Once my servants saw you entering this region, they immediately informed me. And here I am."

"Why have I suddenly become the object of interest to you?" The angel dared to ask.

"Don't flatter yourself." Mara replied, with an evil chuckle. "You are merely a means to an end."

Anthony did not know what the demon was talking about, nor did he care. He only knew that if Mara Di'Vour and her

Rippers were involved, he wanted no part in their plans. With one swift move, the angel unlatched his mace from his belt and held it threateningly in the demon's direction.

"Do you really want to test your skills against *us*?" Mara asked haughtily, pulling her dark cloak back to reveal the hilts of her sabers.

"Certainly, that would not be wise." Came another voice from above the two spirits.

The situation became far worse when Anthony saw both Sinjj and Jinx descending upon the rooftop holding a long dark chain. The angel had no idea what the demons wanted to do with him, but since no option of escape had presented itself, he had no choice but to comply…

*　　*　　*　　*　　*

Cazzbein had been watching the events of his charge's day with great interest. Everything appeared to be flowing smoothly until the human followed Tyler and Booker to the drug dealer's apartment. Now, with a handgun pointed directly at Ethan, things were heating up beyond control.

"Easy!" Ethan screamed, as he moved his hand toward the Glock in his shoulder mounted holster.

Before his hand ever touched the gun's grip, Booker snatched it from his possession.

"What's going on?" Ethan asked, already fearing the answer.

Without saying a word, Tyler got up from his seat and walked over to Ethan with a cross look on his face. He then proceeded to remove a sharp knife from his pants pocket before lifting Ethan's shirt to display the recording device's microphone taped to his chest. Showing no sign of surprise, Tyler used the knife to sever the wire from the recording device, rendering it useless.

Cazzbein could see his charge's pulse begin to rise. This was a life-threatening situation that he was sent to protect the human from.

"You stinking, little rat!" Tyler yelled in Ethan's face, before punching him hard in the gut.

The punch was delivered with such impact that Ethan fell to one knee. After doing so, an angry expression emerged on the guardian angel's face. He unsheathed his scimitars and immediately took a defensive posture in order to protect his charge.

"You were going to serve me and Booker up to the DA?" Tyler continued the verbal assault. "After we took you under our wing?"

"Not a smart move, dog." Booker added. "Now you gotta be dealt with."

Booker was right about you all along!" Tyler growled. "You could never be one of us!"

"Why would I want to be?" Ethan shot back. "You two are worse than the scum we swore an oath to lock up!"

Tyler pulled back his fist in order to strike Ethan in the face, but then stopped himself.

"You know, if we weren't stagin' your death right now, I'd punch you square in the mouth!" Tyler screamed back. "But I don't want to leave a mark on you."

Ethan's mind began to race. They were indeed going to kill him. He began to scan the room for anything that would aid him in an escape. Eventually, his eyes fell upon a revolver strapped into Booker's ankle holster. Since he was still in a kneeling position, the weapon was not so far from his reach. Cazzbein followed Ethan's line of vision to its end and knew what the human was planning. He would back Ethan's play whenever he made the move."

"The Internal Affairs has been recording everything up until this point!" Ethan yelled, in an attempt to stall the men. "They know where we are! How are you going to explain my death to them?"

"Easy." Booker replied, nonchalantly. "Evil killed you during a drug bust."

Tyler pulled an arrest warrant out of his jacket pocket and unfolded it for Ethan to see.

"Let me ask you something, rookie." Tyler said, coolly. "How do you think all the judges and District Attorneys get to live so extravagantly? Ever give it much thought?"

Ehtan did not respond to the questions, therefore letting Tyler know he had no answer.

"They take bribes. A lot of them." Tyler answered. "I learned that lesson early in my career. That's why me and Booker have remained off their radar for as long as we have."

"They all like tastin' the cream." Booker interjected. "So, what do you think crossed my mind when I got a call from the District Attorney's Office this morning, telling me you were talking to IAD?" Tyler asked, plainly.

Ehtan didn't see the need to answer, because the scenario playing out before him was enough for him to figure it out.

"What I don't get is…once Evil kills me, what are you going to do about him?" Ethan shrewdly inquired. "If that warrant is for his arrest, then you only have two options. You either have to arrest him or kill him too."

"Hey! What are you guys tryin' to pull?!" Evil shouted, after finally figuring out his part in their scheme.

The little Latino received his answer in the form of a hail of bullets, as Booker shot him repeatedly with Ethan's gun. In the mix of all the excitement, Ethan seized his opportunity and dove toward Booker's ankle holster. In the process of removing the gun, he managed to fling the man's leg backward far enough for him to land flat on his back. With all his might, Booker tried to aim his weapon at Ethan. Little did he know, a guardian angel held his arm from doing so.

"Hey! Stop him!" Tyler screamed, before removing his Beretta from its holster.

Ethan did not allow him to use the weapon, however, due to the fact that he unloaded three shots of his own in Tyler's direction before diving behind the kitchen wall for cover. The bullets missed their mark by only a short margin, as Tyler leapt behind the couch before the hot lead ever reached him. By this time even Booker had regained himself and scurried behind the couch next to his partner.

"Put that gun away and get the one in Evil's hand." Tyler ordered Booker, as he began making a call on his cell phone. "When the crime scene guys get here, I don't want 'em finding any of *our* bullets."

"What are you doin'?" Booker asked, looking at the device in his partner's hand.

"I'm buying us some insurance." Tyler answered.

"Looks like we have a standoff!" Ethan shouted, from behind the kitchen wall. "How's this going to end?"

"Either way, it's not looking too good for you!" Tyler screamed back. "I just called some of the bangers I got on my payroll and they're heading to your house! What do you think they'll find when they get there!?"

During the brief exchange Booker managed to pull the gun out of Evil's hand and move back into cover. He leveled the barrel in the last direction he heard Ethan's voice and peeled off three shots of his own.

Seeing the bullets soaring toward his charge, Cazzbein used his scimitars to deflect each one away. The slugs tore through the drywall two inches from where Ethan's head was resting on the wall. They would have found their mark had Cazzbein not been present to thwart their path of flight from reaching the intended target.

Although the bullets nearly ended his life, Ethan's thoughts were not on the flying pieces of lead, but instead on his wife. Wisely the young man dialed his home number in order to warn Becky to leave the house. Unfortunately, on several attempts at trying, Ethan only got the answering machine. Seeing no other way around it, Ethan knew he had to end the shoot out quickly and then race home to personally protect Becky from Tyler's death squad.

Cazzbein saw the predicament Ethan was facing. Trying to help the best he could, the angel wafted into the bathroom and moved the mirror from the medicine cabinet into the correct position. He then moved back to Ethan's side and whispered advice into his ear.

"Look into the bathroom."

Ethan disengaged his thoughts from the shootout for a moment and happened to glance in the direction of the bathroom. Using the reflection from the bathroom mirror, Ethan was able to pick a location on the couch where he took aim and fired his weapon once. The bullet ripped through the couch right between Tyler and Booker's heads.

"That was close, dog." Booker whispered.

"You got this situation under control?" Tyler asked.

"What do you mean?" Booker queried, unsure of his partner's intent.

"Give me some cover fire." He ordered. "I'm gonna go out the door and come in through a window in the back bedroom. Then we can get him in a crossfire."

"A'ight, dog." Booker replied. "I'm with you."

After saying so, Booker unleashed five successive shots from evil's gun. Ethan barely had enough room to dodge the spray of bullets, but managed to lean just far enough away from the assault that he did not get exterminated. However, one of the rounds did manage to graze his neck during the rampage, causing him severe pain. He moved his hand to the wound and felt the warm, moist blood flowing freely between his fingers. Even though he managed to survive the succession of gunplay, the diversion had worked to perfection, allowing Tyler to slip through the door undetected.

"You still alive, rookie?" Booker asked, evilly.

Ethan did not answer. Instead, he peeked through one of the bullet holes Booker made with his shooting. The hole allowed him a perfect view of the living room, where he saw only one set of legs crouching behind the couch. Moving his revolver around the corner of the wall, Ethan was able to take careful aim while not exposing himself.

"Hey Booker!" He yelled.

"What?!" Booker screamed back.

"I'm doing better than you!" Ethan announced, before firing a round into the dirty cop's knee.

"AAHH!!" Booker screamed, before inadvertently jumping to his feet. Once he was no longer behind cover, Ethan fired the last hollow point from the revolver.

Cazzbein knew it was Ethan's final bullet and that the human's life depended on the accuracy of the shot. The angel also knew that the projectile was going to miss its mark by less than an inch. Seeing this, Cazzbein grabbed the bullet out of the air and sent it on a new trajectory, where it tore through Booker's head, killing him instantly.

Having no time to gloat over the shot, Ethan ran over to Booker's fallen body and plucked his Glock out of the dead man's hand.

"It didn't have to end like this...*dog.*" The young detective said, before bolting through the open door to find his wife.

Cazzbein was about to go with his charge until a voice called to him, stopping him in his tracks.

"Cazzbein wait!"

The angel turned to see his friend Gunthar. The expression on the big guardian's face did not sit well with him.

"Gunthar...?" He asked, truly perplexed by his friend's appearance. "What is wrong?"

"Anthony has been taken."

The dilemma that presented itself was nearly more than the angel could handle.

Chapter 23

All the kids in the neighborhood had at one time or another been dared to stay overnight in the house on the corner of Scenic Drive and Antelope. The dilapidated, old structure had been the target of many scary tales by the children in the community ever since it was condemned some ten years ago. It was simple enough to understand how the frightening stories were devised, since on many occasions the owners of the surrounding homes have reported hearing loud noises erupting from the house late at night. However, to date nothing has been seen with the naked eye to explain the commotion.

Truth be known, from the human viewpoint, the aged structure may have been nothing more than an eyesore bringing down the property value. However, to the creatures of the spiritual realm, whether they be angel or demon, the land the house was built upon, has been and always will be, neutral ground.

Since fighting of any kind was forbidden on this particular soil, it was no surprise that Dartamus chose this spot for his expected meeting with Cazzbein. The demon's shifty eyes seemed to dash about in their sockets even more quickly than they usually did, since his level of anxiety was tweaked to an extra high level.

Underneath his long black cloak, his scrawny hand moved up and down, as he continually reassured himself that his hidden dagger was still in place. The shifty demon kept the weapon close, just in case the meeting took a turn for the worst. He doubted the blade would be needed, considering combat of any kind would result in the instant destruction of the instigators, but it still did not hurt to be prepared.

As Dartamus grew more nervous, he unconsciously began to pace. His involuntary journey took him by the window several times before he caught sight of several young boys sneaking through the chain link fence that surrounded the property. A grin spread across his face as a mischievous idea formulated within his thoughts. Just as he was about to put his idea into action, the demon heard the one sound that was able to send chills down even *his* crooked spine.

"Tell me what you've done with Anthony, fiend, or I'll wet my blades with your dark essence!" Cazzbein screamed with hostility, as he and his companions soared through the house's ceiling at record speeds.

"Easy, guardian!" Dartamus countered. "Remember…the ground on which we stand is to remain a safe haven for our two kinds to assemble!"

"Cowardly scum!" Gunthar growled.

"What you interpret as cowardly, brute, I view as a vital necessity." Dartamus purred, causing the trio to grow even angrier.

"Let us begin then." Glistinia put in, trying to bring the two parties into a more communicative role.

"I agree." Cazzbein replied, in an angry tone. "What does your master want with Anthony?"

A malicious grin formed on the demon's lips, as he paused for dramatic effect.

"Absolutely nothing." He at last answered.

"Well, that makes no sense at all…" Gunthar said, his last words trailing off as he tried to figure out his enemy's motives.

"On the contrary, my friend," Cazzbein replied with certainty, as he knew precisely what the demon meant. "Anthony is being held as bait."

"But for what?" Gunthar asked, still not caught up to speed.

"Me." Cazzbein said, grimly.

"It appears you are as quick with your wits as you are with your blades, guardian." Dartamus interjected. "I think it fair to inform you that it is not just Hunter that wants me to bring you to him."

"Who else then?" Cazzbein questioned.

"It seems your exploits have caught the eye of Hunter's master as well, Mistress Vixanna." The fiend explained.

"Vixanna..." Glistinia gasped, without realizing she had done so.

As if a spark was suddenly triggered within Cazzbein's mind, he narrowed his brow, heavy in contemplation. Maybe this turn of events could be made to his advantage, and inevitably benefit Ethan. He had been debating on whether or not to go in search of the powerful archdemon, but Vixanna took the trouble to seek him out instead. The guardian knew he could not squander the opportunity that had just been openly presented to him.

"This is madness!" Glistinia shouted, as she slung the bow from around her slim shoulder. Once her fingers enclosed the string it caused the weapon to begin glowing brightly, as an arrow of pure light materialized within the bow's curved chassis. "We will not idly stand by and watch as our friend is carried away to be sacrificed for that witch's pleasure!"

At that moment the house began to shake violently as the ground sensed the amount of growing hostility. Chunks of the old plaster fell from the walls and crashed to the floor in heaps, while large wooden beams broke away from the ceiling and followed suit. The display of power was even more impressive in the spiritual world. Tiny orbs of light began to tear away from her beautiful body, as she was beginning to be torn apart one small piece at a time.

"Your weapon! Put it away! The land will absorb you if you do not respect its peaceful existence!" Cazzbein warned.

Glistinia quickly heeded her companion's advice and whirled the bow back over her shoulder. Once this was done, the tiny glowing orbs that had been tore from her body returned to the angel, making her whole once again. The house then ceased its intense thrashing, satisfied that the meeting had returned to a passive status.

"You see," Dartamus began, as a cocky grin adorned his lips. "There is really no choice. If you want us to release Anthony, Cazzbein will have to come with me."

"There is one thing I still do not understand…" Gunthar said, rubbing a hand through his beard as he spoke. "Why would we trade one friend for another? There is nothing to be gained from this situation. Either way, one of our friends will be taken.

"Not necessarily." Dartamus responded. "Mistress Vixanna merely wants Cazzbein for a duel."

"What duel?" Glistinia asked, casting the demon a suspicious glance.

"Mistress Vixanna was very displeased when she heard the human known as Ethan Brooks, asked forgiveness of his sins. To make matters worse, after she found out that Hunter was the one that interfered when Mara Di'Vour was about to deliver the ending blow to Cazzbein, she nearly destroyed him. The only way Hunter can now regain his standing with Vixanna, is to defeat Cazzbein in a one-on-one duel. However, if the guardian defeats Hunter, he will have earned his freedom."

"Hunter can never defeat me in swordplay." Cazzbein said, confidently.

"Either way, Vixanna cares little." Dartamus responded. "The duel will decide whether one of our most hated enemies is defeated, or if Hunter is punished for his arrogance. If the latter is true then Vixanna will show all of her underlings that she is, as always, in total control."

"If Cazzbein goes with you, what guarantee do we have that you will release Anthony?" Gunthar inquired, genuinely concerned with the welfare of both of his comrades.

"None." The demon answered. "You will just have to take my word for it."

"Bah! Everyone knows you monsters cannot be trusted!" Gunthar scoffed.

"Have no fear, my friend." Cazzbein said, taking his companion by the arm and moving him off to the side to speak with him quietly. "This is the only way to get Anthony back. Even if they do not keep their word, once I am in their lair I can help Anthony escape."

"I do not like this arrangement." Gunthar replied, honestly.

"What would Jesus do, Gunthar?" Cazzbein asked, firmly. "It was He Himself that said, "Greater love hath no man than this, that a man lay down his life for his friends.""

Cazzbein stopped for a moment so that Gunthar could grasp the full weight of his words. Once he saw the wave of submission wash over the powerful angel's visage, he knew his friend at last understood.

"Make sure you do not destroy all of those accursed dogs,' Gunthar said, with a smile slowly replacing his gloomy expression. "Take care to leave some for me."

"I would not think of depriving you of such pleasure, my friend.' Cazzbein answered, with a wink and a sturdy slap on one of Gunthar's broad shoulders.

"Shall we go then?" Dartamus asked, growing leery of the two conversing angels.

"Take care, Gunthar, and you as well, Glistinia." Cazzbein said, before turning back to face the demon. "I am ready."

"Good. I am glad to see you are being compliant." Dartamus muttered mockingly, drawing a look of disdain from the angel. "I will need to take your weapon though." He continued, pointing a long misshapen finger at the spectacularly crafted scimitars strapped around the guardian's waist.

Cazzbein hesitated. Other than when he was held captive at the hands of Vermillion, he could not remember the magnificent blades being anywhere but sheathed at his sides, or being put to good work in his capable hands. He never imagined having to relinquish them to the enemy once again.

"Surely you did not think I was going to let you keep them?" Dartamus asked, raising an inquisitive eyebrow, as he crossed his bony arms across his chest.

Tentatively, Cazzbein moved his finger toward the latch and triggered the button that would allow the belt to be loosened. As the weapons fell from his torso, it felt to the angel as if one of his very own limbs had just been removed. After he wound the strap around the sheathed scimitars, the guardian then passed the blades that had destroyed a countless score of demons into the gnarled hand of the very thing the weapons were crafted to slay.

"Excellent." Dartamus purred, almost salivating with excitement. At long last he would do something that even his superior, Hunter, could not do. He was going to be the one to bring Cazzbein to Mistress Vixanna. Little did the low-level demon realize, Mistress Vixanna only sent him on the trek because he was expendable, and would not be missed if the meeting turned out for the worst. "Now…I must bind you." He continued, showing the angel a pair of shackles attached to a long black chain.

Cazzbein recognized the restraints immediately, and knew the bonds could never physically be broken, because each of the chain's links were constructed from the same imperishable material as the weapons the creatures of outer darkness wielded in battle. Once the fetters were around his wrists, he knew that he would truly be at the mercy of his enemies. And to be left to the compassion of monsters that shared no such emotion was a frightening feeling indeed.

Nevertheless, the valiant angel held his wrists out with courage and did not so much as flinch as the restaurants were fastened into place. Once this was done, Dartamus conjured up the gateway that would take him and his captive back to Vixanna's keep. The shimmering oval portal sliced its way through the darkness of the room until it reached its maximum height of eight feet. After doing so, thick clouds of smoke poured forth, engulfing the entire floor. Cazzbein tried to peer his way through to the other side, so he would know what to expect once he arrived within the walls of the evil stronghold. Nevertheless, even with his extraordinary vision, he could see nothing but a kaleidoscope of optical light.

Dartamus was just about to take his first steps into the gateway when he remembered something that stopped him.

"I nearly forgot." He mumbled incoherently, before turning in the opposite direction. The demon then disappeared through the walls of the house with Cazzbein in tow, leaving Gunthar and Glistinia staring at each other confusedly.

Dartamus soared his way toward the ground where the young human boys were about to enter into the house via an opening between one of the plywood boards that was supposed to be sealing off a broken window. When he arrived, the demon silently made his way up behind them, where he then made himself visible, shrieking in a hellish manner as he did so.

The boys were so terrified at the demon's sudden appearance that they ran straight for the gate that they had originally entered, not stopping once to see if they had left anyone behind.

"Cowardly humans!" Dartamus proclaimed. "I think two of them even wet themselves. What does God see in these creatures anyway?"

"Is this what demons do to preoccupy themselves before Judgment Day?" Cazzbein asked, referring to the everlasting punishment all the demons knew they were going to endure by means of a lake of burning fire.

Dartamus turned to the angel and shot him a menacing glare, not happy one bit to be reminded of the rapidly approaching damnation.

"You need not worry about me, guardian. You should be more concerned for yourself at the present." He sneered.

With that said, the demon gave the chain a sharp tug and drug the angel back into the house where the portal still awaited. Dartamus glanced around the room and was delighted to see that Glistinia and Gunthar had already left the premises.

"Looks like your friends could not wait to abandon you." He said with an insulting grin.

Cazzbein had no reply. He hung his head so as not to look into the demon's eyes. The angel knew that his friends could not stand idly by and wait for his return because they had to get back and look after Ethan.

"Come." The demon ordered, giving the chain another quick jerk to let his prisoner know who was in charge.

Once he was satisfied with the display of dominance, the demon stepped into the depths of the glowing portal with his captive slowly making up the rear. The gateway seemed to tug at them as they sunk within its sparkling energy. After they were both swallowed up by the portal's current, they were transported to their destination at speeds faster than a human's ability to produce thought. Cazzbein had little time to worry about their arrival, but let it be known, he dreaded it with every fiber of his glorious being.

*   *   *   *   *

Tyler heard the shooting from the outside of the house. He had hoped to find Ehtan's dead body on the ground courtesy of one of Booker's bullets, as he climbed through the window in the back bedroom. However, he feared the worst when he rounded the corner and found no one in the kitchen.

A few droplets of blood remained from where one of the rounds scraped Ethan's neck. Other than that, the kitchen was unoccupied.

Tyler instantly took a defensive stance, leveling the sights of his Beretta in case the need arose for him to fire. He cleared the kitchen and then leapt from the open doorway to the bathroom, being mindful to keep his weapon trained on the open room.

The bathroom was vacant of anyone other than himself. Satisfied with his search, he then took position up against the room's door frame, leaning his head out just enough to sneak a peek into the living room.

"No…" Tyler gasped, when he saw the blood spattered all over the wall behind the couch.

Taking no care for his own well-being at that moment, Tyler rushed behind the couch, dreading what he'd find waiting for him.

"Booker…" He said, aloud to himself, as he fell to his knees, overcome with grief.

He stared in disbelief at the body of his partner of nearly ten years. Together they had amassed an enormous amount of money and an empire of illegal schemes that would keep the cash flowing in for years to come. And now, all because they had to take this *rookie* into their midst, his partner lay here in a lifeless puddle of his own blood.

Gathering his thoughts, Tyler pulled himself together. The plan had been flawless. Evil was going to kill Ethan and then he and Booker were going to kill Evil. The little Latino had been proving himself to be such a liability as of late, his replacement would have been welcomed with open arms. The whole scene would have appeared as a drug bust gone bad.

That mattered little now. The plan had come unraveled. Tyler knew he would be lucky to come out of this alive himself. The blonde haired slickster had already determined since the day he and Booker began the trek down their dark path that he was not going to prison. There was only one way this mess could be salvaged now. And that would be handled by means of several well delivered phone calls.

*   *   *   *   *

Ethan drove as fast as his car could safely handle, as he veered in and out of traffic at harrowing speeds. Since he was not driving an emergency vehicle, he had no lights or sirens to warn the pedestrians to curb their vehicles. So, needless to say, that made his job of beating Tyler's gangbangers to his house that much more difficult.

Ethan didn't know where Tyler's crew would be coming from, so therefore, he didn't know how soon they would be arriving. Seeing as though he was still in good standing with the police force, Ethan wisely called 911 on his cell phone.

"911, what's your emergency?" Came the expected answer.

"Yes, this is Detective Ethan Brooks with the Winnebago County Sheriff's Department. Badge number 2460. I need backup sent to 3024 Ellen Avenue…"

"Can you repeat your name and badge number again, sir?" The operator interrupted.

"Excuse me?" Ethan asked, in a perturbed tone.

"Could you please repeat your name and badge number?" She asked again.

"My name is Ethan Brooks, badge number 2460." He responded.

"What is your current location, Detective Brooks?" The operator asked, offhandedly.

"*My* location? Ethan asked, in a confused manner. "No, you don't understand. I need backup sent to-"

Before Ethan finished the sentence he had figured out what was going on. Immediately he ended the call before saying another word. He followed his thoughts through to the conclusion and determined that Tyler had used the police two-way to call him in. Booker had been using his Glock to spray bullets all over Evil's apartment. Tyler had obviously beaten him to the punch with the call and was trying to make it look as though Ethan had gone rogue. The young detective had no choice but to try and save Becky on his own.

It was at that moment Ethan's cell phone chimed. He had expected it to be the police dispatcher calling him back to find out his location, so they could bring him in for questioning. Ethan knew he would surely be able to prove his innocence in the matter, especially when a simple phone call to the Internal Affairs Department would explain everything away. Nevertheless, the time could not be spared. Becky's life depended on it. However, when he looked at the caller ID, he was somewhat shocked to see Tyler's name appear.

"Yeah?" Ethan answered, angrily.

"Hey, rookie, your name just came up over the two-way." Tyler said arrogantly. "Looks like you're a wanted man." Ethan said nothing, as he whipped his car around slower moving vehicles.

"You might as well not stop by your house." Tyler continued. "My boys already snatched your wife. Besides, by the time you get there, cops will be swarmin' the place with itchy trigger fingers lookin' to take down a cop killer."

"Where's my wife, Tyler?" Ethan growled.

"She's safe." Tyler answered, coolly. "For now."

"Where is she?!" Ethan asked again with venom, as he slammed a fist into his steering wheel.

"Now, now, now. You better calm down, rookie." Tyler teased.

"You're just wasting time." Ethan said. "When the boys downtown finally take my statement, all they'll have to do is call IAD and they'll find out I was working for them to take you down. The only thing you're doing is buying time until they haul your sorry butt in."

"Wrong again, small timer." Tyler shot back. "You must not have heard. Detective David Grimes and his little tech freak just got killed in a drive by shooting."

"What…?" Ethan gasped.

"And since my buddy down at the DA's office intercepted your immunity papers, looks like you're flyin' solo. Face it *rookie*, there's nobody left to back your story. That deal you made ain't lookin' too good now, is it?" Tyler said, smugly.

Ethan could not believe his ears. If Tyler's story was true, then he really was all alone. Maybe he had locked horns with a more capable opponent than he was capable of handling.

"So, what do you want?" Ethan asked in a defeated tone, as he pulled the car to a stop in a vacant parking lot.

"Ahhh!" Tyler gloated. "Now you're beginning to understand that I have you in the palm of my hand."

"Cut the sarcasm!" Ethan yelled. "My wife didn't do anything wrong! She doesn't deserve this! So, what do you want?!"

"As far as I can tell, rookie, there's only one more mouth left to silence, and that's yours." Tyler answered, in a point-blank fashion. "I'll let your precious little wife go, as long as you meet me at the abandoned industrial building down by the docks in two hours. Try not to get picked up by the boys in blue until then or I have no reason to honor this agreement."

"Tyler! Don't you-" Ehtan tried to get one last warning in, but was unable to before the phone went dead.

The young man's mind raced. Ehtan did not know if his wife was still alive or not, and that thought alone drove him mad. By all aspects Tyler appeared to have him cornered. He could not go to the police or he would be arrested. Furthermore, there were no witnesses left to come forth on his behalf and vouch for the fact that he had been working for Internal Affairs to take Tyler and Booker down. To make matters worse, if he were spotted by any patrolmen, he would be arrested on the spot, and Tyler would kill Becky when he missed the arranged meeting.

Ehtan did not believe in the least that Tyler would ever let Becky walk out of the encounter alive. There was too much at stake, and Tyler lacked any shred of honor. Nevertheless, if Becky stood any chance at getting out of there safely, it was because he showed up and personally saved her himself. In the meantime, Ethan had two hours in which to keep low. He already knew home was not an option, and going back to the station house would mean certain death to Becky.

Where would no one think to look for him? He wondered. Before a thought could formulate within his manic brain, Ethan's cell phone chimed once more. He looked at the caller ID with uncertainty, not knowing if the person on the other end of the line was going to help him or hinder him even further. With no other solution presenting itself, Ethan

hesitantly put the phone to his ear and began the
conversation.

Chapter 24

When Dartamus strolled into Vixanna's throne room with the mighty Cazzbein in shackles, a satisfied utterance that could only be described as a deep growl escaped her lips. She looked upon the great angel with her cruel gaze as the look of contempt never left her glistening orbs. Standing before her was the sole angel that had been credited for sending several of her legions spiraling into the depths of the abyss. Nothing could be more satisfying to the arch demon but to know he would cause her no more strife, since he would never leave this place again.

"Mistress Vixanna." Dartamus cooed, as he stooped into a gracious bow. "It gives me great pleasure to present to you, the warring angel, Cazzbein!"

Vixanna paid the sniveling minion no care, as her thoughts were fastened completely on the angel. Truly, God created this creature specifically for the art of swordplay, as the craftsmanship of his flawless presence shown clearly throughout his frame. Cazzbein's lean, taut muscles were chiseled as if crafted from marble, allowing him to wield his scimitars with the perfect balance of speed, strength and dexterity. His sparkling azure eyes were as keen as a hawk's, allowing nothing to escape his attention, while his gorgeous white wings possessed the perfect span in which to allow him to soar like an eagle.

Unaware of the fact that she too was being sized up, Cazzbein studied the six armed she-demon with a scrutinizing gaze of his own. Never had he seen such a creature control so many limbs with such precision that Cazzbein wondered if the demon's thought process was that much more superior to his own. When the opportunity presented itself, he would surely find out.

As to date, this was the first time either of the spiritual beings had ever seen one another. Their paths had always taken them in separate directions, but continually both of them seemed to have an indirect impact on the others' agenda.

"The mighty warring angel, Cazzbein…" Vixanna said, in a deeply evil intonation. **"…You have caused me considerable anguish over the centuries. However, all that ends today."**

"It will certainly end for one of us, I agree." Cazzbein said, definitely, as he stared into the demon's hate filled eyes.

"A hero to the end, eh angel?" Vixanna asked. **"You still have not grasped the fact that your accolades end here."**

With that said, Vixanna motioned for Dartamus to take him through a doorway off to the side of the room. Cazzbein was surprised to see the throne room barren of all but a few guards. He was not aware of the fact that the archdemon's hordes were scouring the region, marking prospective candidates for the upcoming battle that would soon be taking place.

Turning his thoughts from the loosely garrisoned throne room, Cazzbein's eyes fell upon the key fastened to Dartamus' belt. After the demon tugged him over to the door Vixanna had gestured to, Dartamus plucked the key off his belt and used it to lock the entryway.

"Enter!" Dartamus barked, in a tone that did not match his authority. "Hunter awaits you within."

"My scimitars?" The angel rightly asked.

"I think not." The underling said in a nonchalant tone, as he used the key to unlock Cazzbein's shackles and then placed it back upon the belt where it had been taken a moment before. "These belong to me now. A reward for delivering you here."

"No, I think not." Cazzbein proclaimed, before head butting the demon on his large snout, and snatching the weapons from his possession.

After doing so, the angel rushed down the corridor where his most deadly enemy awaited. When Dartamus had finally regained his wits, he closed the door and was about to lock it when he made a horrifying discovery.

The angel had stolen his key during the attack.

It was true that the little imp did not possess near the intelligence as his superiors. However, even his primal instincts were enough to calculate Vixanna would utterly destroy him if she were to find out the angel held the means of escape within his grasp.

Subtly, Dartamus slipped through the doorway, being mindful to shut it behind himself.

When Cazzbein reached the end of the corridor, he was standing within a wide opened cavern. In the midst of the hollow, Hunter stood defiantly with his saber and serrated dagger well in hand. At the demon's feet laid Anthony, bound in the same sort of unbreakable shackles as Cazzbein had taken off his own wrists only moments ago.

"Salutations, Cazzbein." Hunter purred.

"Salutations, Hunter." Cazzbein replied, as he closed the gap between them.

"We meet once more." Hunter said, calmly, as if talking to an old friend.

"So we do." Cazzbein replied, in the same intonation, while slowly unsheathing his scimitars.

The two had gained respect for one another over the course of their many battles. Hunter now knew that his rival's reputation was well deserved. While Cazzbein, likewise, held his enemy's swordplay in high esteem, and also owed him a debt of gratitude for saving him when Mara Di'Vour was about to incapacitate him at their last meeting."

"The angel at your feet shares no role in this duel." Cazzbein said peacefully, as he gestured to Anthony with the tip of his scimitars.

"I agree." Hunter replied, as he stooped down and unlatched his binds.
Once the shackles were loosed, Cazzbein motioned for Anthony to leave with a quick nod of his head.

"Get far from this dreadful place, Anthony," Cazzbein advised. "And be mindful not to interfere."

The young-looking angel heeded his friend's words and moved out of the way of the two warring spirits with haste.

"Shall we begin?" Hunter queried.

"We shall." Cazzbein replied, through gritted teeth.

With that said, both combatants leapt at one another with the tips of their weapons aimed at lethal locations. Seeing this, Cazzbein wisely altered his attack and deflected each of Hunter's weapons away with a quick flick of each wrist and then countered with a sharp kick to his enemy's midsection.

The blow knocked Hunter back a couple of steps, but did not slow his pace in the least.

The ivory haired demon pressed on with a successive number of thrusts aimed at the angel's exposed neckline. Cazzbein parried each attack away an inch before they were able to do any damage. After fending off the fifth thrust, Cazzbein fell into a low crouch that he swiftly turned into a spinning slash attack directed toward the demon's legs.

Sensing the move, Hunter used his powerful wings to carry him a safe distance away a split second before the scimitar's razor-sharp edge sliced off a section of his long, black robe.

Cazzbein let the momentum of the spin carry him around and then leapt into the air to continue the duel in the form of aerial combat. He soared into his enemy with a closed fist that connected to the demon's jaw. The blow did minimal damage at best, but was successful in jolting Hunter out of his rhythm.

With the energy of the fight now on Cazzbein's side, the angel pressed onward with two slashes targeting the demon's esophagus and a third aimed at his hip. As expected, Hunter was easily able to deflect the swipes to his throat, but since the third attack was purposely thrown into the mix in order to confuse him, the scimitar sunk deep into the demon's side, emerging wet with his dark essence.

"AAAHH!" Hunter shrieked in anguish.

"First blood is mine." Cazzbein declared, as he continued the assault, never slowing for an instance.

The stinging pain was almost unbearable. Nevertheless, Hunter knew his existence in this realm would be decided by the outcome of this battle. And since the searing pain of hellfire was far worse than a scimitar cut, Hunter decided something unorthodox needed to be done in order to turn the tide of the battle in his favor once more.

Risking all, the snowy-haired devil lunged at his rival, seizing his left arm in the process. After doing so, Hunter dove toward the jagged rocks below taking the angel with him as he went. With all of his weight placed squarely upon the limb, Hunter drove Cazzbein's arm into the surface of the rocky cavern with massive force, causing the scimitar in that hand to fall from his grasp.

Cazzbein's armor absorbed much of the blow to his shoulder area, but his exposed bicep was deeply bruised. The demon's attack had been a success.

Cazzbein barely had time to get to his knees before Hunter swung the dagger in his left hand toward the top of his golden-haired cranium. In order to defend against the strike, the angel pulled back his head just far enough to change the weapon's intended target. Instead of a finishing blow, a fine line was cut below the angel's right eye.

Seeing his foe on his knees, Hunter came in again with a slash from the saber in his right hand. However, Cazzbein did not allow the attack to flourish. The angel used his empty hand to grab Hunter by the wrist just as the strike was coming down upon him and then punched three solid fists into the demon's Adam's apple.

The blows had been unleashed with tremendous impact. Had Hunter been a mortal creature he would have surely been killed. The demon stumbled backward, trying desperately to put distance between him and the angel while he struggled to regain his composure. As he backpedaled, his foot dipped over the ledge on which they fought, where the jagged rock floor beckoned far below.

Cazzbein used the opportunity to lunge for his discarded scimitar. Once the weapon was within his grasp, he again pressed the attack. Using the scimitar he had just retrieved, the angel sliced the weapon through the air intending to decapitate his foe.

Still feeling the effects of the damage done to his Adam's apple, Hunter instinctively enshrouded himself within the confines of his wings. If more time had been available for the demon to formulate another defensive move, he surely would have chosen a different course of action. Hunter's thick, leathery, bat-like wings had sufficiently protected him from certain doom, but the mutilation was catastrophic. The sharp blade's pass was unhindered, as it hacked the limbs into useless stumps.

Predicting the end was near, Cazzbein moved in to finish the duel. He pulled both scimitars back and prepared to drive them through his enemy's midsection, when he felt a dagger sink deep into his ribs. Apparently, there was more fight left in Hunter than he had originally assessed.

"I have won…" Hunter gasped, as he saw the angel's eyes grow wide with astonishment.

Cazzbein fell to his backside, the serrated dagger tearing the wound even more as it pulled free. The angel moved his hand over the lesion to slow the loss of essence from his body, but the glowing fluid poured out relentlessly. As much as he dreaded to admit, Hunter may have spoken true. The demon may have well just defeated him with the unexpected move.

Hunter slowly moved away from the ledge to tower over his fallen rival.

"I can hardly believe it…" The demon said absently, as he slowly dug the tip of his saber further into the angel's wound. "I *have* won…"

As Hunter opened the injury even further, Cazzbein thought of his charge Ethan. The young man was at this moment facing the greatest challenge of his life. If ever there was a time when the human needed him, it was now.

With speed as quick as thought, Cazzbein leapt from the ground, allowing the saber's blade to run through his body and emerge out his backside. The move caused him tremendous pain, but allowed him to get within range of his greatest enemy. Once Hunter was within reach, Cazzbein took hold of each of his shoulders and plunged both of them over the side of the ledge on which they fought.

Hunter's face twisted into an expression of terror as he realized what his enemy had just done. With his wings decimated, there was no way for the demon to slow their descent. He was helpless to do anything more than watch as the ledge they had just descended over rapidly disappeared.

With a swift pace, the two spiritual warriors crashed into the jagged rocks of the cavern floor with an unforgiving collision. And then…the duel was over.

*　　*　　*　　*　　*

Ethan pulled his car into a stall within the Spirit Led Church parking lot, and shifted it into park. He had told no one about his experience last Sabbath morning, and therefore no one would think to look for him here. The young detective determined this would be the best location in which to pass the next two hours while contemplating a strategy for his former partner Tyler Lynch.

Ethan exited the car and then strolled up the lilac lined sidewalk to the doorway. When he tugged on the door's handle, he was relieved to see that it was unlocked. Thinking the chapel was left opened for congregation members to pray, Ethan entered, showing no signs of concern. It wasn't until he walked into the sanctuary that he discovered something was unusual.

"Hello, Ethan." Pastor Joe Horton greeted, from the front of the chapel. "I've been expecting you."

"You have?" Ethan asked, truly not understanding how the preacher could have known he was coming.

As Ethan approached Joe, he noticed the pastor had several artifacts displayed upon the front row seat before him. The objects looked extravagant. To Ethan, the items appeared to be some sort of ancient weaponry that could have easily passed for priceless works of art.

"Yes, Ethan, I have been waiting for this day for twenty-four years." Joe answered, with a disarming smile.

"What?" Ethan inquired, in a perplexed tone. "I'm sorry, but I don't quite understand. Didn't we just meet the other day for the first time?"

"Please take a seat." Joe replied, as he gestured to a spot on the seat before him. "I'll be happy to explain."

Ethan was more than a little perturbed by the exchange, but decided to take a seat and humor the preacher in order to get to the bottom of what he was talking about.

"That's funny." Joe said with a laugh, after Ethan stared up at him waiting for an explanation. "I've practiced for years what I was going to say to you when I at last had the opportunity. Now that you're actually here, I don't know where to start."

"How about starting from the beginning." Ethan advised.

"I guess that would be best." The pastor said, before clearing his throat. "Well, Ethan, I was present the night your mother passed away. That was the same night you took your first breath."

"Wha-? You knew my mother?" Ethan was barely able to stammer, the unexpected comment throwing him for a loop.

"Oh yes. Jody Brooks was a fine young woman." Joe answered. "She attended this very church when I was a young preacher just starting out."

"This isn't your way of telling me that you're my father, is it?" Ethan queried, after he pondered the thought.

"No, no." Joe assured him. "I was just her pastor, nothing more."

"So, what's all this about then?"

"Do you believe in angels, Ethan?" The preacher asked, offhandedly.

Ethan gave the unanticipated question some thought before answering.

"You mean like, the little babies in diapers with wings and harps?" The young detective asked, with a snicker.

"No." Joe replied, in a firm tone. "Those kind do not exist. "I am talking about warring angels. The kind that battles the devil in the service of God Almighty."

"Well…I have to say I've never given it much thought." Ethan answered, honestly. "I guess I do."

"You guess?" Joe asked, in a tone that almost sounded as though he were offended by the response. "Ethan, I know you are just recently saved. But if you believe in God, then you must also know the devil exists as well. And these powerful, Heavenly Hosts, are constantly at our sides waging war on the spirits of darkness that are relentless in seeking out our destruction."

"What are you getting at, preacher?"

Joe let out a deep sigh, as he contemplated his words carefully.

"Ethan, back when I was a young man, I chose an entirely different path for my life than the one I'm walking on today. I wanted to be rich, and I dedicated my whole heart toward that goal. It wasn't until I had met a strange man out of the blue one day, and had a similar conversation to the one we are having now, that changed the course of my life forever."

"What happened?" Ethan queried, seeing that the preacher was genuinely having a difficult time telling him whatever it was he was trying to tell him.

"He told me that he was a powerful exorcist that had been granted certain gifts from God due to the possession of these artifacts that I have displayed here today." Joe explained, as he searched Ethan's face for signs of understanding.

"So, was it true or was the guy some sort of nutcase?" Ethan asked, after a short pause.

"Oh, it was definitely true." Joe replied with the nod of his head. "More than you can imagine."

"How did you come to possess his artifacts?" Ethan inquired, as he visually inspected the beautiful objects.

"Funny you should ask that." Joe commented, before giving his reply. "The man told me that he was dying, and that God had directed me to him in order to become his replacement."

"Sooo, what you're actually telling me is, *you* are a powerful exorcist." Ethan commented, believing he now understood.

"Yes." Joe answered, plainly. "And you should also know, that *I* am dying."

Joe watched as Ethan's eyes grew wide, as the full weight of the conversation finally sunk in.

"Wait, wait, wait! Time out! Time out!" Ethan shouted, as he held his hands up in the form of a large 'T'. "Are you trying to say you want *me* to be *your* replacement?"

"That is exactly what I am saying to you, Ethan Brooks." The preacher answered, plainly.

"You're crazy!" Ethan shouted, as he jumped to his feet. "If that was true, then how come I never felt God pulling me in that direction?"

"Search your feelings, son." Joe responded, as he slowly stood to his feet and placed his hands to Ethan's shoulders to calm him. "Deep down you know God has been directing your path here all your life. Your *'miracle shot'* is all over the news…Tell me how many ordinary people have ever intertwined a bullet with another? Even your birth was a miracle! A runaway semi just happens to come to a screeching halt as if it hit an invisible force…How many times has that ever happened? And, you just happened to show up here today while I had these priceless weapons out on display? Tell me Ethan, how many people knew you were coming here? Up until a few minutes ago, even you didn't know you were going to be here… but *I did*!"

Ethan did not reply. Instead, he searched his heart for any possible scenarios that would explain away what the preacher was telling him. Nevertheless, no matter how hard he tried, the random experiences could not be simply explained away as mere coincidence. When he slowly began to accept the possibilities, the young man looked the pastor in the eyes.

"If I were to believe you, which I am not saying that I am, what is it God wants from me?" He asked, genuinely.

Before Joe answered, he reached in the direction of the seat in front of them and picked up one of the artifacts. It was an elegantly crafted spear that looked as though it dated back to a time during the Roman Empire. Its shaft was forged from solid gold and was polished so brightly that the light of the room danced wildly down the length of its exterior. The head appeared to be fashioned from regular metal, and on either side, four small vials of red liquid had been set within its surface, while golden laced trim surrounded each vessel artistically.

"Take it." Joe said, as he held the weapon out toward Ethan.

"I-I can't." Ethan replied, hesitantly. "It looks far too expensive. If I was to break it, it would take me until my grandchild's retirement to repay you on a policeman's salary."

"Take it." Joe said again, in a much firmer tone than before.

Tentatively, Ethan reached out his hands and took hold of the weapon, using an extra bit of strength so he would not drop it. As soon as his flesh came into contact with the shaft, Ethan could feel an unseen energy coursing through his body. The weapon hummed in his hands as if it had a life all its own. At first glance, the lance looked as though it could have easily weighed around thirty pounds. However, Ethan was able to hold the weapon with only one hand, as if it was light as a feather.

"This is amazing…" Ethan gasped, as he twirled the spear around in his hands like a well-trained martial artist.

"You hold within your grasp The Spear of Destiny." Joe explained. "It is the same spearhead that the Roman centurion used to pierce Christ's side. The metal has never lost its razor-sharp edge since the day Jesus' blood covered it. Many wars have been waged in search of this magnificent weapon and yet here you hold it in the palm of your hand."

"The Spear of Destiny!" Ethan gasped.

"So, you've heard of it?" Joe inquired.

"Yes, I have." Ethan answered, in an unusual tone. "I heard about it from two Federal Agents when they questioned me one day. They said it was the same spear Hitler had in his possession when he tried to take over the world."

Joe snickered at the comment.

"It's true." The pastor responded. "That spear in your hand is the spear Hitler was *searching for*. However, had he ever possessed the true Spear of Destiny, his armies would have been unstoppable, and we'd all be speaking German."

"So, what did Hitler have then?"

"A replica." Joe answered. "The real spear was purchased by Jesus' followers right after the Crucifixion and has never been out of the possession of The Order. Could you imagine the actual spearhead that pierced Christ's side on display at some museum? This weapon is far too powerful to be treated in such a way!"

"What is that?" Ethan asked, turning his attention to a golden cross about two feet in length that looked as though it should be mounted on the steeple of a church.

"That is 'The Exorcist's Cross'." Joe replied, as he picked the artifact up and brought it over to Ethan for him to examine.

Ethan placed the spear back down upon the row of padded seats, and then took hold of the cross. Amazingly, the object possessed the same tingling energy as the spear. It had been elegantly crafted by a talented metal smith and kept highly polished. There were also eight vials of red liquid set within its surface at precise locations.

"I've never heard of it before." Ethan said truthfully, as he inspected the beautiful piece of art.

"No one has." Joe replied, as he picked up a stunningly gorgeous dagger from one of the seats. "Nor has anyone heard of 'Hellfire's Blade'."

Ethan reached out and slowly took the dagger in his hand. Just as the other relics, the young man felt a volt of power surging through his body as soon as his skin came into contact with the artistically crafted metal. The dagger's hilt felt warm to the touch as it reverberated in his grasp, firmly seating itself within his hand. The young man held the artifact up to the light and twisted it in his hand, watching the illumination of the room move freely down its silver blade.

"Both The 'Exorcist's Cross' and 'Hellfire's Blade' were fashioned out of the nails that hung Christ by his hands and feet." Joe said, as he watched Ethan examining the weapons with a childlike fascination.

"Amazing…" The young man said, as his voice trailed off. After Ethan's close inspection of the blade, he then examined the golden hilt, and it did not escape his attention that it had been lined with several vials of the same red liquid as the other relics.

"What are these?" He had to ask.

"Those are vials of Christ's very Blood." Joe answered. "These weapons serve a purpose."

"What purpose would that be?"

"They are used to exorcize demons from this world." Joe replied. "Each artifact has been coated with the Blood of Christ, making them powerful enough to send even an arch-demon to Hell."

"Really?" Ethan asked, with the sound of skepticism in his voice.

"You can't tell me you don't feel the power surging through your body right now."

Ethan could not deny the energy he felt coursing through him. It was the sensation of absolute supremacy. Nothing he had ever experienced in his lifetime could measure up to the influence that had just awakened every fiber of his being.

"These weapons are yours now, Ethan Brooks." Joe said, as he slipped into his seat once more, drained by the transfer of energy.

"Wait! No! I can't take them!" Ethan shouted. "I don't know the first thing about exorcism!"

"You don't have to." Joe responded, in a weakened tone. "The weapons do most of the work for you. It is your faith in Jesus Christ that fuels them. The stronger you grow as a Christian, the stronger they will become. Think of them as having their own life source. The more you feed them, the more influential they will be."

"I can't deny how powerful I feel now that I have touched them." Ethan said, as he carried the dagger through several stabbing and slashing gestures. "But I can't shake the feeling I'm going to get mugged as soon as I leave here. These things must be worth a fortune."

"You are the relics' rightful owner now, Ethan." Joe said, as he watched the young man move the dagger through several attack routines as if he had been trained in the art of swordplay all his life. "They will not allow anyone else to possess them."

"Hey, you mentioned something about the weapons granting the owner certain gifts from God…" Ethan commented, remembering an earlier portion of their conversation. "What kind of gifts exactly?"

Joe did not answer right away, giving Ethan the impression that he was holding something back that he did not want to know.

"It's probably best that you find that out on your own." The preacher at long last responded.

"Well, whatever it is it can't be that bad, right?" Ethan said, as he placed the cross on the pew and picked up the spear in his free hand. He then sliced both weapons through the air as if bred for the art of melee combat. Ethan was not even aware that he was wielding the weapons in such a way, due to the fact that the relics danced in his hands with a life all their own.

"Let's just say, you will deal with it as all the weapons previous owners have." Joe answered. "No amount of talking about it will prepare you."

"You're not filling me full of confidence here, preacher." Ehtan replied. "I guess I'll cross that bridge when I get to it. In the meantime, these weapons are going to really come in handy with my showdown with Tyler."

As soon as the words had been uttered, the weapons leapt out of Ethan's hands and dug their blades deep into the chapel floor. A second later the cross jumped from the surface of the seat it was on, and clung to the side of the dagger as if a magnetic force had summoned it.

"Hey! What just happened?" Ethan asked, as he walked over to the weapons and tried to pull them free. Nevertheless, no matter how hard he tugged, the relics would not come loose.

"I forgot to tell you," Joe began. "The weapons are crafted for battling spiritual beings only. They will not allow you to wield them against another human."

"Alright…" Ethan said. "So, how do I remove them from the floor?"

"You must clear your mind of using the weapons against a human entirely." Joe answered. "The weapons know your thoughts. Once they feel you understand, they will come to you once again."

Ethan closed his eyes and concentrated. It took a moment for him to change his thought process, but once he had fully grasped the fact that the relics were not to be used against another human, he could feel the ancient weapons slowly releasing their hold on the floor. Once they were entirely free, he stood to his feet and once more considered the magnificent artifacts.

"Amazing…" He said aloud, not even realizing he had just spoken.

"There is one more item I have left to give you." Joe said, as he picked up an ancient looking tome from the seat from where the relics had originally been displayed. "This is a volume dating back to the time in which The Order was founded. Every previous owner of the relics took time to add something to its pages, because each one has discovered a new ability the weapons had granted them. Truth be told, I believe the artifacts hold a limitless supply of power."

Joe went on to warn Ethan, "more than a few of the relics' previous owners have fallen to evil, and tried to use the weapons for personal gain. However, The Order has safeguards in place in case this ever happens."

"Who is The Order you keep referring to?" Ethan asked, as he held the spear out at arm's length. With nothing more than a mental command the seven-foot shaft disappeared into the spear's head, making it easier to transport.

"The Order is a collection of members from around the globe that have dedicated their lives to fight against Lucifer and his fallen angel horde." Joe answered. "There is nothing unusual about them. That is to say, if you were to pass a member on the street, they would not stand out."

"Then why were they chosen to become a members?" Ehtan queried, as he took his seat alongside the preacher again. "I mean, what makes them qualified to be part of such a vast organization?"

"No one rightly knows." Joe replied honestly, with a shrug of his shoulders. "It is not humans that choose the members. They are all chosen by God. But I believe they are chosen due to the strength of their faith."

"Really?" Ethan asked, in a tone that suggested he was honored to have been picked.

"Oh, yes." Joe continued. "God sends one of his divine messengers to another member of The Order with contact information, and then we wait for the new candidate to arrive, just as I have been waiting for you."

"That's incredible…" Ethan commented.

"Not really. If you truly give it some thought, God is in command of the largest, most well-organized army ever created." The preacher said, in a nonchalant manner. "His lines of communication are far greater than we could ever conceive. With that said, it is time I explain to you your part in the grand scheme of things."

"I'm listening." Ethan said, harkening his ears for what the pastor was about to tell him.

"There has already been one war fought between God and Lucifer. It all began with The War in Heaven. Lucifer and his followers were utterly defeated and cast down to Earth. However, Lucifer was never satisfied with the outcome and has never stopped seeking ways to hurt God Almighty. As soon as Lucifer and his fallen angels were cast out, they waged The War for the Souls of Man, and now seek to blind humans to the love of God. When they succeed in keeping a human from asking for forgiveness of their sins, that soul is then cast into the Lake of Fire that has been prepared for Lucifer and his angels, forever separated from the love of God. Throughout the centuries, many battles have been fought between angels and demons in this war. The Spanish Inquisition, The Holocaust, World War I and II, The Salem Witch Hunt, all of the world's darkest atrocities were actually major battles fought between good and evil."

"So, what part do I play?" Ethan rightly inquired.

"Ethan, the Earth is about to witness the darkest era it has ever known. The Book of Revelation found within the pages of The Holy Bible describes these days as The Great Tribulation." Joe explained. "It will inevitably lead mankind into The Battle of Armageddon, the final battle between God and Lucifer. You are to be God's General in this army."

"Wow…that's hard to imagine." Ethan said, as he thought of the possibility. "I'm still just a rookie detective and you're telling me I'm going to be a General? This is too much to take in, especially at this time in my life."

"Don't worry, Ethan." Joe replied, as he placed a consoling hand upon the young man's shoulder. "God has a way of grooming us for positions of power. You will be ready when the time comes. Just keep in mind, Lucifer is merely a fallen *angel*, and God is…well…*God.*"

"Oh, no! Look at the time!" Ethan shouted, "I still have so many questions, but I have to be somewhere!"

"I understand." Joe said casually, as if he already knew the reason behind the young man's haste. "Just remember what Jesus said, Ethan, 'Greater love hath no man than this, that a man lay down his life for his friends'."

Ethan looked at the preacher with a perplexed expression on his visage. He wondered if the words were meant for him, because he was about to risk his life to save Becky. However, when he gave it more thought, Ethan did not understand how the pastor could have possibly known what he was about to do when he had never mentioned it to him.

"I promise I will return, so that you can teach me how to perform the art of exorcism." Ethan said, as he gathered the artifacts together. "But right now, I have an important meeting that cannot be missed."

"I only have enough time to show you one exorcism." Joe responded. "Don't worry though. The artifacts pretty much do most of the work."

"Alright then." Ethan said, as he extended his hand for a shake goodbye. "Until next time, preacher."

Joe Horton took hold of Ehtan's hand and gave it a hardy shake, but he never said another word to the young man. The preacher merely watched as Ethan hustled himself out the chapel's exit. When Joe was sure the church was empty, he stood to his feet and pulled a Remington 9mm semiautomatic pistol out of the shoulder holster he kept underneath his suit jacket. After pulling out the clip and checking to make sure it held the maximum amount of hollow point bullets, he slid the container back into the handle and chambered a round.

"To God be the glory." He said to himself, before holstering the weapon and heading out the exit.

Chapter 25

The angel's movement was so subtle at first that it was barely noticeable. Nevertheless, no matter how faint it had been, the movement had indeed been made. The battered guardian fought to cling to consciousness before the pull of Heaven drew him in, because he knew he would never find his way back to Mistress Vixanna's lair if he was taken now. Cazzbein moved his shaking hand to the hilt of his scimitar. The weapon had fallen from his grasp during the descent over the side of the cliff and now laid mere inches away. Even though the blade was close, it felt as if it were miles away, as the angel strained against the saber still penetrating his torso.

When he at last felt the comfort of the weapon's hilt settle into the palm of his hand, Cazzbein maneuvered the tip toward the ground. Once the scimitar was in position, the angel used it to push himself off Hunter's broken body. With every inch he gained, he could feel the saber's sharp blade slowly slicing deeper into his body, causing the laceration to open further.

At last, when the angel thought he could tolerate the pain no longer, the saber's tip fell free and dropped to the ground with a clang.

"AAGH!" the guardian screamed, while pressing the wound with the backside of his hand.

"You…have…won…" Hunter said weakly, taking the angel by surprise.

"It would appear so." Cazzbein responded, as he examined his enemies' shattered form lying crumpled upon the rocks of the cavern floor.

"You…are truly…a worthy…opponent…Cazzbein…"

"As are you, Hunter." Cazzbein added, returning the sentiment. The two combatants had come to earn a great deal of respect from one another after every encounter they shared.

"I wanted…no part…in this war…" Hunter continued. "Lucifer…filled our heads…with such lies…"

"You should never have turned on our Creator." Cazzbein said, soberly.

"A decision…I will forever…regret…" Hunter responded, with a heavy sigh.

For the first time since The War for the Souls of Man had begun, Cazzbein felt a moment of pity for his enemy. Truly Hunter was a commendable adversary, worthy of his praise. The angel could not help but wonder if the demonic hierarchy possessed any more praiseworthy combatants within their legions that could compare anywhere near Hunter's caliber once the Lake of Fire accepted his dark spirit into its bowels.

"May I ask…a favor of you…my brother…? Hunter asked, his voice growing noticeably faint with every word.

"Ask it." Cazzbein replied, as he sheathed his scimitars.

"May I have…a few moments alone…to ponder my…mistakes…before I am forced into…The Abyss…?

Cazzbein gazed at his enemy with his azure orbs for a short time. His body was battered to the point that the angel felt he could not possibly cause any further harm to the world of man or angel. The request seemed a simple one.

"Go in peace, Hunter." The angel replied, before taking to flight and exiting the cavern all together.

From the shadows, a dark, little imp watched as the guardian soared over the lip of the grotto. When the misshapen demon was sure the angel was not coming back, he scurried his pudgy form to Hunter's side.

It was Dartamus. He had watched the duel in its entirety, being mindful not to interfere as his master requested. The filthy minion took Hunter's hand within his own, so as to make his presence known.

"Fear not, my master." The fiend assured. "If there is anything I can do, just ask of it."

*   *   *   *   *

Ethan pulled his car to a stop at the location Tyler had given him directions to. It was an abandoned building in the business district of Rockford, overlooking the frozen waters of the Rock River. He realized he was at the right place when a remote operated garage door opened up to allow him access to the lover level. Ethan took in a deep breath to settle his nerves and then reluctantly drove the car into whatever fate awaited him. He parked the car next to Tyler's '69 Caprice that he saw waiting inside. After doing so, the garage door closed behind him, sealing off any visible exits.

"Glad to see you could make it, rookie!" Tyler yelled, from the level above.

"Where's my wife?" Ehtan asked in a hostile tone, as he stepped out of his sedan.

"She's safe…" Tyler acknowledged. "For now."

"So, now that you got me here, what do you want?" Ethan rightly inquired.

"Well, rookie, to give you the simple version, I wanna watch you bleed." Tyler answered, as he pulled his Beretta 9mm out of its holster and trained the sights on his former colleague.

Ethan went for his weapon, but Tyler already had him beat.

"Ah, ah, ah!" Tyler teased. "I wouldn't do that if I were you. Remember, *we* still have your wife."

"We?" Ethan pondered, aloud.

It was then that a large group of gangbangers started descending the stairs, and another bunch burst through an office door on the same level in which he stood. Ethan didn't have time to do an accurate head count, but he guessed there were about twenty thugs in total. A sinking feeling came over him when he realized his situation had suddenly gone from bad to worse.

"You killed my partner, you little rat." Tyler growled, as he slowly walked down the stairs with his gun still pointed at Ethan. "Everything was running smoothly, until you came along!"

"I can't say I'm too sorry to have messed things up for you." Ethan responded.

Tyler did not appreciate the insult, and proceeded to give his retort in the form of a smack to Ethan's mouth with the side of his gun as soon as he was within range.

"I wouldn't be such a smart-aleck if I were in your position, rookie." Tyler sneered. "That is, if you ever wanna see your woman again."

"Where is she?" Ethan asked again, after spitting some blood from his freshly cut lip.

"She's keepin' some friends of mine company." Tyler replied, with a snicker.

"You better not hurt her." Ethan snarled.

"Take his piece.' Tyler said to one of the gangsters. "And make sure he doesn't have anything else on him."

The thug did as he was ordered, and removed Ethan's Glock from its shoulder holster and thoroughly patted him down.

"He's clean." The henchman said, before slipping the gun into the waistband of his baggy pants.

"Those miraculous shootin' skills of yours don't seem to do you much good in a situation like this, do they, rookie?" Tyler asked, before punching Ethan solidly in the jaw.

Ethan saw stars for a moment and then fell to one knee under the force of the blow.

"Have you ever seen a gang initiation before, rookie?" Tyler inquired. "Well, don't worry, because you're about to witness one first hand. It's where my boy's here beat you like a pinata. If you survive the beatin' then you're an official member. But I think we all know you're not going to survive."

Ethan watched as the group of thugs encircled him. He barely had time to make it to his feet before the first punch hit him directly in the mouth. The attack was quickly followed by a fist to his kidneys. Those were the only blows the young man remembered before the full assault was unleashed. Fists pummeled every square inch of his body. If there was any positive spin he could put on getting beaten by so many opponents at once, was the fact that none of the punches or kicks were able to land squarely where they were aimed due to the overcrowding of brawlers. There were so many attacks coming in at the same time that one man's punch inadvertently knocked another away.

Ethan walked into the meeting with Tyler blindly. The young man was not familiar with the location as his former partner was, nor did he know what Tyler had done with his wife. Those aspects alone made it impossible for him to formulate a plan. If he were going to save Becky, and himself, Ethan knew he was going to have to improvise quickly.

A solid punch in the temple staggered him to his knees once more. Ethan felt as though he was going to collapse completely, but he knew if he did, he would surely be killed and there would be no hope for Becky.

Out of his peripheral vision, Ethan saw his gun hanging loosely from the pants of the thug that had searched him. Swiftly, he grabbed the weapon and squeezed the trigger. An explosion filled the room as the Glock discharged a round. As soon as the shot was fired, the pummeling stopped for a brief moment, allowing Ethan to regain his footing. The gangster that he unloaded on, however fell to the ground clutching his wound. Ethan did not know exactly what area he had put the bullet into, nor did he care, as he waved the weapon around the circle of thugs in order to back them away.

"What do you think you're doin' rookie?" Tyler asked, still pointing his weapon at him. "Did you forget we still have your wife?"

"If you kill me here and now, she'll be dead too." Ethan replied, turning the weapon on Tyler.

It was then that the sound of many police sirens could be heard drawing near to their location.

"Hear that, rookie?" Tyler taunted. "Things aren't soundin' too good for you."

"On the contrary…" Ethan retorted, with a smile. "That's like music to my ears."

Tyler furrowed his brow at the comment, not following what his former partner was saying. Last he knew, the police were still searching for Ethan after he killed Booker.

"All you bangers probably haven't heard, but Tyler here isn't even a cop anymore." Ethan said, his smile growing wider with every passing word.

"What…?" One of the thugs asked, in a concerned tone.

"That's right." Ethan replied, as he looked Tyler dead in the eyes. "Captain Watkins called me. They found the recorder that contained my meeting with Internal Affairs on Detective Grimes' body. It seems your boys are good at performing drive-by shootings, but not so good at searching the body afterward."

"So, what are you saying?" Another of the gangbangers asked.

"I'm saying, whatever Tyler had over you, is gone. Whatever he promised you, he can't give, and if he said he was going to be able to cover up your involvement in my attempted murder here today, and the kidnapping of my wife, he has no power to do that anymore.'

As the sound of sirens grew closer, the gangbangers grew more nervous. They were not the smartest group of guys in the world, but even they had the brain cells to figure out what Ethan was saying. Hastily, they began to scatter, everyone searching for an exit.

"Hey! Come back!" Tyler screamed. "He's lyin' to you! If you don't stop running I'll have cases on all of you!"

"Looks like it's just you and me, big boy." Ethan said, with a grin. "Now, where's Becky?"

Tyler wondered if the rookie was trying to call his bluff, or if he had spoken true. Nevertheless, it only took a short while for him to put the clues together. When the sirens were almost upon them, and Ethan had made no attempt to flee, Tyler knew the rookie was not just trying to deceive him. Obviously, there had been a recorded meeting between Ethan and David Grimes that most likely incriminated the blonde-haired slickster in enough illegal deeds to put him away until his grandchildrens retirement age. When Tyler at last figured out that he had been outsmarted by the rookie, he bolted for the '69 Caprice.

"Hey! Stop!" Ethan shouted, before firing a warning shot into the air.

Tyler never slowed his pace. Instead, he turned his Beretta on Ethan and squeezed off three shots of his own. Ethan had wisely dove out of the way when he saw his former training officer turning to fire, and took cover behind one of the building's metal supports.

Even though Tyler's bullets missed their mark, they were successful in hindering Ethan just long enough for him to get to his car. Once he was in the driver's seat, Tyler fired up the engine, threw the car in reverse, and nearly drove over some of his own fleeing henchmen as they tried running through the slowly opening garage door.

When he at last reached the parking lot area, Tyler spun the car around and headed for the exit. However, by the time he arrived a flock of squad cars had sealed it off. Not wanting to spend the rest of his remaining days behind bars, Tyler quickly whirled the car around again and headed toward the dock. In his frantic thinking, Tyler knew the policemen would not dare risk their lives in what appeared to be a suicidal feat. Knowing this, Tyler never slowed his car down when the dock ran out of space, and he tore through the wooden guardrails as if they were made of confetti. The suspension of the '69 Caprice was tested to its limits, as the car's exhaust system bottomed out on the frozen river after the fifteen feet drop. Even though the impact was tremendous, the vehicle and the ice on which it landed held together.

Ethan had watched the reckless move from the confines of his own driver's seat. Knowing that Tyler was the only one who could tell him where Becky was, Ethan saw no choice but to shift his sedan into drive and tear off after him. When all four wheels of his car left the ground Ethan could literally feel the gravity tugging him back to the Earth. His sedan slammed into the frozen Rock River with such force Ethan thought as though he swallowed his own tongue. Fighting through the pain, Ethan pushed his accelerator to the floor in hot pursuit of his enemy.

*   *   *   *   *

Cazzbein used the keys he plucked off Dartamus' belt to get through the door leading back into Vixanna's throne room. His injuries were far from healed. The angel inspected his midsection and was disheartened to discover that it still gushed glowing essence upon the ground, while the damage inflicted to the bicep on his right arm hindered him from effectively using the scimitar in that hand. However, he had chosen his path and would not be diverted. The angel had already determined Vixanna must not survive their meeting.

Cazzbein peered into the throne room from the antechamber and could not help but wonder why it contained so few guards. An archdemon was housed here after all, it should be lined wall to wall with demons ready to tear him to shreds. The angel was unaware that Vixanna's evil legions were currently searching mankind for potential members into the dark army they were creating for the upcoming battle. Seeing no reason to waste time, Cazzbein pulled his scimitars from their sheaths and kicked the door wide open, ready for engagement.

The sudden emergence startled Vixanna at first. Then when her serpent-like gaze clearly focused on the angel, a wicked grin formed on her lips. His current condition did not escape her attention.

"I assume Hunter has been defeated." The archdemon said, in her naturally hate filled tone, while each of her six hands discreetly reached for her weapons.

"You assume correctly." Cazzbein answered, as he stepped closer. "And now, you too will feel the sting of Hellfire."

"I think not." Vixanna snarled, before motioning for her four remaining guards to attack.

The demon guards unsheathed their swords and rushed toward Cazzbein at full speed. However, before they came within ten paces of him, four glowing arrows sunk deep within their chests, dropping them instantly.

"He is not alone, she-demon." Glistinia said, as she and Gunthar emerged from the shadows.

"How…?" Cazzbein asked, truly not understanding by what means his friends had arrived.

"We leapt into the portal when Dartamus scared those children at the meeting in the neutral territory." Gunthar answered, with his enormous war hammer already in his grasp.

"Do not forget about me!" Anthony announced from the doorway Cazzbein had previously come through. "I know you told me to leave, but I could not until I knew your fate."

"Your assistance will be well appreciated." Cazzbein assured.

With the odds greatly improved than what they had been moments before, the foursome was still faced with a daunting task. They were merely angels; the lowest ranked spiritual beings in all the Angelic Hierarchy. And here they faced an archdemon. Never in the history of creation had such a small number of lower ranked angels been able to defeat such a powerful foe without the assistance of one of the Archangels. Nevertheless, Cazzbein could not imagine facing such an insurmountable undertaking with any other angels than the ones standing by his side at this very moment.

"Shall we begin?" The angel asked, after turning to face the evil creature once more.

"We shall." Vixanna growled, before lashing out with the wicked scourge in one of her left hands.

The weapon bit neatly into Cazzbein's thigh, creating six deep lacerations that caused him to drop to one knee. She then swung downward with an overhead cleaving chop from one of her five flaming falchion swords with enough force to split him in two. Cazzbein had to cross both blades and brace himself with all his strength in order to fend off the blow, causing further discomfort to his already injured bicep.

Seeing his friend in trouble, Gunthar rushed to Cazzbein's aid and swung his huge war hammer into the elbow of the arm that had his ally pinned. The attack connected with a nauseating crunch, causing the demon to relinquish her hold over the angel, and smashing the limb into uselessness. Seeing an opportunity, Anthony then descended from above and pelted the arm holding the scourge with three consecutive blows to the wrist from his silver mace. The quick attacks were fierce, and managed to get the demon to drop the scourge to the ground. Once Cazzbein was no longer being targeted, he used one of his scimitars to pry the brutal barbs free of his leg, and then rubbed the appendage vigorously in order to regain feeling.

Vixanna was impressed with the angels ability to function as a well-oiled until. Two of her weapons now laid on the ground, and one of her arms dangled uselessly by its crushed elbow. However, she was far from finished. Lashing out with two of her arms, Vixanna was able to connect with Gunthar's hammer with enough force that it flung him across the room with little effort. While on the other side of her torso, she clubbed Anthony out of the air with another of her forearms, sending him hard into a nearby pillar that then collapsed on top of him, taking him out of the battle entirely.

From a distance, Glistinia pelted the demon with five successive arrow shots that sunk deep into her hide at several random areas around her torso. The glowing projectiles put Vixanna through severe pain, causing her to lash out at the angel wildly with her other cat o' nine tails. However, even with her second scourge adding to her reach, she was still unable to come close to the bow wielding angel. With her ranged weapon giving her an enormous advantage, Glistinia continued her assault and unleashed wave after wave of glistening arrows.

Cazzbein could not believe the speed of the hateful creature. Her multiple limbs were more than capable of launching simultaneous attacks on him and his colleagues with uncanny precision. The angel knew the only way they were going to defeat the archdemon was to take away that advantage. Knowing exactly what he was in for, Cazzbein soared in, attempting to challenge the beast at a closer proximity from the air. Just as expected, when Vixanna saw him coming closer, she attacked him with every limb she had left. Cazzbein knew her power was unable to be challenged by the way she had previously pinned him to the ground, and by the way she shrugged Gunthar away with such ease. So, when her flaming falchion swords came at him, the angel wisely set his scimitar between his torso and the razor-sharp edge of each attacking blade and then twirled his entire body over it, using his momentum to keep him from straying off course.

The maneuver was a success against all three remaining swords. Cazzbein was now able to fly in close and perform a double-bladed slash to the left side of Vixanna's torso. Both scimitars struck home, burying each blade up to the hilt in arch demon flesh.

"AAAGGHH!!" The powerful demon shrieked, in a volume that shook the room.

The pain was overwhelming. Never had Vixanna tasted the sting of an angelic blade. Her dark essence poured from her side like tar. She was forced to move her free hand to the wound in order to slow the loss of black liquid.

The pendulum of the battle had now swung back into the favor of the angels, as Vixanna now only fought with four of her six limbs. It did not escape Gunthar's attention that the marred limb and her opened wound were both on the left side of her body. Seeing the tactical advantage, the burly angel sprinted up to her snake-like coils and began landing one hammer strike after another upon the thick scales until one at last broke free to reveal the flesh beneath. Glistinia spied the opening from across the large room and sent three arrows at a time into the exposed area, causing yet another perforation to appear into her demonic body.

Vixanna recoiled from the intense pain. Without realizing it, she slithered backward several yards in order to regain her bearings. She was retreating!

"She's weakened!" Cazzbein screamed, in a triumphant tone. "We must press onward with even more vigor!"

Vixanna could sense her enemies' confidence. However, she did not share their opinion. The crafty archdemon was actually setting them up for a trap. She moved her gigantic tail behind her torso, so as only to appear to be moving backward. When Gunthar raced after her to quench his war hammer's taste for the demon's hide, she launched her tail into the center of his chest plate, hurling him into the air where he then collided with Glistinia, knocking them both to the unforgiving floor.

"Only you and I remain now, Cazzbein!" Vixanna taunted, as a portal began to form behind her.

She was fleeing the field of battle! Cazzbein and his team had pushed the archdemon to her near destruction. The angel realized the chances of him ever reaching this point again were not only slim, they were nil. Knowing Ethan Brooks needed the archdemon to be slain before he could begin his destiny, Cazzbein thrust himself into the portal's murky depths after Vixanna, leaving his friends behind to recuperate from their wounds.

*　　*　　*　　*　　*

Ethan knew his sedan could not match the horsepower of Tyler's muscle car in a regular race. However, he watched as Tyler struggled to keep the rear-wheel-drive vehicle guiding in a straight line on the slick surface of the frozen river.

"You've got guts, kid." Tyler said aloud, as he watched Ethan gaining ground on him.

Tyler knew if he stayed on the icy surface any longer, Ethan would surely catch him. Quickly he scanned his surroundings for a point of exit. His eyes then fell on a pier complete with a cement made loading zone used for fishermen to lower their boats into the water in warmer conditions. He then eased the car in that direction, being mindful not to spin out upon the frozen surface.

Ethan saw what Tyler was trying to do and wanted to cut him off before he was able to get the more powerful vehicle on land once again. Punching his accelerator to the floor, he was able to push the front-wheel-drive vehicle to its limits, gaining some much needed ground on his enemy.

It was then that Vixanna took possession of Tyler's body. The archdemon had been controlling the human for years. It took little effort for the demon to find a point of entry within him. With Tyler's lustful desires and carnal needs controlling his thought process, it was as if he was leaving an open door for the influential demon to stroll through whenever she wished. Once she had taken full control over Tyler Lynch, the amount of jeopardy Ethan faced had been raised even higher.

She moved Tyler's hand to his cell phone, where she then searched his contact list for the appropriate digits. When she had found them, the demon used Tyler's fingers to hit the send button that would activate the call.

"Yeah, it's me." She said, using Tyler's vocal cords. "You know what to do."

Once the brief conversation was at its end, Vixanna pressed the car's accelerator down hard ,and headed for the loading ramp at full speed.

Ethan saw the '69 Caprice lurch forward and could hardly believe his eyes. If Tyler hit the ramp at such a high rate of velocity, he would surely overshoot the road and fly into the highly populated residential area that surrounded it. The feat was obviously suicidal. Ehtan knew he had to somehow incapacitate Tyler's vehicle before anyone got hurt, but didn't know how he was going to do so considering his car was running at top speed on the frozen river.

It was at that moment when Cazzbein fell through the portal above the car chase. He scanned the situation quickly and figured out exactly what his charge was trying to accomplish. The angel then soared through the rooftop of Ethan's car and looked through the hood. The angel instantly determined the engine was producing its maximum amount of horsepower, and nothing he could do from the inside of the vehicle was going to help. It wasn't until Ethan saw something out of his peripheral vision that they both made a startling discovery.

Cazzbein was in full view.

"AAAAAHHHH!!" Ethan screamed in pure terror, as the hair on the back of his neck stood straight up.

He grabbed his pistol from its shoulder holster and hastily unloaded the clip on the angel. Ethan watched with sheer astonishment as each bullet passed through the intruder's body and decimated his car door.

"Fear not!" Cazzbein said, after placing a comforting hand on the human's shoulder. "I am an ally sent to aid you."

When the angel had said his piece, Ethan observed as he wafted through the back end of the car to the outside. Once there, Cazzbein gave the vehicle a sturdy shove that mashed the trunk area into the backseat and jolted the entire sedan as if a rocket had suddenly been strapped to its exterior. Under the pressure of the G-forces, Ethan's head was pinned to his headrest. His eyes grew wide with shock as his front end smashed into the back fender of Tyler's '69 Caprice. The muscle car was knocked off course, where it hit the ramp at the wrong angle, and crashed through the roof of an unfortunate greenhouse in someone's backyard, where it was totaled entirely.

Ethan's car fared no better. The front end now matched the rear, making the complete vehicle resemble nothing more than a giant metal accordion. When Cazzbein reached the driver's side door, Ethan's head rested on the inflated airbag from his steering wheel. Thankfully the human had been wearing his seatbelt and his injuries were minimal. Other than receiving a large cut that transcended down his forehead, and a few other bumps and bruises, Ethan was alright.

Cazzbein ripped the door straight off the car, and began gently shaking the human back to consciousness. Slowly, Ethan responded. When his eyes had at last regained their focus, he screamed in terror once again. Instinctively, he grabbed his pistol off the dashboard and began pulling the trigger, where it responded with nothing but empty clicks. In his panic-stricken fear, Ethan had forgotten he had already emptied a full clip of bullets on the angel and it had no effect.

"You'll be needing this." Cazzbein said, in a calm tone, as he displayed a full clip of bullets for Ethan to take. "Your true enemy awaits within."

Hesitantly, Ethan took the bullets from the angel's large hand. The sheer size of the creature was unbelievable. The fact that he could see the angel at all was inconceivable Being able to see the beautiful angel had to be one of the gifts from God Joe had mentioned to him. The gifts that the preacher said nothing could prepare him for. God had called him to be the next possessor of the artifacts, and with them came the ability to see within the Spiritual Realm.

"Y-You're an angel…" Ethan stammered, while loading the clip into the handle of his Glock.

"Yes." Cazzbein answered. "Your guardian angel to be exact."

"W-What do you want from me?" Ethan asked, stupidly.

"I am here to protect you from all manner of harm." Cazzbein replied, in a straightforward tone. "And right now, you have to exorcise the demon out of the human named Tyler Lynch, so that we can send it to the Abyss."

"B-But I don't know how to exorcize a demon…" Ethan said, honestly.

At the end of the loading ramp on which Ethan's mangled car was sitting, a loud screech could be heard as a set of car tires came to a halt.

"Fear not, Ethan Brooks." Cazzbein responded, casually. "The previous owner always shows his replacement how to perform the first exorcism."

Ethan understood exactly what the angel was telling him. He remembered Joe saying he only had enough time to show him one exorcism, and the one he spoke of must have been the exorcism of Tyler Lynch. Ethan reached into the passenger side floorboard and took hold of the duffle bag that he had stored the artifacts in. After slinging the strap around his neck, he exited the vehicle and ran up the ramp to meet Joe.

"Are you ready for this, Ethan?" The preacher asked, in a rushed tone.

"Ready as I'll ever be." Ethan answered, as the two ran in the direction of the destroyed greenhouse.

When they at last arrived, Ethan's heart sank. There was a man-sized hole in the windshield of the Caprice. Tyler must have been tossed from the car when it crashed into the ground. He could not help but wonder if Tyler yet lived or if his wife's whereabouts had been taken to the grave with him. Chills then ran the course of Ethan's spine when Tyler somehow managed to pull himself out of a pile of broken glass.

Tyler stood before Ethan with cuts and open wounds covering nearly every inch of his body. Ethan easily recognized his ex-partner despite the severe damage that had been done to him. Yet, there was something a little off about the man's demeanor. His eyes now bore a solid ebony hue and a chillingly evil smile adorned his bloodied face. Even though blood rushed out of hundreds of lacerations, the man was able to stand as if he felt no pain. Little did Ethan realize, Vixanna now controlled the man he once knew. The young man was standing before an ancient evil few had ever witnessed, and even fewer had survived to speak of.

At first, Ethan thought the smoke rising from Tyler's battered muscle car was distorting his vision or that he was feeling disoriented from the impact of hitting his head on the airbag of his steering wheel during the wreck. The reason Ethan questioned his vision was because whenever he looked upon Tyler, he saw the shadowy silhouette of Vixanna, the demonic creature that had immersed him.

"Where's my wife, Tyler?" Ethan demanded, while pointing the gun squarely at his ex-partner's forehead.

"Your wife is of no consequence, Ethan Brooks."

Ethan's jaw dropped when he heard the demon's raspy voice coming from Tyler's mouth.

"Soon, you will join her!" Vixanna growled, as she used Tyler's hand to slowly take aim at Ethan.

"Ethan! The cross! Use it!" Joe screamed.

Hastily, Ethan took cover behind the wreckage of Tyler's car and then dug the 'Exorcist's Cross' from the duffle bag before a barrage of bullets pelted the twisted metal all around him. Once again, the artifact sent a wave of energy coursing throughout his body, and for some unexplainable reason, his fears were drowned out. It was as if the cross bolstered his courage, and gave meaning to his life. Ethan also noticed the hail of bullets had ceased since the moment his hand grasped the artifact.

"You…" Vixanna gasped. **"You are the new heir to the Holy Relics!?"**

Suddenly, the momentum of terror had changed sides. It was now Vixanna that was petrified with mind numbing fear as she sensed the Holy objects within her proximity. The archdemon now realized how grievously she had erred by revealing herself to the human named Ethan Brooks. All the years that she and her henchmen had struggled to figure out what God's purpose was for the human's life had now been realized in one frightening moment.

"Make the demon reveal its name to you, and you will have control over it!" Joe advised. "Then compel it by the power of the Lord Jesus Christ to leave the host body and reveal itself to you. Only then can you use the 'Spear of Destiny' or 'Hellfire's Blade' to destroy it entirely!"

Drawing from the power of the Holy Relic, Ethan stood to his feet and slowly walked toward the demon possessed body of Tyler Lynch. He held the cross tightly in his grasp with his arm fully extended. Every footfall that brought him closer to the monster made the demon recoil in anguish.

"Demon!" Tell me your name!" Ethan demanded, as a wave of golden energy washed over Vixanna.

"Never!" The creature hissed in the most demonic tone Ethan had ever heard.

"Demon!" I command you in The Name of Jesus Christ to tell me your name!" Ethan pressed, forcing the cross into the fiend's line of vision.

The dose of electrifying power that immersed Vixanna after hearing Christ's Name made her feel as though she had already been doused in the Lake of Fire. An ear-splitting shriek burst out of Tyler's mouth that was so shrill it broke the windows of several nearby houses.

"Vixanna! My name is Mistress Vixanna!" She at last shouted, when she could no longer tolerate the influence the Name of Jesus held, combined with the sight of the 'Exorcist's Cross.' **"I am the Demonic Principality of the Kingdom of the North! And devourer of the lives of men!"**

"You are mistaken, demon." Ethan said, in a tone lacking fear. "You *were* those things…."

The demon thrashed about in tremendous agony. In her weakened state, Vixanna could feel herself involuntarily relinquishing control over Tyler.

"By the power of Jesus Christ, I compel you to exit the body of Tyler Lynch and stand before me in your true form!" Ethan commanded, while moving the cross in closer.

"AAAGGHHHH!!" The archdemon squealed in anguish.

Vixanna knew that she had lost. The influence of the cross, and the authority Ethan displayed in the Name of Jesus while wielding it was far too much for even her powerful form to withstand. The demon had no choice but to relinquish control of Tyler's body.

Ethan watched as his ex-partner's bloodied form fell to the ground. And there, standing in all her horrific evil, stood the six armed, snake-like archdemon, called Mistress Vixanna. Chills ran the course of Ehtan's spine. He could never have imagined something so hideous even existed before this moment. For an instance he was frozen, staring in awe of the beast, not quite sure what to do next.

"Use the spear or the dagger, Ethan!" Joe screamed, trying to get the young man to regain focus on the matter at hand.

Ethan shook his head to clear his thoughts, and then holstered his gun, since he would need the free hand to retrieve one of the weapons from the duffle bag still draped about his neck. He then reached inside the bag and took hold of the hilt of 'Hellfire's Dagger' and pulled it out. Vixanna's evil orbs grew wide with terror as she realized what was about to transpire.

"Allow me." Cazzbein pleaded, as he held his hand out for the weapon.

Ethan looked at the angel for a moment. No longer did he fear the stunning creature. He now fully understood that he and the spirit were a team. Ethan took hold of the dagger by its blade, holding the hilt up for Cazzbein to take. The angel grasped the weapon in the palm of his huge hand, and then gave the human a nod. Afterward, Ethan observed the guardian angel as he soared toward the thrashing archdemon with the tip of the dagger's blade aimed squarely at her heart.

Easily, the weapon sunk through her thick hide, sinking deep into the most vulnerable area of her body.

"To Hell with you, she-demon!" Cazzbein announced, with grim satisfaction.

Vixanna stared into Cazzbein's azure eyes with disbelief. The mere angel had defeated her, just as he proclaimed. Never had the archdemon felt the sensation of vulnerability. One by one, her remaining weapons fell from her hands to the ground. With a fleeting effort she tried to pull the blade free from her bosom, but as expected, it did not move. Instead, the hilt burned her flesh with an intense heat. Slowly, Holy light began to consume her wicked form from the inside. The illumination traveled the course of her body, finding cracks between her scales and every crevasse of her hideous form in which to escape through. Once the light successfully chased the darkness away, and Vixanna was vanquished to the outer limits of the Abyss, the dagger fell to the ground with a clang and the confrontation was over.

Ethan looked at Cazzbein, and the two returned satisfied smiles to one another. He then stepped forward to retrieve the dagger, but was met with one final obstacle.

Tyler stood to his feet with his Beretta 9mm still in hand. Ethan quickly reached for his own weapon that he had previously holstered, but it was too late.

"You're dead now, *rookie*." Tyler snarled.

Then the sound of gunfire filled the air.

The next thought Ethan remembered was seeing Tyler stagger backward, smoke rising from the barrel of his pistol. Ethan ran his hands over his body, as he hunted for a bullet hole. However, after a vigorous search, he found none.

Had Tyler missed? He wondered.

It wasn't until Tyler fell to the ground with a hole in his head that Ethan realized what had happened.

"Joe!" The young man screamed, after turning to see the preacher slumping over with his shirt covered in blood, and a smoking pistol in his own hand.

Joe had saved him! That is why the preacher told him that he was dying! Joe knew he was going to sacrifice himself! Ethan ran to the preacher's side and helped him to the ground. He then grabbed his cell phone and dialed 9-1-1.

"Yes, this is Detective Ethan Brooks, badge number 2460, I am in need of an EMT…"

Before Ethan could continue the call, Joe pulled the phone away from his ear. The young man could tell by the expression on Joe's face, there would be no last-minute save for him.

"R-Remember w-what Jesus said, E-Ethan…" The preacher stammered, as his mouth filled with blood. "Greater love hath no man than this, that a man lay down his life for his friends."

With those last words of wisdom, Joe Horton entered eternity.

"He is with the Lord now, Ethan Brooks." Cazzbein said in a comforting tone, as he placed a hand on the human's shoulder.

"He was a good man." Ethan replied, as he slowly closed the preacher's eyelids with his fingers.

After replacing Joe's head back down upon the earth, Ethan rose to his feet and walked over to Tyler. The young man looked down upon his ex-partner's body with anger. He was clearly dead.

"How am I going to find Becky now?" He wondered aloud.

As if a light switch was suddenly turned on in his head, a thought occurred to Ethan. He stooped down and plucked a cell phone from Tyler's pocket. Using his fine detective skills, he then searched the recent calls list and found a number that had been dialed several times throughout the day, the last time being while their car chase was going on. A sense of dread came over Ethan when he realized the timing of the last call. As furious as Tyler had been with him, Ethan doubted he was calling the number to have Becky set free.

Ethan fought to keep himself from panicking, as he ran to the wreckage of the '69 Caprice. Since the car had been outfitted with police equipment, a laptop computer had also been installed, and sat innocently enough between the two front seats.

Hastily, Ethan flipped open the screen and tried to boot it up. Unfortunately, he was met with nothing more than a blank screen. It must have been damaged during the crash.

"Let me assist you." Cazzbein said, as he ran his hand over the top of the computer. Afterward, the computer flickered to life.

"Thank you." Ethan said, before typing the number into the laptop.

When he was finished, Ethan hit the enter button and then the computer tracked down the location of the sim-card that the number had been programmed into via the form of sophisticated targeting satellites. After this was accomplished, it was only a matter of seconds before the cell phone was tracked down. Once he had the address, Ethan dialed 9-1-1 again.

"Yes, this is Detective Ethan Brooks again." He said, with grim determination. "Cancel the EMT. I need the S.W.A.T. team…"

Epilogue

The S.W.A.T team arrived at the address shortly after Ethan. After a quick assessment of the situation, they determined the house was empty. Wasting no time, they rushed the door and busted it open with a battering ram.

"Stack it up! We're going in!" The team leader yelled, as they entered the house and began clearing the rooms.

The men moved from chamber to chamber, making sure there were no gunmen lying in wait. Nevertheless, nothing seemed out of the ordinary until they reached the back bedroom.

"I've got something!" One of the team members announced.

Ethan wasted no time making his way into the room. He was horrified at what he found once he arrived. Seated in an ordinary kitchen chair with her arms bound behind her back, sat Becky. Her lips were blue and her skin was a dark lavender. She had been the recipient of three gunshots to her bosom.

Becky was gone.

"NO!!" Ethan screamed, before running over and cutting the binds off her petite wrists.

After doing so, the young man took his wife's body and collapsed to his knees, holding her in his arms as tears rolled unhindered down his face. Ethan knew he should have waited for the crime scene investigators to search for evidence before he tampered with anything in the room. However, at that moment, Ehtan only wanted to hold Becky one last time.

"I know you're in Heaven Becky…" The young man sobbed. "Wait for me… I'll be there soon… But I promise you… I won't go until I've found the one who did this to you…"

*　　*　　*　　*　　*

Lars stood atop a tall hill watching the Rockford horizon as a dark cloud moved in. At first glance it looked as though a storm was about to break out over the city. However, at closer inspection, one could see that the black mass was actually moving as if it had a life all its own. That is due to the fact that they were not clouds at all, but instead hundreds of thousands of evil spirits moving together as a well-trained army in the sky.

The enormous demon crossed his massive arms across his barrel shaped chest, as he looked upon the legions swarming together with grim satisfaction. His reptilian eyes gazed upon the scene with an intense hatred for the residents of the city below. When the army was in place, the chief prince gave a simple hand gesture to his generals and the attack began.

With blood curdling screams, the demons rained from the sky upon the helpless city. Their mission was well in mind; target everyone that did not bear the Seal of God and take possession of them. It was not until Lars felt the weight of someone's stare upon his back that he decided to divide his attention between the view and his expected guest.

"Can you be trusted?" Lars asked, never taking his eyes off his legions.

"I can." The visitor answered plainly.

"Mistress Vixanna did not trust you." Lars felt the need to comment.

"Vixanna was wary of my talents."

"I do not fear your blades." Lars said flatly, as he turned to consider Hunter. "You could not defeat the guardian angel known as Cazzbein. Yet, *I* swatted him like a fly."

"Cazzbein is a worthy opponent." Hunter replied, never breaking eye contact with the gigantic Chief Prince.

"The only reason I am giving you a second chance is because you personally rescued me from the Abyss. I owe you that much." Lars commented. "But do not fail to bring Cazzbein to me when you and the Rippers capture him."

"Yes, Chief Prince…" Hunter replied, as he stooped into a low, courteous bow.

"I want that angel locked away in the lowest recesses of our most intolerable dungeon for what he's done." Lars growled. "There we will keep him hidden away from even God's sight for the rest of eternity!"

www.ingramcontent.com/pod-product-compliance
Lightning Source LLC
Chambersburg PA
CBHW060610300726
48975CB00005B/1513